PRAISE FOR RICHARD B. SCHWARTZ

Proof of Purchase

I0588037

It's like this guy is just channeling Raymond Chandler on every page. . . . The ending . . . would make Mike Hammer proud.
— Jochem Steen, *Sons of Spade*

In this engaging hard-boiled mystery, one of three in Schwartz's Jack Grant series (Frozen Stare; The Last Voice You Hear), the seasoned California PI looks into the disappearance of an ex-girlfriend at the request of the woman's husband. When her mutilated body turns up in the woods, Grant makes it his mission to track down her murderer. With the assistance of Lt. Diana Craig, an attractive fast-riser in the San Bernardino police department, Grant follows leads that point to his client, as well as to a consortium of underworld bosses who are branching out into a mega-real estate project. The pair find time, between car chases and gun battles, to begin a relationship. . . . Fans of Robert Parker will enjoy encountering Grant . . . .
— *Publishers Weekly*

The Last Voice You Hear

It's not often that an author's second book is as good as the first, and even less frequent are the instances when an author . . . top[s] it with an extraordinary second . . . deliver[ing] a walloping good tale as well. Richard B. Schwartz has done just that. In *The Last Voice You Hear*, Mr. Schwartz places himself on par with our finest contemporary murder-mystery writers. This is a book you won't want to miss. . . .
— Alan Paul Curtis in *Who Dunnit*

The author . . . writes vividly, putting the reader right into the scene. Schwartz explores the meaning of right and wrong, crime and justice.
— Mary Helen Becker in *Mystery News*

The story rockets along . . . a fast-moving, well-told story with a surprising conclusion that blurs the line between crime and justice.
— Joseph Scarpato, Jr. in *Mystery Scene*

Jack Grant, the Vietnam vet and Pasadena-based PI who debuted in Frozen Stare (1989), returns in this engrossing sequel by Schwartz, author of several scholarly studies of Samuel Johnson. Schwartz knows his London, but surprisingly he evokes California with equal ease, mainly with vividly etched strokes. An apparently maniacal killer is on the loose in London, someone strong and very practiced at impalement. So far, so nasty. But when a victim is dispatched in similar fashion in Disneyland, of all places, Jack Grant is called in. He discovers the killer's identity, but there's a problem: there's a method to the killer's madness. Moreover, Grant has an ethical problem of his own: he's plagued by his conscience, since he understands and even sympathizes with the murderer's cause. The cinematic climax takes place high above the floor of the California desert, and Schwartz squeezes every last drop of suspense from his setting. . . . The result is a high-tension thriller awash in sanguinary detail. Paper towels, anyone?
— *Publishers Weekly*

Frozen Stare

I welcome Richard Schwartz to the club. It's been a long time since I've seen two more engaging characters entering the series scene.
— Sandra Scoppettone

Grant and White play nicely off each other and the switch-on-a-switch works well.
— *Kirkus Reviews*

This tale, in the California private eye tradition, has a rousing finish and is an enjoyable read.
— *Publishers Weekly*

A new author devoted to the hard-boiled tradition. . . . Schwartz has the hard-boiled formula down pat. . . . Schwartz does not break any rules in Frozen Stare. . . . He writes crisply. The narrative moves at a slam-bang pace as bodies

pile up. . . . As a dedicated student of the hard-boiled school of detective fiction [Schwartz] has learned his lessons well.
— *The Washington Post Book World*

Gives a whole new meaning to the phrase 'cold-blooded murder'. . . . This is a quick read with plenty of action. Schwartz's first novel is a winner!
— *Sarasota, FL Herald Tribune*

This is a delightful tale, full of amusing touches, and the relationship between Grant and his good cop friend, black Frank White, is a joy. I hope that Schwartz can keep this standard up for a long time to come.
— *The Armchair Detective*

Nice and Noir: Contemporary American Crime Fiction

Opinionated but always fascinating, shrewd and smart, but always readable. . . .
— *The Thrilling Detective*

BOOKS BY RICHARD B. SCHWARTZ

FICTION
The Jack Grant Novels

Frozen Stare
The Last Voice You Hear
Proof of Purchase

The Tom Deaton Novels

Into the Dark

CRITICISM

Samuel Johnson and the New Science
Samuel Johnson and the Problem of Evil
Boswell's Johnson: A Preface to the Life
Daily Life in Johnson's London
After the Death of Literature
Nice and Noir: Contemporary American Crime Fiction
The Wounds that Heal: Heroism and Human Development
(with Judith A. Schwartz)
ed. *The Plays of Arthur Murphy*, 4 vols.
ed. *Theory and Tradition in Eighteenth-Century Studies*

MEMOIRS

The Biggest City in America: A Fifties Boyhood in Ohio
Accidental Soldier: A Reserve Officer at West Point in the Vietnam Era
Postwar Higher Education in America: Just Yesterday

EBOOK

Is a College Education Still Worth the Price? A Dean's Sobering Perspective

A TOM DEATON NOVEL

INTO THE
DARK

RICHARD B. SCHWARTZ

DARK
HARBOR
BOOKS

INTO THE DARK

Published by Dark Harbor Books
Revised Edition 2021

Cover design: Jana Rade.
Photo of horses on cover copyright © Claude Valette, used under Creative Commons license unmodified https://creativecommons.org/licenses/by-nd/2.0/legalcode
https://flickr.com/photos/cvalette/31236434055/

ISBN: 978-1-7374748-1-4 Paperback Edition
         978-1-7374748-2-1 Hardcover Edition
         978-1-7374748-0-7 Digital Edition

Library of Congress Control Number: 2021912929

Author services by Pedernales Publishing, LLC
www.pedernalespublishing.com

10 9 8 7 6 5 4 3 2

Printed in the United States of America

for Judith Alexis
always the light in the dark

And these are the gems of the Human Soul
The rubies & pearls of a lovesick eye
The countless gold of the akeing heart
The martyrs groan & the lovers sigh
                                William Blake

If all the world were just, there would be no need
of valour.
                                Plutarch

.

I

DEAD SO SOON

CHAPTER ONE
Laguna Canyon Road
Sunday, 3:00 a.m.

Death and grief on a canyon road, the reports breaking the silence.

"I'm here about ten minutes now, Chief. Best guess is that it was self-inflicted. Nautical rope. Expensive. Nobody seems to know where it came from. Simple loop. Over the chin and into the air. Long fall. Quick snap. A shudder or two and it was over. Good muscles; everything held. Probably been here a day or a little less, but that's just a guess. Streaked and purply but no Mr. Potato Head yet. Except for the rope, everything else standard issue. Nothing odd or out of place. No hands or fingers caught in the rope. Body fully clothed; feet and ankles free to kick around. Your basic slump. Head off to the side, like it doesn't belong to the rest of him anymore."

Carl Albers. Officer, Laguna Beach PD. Tall and straight, with a closely-cropped, flat stand of salt-and-pepper hair. Expecting a quiet eight-hour watch, but instead parked beside a canyon wall, lit by flashing roof lights from black-and-whites beached in the burn at odd angles, standing beside the dusty front fender of his cruiser, balancing the radio mike on a cramping shoulder and watching rubberneckers crawl through the strobing lights.

"Who, when, and how, Carl?"

Chris Dietrich, Chief of Police, LBPD. Shaking off sleep. Standing in the kitchen of his Laguna Hills condo, an internal unit. Still barely affordable. Facing the gray night sky, looking over the hazy glow of lights flickering along the coast.

"Chippies catching the Canyon Road from the **5** to the **PCH**, Chief. Making their usual rounds. Cloudy night, even this close to the coast. There's a lot of dust and wind coming down the canyon. They keep tooling along. Suddenly, they see a woman's silhouette in their headlights—standing in the grit on the northbound shoulder, shifting from foot to foot, waving her arms. Fully dressed, but distraught. They stop; she takes them inside. At first they think it's a rape or assault, because she isn't saying anything, just choking and shaking. Then she points toward the ceiling and they see the body."

"How long ago, Carl?"

"Around 1:30. They called the duty sergeant; he called me."

"Anxious to hand it off."

"Probably. They said the guy's famous, Chief. They thought we'd want to gear up for the media response. His name is David Bennett."

"Rings a faint bell."

"He's a painter, Chief. Artist-type. Very heavy rep; very heavy price tags. The woman is his sister."

"Oh yes, that's right. I didn't know he had a sister."

"Yes. Slightly younger."

"You said she was out on the Canyon Road waving her arms. Why didn't she just call it in?"

"No connectivity."

"A guy that big and he didn't have a landline? I'd figure him for a beeper, a cell, an indoor/outdoor portable for his landline, a new iPad and a couple of stray computers."

"Apparently not, Chief. This is where he went to get away from phones and everything else but his work and an occasional big-time buyer. He used the building as his studio. The place is a former antique furniture store. Some mahogany and cherry, mostly oak and pine. Downstairs was the retail space and upstairs was the refinishing shop.

Probably five, maybe six thousand square feet. Nice place for a painter. Close to the deep pockets and galleries along the south coast. He worked upstairs. It's all been remodeled, with a catwalk connecting two sides of the second floor. The sister found him hanging from a handrail, just under the skylights. He was dangling four or five feet above eye-level on the first floor. When I first saw him he looked like a stuffed dummy—you know, some kind of fraternity mascot or bonfire (what do you call it?) *effigy*. There was so much art stuff sitting around on the floor I blinked and thought he might be a weird decoration or human mobile. Like an ornament that was supposed to make some kind of statement. When I got a little closer it was clear that it was a young man or what was left of one."

"What's happening now?"

"Lieutenant Brighton's inside with a team of our techs. As far as I can tell they haven't found anything worth talking about. They're getting ready to cut him down and take a closer look. I described the situation to the Duty Sergeant; he called the M.E., who should be here in a few minutes."

"Is the sister still there?"

"Yes. She refused to leave. They offered to drive her back home, but she just shook her head. Still in shock and denial. The last time I saw her she was sitting in a chair in the corner, listening and watching without moving."

"Any idea where she lives?"

"No. She hasn't said anything since I got here."

"The press'll be on it soon. I'll warn the PR's downtown. Get the M.E. inside as soon as he arrives and when the media get there tell them we'll report whatever we can as soon as possible. Impress on them that the investigation is just beginning. Keep them at a distance from the building."

"Will do, Chief . . . here's the M.E., just pulling up now." Albers put his hand over the speaker.

"Good morning, Doctor. They're expecting you inside."

"Thanks, Officer."

Dr. Leonard Barnes, Laguna Beach Medical Examiner and surgeon in private practice. Removing his bag from the passenger seat of his Avalon, locking the door, checking the traffic on the highway, and walking through the dust, fog, and flashing lights to the death scene.

Rooting around in his jacket pockets now . . . finding some cellophane-wrapped antacids, taking two in his mouth and chewing them while he returned the wrappers to his pocket, keeping the scene clear of stray paper.

He stopped at the entrance and looked up at David Bennett's studio: two stories, three gables; moonlight reflecting off the windows and porch door; cedar siding and a shake roof; flower planters both on the porch and at the edge of the parking lot: Orange County alpine. Climbing the grass-and-railroad tie steps, he slipped a used tissue out of his back pocket, wiped off his lower lip, and returned it to his pocket. There was a sawed barrel half next to the door which the techs had already been through. It had a musty wine smell cut by the scent of earth. In the faint light the flowers inside looked like fresh marigolds.

Four men were easing the body onto a plywood table: ¾" on oversized sawhorses. The head tech, a man named Sloat, put a small recorder next to the outstretched right arm of the corpse and hit the **record** button. Dr. Barnes walked toward them slowly, then paused, standing off to the side, leaning on the top of a gnarled, pressed-back oak chair with a mismatched pine seat, a remnant from earlier days. Functional, not for sale.

The smells of the escaping body gases were mixing with the hints of paint and glue and thinner. Some of the younger techs were shifting their weight from foot to foot, trying their best to look as if they were glad to be there. The wind had slowed outside and the single-pane windows had stopped rattling. The room was suddenly silent.

"The decedent is a male caucasian, approximately forty years of age," Sloat said. "He is five feet eleven inches in height and approximately one hundred sixty-five pounds in weight. His body was discovered at one thirty-five a.m. at his studio on Laguna Canyon Road. His sister, who found the body, has positively identified him as David Charles Bennett of Laguna Hills and Topanga, California. The body was found suspended by the neck from an iron handrail on the second level of the building. The cervical vertebra was severed in the fall; death appears to have been instantaneous. We are poly-bagging the decedent's hands and we are combing his head and vacuuming his clothing for possible hair and fiber evidence."

Sloat paused until his assistants were finished. He moved back and forth, changing position as three younger men worked on the body. "We are now removing his clothing. With the exception of the usual discoloration of necrotic tissue, the body appears to be in normal condition."

Barnes looked at Bennett's sister, seated in the shadows in the corner of the room. Her head was turned away. She was wearing dark slacks and a jacket in a soft fabric and black leather shoes with short heels. In her left hand was a wadded kleenex which she was squeezing hard.

"We are combing the genital area, which, again, appears to be in normal condition. [Here, help them lift him up.] We are swabbing the anal region. That area of the decedent's body is—on visual inspection—free of any trauma. There are no abnormal markings around the ankles or wrists, no evidence of blows to the skin, no entry or exit wounds of any kind. The decedent's teeth are all intact. Any materials trapped beneath the fingernails will be collected and analyzed later, but the nails appear to be clean. Initial visual inspection confirms the tentative conclusion of investigating officers that the decedent's death was self-inflicted."

It started as a whisper. "He . . . didn't . . . kill . . . himself."

The second time it grew louder, a mixture of pain and rage. A wounded animal sound. Short, threatening. "He *didn't* kill himself."

The dead man's sister was walking toward the makeshift examining table, her head locked, her mind and senses refusing to turn away from the facts of her brother's lifeless body.

"Miss Bennett . . ." Sloat said.

She looked over at her brother's naked body, stained and distorted, swollen and marked with pooled blood. His mouth was open, his head fallen to the side. The even, purplish-red line around his torn throat was flaked at the center, like the back of some dried reptile. It lightened as it found its way to the back of his neck, as if it had attached itself to its host and then melded with his tissue.

She turned and stared into Sloat's eyes but didn't speak. Barnes approached her and put his hand on her arm. "Why don't you sit down again for a little while and let me look at your brother's body," he said.

She didn't move at first, but looked down at her brother and up at Sloat and his now-silent assistants. Then she turned and walked back toward her chair. Barnes put his left hand at her right shoulder—supporting rather than urging. Lieutenant Brighton had been standing in a distant corner, working his cell phone. When Diana Bennett returned to her seat with the M.E. he pocketed his cell and joined her, sitting quietly at her side.

Barnes could feel narrow eyes on his back as she and Brighton sat down in their chairs. When he returned he reached into his jacket pocket for a packet of clear plastic gloves. He put the packet on the table and reached into his pocket again, retrieving a flashlight in a green elasticized sling which he flipped on and slipped over his forehead. He opened the vinyl packet, removed the plastic gloves, snapped them on, and walked toward the head of the table.

"I think you've done a very good job," he said, releasing some of the tension, "and I doubt that I'll find anything that you didn't already see, but I'd appreciate it if you'd give me a couple of seconds."

Sloat shrugged and stood back from the table. His men looked at Barnes skeptically. Big time O.C. doc visiting the provinces. He started with the dead man's neck, working it slowly from left to right. Then he moved his hands across the length of the man's body, touching, palpating, tracing lines and ridges, feeling along the folds and inside the creases. He examined the feet, looking between the toes for needle marks. Except for a tiny bit of dark blue sock lint the feet were unusually clean. He checked the vein line of the penis and the area beneath the eyelids for needle marks. He looked into the ears, redirecting his flashlight. He asked for a clean swab and checked one of the ears, but there was nothing there beyond the dried remains of some crumbly, yellow wax which fell off of the swab and into the waiting evidence bag.

He looked into the right nostril and then the left, asked for another swab, and probed with it. He put the swab into a fresh evidence bag and shined his flashlight into the dead man's mouth. Leaning closer and moving the flashlight from side to side, he inserted a series of swabs, placing each of them in a third evidence bag.

"What is it?" Sloat asked.

"I'm not sure."

"What is it? What have you found?" the woman asked. She was out of her chair now, approaching the table, the sound of her heels suddenly filling the room.

"Ms. Bennett. Do you know if your brother used snuff?"

"Snuff? Of course not."

"Are you certain?"

"Yes, I'm certain. What did you find?" She put her hand on the base of the table, pausing momentarily at the full sight of her brother's nude body.

"Look here," Barnes said, guiding her toward the corpse's head and forcing open his mouth. "Lean down . . . do you see it?" He took the flashlight from his head and angled it for her.

"Let me see it," Sloat said.

"Just a second," Barnes answered. He rested a swab on the dead man's tongue, using it as a pointer. "There . . . do you see that?"

"Yes," she said. "It's red, almost like makeup powder, but it looks thicker."

"There's some caught between the bicuspids on either side of the mouth and a little inside the throat. Look, there . . . there's some on that molar on the left. It's also in the nostrils. There's a good-sized piece trapped in the hairs of the left nostril. Look . . ."

"It's probably just dirt," Sloat said. "Did you see the dust outside when you came in? There's enough blowing around in the air to choke you."

"Yes, but the soil here isn't red," Barnes said.

"Maybe it's some kind of dope," one of the assistants said. The sister snapped her head toward him.

"Addicts don't rub dope on their teeth," Barnes said. "They rub it on their gums under their lips."

"My brother didn't use drugs," the sister said.

"Here," Barnes said, handing one of the swabs to the assistant. "Check some of it out. Make sure."

He returned a few minutes later. "It isn't heroin or cocaine," he said.

"What do you *think* it is?" Barnes asked.

"I don't know what it is."

"None of us do. Just tell me what you think it is."

"I think it's dirt," the assistant said, turning his head away from Sloat. "It looks like it was tinted red."

"What in the hell would a man be doing with red dirt in his nose and mouth?" Sloat asked.

"Here, look," Barnes said. "Look at his nose and lips. Then look at his cheeks, ears, and neck."

"What am I supposed to see?" Sloat asked.

"His face looks clean but he's got dirt in his nose and mouth. I'd expect to see evidence that his face had been scrubbed, especially around the cheeks, mouth and nostrils, but everything looks the same, even down below his neck."

"The body's too far gone to really tell."

"No, I don't think so," Barnes said, directing his flashlight. "Look here. There are some particles of blood at the base of his left cheek, right where it meets his chin. A shaving nick. If his face had been scrubbed, those flakes of blood would have come off. Come here, look at his feet and tell me what you see."

They walked around to the end of the table.

"I don't see anything," Sloat said.

"That's right," Barnes said. "His feet are clean. There's no dirt, red or otherwise. Look at the ridge lines left by his socks. They're clean too."

"So what am I supposed to conclude?"

"I don't know," Barnes said, "that's the point."

"I don't understand. *What's* the point?"

Barnes tried to keep from shaking his head in frustration. "Look, gentlemen, we have to assume that the man did not eat and snort dirt. Even if he had wanted to, *this* dirt had to have been either imported or homemade. Right?"

"Go on," Sloat said.

"OK. To get dirt in your nose and mouth—something that most people don't generally want to do—you'd have to fall in it and get a faceful. Right?"

"So what you're saying is that the man didn't kill himself, that he died somewhere else and was brought here."

"No, I'm not saying that at all," Barnes said.

"Well what *are* you saying?"

"This man shows no evidence of dirt on his feet or ankles. Assuming for the sake of argument that his *face* was in the dirt it would take a serious effort to clean him up afterwards. None of us has seen any evidence of such an effort. His hair is clean, his ears are clean, his eyes are clean, and there is no dirt on his clothing.

"If he actually *was* in the dirt somewhere he didn't walk around in it. He was an artist, not an angel, so we know he didn't hover over a pile of red dirt and then drop down for a sniff and a taste. Let's say he died elsewhere, some place we might be able to identify, some place with red dirt . . . if his body *was* brought back here and doctored to make it look like a simple suicide somebody did a world-class job on the outside of his body and then forgot completely about the inside. Does that seem likely?" Barnes paused for a moment before continuing.

"We know he died from hanging. That's clear from the marks and the blood pooling . . ."

"But look at the rope," Sloat interrupted. "If there really was foul play and somebody wanted to make it look like a suicide they wouldn't use nautical rope. They'd use something from around the studio. That stuff is a dollar a foot; what's it doing here? It raises questions. Somebody fabricating a suicide wouldn't want to raise questions. Maybe he was working with some powder for clay or something . . ."

"Working it in his mouth?" Barnes asked.

"Somebody said something about makeup. Maybe that's a woman's makeup. Maybe he was kissing and nuzzling her and really started to get into it."

"She'd have to be an Apache, painted up to go after the Union Cavalry," the M.E. said.

"With all due respect, Dr. Barnes, how long have you worked sex/drugs/and violence cases in southern California? Are you going to stand there and tell me that you haven't seen things a lot stranger than this?"

"Look at his hands," his sister said. They both turned to her simultaneously. Sloat's assistants stepped closer to the table.

"Leave the bags on," Sloat said. "I don't want any contamination."

"Of *evidence*?" the sister asked.

Sloat didn't answer her.

"The right hand looks clean. I don't see anything," the youngest assistant said.

"Look here," Barnes said, angling his flashlight. "The nails of the left hand appear to be clean, but look at the back of it, especially the ring and index fingers."

The sister stepped in, blocking Sloat's way. She bent over as Barnes adjusted the poly-bag and spoke. "There are red particles in the creases, but nothing under the nails and nothing on the front of his hand. That doesn't make sense . . . unless his hand brushed against something or he used the back of his hand to wipe his nose. There should be dirt under the nails and on his palms and fingertips. And if he washed his hands there shouldn't be dirt on the back of his fingers. It looks as if he might have wiped his hand and left a little residue."

"Assuming you're right—that it *is* dirt—what does that prove?"

"It doesn't *prove* anything," Barnes answered. "It shows that there's something going on here that we don't understand. It's certainly not some woman's makeup, because if he was kissing and nuzzling and really getting into it (as you said), there would be some residue on his fingertips and palms. There isn't."

"Detective . . ."

It was one of Sloat's assistants.

"What, Gibson?"

"I'd like to go downstairs again."

"You said there was nothing there."

"Maybe there's some dirt down there, something that would explain this."

Sloat's impatience turned into expectation. "OK, let's take a look. Maybe there's some crud on the furnace or hot water heater. Maybe he lit a pilot light and got a mouthful of rust and dirt."

The entrance to the cellar was next to a converted kitchenette at the rear of the building. There were wooden steps lit by a cobwebbed bulb. Sloat's assistants checked the furnace first. The pilot light was off and the gas valve arm was perpendicular to the line. "It's been shut off," Gibson said.

"The hot water heater's electric," Barnes said, "safer for earthquakes.

Look along the top of the foundation, beneath the subfloor. Maybe something was stored along there. Some people use those areas as shelves."

After a thorough search of the forward area of the cellar they were standing together under the light. "There's nothing back there at all," Sloat said. "No tools, newspapers, mowers, no garbage cans, nothing."

They walked through the single remaining portion of the cellar. One area at the rear had track lighting, a set of stationary tubs, and a jack for a phone. It was a large space: at least fifteen by twenty-five feet. There was some gray powder and gravel on the floor and some scrape marks in the cement. In the center of the nearest wall were double, steel doors.

"Loading ramp?" Barnes asked.

"I don't know," the sister said. "I've never been down here."

"We're in the back section of the building," Barnes said. "There must be a driveway at the back of the lot that leads to those doors. Materials could be unloaded here and items stored for pickup."

He walked over to the doors and shined his flashlight along the edges and into the lock. "Did you dust this?" He could see that they hadn't.

"No," Gibson answered. "I will."

Barnes returned to the center of the room and shined his flashlight on the floor. "This dust looks like pieces of green cement. It's not from this floor; it's too fresh."

"It could be anything," Sloat said. "Grit from somebody's shoes. Something that fell off a dolly from a delivery truck. Something from the driveway or parking lot. If this is where they made deliveries you'd expect grit on the floor and scrapes and gouges in the cement."

"Find anything on the door or handle?" Barnes asked.

"No," Gibson said. "Nothing."

"Nothing? On a delivery door?"

"I'll check the outside," Gibson said. "Maybe they always opened the door from that side."

"Makes sense," Barnes said. "You'd have to show the driver how to get in, so you'd direct him around to the back and open it from that side. The porch encircles the building. It would be easier to just walk around and open the doors from the outside than go into the house and take those old wooden steps. Especially if you were expecting a driver; you'd have your keys with you and you could open it right up." He didn't believe all of it, but he could see that Sloat wanted to.

"I'm not getting anything on this side," Gibson said.

"Nothing at all?" Sloat said, impatiently.

"No, sir. There's nothing here."

"The D.A. is unlikely to proceed with this. I'm sorry," Lieutenant Brighton said.

"I know," she said, "I felt it five minutes after the lab people arrived, but I still can't understand why. How can they just let it drop?"

It was the first words they had spoken after she had agreed to let Brighton drive her home in her car. Albers was following in his cruiser.

"The unanswered questions are immaterial, no matter how many there are, because there's no evidence of foul play. At least not yet. They could find something lethal in his bloodstream, but unless it's fast-acting they could claim he ingested it himself. And why would someone who wanted to kill him do it twice? You can make a poisoning look like suicide just as easily as you can a hanging."

She sat quietly, staring through the scattered lights of oncoming traffic. "Your brother was an artist, Ms. Bennett," Brighton said. "Artists work in multiple media. They're always getting their hands dirty in some way. Unless the dirt on his body has some criminal dimension to it it's just not enough to build a case on. We can make some enquiries and we'll certainly do additional tests, but I don't want you to get your hopes up . . ."

A few minutes later she broke the silence: "It's funny . . . there's always someone on these roads, even at five in the morning." Brighton turned toward her, thinking about a response, but her head was turned away as she spoke into the void.

CHAPTER TWO
Angeles Drive, La Cañada
Sunday, 6:40 a.m.

Diana opened the glove compartment as Bill Brighton turned onto Angeles Drive. The garage door opener was clipped to a bracket on the side nearest the driver. Except for the owner's manual the box was empty. "It's the third one on the left," she said. The house was a low-slung, pale-yellow stucco two-story with a shake roof and a deep rear yard. The front yard was covered in dusty ivy that had been trimmed neatly along the edges. It projected four or five inches above the ground, its roots rising like miniature, woven mangrove. In the center of the yard was a configuration of young fan palms; along the lot line on either side were decorative, shoulder-high, redwood fences with sprays of purple and red bougainvillaea. The yard had been professionally designed and maintained.

She hit the button and the door slowly rose. "I want to get something from the other car," Brighton said. "I'll only be a second." He pulled Diana's car into her garage, got out, and walked down the driveway. Albers had pulled up to the curb and turned off the motor on the police sedan. "Her brother called her right before he died. I want to record the message on her answering machine," Brighton said. Albers reached around and retrieved a thick, faded attaché case from the back seat. He popped open the pitted brass locks, exposing a pair of miniature tape recorders and other electronic gear. The recorders were secured by small rubber straps. "Take your pick, Lieutenant," he said.

Brighton went in through the garage. The door opened onto the kitchen. Diana was standing next to the double, stainless-steel sink, drinking a glass of water. "Can I get you anything?" she asked.

"No thanks," he answered, "I just want to listen to the phone message and then get out of here so you can be alone and get some rest."

"It's right there," she said, indicating a phone on an antique pine washstand in the corner of the kitchen. When she put her black bag on its lower shelf he saw that it was too big to be a purse.

"You're a doctor?"

"Yes," she said.

"I'm sorry," he answered. "I didn't notice the bag in the darkness."

"I could never bring the joy to people that David brought, so I decided to do what I could to alleviate their pain. David took care of one side, so I thought I'd try to take care of the other. I started to practice just as David made his first big sales. After a year and a half he asked me to help him invest his income. I asked a friend of mine to help. David's money was invested conservatively but he was still very successful. When he saw the numbers he urged me to keep half of the return. He cared little for the money and wanted to be sure that I was secure. I refused and suggested instead that we establish a foundation. He lived modestly, returning most of his personal income to principal. Later he issued instructions to set aside one-fourth of the return on the investment for me. He was adamant that I accept it. I decided to give up my private practice and do other work. I help out with several clinics in the city and at two VA hospitals."

Brighton stood there silently. "I know what you're thinking and I don't mind your asking," she said. "These things will all come out if you proceed with the investigation. I told you that we were very close. The two of us were all that remained of the family and he felt strongly that he should share his success with me."

Brighton let her continue.

"The value of David's investment portfolio now stands at approximately $58,000,000 and the recent returns have been hovering between 6 and 8 percent. Lately I've been returning most of my share to the foundation account."

The kitchen was a mix of textures. The main wall was brick. Brighton had seen the materials before in a house in Newport Beach: sections of thin bricks mounted on board that is then secured to the wall. Mortar is used for grout and the final product looks like authentic, standard-weight brick. Upscale decorating. The soffit above the sink was painted a muted maroon; the counters were granite, the cabinets cherry and the kitchen table clear glass . There was no artwork.

He took out his recorder and looked at Diana for approval. She nodded; he clicked it on and hit the *play back* button on the answering machine. The message was just as she had remembered it. There was desperation in her brother's voice: "Diana, it's David. This project I'm working on . . . I just can't do it, I can't. I have to talk to you immediately. I'll be at the studio. Come at once."

There were no other messages on the machine. Brighton played it back on his recorder.

"The urgency in his voice . . . that wasn't David's way," Diana said. "Something was wrong, very wrong. If only I had responded sooner . . . I was at the VA hospital all day on Saturday. By the time I got the message it was . . . too late. He should have called my cell; I would have gotten it instantly."

"So it was something like fifteen hours between the time that he called and the time that you arrived at his studio," Brighton said.

"Yes, I worked at the hospital all day, got some dinner and then went back to the wards that evening to check on a few patients. It was very late when I got home. I got David's message and tried to call him, but there was no response. I drove to Laguna and found him . . . dead."

"I don't think you should blame yourself or your brother," Brighton said. "From the condition of his body I would say that he died very soon after placing the call to you."

"If I had been able to talk to him I could have learned what was happening to him and called the Laguna police," she said.

Brighton didn't respond right away. He knew that what she said was true. Finally he spoke. "I'll see what I can find out. I'll do some checking, make some calls. I won't just let this drop."

"I'd appreciate that very much," she said. "David could *not* have killed himself."

He nodded silently. "Before I leave, could I ask one more favor?"

"Of course."

"It doesn't have anything to do with the case. It's more a personal thing."

"What is it?"

"When we were on the freeway . . . you told me about the portrait your brother did of you. I'd like to see it."

"It's in my bedroom," she said. "At the end of the hall."

He walked past the living room and saw a number of pieces hanging there beneath a line of miniature track lighting: an old man in a stand of scrub pine, balancing against a rusted, black pickup as he tightens the strings on his scuffed boots; an elderly Asian woman in a neatly-buttoned, faded cloth coat waiting for her bus; women with straw hats and pastel scarves, sipping iced tea as they rest in chalk-white deck chairs; student pastry chefs with tilted hats tracing lines across the tops of napoleons and lining charlotte molds with strips of yellow ladyfingers; a female nude with a towel around her shoulders, sitting on a bare, bleached deck with her eyes closed in the afternoon sun; the face of a man in close up, his lips narrow and dry but with bright white teeth and the beginnings of a smile.

The picture of Diana had been done many years before. It was hung on the wall opposite her bed, above a table with a large, signed photograph of her brother. The inscription read, "To my beloved sister, Diana." The portrait was smaller than he had expected, approximately 12" x 20". Diana was thirteen or fourteen at the time. The figure was

3/4 length. She was wearing a loose-fitting sundress that clung to her just enough to outline her young woman's body. She was holding a small note between her fingers, its prominence in the portrait suggesting its importance. Her hair was longer then, swept back behind her neck and across her shoulders and back. She seemed absorbed, perhaps even sad, but comfortable with herself, her eyes turned toward the left and the lids half-closed, alone with her thoughts.

"He said it was clichéd, assembly-line stuff."

Startled to hear her voice, Brighton turned to see Diana standing in the doorway. He hadn't heard her footsteps along the hall.

"I don't know very much about art, but I wouldn't say that," he said. "I think the picture of you is how all teen-aged girls would like to see themselves. There's no awkwardness. There's maturity but there's still youth. Innocence but not ignorance or silliness."

"You sound as if you could be an art critic," she said.

"No. I just see a lot of people who wish they looked different than they do. When I was a kid and I brought home my school photographs I could always tell when my parents liked them. They would say that they looked good and that they also looked like me. I figure that's what we want from somebody when we ask them to do a portrait of us. We want to look good but we also want people to be able to recognize that it's us. It seems to me that's what your brother was trying to do here."

She smiled and for a brief moment he could see in her eyes a part of her that her brother saw when he sketched her years earlier. "I'll be in touch with you as soon as I can," Brighton said. "I'll need to speak to the Chief. Any approach to the D.A. in a case like this would go through him. We'll see what we can do."

"I appreciate it," Diana said. "I know what you're saying and what that man Sloat said, but you've got to believe me; I knew my brother and he would never have taken his own life."

Brighton nodded sympathetically, but didn't speak.

She thanked him again for driving her home and he told her to get some rest, that she'd had to absorb a lot of pain in a short time and that she should let it sink in so she could move beyond it later. He dealt with this kind of thing all the time, he said, and he knew what worked and what didn't work. She smiled appreciatively and walked him to the door. When he got into the cruiser with Albers she was standing in the living room window, watching. Brighton raised his right hand to the side of his face and Albers pulled away from the curb. "How'd it go, Lieutenant?" he asked.

"I've got a tape of the brother's voice. I'll play it for the Chief when we get back to Laguna. It doesn't sound good, but unfortunately I doubt that there's much we can do."

"I guess I don't have any choice but to take the **210** and then drive through Pasadena again to get back to the **5**," Albers said. He was making small talk, moving the dead body of David Bennett into some remote file in the back of his head.

"No. Maybe we'll stop somewhere on the parkway. Get some coffee."

"Right," Albers said. "How's the sister doing?"

"She's not saying much. She and her brother were close, a lot closer than usual. She told me that her brother told her everything. I think that's nice. You take my family, hell, one half barely speaks to the other half . . ."

"I know what you mean," Albers said. "With ours it's always an uneasy peace . . ."

Diana got out of the shower, her body moist with steam, toweled off and slipped into some gray jeans, a dark blue tee shirt, and running shoes. She combed her hair back and pinned it, picked up her purse, and walked to the hall closet. She pulled out a light beige jacket and slipped it on. Then she reached back to the left corner of the closet, slid a garment bag out of the way, and searched the darkness, her hand eventually finding the vintage Walther .32 pistol that had been a gift from her brother. It hung from the end of the closet bar in a simple sling holster. She paused to recall the procedure in which she had been briefly trained, checked to make sure that the weapon was fully loaded, slipped it carefully into her purse, and hurried to her car.

CHAPTER THREE
The Harbor at Dana Point
Sunday, 7:45 a.m.

The morning sky was still dense with clouds as Detective Tom Deaton made his way along the line of guest slips at the harbor. He was looking for his father's boat, which carried his mother's name, the *Katharine Elisabeth*. A 47' Chris Craft with twin diesels and two staterooms, it was now his father's home, his cottage in the Laguna hills on permanent loan to Tom.

His grandfather, Ralph Deaton, had brought the family from northeastern Kentucky to Orange County after the war. His aunt had moved to Ohio with her own family a generation later, but his father, Wayne and mother Kathy had stayed in California. Wayne began his adult life as a fisherman, but as business and demography changed, the wooden boats on the salt were replaced by 60' motor yachts; the family homes at the outer extremity of L.A. commutes rose in cost from the low 6 figures to the low 7 and the bluffs above the Pacific were blanketed with industrial parks, shops, and restaurants, as the smells of fish and light industry were replaced by the smells of new money.

Wayne Deaton had followed the market, first managing the ferry service to Catalina and eventually working his way up to the position of harbor master at Newport Beach. The long slip that had once contained a group of fishing boats, including his own, now served a 72' Hatteras that cost more than the combined value of the 27 houses in his father's neighborhood in the Bourbon County town of Paris, Kentucky.

When his wife Kathy died in 2005, Wayne turned over his house to his son Tom and began sleeping in the boat that bore her name. She had lived to see it and enjoy it and somehow he felt her presence there more than he did in their cottage in the hills.

"Dad . . . ?" Tom said.

"I'm in the galley; come on down."

"I felt the boat list to starboard a little when you stepped onto the deck. It was a good feeling. How about some coffee?"

"Sounds great," Tom said. "It's a little cool out."

"I've got some bagels too and some of that whipped cream cheese you like," Wayne said.

"I'll have one if you'll join me," Tom said. The coffee was hot and black, with wisps of steam drifting on the surface and over the edges of the oversized mug. Tom sipped it carefully.

"Have a seat," Wayne said. "I'm been looking forward to seeing you. I figured it might be fun to sail down the coast rather than having you face the morning traffic."

Tom smiled. The thirty-five minute morning drive was an easy shot, compared to the water route. His father had come in the previous afternoon and logged some quality time with his friends in the local marinas.

"The coffee tastes great," Tom said. "So does the bagel. When did you get the toaster oven?"

"A couple of weeks ago," Wayne said. "Your mother would have approved. She always thought I needed to be domesticated a little."

"How's the boat?"

"She's a kind mistress," Wayne said. "As long as I spray off the chrome and teak at least twice a day and have her serviced three times more often than an antique Austin-Healey, she's fine. I figure she doesn't require more than about 6 hours of attention a day, which works out with my schedule. I'm thinking about getting a dog to fill the rest of the available time. Now that we've put in that patch of grass and plastic fire hydrants for the yachters it wouldn't be too hard to walk it a couple times a day. I need a homebody with a large bladder. Wally Carter recommended a miniature bull terrier."

"Might even protect you," Tom said.

"I'd have to protect *him*. They cost a small fortune."

"We always had nice dogs," Tom said.

"Yes, we did," Wayne said. "They were always your mother's dogs, but that was OK. She spent more time with them. How are you feeling, Tom?"

"Better than I thought I would," he answered. "I'm not yet as steady on my feet as I'd like to be, but that should change. I figure I'm at about 75 or 80 percent."

"It's good to see you vertical again," Wayne said.

"The first couple weeks are the hardest. You don't know whether the operation is going to work or not. I mean . . . you figure it will help, but maybe it won't do the complete job . . . or maybe there's no such thing as a complete job under the circumstances. You feel helpless lying there, waiting for results . . . any results. Then you start to notice changes and you wonder how many more changes there will be . . . whether you've reached the first step or the final plateau. I appreciated your checking in on me so often."

"I was worried," Wayne said. "Who else would help me drink this kind of coffee?"

"It's good, Dad. It really is."

"I don't know . . ." Wayne said. "It seems to taste better when you're working. I suppose it's because you *need* it more. When you're semi-retired you miss the . . . I don't know . . . the structure . . . the *rhythms* of your life . . . the breaks, the vacations, the holidays."

"I know what you mean. I've had to look at the calendar to remind myself what day of the week it is."

"Your Aunt Jean sent me a bottle of scotch for Christmas. Probably cost her a small fortune. *Cask strength* it said on the label. I didn't know what that meant. I asked the guy at the liquor store by the harbor. He told me. *Cask strength* means it's pure alcohol."

"You can add your *own* water," Tom said. "It's a good deal. You're getting twice as much scotch in each bottle."

"That's right," Wayne said. "And they say it's delicious. Been in special casks . . . gives it additional flavor . . . but you know what?"

"What's that?"

"I haven't tasted it. It's right up there in that far cabinet. Came in a special tube, with a picture of the place where it was made. I haven't had a drop of it."

"You should give it a try."

"I will," Wayne said, "but when you can do it anytime it's not the same as when you had worked all day and really *needed* it."

"I understand," Tom said. "There's a good side to that though."

"Of course there is," Wayne said. "And I'm grateful every day. After all, I'm still around, when a lot of people aren't. It's just . . . *different*. When do they want you back at work?"

"Pretty soon, I think," Tom said.

"You're a good detective, Tom. You'll continue to be."

"Thanks," Tom said, as he poured himself and his father a second cup of coffee.

"Have you seen Sarah lately?"

"I saw her about two weeks ago," Tom said. "She came by the hospital to drop off my mail."

"I've always liked her," Wayne said.

"Yes, me too," Tom said.

"Did you happen to catch any of the news this morning?"

"No," Tom said. "I checked the national news on the internet. There wasn't anything special in the paper."

"It happened last night," Wayne said. "Too late for the morning papers. The national media will pick it up as soon as the details come out."

"What happened?" Tom asked.

"One of my clients told me. Made a special point of it. Maybe he figured I could find out some of the details and pass them along to him. He knows you work for the force and all."

Tom sipped his coffee and waited for his father to go on. Wayne took a drink, said, "This really isn't all that bad," and then continued.

"It was up on the Canyon Road. The early indication is a suicide."

"Who was it; do you know?"

"A painter. Very big locally. Probably nationally as well. The guy who called me has one of his paintings. Said he paid eight hundred thousand dollars for it."

"David Bennett?"

"Yes, that's him. The police haven't released the name yet, but somehow this guy had already heard. He probably knew where the studio was and talked to somebody who saw cruisers and police tape there."

"That's really interesting," Tom said. "I knew his stuff was good and that it was expensive, but I didn't know that it was that expensive. Usually paintings don't draw big dollars until after the artist is dead. David Bennett was a young man. In his thirties or early forties still, I think."

"Right."

"And he was cranking it out. It's not as if his best work was all behind him and people were scrambling to buy up the good pieces that remained. I passed one of the galleries in Laguna on my way down here. There was a sign announcing a new show of his work."

"That's interesting."

"So why on earth would he kill himself?" Tom asked.

"I don't know; that's what my guy wondered. That's why I thought I should mention it to you."

CHAPTER FOUR
Carlton Road, Topanga Canyon
Sunday, 8:45 a.m.

She parked in the trees at the bottom of the gravel road, circled around to the hillside at the back of the house, and walked quietly from the southwest, approaching the corner with the small, shuttered window. The pine needles were dry and the lichen on the side of the trees was greenish gray. She heard the grackles expressing their opinion about her presence as a few lit upon the ground and then flew quickly back into the trees.

There were no vehicles parked near the house. The door of the two-car garage on the southeast slope was closed. She looked for tire tracks in the earth on the sides and end of the blue-stone cul de sac, but the winds and canyon rains had rearranged the dust and pine needles and obliterated any obvious traces.

She moved closer to the house, listening beneath the window for footsteps or voices. Her pistol was out of her purse now. She was carrying it in her right hand, her index finger snug against the trigger housing. As she approached the front porch she heard a rustling sound in the woods beyond. She raised the pistol higher and edged around the corner of the house. The noise stopped. Probably a squirrel or a local dog. She waited. Still no sound. She eased around the corner, climbed up on the edge of the porch and sat beneath the picture window of the living room, listening.

After a full minute and a half she took the key from her purse and approached the front door. She inserted it into the lock, turned it quickly, and pushed open the door. She was still on the porch, her back against the left side of the door frame, the pistol in her hand, clutched against her waist. She listened for ten seconds, counting them off in her head, and then slipped inside.

The family's summer home was a two-story craftsman, constructed of redwood, pine, and California cedar. The front porch, of highly polished pine, led to a living room/great room with a Franklin stove on the west wall. The living room ran the full width of the house. In the rear were the dining area, the kitchen, a half-bath, and Carlton Bennett's study. On the second level were the original master bedroom, now a small studio, and—at opposite ends of the hall—the childhood bedrooms of David and Diana, which were separated by a common bathroom.

David had stretched a piece of heavy canvas across the length and width of the studio to protect the pegged plank floor from spattered paint and thinner. The master bath in the east corner had been converted into a kitchenette, with a long sinkboard and counter tops to hold his brushes, pigments, oils, and a small coffee maker.

Diana walked across the living room and stood at the base of the stairway to the second level, listening. After a few seconds she returned to the front door, closed it, locked it, checked her pistol, placed it in her purse, and began to work her way through the house. She started at the Franklin stove. The cast iron was cool to the touch. Inside there were a few ashes and the remains of a piece of scorched oak. She raked through the ashes with the fireplace pick but found nothing more than some charred fragments of newsprint.

She checked the drawers in the living room occasional tables and opened the books scattered throughout the room, looking for anything that David might have left. David used notes, checks, bills and letters for bookmarks, anything that was within reach, but there was nothing in any of the books except for an old Rizzoli bookmark and some simple slips of white paper. David had always surrounded himself with stacks of journals and piles of magazines, newspapers, and books, all with protruding paper markers. Where were they? Someone had been there before her. Who? And why? Were the intruders David's killers? Did they know of her or did they underestimate her? Why would they call attention to their presence by rearranging the objects in the room and confiscating or burning nearly every loose scrap of paper?

The dining room was empty except for the table, four chairs, and sideboard. The plates and tablecloths inside appeared undisturbed. David seldom entertained at home and usually ate while he was working. He "grazed," he said. Diana thought of the empty glasses with dried milk along the rims and the remains of his sandwiches, drying on cardboard plates, with paint smudges along the tops of the crusts.

She went through the kitchen cabinets. Nothing. There were no reminder notes pinned to the corkboard and nothing written on the blackboard above the telephone. She lifted the receiver and hit the redial button on the phone and got the weather line. David never called the weather line. He didn't care about the weather unless he was painting it or its effects.

There were a few books stacked on the library table in the den but nothing inside them. There were three novels, two books on Mediterranean architecture, and two large books, one containing photographs of antique pinball machines, the second an Abrams art book on Christopher Wren and the rebuilding of London after the great fire of 1666.

The studio on the second level looked as if it had been recently cleaned and straightened. David's paints were all arranged in the cupboards and on the countertops of the kitchenette. His brushes were clean and dry. The easels were empty and there was no work in progress anywhere, not even pencil sketches or scribbles. The coffee maker was clean, dry, and unplugged. There was no food except for an unopened box of Peek Frean biscuits, a package of Darjeeling tea (David preferred English Breakfast), and a sealed tin of Maxwell House coffee (David bought $14 a pound coffee from a place in Malibu). It looked as if someone had just returned from shopping. She opened the doors under the sink. The waste can was empty but it had a fresh plastic liner.

Diana walked back through the studio, crossed the hallway, and paused for a moment in her former bedroom; she still slept there whenever she visited David. She checked the chest of drawers and the cupboard but there was nothing there: a few clothes, a rose sachet, some cologne. She looked at the pictures on the top of the chest: she and David in their teens, standing in tall grass, carrying a heavy picnic basket and shielding their eyes from the glare of the sun; David standing at his easel, caught unawares; Diana with her swimming and gymnastics medals, David beaming at her side.

A more recent picture: she and David standing at the edge of a tree line behind the house, she in the shadows beside him. They had quarreled about it. She told him she would always be in his shadow but that she could handle that fact. At first her words had angered him, though he spoke gently to her, assuring her that she would never be in the shadows. "I don't mind being the sister of a great painter," she said, "it's rather nice."

"And his best friend," he had added, "who will do many great things, greater things than painting."

She thought of how they had embraced and made promises to one another. She remembered believing in David, in his trust and affection, if not in his words. The shadows could be a comfortable place, particularly with him nearby.

The bathroom was devoid of anything human except for a bar of English soap, still in its heavy, expensively-printed cardboard box, toothpaste and brush, a razor, a set of five blades, a plastic container of shaving cream, and a twist-tube of deodorant. It looked like a hotel bathroom after a traveler had set out the few essentials he routinely brought. She had a thought. She got the flashlight from the downstairs closet, checked the drain in the sink and tub, then the drains in the kitchenette and the kitchen sink and powder room sink downstairs. She had no idea what she was looking for, but so far everything had been too neat, too pat, too clean.

There was nothing. No hair, no residue of blood. She went back upstairs to his bedroom. His clothes were clean, neatly stacked in drawers or neatly hanging in his closet. His bed was made. She put her purse on top of his chest of drawers, slumped down in the armchair next to his favorite window, and looked out into the trees. When he was young he had done that for hours—thinking, musing, daydreaming.

"What are you looking at?" she asked him once.

"Everything," he said.

The trees were smaller then and you could see for at least two hundred yards down the southern slope of their property. Gulls came up from the coast from time to time looking for an easy meal and the hummingbirds fluttered about the nectar feeders their father had installed beneath the roof at the corners of the house. At night the coyotes took over the canyon, filling the air with their cries.

Most of all she remembered the light, its changing tints, the ways in which it was filtered by the treetops, the way it glistened on the sea and reflected off the heavy chrome bumpers of cars working their way to the top from the canyon below. David watched it, studied it, talked about it, and painted it.

"It's the first thing and the last, the only thing," he used to say. "Look," he said to Diana, squeezing the tubes of pigment and mixing reds and yellows and whites on his palette. "Look there . . . see that rose and pink. You can only see those colors in the skies of Italy. When Canaletto painted London he painted it with Italian light. You see it immediately. It's wonderful, but it's not real. Even at the height of his powers—doing Greenwich from the Isle of Dogs or looking down river at the City from Lambeth Palace—it's painfully beautiful but it's still only art. The skies on his canvases melt your heart with envy and admiration, but they're not the original. The sun sets every day but people still line up all along the coastline to watch it. They've been watching it for millions of years. Every day. And it doesn't work without the color, without the oranges and pinks and reds. The god has to bleed before he slides into the sea. And we have to know in our hearts and minds and spirits that he'll return. He always has, each and every one of those days and each and every one of those years. He has to leave and he has to return. Without each step, each act—each one just like the one before—each of those days would lose some part of its special meaning."

She could hear him in the back of her head as if he was still sitting beside her. She looked around the room, imagining him there, seeing him there, hearing the timbre of his voice, sensing his presence. She remembered the day she began to study art. She couldn't do it as he could, but she could read of it, learn of it. It would be her way of staying in his world. He encouraged her, though he never fully understood why she was doing it. He suggested things to her, loaned her books and magazines, talked to her, asked her for her advice and opinions.

She thought of him in his room as a child, then as a teenager, and finally as an adult. This room was one of the few constants in his life. She leaned forward in the chair, David's chair, staring at the far wall. She looked a second time and then a third. There was something about the wall and the bed that was not quite right. She thought back through the years and it suddenly struck her. David's poster. It had been removed and the bed moved slightly to the side.

Their mother had continually been at David to pick up his clothes; she told him again and again that the laundry hamper was only a few steps away, in the bathroom. She would do his laundry, but he must help her; there was no reason for him to leave his clothes lying on his chair or bed or floor. Time and again she would find him in his room, reading, forgetting about all other things, lost in his thoughts. Sometimes slumped in his chair, sometimes curled up in his window seat, his eyes fixed on the pages of a book, he had passed through the gates of a world no one else could enter. "David, your shirt," she would say, or "David, your socks," and he would nod, momentarily remembering.

Once when she was away he took a drywall knife and cut a large rectangular hole in the wall next to his bed, just on the other side of the bathroom wall. It was large enough that he could slip his clothes into it at a moment's notice, saving the moments it would have taken him to walk to the bathroom. Everyone would then be happy. He covered the hole with a poster and left the bottom portion untacked. It was one of the secrets he shared with Diana.

A few months later he built a small, three-sided frame inside the wall. He attached pieces of wood to the parallel studs, making miniature shelves. He stored personal things there—notes from girlfriends, clippings from magazines, pictures, photographs. Diana knew that it was his private place and she had always left it undisturbed.

She pulled herself up from the chair and hurried to the side of the bed, moving it with her hip. It slid easily. When the headboard was out of the way she could see the hole. David had covered it with a piece of snug plywood on a single, tiny hinge. The plywood was flush with the wall and both it and the center-top hinge were painted the same tone of off-white as the wall. It could easily have been missed by someone going through his room. She used her fingernail to free the piece of plywood. Then she lifted it with her left hand and reached in slowly.

Twenty minutes later, sitting at the desk in the den, she finished sorting through the images she had found there. She took an empty shoe box from the den closet and filled it with the pictures which David had left behind. Her eyes were moist and as she put the last item in the box she put her hands flat against the desk to stop them from trembling. "So that's what you were doing," she whispered audibly. "Did you trade your life for them?"

CHAPTER FIVE
The LBPD, Investigations Division
Sunday, 2:00 p.m.

"I just talked to the D.A., Bill," Chief Chris Dietrich said. "He thinks it's a *nonstarter*. That was the word that he used. You've been a street cop for twelve years and a lieutenant for seven. What do you think?"

"I can see where he's coming from," Brighton said. "He's like a football referee studying the videotape. If there really is no positive evidence supporting a different call, the original call stands. It has to, at least from his point of view, because he's spending the public's money and he's got many more potential cases than he has dollars to prosecute them. In this case there's nothing substantive jumping out at us. Murder requires motive. If someone killed him they didn't do it for money. His studio was filled with paintings. Most were in progress, but that doesn't mean they weren't valuable. There was eight hundred and fifty dollars in his wallet, credit cards with credit lines from here to Cabo, an Omega watch . . . lots of things to steal."

"He lived in L.A. but did most of his work here," Dietrich said. "Everybody we've talked to loved the guy. They used words like *quiet, unassuming, decent* . . . A gallery owner here said that for an artist he showed no temperament. None whatsoever. So the next question is obvious: if he was pure Frank Capra, with no dark side, why would he ever kill himself?"

"Very hard to say, Chief. Especially when he was pulling down huge bucks for his work and had a devoted sister. The art critics loved him too. I wish we had a suicide note or a note that said he's as happy as he could possibly be. The phone call to his sister suggests that he was in distress, but it doesn't seem like something worth killing yourself over. Why would he do it?"

"I asked the D.A. that question," Dietrich said, as he refilled their coffee cups. "Like you said, he's got to be like the referee. He can never really see *everything* and never really *know* everything, so all he can really judge is what he *can* see and what he *can* prove. Since none of us can read minds either, the physical facts trump everything. I pressed him a little and he said something about God judging intentions, but men judging results. I'm not sure who he was quoting, but it sounded good. Anyway, he's trying to be reasonable and think through this situation fairly. You know the D.A.; he's pretty no-nonsense, but he's also very experienced when it comes to human behavior. He ran a riff on me about how the rest of us see things versus how artists see things. 'Maybe the guy was trying to achieve something he couldn't quite reach,' he said. 'In *his* league the acclaim becomes irrelevant and the money is a foregone conclusion. He understands what he's trying to do at a far greater level than anybody standing on the sidelines, even if they're bankrolling him or leading the cheers. If *he* thinks he's failed then he's failed and it could be over something that the rest of us wouldn't even begin to see. He's trying to mix his colors in just the right way and it's not working. He sees something that some dead Frenchman was able to do, but he can't. He gets buried in praise for a work that made everybody happy when they were all supposed to feel sad. We're talking world-class talent and that means world-class aspirations and the potential for a world-class feeling of failure.'"

"I can't disagree with any of that," Brighton said.

"No, neither could I, Bill," Dietrich said. "But there's still that red dirt in his mouth and on the backs of his fingers. If we're talking about facts that's a big one, one with no quick and easy explanation."

"I keep coming back to that too, Chief. What did the D.A. say about it?"

"Nothing really. Oh, he repeated the fact that this guy was a heavyweight and that the rest of us were mere mortals who could never see things the way he would. People like that, he said . . . at that level . . . they're different from the rest of us. We put dirt on our gardens; maybe they taste it. They want to paint it so they want to know what it's all about . . . how it smells . . . how it feels . . . even how it tastes. It doesn't prove that somebody killed him. It doesn't prove *anything*, for that matter, except that this guy lived and worked very differently from the rest of us. Which we already knew."

"So you think he'll want us to drop the investigation entirely?"

"He doesn't have any enthusiasm for it; that's for sure. At the same time, it's very clear that he's anticipating the heat that's going to come from the media lights and the questions that are going to come from the people in the art community. If the guy wasn't so well-known and, apparently, so loved, the case would sink like a stone, the waters would close over it, and we'd all move on. But that's not going to happen. There are going to be questions from both local and national reporters and questions from the people who collected his paintings— prominent people—the kind whose first calls go to people much farther up on the food chain. He can't simply drop it all and stonewall their questions.

"What he'll do is make some comments designed to reduce expectations. He'll say something like, 'This is a terrible loss but sometimes, tragically, these things happen.' Then he'll backtrack a little and say that he shares the concerns of those who loved David Bennett the man and David Bennett the artist. He'll announce that, *of course*, the investigation continues, but that we shouldn't get our hopes up. He won't put it that bluntly; he's too smart for that. He'll say something like 'Please join me in praying for some answers to the questions we all have,' the point being that he's hoping against hope to find those answers, but the subtext being that we're going to need the Almighty on this one, because the facts are all pointing in another direction."

"So we can continue the investigation . . ."

"Yes, for the moment at least."

Brighton smiled approvingly.

"However . . . I'm going to take a little different tack on this one."

"What do you mean, Chief?"

"Well, I can't commit the full resources of the Department to a long shot. There are too many other things facing us. Plus there's the likely reaction from the other side—pointing out that we're always ready to invest resources when the rich and powerful die, but when the concerns of everyday people are raised we stand by and let them slide."

"So what are you going to do, Chief?"

"Like I said—take a different tack."

"Yes, sir . . . ?" Brighton said, waiting for the second shoe to land.

"I'm going to ask Tom Deaton to take a look at it."

Brighton paused before asking his next question. "Is he well enough to do that?"

"I'll have to talk to him. He was released from the hospital a couple days ago. I had lunch with him yesterday. He's a little tired, but he's certainly alert and ambulatory. You can't lay in a hospital bed for weeks and then suddenly jump up and start running down the beach. Still, I think he could do it. I think it would be *good* for him."

Brighton paused, not wanting to fill in the blanks. Deaton had been recently passed over for Lieutenant, not because of any problems with his record or his abilities. Charlie Castle retired; the Chief needed a Lieutenant and he had two candidates: Tom Deaton and Alonzo Williams. Lon's record was strong and Tom was recovering from surgery, his long-term prospects uncertain at best. When he checked into Saddleback Memorial nobody was sure that he'd ever come out again head first and when he actually did it was weeks later than even the moderate optimists had expected.

"I'd be happy to help in any way that I could," Brighton said. "I'm sure Lon would say the same."

"I appreciate that," Dietrich said. "If he feels up to taking the case I'll tell him that he should feel free to draw on all the resources of the Department. I won't tell him you've volunteered. I don't want him to feel as if we think he'll need to be propped up."

"I understand, Sir."

"Tom's a good detective. Maybe he'll see something that no one else has seen so far."

"Right."

"Or maybe I'm just trying to be one of the optimists."

"About Tom or about the case?"

"Both. I like the fact that Tom goes way back with the town and the county. I came in from L.A. and you and Lon started out in San Diego. Tom's an O.C. cave dweller, at least by O.C. standards. His grandfather came in after the war, from Kentucky, I think. His dad's worked at the harbor in Newport Beach for decades. I don't know how much Tom knows about art, but he knows how important the shops and galleries and artists have been to this town. I'm not big on touchy/feely approaches, but when you live somewhere for as long as he has you *do* get a feel for the place and what the people who live there do. Like I said, I'm going to try to be optimistic on this one."

CHAPTER SIX
Wilshire at 2nd, Santa Monica
Sunday, 2:30 p.m.

By the time Diana left UCLA the west side was blanketed with smoke-gray cloud cover. The wind was up and the drizzle was blowing in from the coast, smearing her windshield and streaking the sides of her car with swipes of moist dust and grit. She flipped off the wiper control as she pulled into the four-car lot behind David's Santa Monica gallery. A second car was already parked there, the administrator's, Sandra Harkin. Diana took her key from her purse and unlocked the steel door at the rear of the building without pausing to knock.

Sandra came out of her office, her faced marked by displeasure at what she considered to be an intrusion. She was tall and gym-and-diet slim, holding back middle age. The sunlines on her face meshed with the hard outlines of the body beneath her black skirt. "Hello, Diana," she said. "I'm very sorry about your loss. I don't understand this at all. I really don't know what I can say."

Diana nodded in response. She was preoccupied, walking from room to room through the gallery. "Are there any pieces not on display?" she asked.

"Not really," Sandra answered. "There's a small watercolor packaged for delivery. It's next to my desk. There's also an older canvas I've agreed to reframe, but that's all. It's the one of the woman in the park, the one with all the greens. Everything else is out."

"Everything?"

"Yes, Diana, everything."

"Did David say anything to you about any other projects on which he was working?"

"Nothing specific. Why do you ask?"

"Anything in other media?"

"What do you mean, other media?"

"Something unconventional."

"Such as?"

"Did he say anything about any projects that you would consider out of the ordinary?"

"No, as I told you . . ."

"Thank you," Diana said and walked toward the door. She paused for a moment and turned. "I know that you were close to David also, Sandra. I'm very sorry."

Sandra nodded. "What's happened, Diana? What are they saying?"

"They're saying that David killed himself."

"That's preposterous."

"I know."

"Why did you ask me about an unconventional project? What was David doing when he died?"

"Painting," Diana answered.

"How is that unconventional?"

"I really can't say. I'm really not sure," Diana said.

"I don't understand."

"Neither do I, yet. I'm sorry, there's nothing more that I can tell you at this point."

"It's hardly the time to say so, but this will make you a very wealthy woman, Diana. The price of David's work will double at least."

"I don't care about that," she said. "I want to find out what happened to my brother and why."

"What about the police? Aren't they investigating?"

"I'm afraid they're going to close out the case. They don't have adequate evidence to pursue it."

"What about a lawyer or private investigator?"

"I don't know. I'll have to see."

As she headed up Wilshire to the 405 she hit a break in the cement and heard the bump in her glove box. She suddenly remembered that she still had her pistol. At UCLA she had left it in the car, fearing she would set off the alarm of the detector frame at the door of the main library. She opened the glove box, took the pistol in her hand for a moment, and rested it against her leg, the weight somehow confirming its reality. She ran her right thumbnail along the hard ridges and logo near the top of the grip. After slipping it into her purse she caught the slight smell of oil on her palm and fingertips. She held her hand near her face, catching the scent as she moved her fingers, imagining a cologne sample sprayed on a cardboard sheet, waving rhythmically in a hand with pink-white fingers and polished red nails.

It was 4:10 by the time she pulled into her driveway, parked her car in the garage, and began collecting her thoughts. She was holding her open purse in her hand when she hit the garage door button and turned the knob on the door connecting the garage with the house. Halfway through the kitchen she sensed something was wrong. There was something in the air, faint but still perceptible. It was heavy, funereal. She thought about the scent for a second, remembering the fresh corsages from her high school dances. Most of the boys bought carnations or sweetheart roses, especially those from above the freeway, measuring their investment against their evening prospects. Her dates had always given her gardenias.

In the living room the smell was stronger. She stopped by the closet, took out her pistol, and listened. She noticed that the closet door was shut, flush with the jamb. Ever since the house had settled, that door had been out of plumb. In the summers when it was hot and dry it fell open; when the winter rains came and it was moist and damp the door caught at the top, but it never closed neatly. Diana never bothered to have it fixed. Someone unfamiliar with her habits had closed it, someone who had been in the house since she left. What were they looking for? For David's things? For her?

She opened the door, ready with her pistol, but no one was there. She turned and walked up the stairs, slowly and quietly, stretching her legs and avoiding the center of the fifth step whose squeak could betray her presence. By now her index finger was resting above the pistol's trigger guard. She searched the house room by room but there was no further evidence of the intruder's actions.

She went to the bedroom at the northeast corner of the house. The windows were covered with heavy green drapes. She walked to the left corner of the window, pulled the drape back just enough to be able to see the street beyond. There were no unfamiliar cars, just the Lawrences' dusty Range Rover and the second-hand, navy blue BMW driven by their daughter, Erin. Diana's mind was running to ugly possibilities: listeners with parabolic microphones, mines on the other side of steel fenders and firewalls, poisoned juice or milk, unscented gas, marksmen with precision sights, waiting for a clear shot.

She went back downstairs to the kitchen and saw the blinking red light on her telephone answering machine. She hit the play button.

"Dr. Bennett . . ." the disembodied voice said. "This is Lieutenant Bill Brighton. I hope you're all right. I just wanted to let you know that I spoke to the Chief here in Laguna. He's spoken to the District Attorney and they all agree that we should proceed with the investigation, even though the facts still point in . . . another direction. We'll be in touch soon."

I can't stand here waiting for a call, she thought and hurried down the hall, took a small suitcase from the closet, entered her room, put the case on her bed and started to go through her drawers for clothes to pack. She found some blouses and slacks, some shoes and underwear, and packed as quickly as she could. She went into the bathroom, put some essentials in her cosmetic bag and added it to the suitcase.

Five minutes later she was pulling out of her driveway, hitting the button for the garage door, and accelerating down Angeles Drive. For a second she smelled it again: the heavy scent of gardenias. She moved her shoulder toward her and then away. She was carrying it with her.

CHAPTER SEVEN
Green Street at Raymond, Pasadena
Sunday, 4:55 p.m.

They had entered her house; now they could be following her. She had driven quickly to Pasadena where she could lose them easily. She signaled a left turn at the Parkway, turned sharply north, and then abruptly turned west on Colorado Boulevard, trying to elude them without signaling any awareness of their presence. The pedestrian traffic in Old Town was heavy; the late afternoon break at the *UA* Cineplex released a wave of people, blinking their eyes in the late afternoon sun, crossing kitty-corner at the light as the bell sounded. Early diners were lining up at *Louise's* and shoppers were moving in and out of *Barnes & Noble* and the adjoining *Starbucks*.

Diana doubled back to Green, crossed the Parkway, drove east to the mall, turned into the underground lot, and shuttled quickly between different levels. Slaloming between lines of traffic and rows of parked cars, she stopped at the end of a darkened row where she could observe any cars that might be following her. After eight minutes she exited on Colorado. If she *was* being followed and they were still with her they were very good. She wove in and out of traffic, moving from block to block, finally heading south on Euclid and then cutting over to Fair Oaks, heading toward South Pas and the freeway interchange.

The traffic on the 110 was surprisingly heavy in both directions but that on the 5 was reasonably light. The 60 miles to Laguna Niguel would take an hour and ten minutes under optimum conditions; she made it in an hour and a half, watching her speed carefully and checking constantly on the adjoining cars. She pulled into the *Ritz-Carlton*, took the valet parking ticket from the attendant, and popped open the trunk so he could get her bag. She carried David's materials from the Topanga home in her left hand and cradled her cell phone in her right. It was in a zippered bag of black nylon. Her pistol was in her purse, which she carried on her shoulder.

She took an ocean-view room, tipped the boy four dollars for carrying her bag, declined his offer to get her some ice, double-bolted the door, and opened the bag and removed her cell phone. She found Bill Brighton's number in her purse and called.

"I'm sorry, ma'am, he's not here now," the desk sergeant said.

"Could I have his home number please?"

"I'm sorry, ma'am. I can't release that information. Can *I* help you in some way?"

"Please connect me with Lieutenant Brighton's supervisor."

"The Chief is out of the office also, ma'am. If you give me a number where you can be reached I can leave a message for Lieutenant Brighton or Chief Dietrich to call you."

She gave him her cell number. "I'd appreciate a prompt response. I don't believe that I'm in immediate danger, but this is *not* a routine call."

"Yes, ma'am. We'll get back to you as soon as possible. Who should I say called?"

"Diana Bennett."

"Yes, ma'am. I was sorry to hear about your brother."

"Thank you," she said. "I appreciate it."

"How do you feel by now, Tom?" Chris Dietrich asked. They were sitting in a quiet corner of an Italian restaurant in Irvine, named *Felicità*.

"Better all the time, Chief," Tom answered.

"Any dizziness?"

"Some, but I think that could be because of the break in my routine. I wasn't used to being on my back twenty-four hours a day and I'd always eaten with a knife and fork instead of a feeding tube. I'm sure I got a lot of vitamins with the sugar water, but this linguine is more like my regular diet."

"I understand," Dietrich said. "Whenever I go in for a blood test and have to fast first I come out hungry for pancakes and sausages floating in a pool of syrup. Usually I just eat cereal or toast in the morning. There's something about the change in the pattern that does it. And you went through a very big change . . ."

"Yes, sir, I did."

"How's the salad?"

"Good. Especially with the basket of fresh bread and bottle of red wine on the side. I think this is just what I needed, Chief."

"Glad you're enjoying it," Dietrich said, taking a sip of the wine. "I wanted to get a sense of your progress, Tom. I'm sure it won't come as a big surprise when I tell you that we could use you . . . just as soon as you're ready."

"I saw my dad this morning. He came down to Dana Point in his boat. I told him I felt about 75 or 80 percent. I think that's fair. My head's clear. I can perform all routine tasks. I haven't recovered my full strength. I've lost some muscle tone. I could probably run a couple hundred yards if I had to, but I would hope for a soft surface in the event of an unexpected landing. I don't need physical therapy *per se*, but I need to do some moderate exercise and build myself back up. What have you got in mind, Chief—anything specific?"

"I suppose you've heard about the painter dying on the Canyon Road last night . . ."

"David Bennett."

"Yes."

"The initial report was that it looked like a suicide."

"It did, but the decedent had a sister. Her name's Diana. She found the body. Bill Brighton's talked to her at some length. She says he absolutely could *not* have committed suicide."

"I take it they were close."

"Very. They were orphaned when their parents died in a car accident. They grew up together; he was older."

"So he was almost like a stepfather."

"Yes."

"Hard to bring yourself to believe that someone you love that much could take his own life."

"Right," Dietrich said. "Nothing was taken from the studio and there was a lot there to take, but his sister has a lot of points on her side. David Bennett could pull down mid to high six figure sales, even for a modest effort. No known enemies; he was pretty much a recluse. The art critics loved him and so did the gallery owners and collectors. He was rich and famous and by all accounts happy. No apparent reason why he would want to kill himself, but also no apparent motive for anybody else to kill him and go to the trouble of making it look like a suicide."

"Very odd," Tom said.

"There's something else . . . we've held it back from the press."

"What's that, Chief?"

"There was some red substance . . . earthen material . . . it was found in his mouth and nostrils and on the back of one of his hands."

"But nowhere else."

"No, nowhere else."

"Was it common to this area?"

"No, it wasn't. And the body hadn't been washed or bleached, with those sites somehow overlooked. We found dried razor nicks, for example. All nearby and intact."

"I'd have to think about that," Tom said. "Nothing's jumping out at me."

"No, it's a tough one," Dietrich said. "Would you like to pursue it further?"

"You want me to take the case?"

"Yes, I do, Tom."

He paused and took a sip of water, thinking. Fifteen seconds elapsed before he continued. "I'd need some help."

"Anything you need, Tom."

"I don't mean I can't investigate the case. What I'm saying is that I'll need somebody to watch my back and the back of the decedent's sister. If he *was* murdered the murderer is obviously still at large. I don't want to give him a chance at a second or third victim."

"Of course."

"I'd like Hector."

"Hector Campo?"

"Yes, does that surprise you, Chief?"

"A little. I don't think of Hector as the artistic type. He was once a member of a youth gang. He still carries unauthorized weapons. He doesn't know I know that, but he does. He's a solid officer, but a little rough around the edges, not insubordinate exactly, but *very* sure of himself."

"I know, Chief. That's why I want him on my side."

"If you want Hector Campo, you've got him."

"How soon can we start?"

"As soon as we can put you in contact with the sister."

Diana put her bag on the luggage rack beside the armoire, closed both the sheer drape and the rubber-backed heavy drape at the balcony door, and slipped out of her clothes. She unlocked the door to the minibar, took out two miniatures of Bombay Sapphire gin, poured them into a glass, and lay down on the king-sized bed. Her pistol was beside her, its pebbled, black grip within inches of her fingertips.

When she awoke it was nearly midnight. The room was chilly. She put her pistol on the nightstand, pulled the bedspread around her shoulder and legs and tried to fall back asleep. The room was dark but the light on the hard-wired smoke alarm blinked gently. The red light from the digital alarm clock was stark and real, as real as David's death. She had never felt so alone, not even on the day that David was away and the county sheriff had told her that her mother and father's car had hurtled over a steel retaining wall, taking them to their deaths on the frozen slope of a Colorado mountain.

She was awakened by the ring of her cell phone. She looked at the face of the alarm clock; it said 8:43. She looked at the cell phone screen but didn't recognize the number.

"Hello," she said.

"Ms. Bennett?"

"Yes."

"This is Detective Tom Deaton with the Laguna Beach PD. Lieutenant Brighton told me you called him. I'd like to meet with you and discuss the case."

CHAPTER EIGHT
The *Ritz-Carlton*, Laguna Niguel
Monday, 8:45 a.m.

"I'm at the *Ritz-Carlton* in Laguna Niguel," she said.

"Did you give them a credit card when you checked in, Ms. Bennett?" Tom asked.

"Yes, I did."

"Gather your things, but don't check out. Keep your keycard with you. Don't say anything to anyone in the hotel. How soon can I pick you up?"

"Twenty minutes."

"Good. I'll be there."

"Detective Deaton . . . I've got dark brown hair and green eyes. I'll be wearing a tan jacket."

"I've got sand colored hair and blue eyes," Tom said. I'll show you my shield when you approach the car—a dark Taurus. Don't get in any car that doesn't contain a detective with proper credentials."

"I won't," she said. "I'll see you in twenty minutes."

"Sorry for the hurryup," Tom said, "but I'm proceeding under the assumption that your brother was murdered. If that's the case the person who did it was not some lowlife thief. Your registration is traceable through your credit card. Whoever can pass up the opportunity to steal hundreds of thousands of dollars worth of art would be able to spread around serious money for bribes and private investigators. I don't want to frighten you and I don't want to appear melodramatic, but I believe that we have to consider the possibility that the murderer might strike again and that anyone who is attempting to pursue the case rather than bury it is a likely target."

"Thank you," she said. "My brother did *not* kill himself. And someone *is* following me, or at least investigating me. They've been in my house."

"Tell me about that in a second," he said. "What was your room number at the hotel?"

"Room 368," she answered.

"Could I have your keycard?"

"Of course," she said, taking it from her purse.

He turned off of the highway, drove a block, and then pulled over to the curb. A young Latino man stepped out of a doorway and approached the car. Tom lowered the window, reached across Diana's seat, and handed the keycard to the man. "Room 368," he said. The man took the card and slipped it into his pants pocket. He was wearing a long-sleeve shirt, but Diana could see the tattoos at the edge of his wrist. He was gone in an instant.

"Officer Hector Campo," Tom said. "He'll go back to your room and keep an eye out for uninvited visitors."

"You're very serious about this," she said.

"I have no reason to doubt what you've told me," he said.

"I appreciate that, Detective."

"Call me Tom."

"Diana."

"Diana, how about some breakfast?"

After cutting through some side streets he drove her to the harbor at Dana Point and walked her to a boat on the edge of one of the marinas. The smallest boat among a line of motor yachts, it was called the *Better Days*.

The enclosed cabin had a small galley, a bolted table with four pivoting chairs, a couch that doubled as a bed and a small head with a shower.

"I haven't had the time to do a major cleaning," he said, "but I've got fresh juice, coffee, some bagels and cheese."

"I'll take all of the above," she said.

"How do you like your coffee?"

"Black. And strong," she said.

"You've got it," he answered.

She told him about the smell of gardenias in her home, assuring him that she did not use the scent and neither did any of her friends. "It was new," she said.

"Not your housekeeper's?"

"I don't have a housekeeper."

"Were there any signs of forced entry?"

"Not that I could see. As soon as I realized that someone had been there I left."

"Did you take steps to insure that you couldn't be followed?"

"Yes, I did a full backstreet tour of the San Gabriel Valley."

"Then you followed the book," he said. "That's good. How about some more coffee?"

"That'd be great," she said. When he leaned down to pour it she looked closely at his head. "You've had surgery lately," she said.

"Yes, I have," he answered.

"Serious?"

"Pretty serious."

"An astrocytoma?"

"Yes, as a matter of fact."

"What grade?"

"A I; I guess I was very lucky there."

"Had you had seizures along with the headaches and nausea?"

"No, I didn't. There were no symptoms at all. I caught a blow to the face while I was taking down a robbery suspect and the Chief sent me in for a routine scan. The scan revealed the tumor."

"How did they treat it?"

"Surgery. Then they did an MRI to make sure they had gotten it all. I should be good to go now."

"When were you released?"

"Five days ago."

"Lean forward," she said, looking more closely at his pupils and asking him to go through some basic neurologic exercises.

"They didn't tell me you were a doctor," he said.

"I don't have an extensive practice," she said. "I spent a lot of time helping David with his foundation. He insisted on paying me. I moved most of the money back into the foundation. He was comfortable with that. Money is not an issue in my life; there's plenty of it. I work at several clinics and at two VA hospitals, one in L.A. and one in Long Beach and I log some time at an ambulatory care outpatient clinic in L.A."

"You and your brother were very close."

"Yes. He paid for my medical education as a matter of fact. I told him that no matter how much help he needed with his foundation that I wasn't going to waste that education . . . tell me, Tom, what do you know about art?"

"I went to college at UC-Irvine; my father insisted on it. It's more a pre-med place than an arts place, but it's known for its architecture—the actual buildings, I mean—and I studied enough art along with English and History to gain a basic appreciation of it. In all fairness, though, I'd have to put the emphasis on *basic*."

"You didn't study criminology or law . . ."

"No. I didn't know what I wanted to do then."

"How did you end up as a detective?"

"That's a long story," he said.

"Give me the short version," she answered, as she took a long sip of her coffee.

"I saw somebody treated very unjustly. It made me angry. Very angry. It haunted me and I decided to try to find some kind of work where I could prevent things like that from ever happening. You can't, of course, and most of the time you spend your day filling out forms or going over files, but every now and then you get a chance . . ."

"Does this look like one of them to you?"

"Perhaps."

"Good," she said. "I don't know what you saw earlier, but David Bennett was one of the finest living artists and the most important person in my life. Taking him away was . . . well . . . let me be careful in what I say . . . something that *cries out* for justice."

"Then we should seek it," Tom said.

CHAPTER NINE
Angeles Drive, La Cañada
Monday, 9:35 a.m.

"She's moved out of her house."

"You followed her?"

"Yes."

"Did she see you?"

"No, I was following her at a safe distance."

"Do you know where she's staying now?"

"Not yet, but I will. We're checking her credit card records."

"What happened? Did you lose her?"

"The streets were unfamiliar to me; she took a complex route."

"What are your plans?"

"We'll find her and eliminate her. Her body will be found in her own garage. She will die from carbon monoxide fumes. Everyone will believe that she took her own life because of her grief over the loss of her brother."

"I'm concerned about the police. What if she's told them something?"

"We'll check. If we need to we can eliminate one or more of them as well. We can make it appear to be an unrelated act of revenge."

"Do it soon."

"Certainly."

"Have you removed the surveillance devices from her home? You don't want that additional chore when you're disposing of her body."

"I'm outside of her house now. I've just finished."

"Excellent. Let me know when you've removed her."

Hector rearranged the items in the room to make it appear that it was still occupied. He took the shopping magazines from the desk and put one on the armchair and one on the coffee table. Then he removed the terry cloth robe from the closet and draped it over the back of the desk chair. Checking lines of sight and lines of reflection from the mirrors and picture frame glass he located the corner of the room affording the greatest degree of concealment, put the other armchair there, sat down, and waited.

Forty minutes later there was a tap at the door. "Housekeeping," a voice said. There was no accent. He sat quietly, slipping his knife and sharpening stone under the cushion. When the woman entered he spoke to her.

"Yo estaba dormido."

She didn't respond to his statement. Instead, she said, "Excuse me; I will return later."

He closed his eyes and rested his head against the chair until she closed the door behind her. Then he quickly retrieved his knife and walked as quietly as he could to the side of the door, where he listened for a moment. Then he looked through the fisheye peephole. The corridor was empty. There was no maid's cart.

A few seconds later he gathered his things, locked the door behind him, and slipped into the stairwell closest to the door of Diana Bennett's room. Putting a piece of folded cardboard between the stairwell door and the jamb, he was able to see the corridor between the elevator and her room. Taking the salt shaker which he had removed from a room service tray in the corridor, he sprinkled salt on several flights of stairs above and below him. Then he positioned himself at the door, removed his Sig P320 from the sling holster beneath his left arm and waited.

An hour passed. No one had appeared in the corridor except for three sets of couples going from their rooms to the elevator and a busboy collecting room service trays. Hector went down the stairs to the lowest level, retrieved a white jacket from a laundry bin, slipped it on and went outside through the service doors. Carrying a carton he found on the floor, he went through the wooden gate in the fence that hid the Dempster Dumpsters. The gate swung behind him as he passed through and he turned, looking through the slats. At the far corner of the building, just outside the guest stairwell, he could see a man in a poplin jacket. It was large enough to conceal a weapon. The man was standing at the side of a large fan palm, drinking from a paper cup.

In a place where a basic room goes for $799 a night plus a laundry list of fees he didn't expect to see someone dressed in a jacket that was more likely to be found at *Penney's* than at *Bijan*. Hector took out his cell phone and speed-dialed Tom.

"It's me," he said.

"What have you got?"

"Suspicious behavior. A maid who doesn't speak Spanish and doesn't have a cart. As soon as she saw me she left. I think she's got a friend—a man watching an exit who looks like he should be selling auto parts rather than lunching with the beautiful people."

"Good work. Keep an eye on him, but from a distance. Don't engage."

"Got it," Hector said, and clicked off.

Tom turned to Diana, who was straightening up the galley in an effort to burn nervous energy. "Guess what," he said.

"What's that?"

"We've got uninvited guests at the *Ritz-Carlton*, one dressed like a maid who came to your room, another standing outside watching an exit."

"For what purpose?"

"She came into the room, found Hector there instead of you, and was unable to respond to him in Spanish. She left immediately . . ."

"And the guy was either watching the exit when she went in or came there as soon as she was discovered and had to leave."

"Yes."

"She was probably there to kill me."

"Eventually, probably," Tom said. "It's very unlikely that they'd tip their hand by killing you there. They're not supposed to exist, remember. Your brother's death may be seen as a suicide by some, but nobody's going to swallow the coincidence of a second body being found this quickly. Also, he came to Laguna to work; there's no reason for *you* to be there. Someone would have had to have followed you. It's also too early for something 'accidental'; I figure they'd try to kill you in such a way as to make it look as if you were overcome by grief and chose to join your brother. Since the two of you were so close *that* might be plausible."

"Then this is good news," Diana said.

"It's good in the sense that it reinforces your belief that your brother was murdered."

"But it *is* clear now that he *was*."

"Probably."

"Why do you say that?"

"Because there are those who prey on others when they're most vulnerable—the kind who scan obituaries and burglarize family homes during funerals. You're a rich woman in a state of emotional distress. You could be . . . Diana, do you really want to talk about this?"

"Of course."

"Well . . . you could be kidnapped and threatened or hurt until someone could successfully extort money from you."

"I understand," she said, "but I still think it's good news."

"So do I," Tom answered, "and as I said earlier no one killed your brother in an attempt to get money. The motive here was much more complex."

"I don't know what the motive was," Diana answered, "but I know what my brother was working on when he died . . . and I have no idea why he was doing it."

Before she could say anything else Tom's cell phone rang. He took it from his belt case, said "Yes," listened, said "OK," clicked off, and then said, "I've got to leave for a couple of hours. You'll be safe here."

They exchanged cell numbers and as he hurried along the pier Diana assembled her papers and David's photographs and took out the pistol that he had given her. She checked to make sure that it was loaded and placed it on the adjoining chair, close to her right leg.

CHAPTER TEN
On the 5
Monday, 1:00 p.m.

"He's definitely headed up the coast now," Hector said. "I watched him finish his coffee and then stand there smoking cigarette after cigarette and he never moved. He never even flexed his knees. He must do this a lot. Then his cell phone twitched in his pocket and he took the call. It was brief. He put the cell back in his pocket, turned smartly, and walked up to the street, got in his car, and took off."

"It's good that you didn't lose him," Tom said.

"I was in front of the hotel so I could get out quickly," Hector answered.

"Did you see the woman again?"

"The one who came into the room? No, I didn't."

"Maybe she checked back, realized that you were gone, and told him to pull back."

"Possibly," Hector said.

"Where are you now?"

"I'm on the 5. I just passed Mission Viejo, coming up on the 405 interchange. How about you?"

"Not quite to Galivan, just a few minutes behind you."

"Hope you got a full tank of gas."

"Always," Tom said, "but I hope I won't need it. Call me as soon as he turns off."

"Will do."

"He made his move," Hector said. "He's pulling into the South Coast Plaza."

"Don't lose him," Tom said. "He could be trying to elude anyone who might be following him."

"My sister Elena loves this place," Hector said. "The garden of Eden for shoppers. And believe me, she knows how to shop."

"Nearly 130 acres," Tom said. "Maybe he's staying at a nearby hotel, using that as his base."

"It would be a lot cheaper than the *Ritz*," Hector said. "Plus it would give him 20 or 25 miles of distance and anonymity. Right by the freeway for easy ingress and egress."

"I wonder if the imitation maid is there too."

"We'll find out," Hector said.

"What's he driving?"

"An Audi."

"That's interesting. May be a personal car."

"Right. He's tall; I don't know how comfortable he is in it, but I'm sure he likes the speed and acceleration, especially when a hot-tempered, heavily armed officer of the law is following him."

"Hopefully he doesn't know that. By the way, I'm almost there," Tom said.

"You want me to still keep my distance?"

"Yes. We can't touch him because he hasn't broken any laws; let's see what he does."

"Where are you, Tom?"

"Just pulling into the mall."

"He parked in the north parking structure and he's headed into *Nordstrom's*."

"I'll get there as soon as I can."

"He went into the Men's room about two minutes ago," Hector said. "I'm not surprised. Wait . . . here he comes. He's looking at shoes, probably just killing time. Where are you?"

"I just found a place. I'll be there in a minute or two."

"He's looking at ties now. So far two salesclerks have volunteered to help him and he blew both of them off."

"Any sign of the woman?"

"Not yet. It's almost 1:30. Maybe that's the time for their meet."

"If she shows you can take one of them and I can take the other."

"Right," Hector said. "Wait a sec. This looks promising."

"Where is he now?"

"Men's leather jackets. Those nice lambskin jobs. The ones that go for eight or nine hundred bucks. He's looking at them but he's also looking around, maybe for her."

"Where are you?" Tom asked.

"Back in the *Façonnable* section, the one with the pricey shirts. I'm about 15 feet from him."

"I've got you," Tom said. "And I've got him. He's tall."

"Yes, six-three or four."

"Don't look for me. I'll try to get a good picture of him with my cell phone and I don't want to draw any unnecessary attention."

"Not to worry. I'm looking at $165 shirts. I don't think I'll be buying any though."

"Got him. Two good angles."

"Here she comes, Tom . . . on his right."

She walked past him and began looking at sweaters on a nearby table. He checked the price on one of the leather jackets, took out his handkerchief, blew his nose, and then nonchalantly walked toward the sweater table. Both of their heads were down.

"That looks like a wig," Tom said.

"Yes. She was wearing it before. Maybe she thought the dark color would make her look more working class than like a member of the Newport Beach set."

"The way the sides hang down . . . it's hard to see her lips move. Fortunately I got a good shot of her before she started to look down. Wait . . . he's leaving. Which one do you want?"

"I'll take him," Hector said. "I know where he's parked in case I lose him in one of the stores."

"Good. Stay in touch."

She left *Nordstrom's* and went in *Tiffany, Dior* and *Chanel,* then came back through *Valentino* and back into *Nordstrom's.*

Perfunctory, Tom thought. She mustn't believe she's being followed. Her car was parked close enough to Tom's that he could identify it and get back to his before she got too far ahead of him in the line of traffic exiting the lot.

The car was a Jaguar XJR. About eighty thousand bucks, Tom thought, not your standard maid's car.

A few minutes later he called Hector. "Where are you?"

"Heading back toward Laguna," he said. "How about you?"

"Me too."

"I wonder why they didn't just meet at the beach and have an ice cream."

"Trying to be more cautious than that."

"Right. I'll call you as soon as he stops."

"Good," Tom said.

Twenty minutes later Tom's cell rang. "He's back at the *Ritz,*" Hector said. "He spent some time rooting around in the trunk before he went into the hotel. I couldn't see what it was that he was looking for. How about the girl?"

"She just stopped and parked. In the Hills. Three doors down the street from my house."

CHAPTER ELEVEN
Avenida Malaga, Laguna Hills
Monday, 3:00 p.m.

Tom called Dietrich's cell number.

"Chief, it's Tom, don't say my name."

"Hi."

"I'm afraid the office landline may be bugged. Just listen to me and give me one- or two-word answers."

"Sounds good."

"I moved the subject out of her hotel room and asked my colleague to keep an eye out. A person came to the room, impersonating a maid."

"How so?"

"She was wearing a wig; she didn't have a maid's cart and she didn't recognize words in elementary Spanish."

"Go on."

"Later my colleague saw a colleague of her's, watching an exit at the hotel. A few minutes later he received a call. He drove to Costa Mesa where he met with the woman. He then returned to the hotel, followed by my colleague. I followed the woman and she is now parked outside of my home."

"Say again."

"*My home*. My dad's place; in the Hills."

"Very interesting."

"They probably located the subject through her credit card transactions."

"Yes."

"That means we're not dealing with amateurs or people without means."

"True."

"It also means that David Bennett was murdered."

"Probably so."

"If they know that I'm on the case they either have your office bugged or they've been following you."

"That's true."

"I wanted you to be aware of the fact that you could be under surveillance."

"Thanks very much."

"When I know more I'll be back in touch."

"I look forward to talking to you. Bye."

Diana secured the sliding door that closed off the boat's cabin, locked it, and returned to the table. She spread her notes and her brother's photos across it and took out a pad and pen.

It had taken her hours to accumulate and then sort through her own xeroxes and notes taken on the library materials and compare them with the materials left by David. The UCLA library had been crowded when she got there and half of her time was devoted to finding maps and pictures and then locating a copier that wasn't broken or already taken. Finally, she could think through what she had found and what she believed she had learned.

She looked at the human timeline she had scribbled in pencil on a lined sheet of notebook paper: tentative dates for the origin of the universe, the appearance of life, the division of cells, the emergence of hominids, *homo erectus*, elementary tools, Achulean tools, brain expansion, language, art, agriculture, religion, war. She made more notes: Stonehenge, Troy, Sinai, Athens, Bethlehem, Rome, Mecca, Paris, Oxford, Florence, Pisa, London, Edinburgh, the Galapagos, Gettysburg, Versailles, Berlin, Washington.

She drew a graph with x and y axes, charting time points, then a spectrum line: the journey from point *a* to point *b*. The whole trip as hunters and gatherers with hunter and gatherer brains and gene pools, with a thin segment at the end, marked **c** for civilization and, after a moment's thought, encased in quotation marks. Then she added David's name above the line and underlined it twice.

She compared photographs, the ones left by David with the ones she had photocopied from UCLA. The Xerox machine took out the color and blurred the shadows, but the outlines were clear. He had been able to do it. She could even see how he had been able to do it. The only remaining question was why.

She needed to sit down with Tom Deaton, show him these things, get him engaged and motivated to help. Where would they start? How much time would he need to make preparations and secure his authorizations before they could leave? Would they be followed? Were there people waiting for them *there*, waiting to kill them as they had killed David? Again the question: Why? David had completed his work and it had been brilliant, stunning, even transcendent in its simplicity. And now it was gone, with him. Work that no one else could have done, work that resulted in his death. She had to find it and she had to find whoever had taken it. Find them before they found her. She liked Deaton. He was alert and smart, even after major surgery. But what of the jurisdictional lines and the limits of his authority? Perhaps he would not be permitted to accompany her. If not him, who then? And how? Meanwhile they were watching her, or trying to. There was no time to sit and wring hands; they had to act. *She* had to act, even if she had to act alone.

"We have lost her."

"What do you mean you've lost her?"

"She registered at the Ritz-Carlton Hotel in Laguna Niguel, using a personal VISA card. We accessed their registration system, found her room, and Helena went in dressed as a maid."

"And?"

"There was no one there except a Mexican. It was a trick."

"What do you mean, a trick?"

"He spoke to her in Spanish, trying to trip her up."

"And?"

"She left immediately. I was outside, watching the rear exit, but no one appeared."

"They must think they are very clever."

"Yes."

"We shall see. Do you think that the Mexican is a policeman?"

"Probably. Helena returned to the room later and took some prints from the bathroom. There was not a great deal of time; she did what she could. Our contact in Washington is checking on them now."

"The Mexican may help lead us to her. Are you outside, ready to follow him?"

"Of course."

"Where is Helena?"

"She is at the home of the policeman assigned to the case."

"So they are still pursuing it."

"For now."

"I am not pleased by these developments."

"As I expected. We will eliminate them as soon as we can."

"See that you do."

Tom watched the woman in the Jaguar for forty minutes before making any moves. When she bent over momentarily he slipped out of the side of his car, closed the door gently, and made his way through some yards and foliage until he could position himself to record her license number. He had caught glimpses of it on the freeway, but wanted to be sure.

Now that she had removed the wig her neck and shoulders were fully visible beneath her bright blonde hair. There were earpods in her ears. Either she was listening to music or she had bugged his house and was trying to detect any sounds of movement or voice communications.

She wouldn't know about the boat, he thought to himself. At least we have that. Her accomplice was staking out the hotel, so they must have assumed that someone would return there. If it was Diana, they could take her. If it was Hector they could follow him in hopes of finding her.

He wondered what else they knew . . . and how much time he and Diana had before they would find them and attempt to kill them.

CHAPTER TWELVE
The Harbor at Dana Point
Monday 5:15 p.m.

"It's me," Tom said as he knocked gently on the sliding door that enclosed the cabin.

"Are you OK?" Diana asked, as she released the dead bolt and slid open the panel.

"I'm fine," he said. "It took me a little while to get back. First we had to track down the people who were watching the hotel, then I had to go by the station. I took the full tour of Laguna after that, so no one would be able to follow me here."

"Did you find out who they are?"

"No. We've got pictures of each of them that we're checking on. We've also got license numbers for each of their cars, but their vehicles were registered to a dummy corporation. We'll try to trace them back to an actual individual, but so far every piece of skin we peel back reveals a new layer beyond it."

"Have you talked to Chief Dietrich?"

"Yes, I have. Twice. He's persuaded that the case is not as straightforward as they first believed. He'll be speaking to the D.A. We're going to proceed with the investigation, but lowkey it. We don't want to draw any unnecessary attention at this point. The press is already making enquiries. Their patience will start to fray in a day or two and they'll demand more detailed answers to their questions."

"We've got to go to France," Diana said.

"France?" Tom said, surprised.

"Yes. David was making a copy of a famous work of art. His copy's now gone. The original is in France."

"I don't understand," Tom said.

"Neither do I," Diana answered, "but we've got to find out why he did it and our only choice is to start in France."

"Why would he make a copy of a unique, known work?" Tom asked. "Forgers usually make copies of prints or other forms that are produced in numbers. I can understand somebody passing off a previously unknown work as the work of a master, but the only reason to make a copy of an original, familiar work would be to substitute it after you've stolen the original."

"I know. I agree," Diana said. "But this work is special. It's one of a kind and I can't imagine how it could be stolen."

"Why is it special?"

"It's a prehistoric cave painting, Tom."

"A cave painting, you mean like a Lascaux cave painting?"

"Yes, exactly."

"Do you have all of the information on it?"

"Yes, I do, and time is of the essence. Whatever is happening, the murderers must be involved. They've eliminated David. That clears the way for their next move. We've got to get to France before they make it."

"Then we'll have to meet with the Chief. We're way out of our jurisdiction, to say the least. We'll need help with the French authorities and that means we'll first need help with the agencies in Washington. I can't do that. The Chief speaks for the Department. He'll need to secure the kind of help that this will require."

"Maybe the governor could help. He owns four of David's paintings. He bought them long before he was elected; he met with David and later maintained a correspondence with him."

"That sounds promising."

"And don't worry about the expenses; I'll cover those," Diana said.

"I'm not sure about the legalities in that case."

"I'm sure they can be worked out," Diana said.

"We've got to meet with the Chief and show him what you have. He'll be pitching on our behalf; he'll have to be convinced."

"I can convince him," Diana said.

"We'll need a secure place in which to meet. He'll be under surveillance now that they know we're proceeding with the investigation and that you and I have suddenly disappeared."

"I know a good place," Diana said. "Let me check . . ."

"We can meet in the private dining room of a winery in Temecula. David and I toured the region several years ago; the owner of this winery was particularly nice. His name is Mike Angioni. I just talked to him. He'll make the room available after the tasting room is closed and the tourists have all left for dinner and bed."

"It'll take a little over an hour to get there, probably closer to an hour and a half with the initial backstreet driving to shake anyone who might be following us," Tom said. "I'll check with the Chief and see if he's available."

Tom and Diana were the first to arrive. She began immediately to arrange her materials. Chris Dietrich arrived fifteen minutes later, apologized for being late, and greeted each of them.

"I haven't had the opportunity to meet you yet, Dr. Bennett," he said.

"Please, call me Diana."

"Chris Dietrich."

"Do you like art, Chief?"

"I don't know very much about it, but I know how important it is to the city and I know how great a painter your brother was."

"My brother completed a work just before he died. That work has disappeared. The original is in France and it is quite special. I do not believe that we can proceed with the investigation without going to France and learning whatever we can there. I'm prepared to cover the costs for myself and Tom and help you in any way that I can to make this possible with the powers that be. The governor owns four of David's paintings and he and David corresponded. I think he could be of help in clearing the way for us at the federal level."

"I could use as much help as you and he could provide," Dietrich said. "The French have a reputation for being . . . *proprietary.*"

"I understand," Diana said, "but they also love art and they loved David's in particular, especially considering the fact that he was an American."

"Tell me about the work that he copied," Dietrich said.

"I've assembled some materials that will help tell the story," she said. "Come around to this side of the table and I'll show you."

"The horses of Pech-Merle," Diana said. "The *Chevaux Ponctués.* The cavern that contains them is near Cahors on the river Lot. Their age is still disputed, but they're older than Lascaux by several thousand years. Seventeen or eighteen thousand years before Christ, fifteen thousand before Stonehenge. If Lascaux is the Sistine Chapel of prehistory, Pech-Merle is its Chartres. The horses are the focal point of a natural structure which, in itself, is breathtaking. Look at the height of the ceiling. Most of the rock shelters and caves of the Dordogne are narrow and confining. Low, curving overhangs and long, tight passageways. Endless head-bumping paths. This is different. Pech-Merle is a cathedral, with vast stalactites and stalagmites. The main hall is 140 meters by 25 and the horses are its centerpiece. The horses were designed to dominate the gallery. Each is nearly 160 centimeters in width."

"Prehistoric cave paintings," Dietrich said.

"Pre-Magdalenian cave paintings," Diana answered. "Probably

Solutrean, possibly even Gravettian. There are at least 68 animal figures at Pech-Merle, 28 human figures, and 595 signs and shapes. The *Frise Noire* which some call the Chapel of the Mammoths is also memorable, but the horses are the image which no one forgets."

"They're painted on a single slab of stone?" Tom asked.

"Yes, it originally fell from the ceiling of the cave. A whole set of slabs fell. This is the one they chose to paint, probably because of its position within the cave. This and the other slabs may have been used ceremonially. That's pure speculation, of course; we don't know anything for certain except that the horses are there; they survived. The slab is now connected with the body of the cave by a flat platform projecting above and beyond it. Some people want to see it as a prehistoric altar."

"This is what your brother was working on," Dietrich said. "It's incredible."

"Here," she said, taking a second photograph from her file folder. It was a freestanding slab in an open room. "The basement of David's Laguna studio," she said.

Tom held both photographs, looking at each in turn and then looking at each again. "The horses are flawless," he said, "even down to the density of the pigments. The lines and dots, the degree to which the pigments have faded, the patterns in the stone, the outline of the horse on the right where the stone is shaped like the horse's nose . . . What are these red markings here?" He pointed at the second photograph.

"It's a fish. Probably the first drawing on the stone. It's usually identified as a pike. The original drawings and markings were done at different times, in some cases thousands of years apart. That's right— *thousands*. This tableau is more than a series of integrated paintings. It is literally a history of the first stages of the human plastic arts."

Tom stared at the photograph, trying to absorb it all.

"Throughout this part of France they've found jewelry and carved objects. Beads, bones, etched ivory. Very impressive, particularly for their time, but nothing like this. One man saw cave paintings in the Dordogne and said that he hadn't known that Marc Chagall had painted on stone walls."

"They just seem to float there," Tom said. "You feel the movement but it's like they're in another dimension. There's no background, no foreground, no setting, just two horses, turned away from us . . . they're just . . ."

"Being horses," she said.

He nodded at her, then moved his head slowly from side to side, as she continued. "When they found David's body he had dust in his mouth. See the hand prints around the horses?"

"Yes."

"They're negatives. The artist held his hand against the surface and then blew dust over it, outlining it against the wall."

"As a signature?"

"Perhaps. Some think the hand negatives were added later. In effect they say 'I was here'. The creation of the negatives would be part of the ceremonies held in the cave. That's the theory, at least."

"How would they blow the dust, with a tube?"

"Yes, possibly a wooden tube or a hollowed piece of bone. What we don't know is whether they put the dust in the tube and blew or put the dust in their mouths and then blew through the tube. David would have experimented with both methods. Nothing less than complete authenticity would have satisfied him. The hand negatives postdate the horses. So do the dots inside the horses and across their backs. He must have just been completing the project when he was killed. If you look more closely at the two photographs you'll see that his work is not quite finished. He would have done the dots in stages. When he took the photograph he had two dots left to do, all of them red. See . . . right . . . *here.*"

"Maybe he was creating materials as he went along and had to stop to replenish his supply," Dietrich said. "This wouldn't be over-the-counter stuff."

"The cave artists used a combination of things. They could have gotten black pigments from manganese dioxide, black iron oxide, or charcoal. Crushed calcite would have given them white powder. Yellow ochres and brown ochres could have been heated so that they would redden in the fire. The cave artists stirred the minerals with sand or clay, crushed them in a mortar, and bound the mixture with water. David would have struggled with it, laboring to get it right. He would be learning a technique that others had practiced for thousands of years. And it had to be perfect. The color is the most important thing after the line."

"The similarity is uncanny," Dietrich said.

"He finished it and then suddenly he was killed," Tom said. "Why? To guarantee his silence or to guarantee the work's uniqueness? Or both?"

CHAPTER THIRTEEN
Rancho California Road, Temecula
Tuesday, 8:10 p.m.

As Tom's questions hung unanswered in the air there was a knock at the door that startled each of them. The door opened slowly. It was Mike Angioni.

"Excuse me," he said. "I thought you might like something to eat. It's just a tray of things from the tasting room . . . still fresh. Some cheese and crackers and fresh fruit. The wine is one of our specialties. It's a Sangiovese that's late-harvested. The sugar level is high; it's a dessert wine. It should taste good with the food."

"Thanks very much, Mike," Diana said.

"No problem. Sorry for the interruption," he said.

They stared at the beautiful food and felt the incongruity of its presence in a room where the most recent discussion had been of death.

"Don't be shy," Diana said. "We're all going to need our strength."

"We'll need pictures," Dietrich said. "For new documents. If these people can access credit card files and snoop on the office of the police chief (it *was* bugged, by the way, Tom) they'll be able to check airline and customs files. Hold on a second . . ."

Dietrich went out to his car and brought in an aluminum briefcase. Among other things, it contained a Nikon camera. "We should use different backgrounds. I'll take Tom in front of a white wall and Diana in front of one that is slightly off-white."

They used a wall in the tasting room and one in a storage area. "I have a secure site in Washington where they will create the documents," Chris said. "You'll also need a local contact when you get to France. In the meantime," he said, picking up his glass and taking a sip of the dessert wine, "you should be thinking about some aliases for your airline reservations, credit cards, and hotel check-ins."

"I appreciate this, Chief," Tom said.

"No problem. We can't have one of the most prominent artists in the world killed in our town and not respond accordingly."

"Question," Tom said.

"Sure, what is it, Tom?"

"How do you think they bugged your office?"

"Probably using the cleaning crew as cover. New outfit. Hired since you went into the hospital. They come and go at night, sometimes together, sometimes singly. This time somebody left something behind besides footprints, one beneath my desk, one beneath the conference table. I'm leaving them there in the meantime."

"Good idea," Diana said. "They should continue to believe that we're not making progress."

"Right. Now what else do we need?" Dietrich asked.

"Besides prayers and luck? Just Diana's call to the governor," Tom said.

"Let's hold off on that for awhile," Dietrich said. "So long as I can promise his support if we need it, I think I can get some help from the feds based on what we have. The more people who are involved in the discussion the more vulnerabilities we create."

Tom and Diana both nodded approvingly.

"They'll be watching the local airports," Dietrich said. "I think you should take a more circuitous route."

"I agree," Tom said. "Meanwhile, we'll get some things together and wait for your call."

"Thank you, Chief," Diana said. "I won't forget the help you've given us."

"Good luck," he answered.

"Why has there been no report?"

"They are being very clever. Do not worry; it is only a matter of time before we discover their location and their degree of progress."

"Are you watching the detective's house?"

"Yes, of course."

"And the sister's?"

"Yes. She has not returned. She has an uncle in New York. We are checking on him and on his house."

"Is there a record of her taking a flight?"

"No, but she might have used an assumed name."

"That is not easy to do without official help."

"Perhaps someone fabricated identification papers for her, for a fee."

"That is possible, but under the circumstances not very likely. I do not like this at all; I want to know where they are; I want to know what they are saying and what they are doing. We need to finish with this business and move on. Bennett's work is finished. I do not want to have to deal with this again."

"I understand. We have placed listening devices in the office of the police department Chief."

"Good, good. But I take it that you have learned nothing from them."

"True, but perhaps that is a good thing. We have learned nothing because they know nothing."

"True. Stay in touch with me. And do not make me call you again for a report."

"Yes, sir. I will call you every three hours."

"Without fail."

"Without fail, sir."

Tom and Diana drove to a small hotel in Escondido. He badged the desk clerk, registered as William Denton, and took two adjoining rooms, prepaid in cash. "We'll shop first thing in the morning," he said. "I don't want to go back to my house and I don't want to tempt fate by continuing to use the boat as a base."

"I agree," Diana said. "We can get some clothes and a bag in Escondido and stay clear of Laguna until we hear from Chief Dietrich. I believe that we should travel as if we're a couple. That would be most plausible."

"Yes. Would you like me to think of a name?

"I already have one," she said. "Justice."

"Wayne and Katharine?"

"Done."

II

THE GREEN DISEASE

CHAPTER FOURTEEN
The Newport Beach *Marriott*
Thursday 9:55 a.m.

He knew that they would tease him mercilessly if they caught him with the candy a second time. They brought it out in the afternoon, during the first post-lunch break. In the morning it was the sweet rolls, the donuts and Danish. Sometimes the miniature bagels. Always the exact same size; how did *Marriott* get them that way? Were they stamped out of a machine like pieces of candy, carefully quality-controlled? Control always managed to trump quality, especially with the bagels. They were always a little too cold, a little too stale, the top and bottom parts joined a little too closely. Then you wrestled them into submission with the plastic knives and tried to make them palatable with the cheese that wasn't always Philly cream.

By the afternoon they were gone, replaced by the bowls of hard candy—anything to provide the sugar rush that would help the conventioneers force their eyes open and continue to stare at the PowerPoint with feigned interest. The pads and pens were aligned with military rigor, as were the complimentary plastic folders with the *Marriott* logo. The only flaws were the widening concentric circles of coffee stains beneath the scuffed plastic tubs, the shutoff valves never quite sealing the taps. Or maybe that was part of the deal, the guaranteed stain. Still, they always chose the same chain. "The quality is not great," one planner said, "but it's at least consistent."

This time the subject of the refresher course was "After Miranda," a tour of the most recent legal challenges and precedent-setting decisions. Hector's attendance had been required. A "command performance" was the LBPD's duty roster notation.

Three months earlier the subject was "Welcoming Diversity" and four months before that, "Managing Change." The only real recompense for a lost workday was the pocketful of hard candy he had taken from the meeting room table—a few from each bowl to divert attention from his action—and passed on to the kids in his neighborhood. Somehow the word got back to the station house, along with his new nickname, "The Candyman." When a quartet of female officers crooned in harmony— "The Candyman makes/Everything he bakes/Satisfying and delicious/ Talk about your childhood wishes/You can even eat the dishes," he knew that any future actions would have to be decidedly more covert. Swearing the neighborhood kids to secrecy wouldn't work; they didn't *do* secrecy. Maybe he'd light-finger a pocketful of creamers and feed the feral cats in the park near his mother's house. At least they wouldn't talk. But would they accept the kind with the almond flavoring?

He turned these thoughts over in his head while the lawyer/ consultant droned on and the clock hands seemed frozen in space and time. At the break he walked down the hall to the stairwell, scaling the stairs two at a time in an effort to get his blood pumping and his leg muscles loose. He felt a little better when he returned to the meeting floor, used the bathroom, and thought about the reward of a fresh hot cup of coffee. Dueling with the motion-sensor towel dispenser, he felt marginally refreshed and mentally prepared for another hour of tedium. Then he walked into the hallway and saw him.

He was staring at the notepad in one of the complimentary plastic folders. The speaker had called it *pleather*, an attempt at humor designed to clear heads and open eyes during a particularly dry discussion of a case that had tanked because of Miranda slipups. This time he was dressed differently than he had been outside the *Ritz*. It may have been his only suit but it was bland enough to help him pass as a coerced conventioneer rather than a *Penney's* customer.

Hector walked to the drinking fountain, took a sip of water, checked his watch, and walked to the end of the hallway, out of earshot. He slipped out his cell phone and called the station. The desk sergeant bounced the call to the Chief's cell phone, which he carried outside of his office.

"What have you got?" Dietrich asked.

"Uninvited guest at the meeting, Chief."

"Someone we know?"

"Yes, a recent acquaintance."

"From the Bennett case?"

"Yes, the man."

"Following you?"

"Seems to be."

"Perfect. Do you think you can tear yourself away from the meeting for awhile?"

"No problem, Chief."

"I thought you might say that. Here's what you do . . ."

CHAPTER FIFTEEN
Route 91, East
Thursday 10:50 a.m.

"Where are you?"

"I'm following the Mexican."

"Where is he going?"

"I don't know yet. He's headed toward Corona. He was at a conference earlier this morning, some sort of mandatory course that the police are forced to take."

"And he just left?"

"Yes."

"That is interesting. His attendance was probably a diversion. He is headed toward the desert, perhaps to meet Bennett's sister and the other detective."

"That is my assumption. They have been hidden well, but perhaps not so well that we can't find them."

"I must know what they are doing and I must know how much they have learned."

"I understand."

"Where are you now?"

"On the 60, just beyond Riverside."

"Is there any chance that he might have seen you?"

"No. After I followed him to the hotel this morning I put a tracking device on his car. I am able to follow him at a safe distance."

"Good. Did he appear to be acting routinely?"

"At first, yes, but at the break he made a phone call in the hallway outside the meeting room. As soon as the call was completed he left."

"He received new orders perhaps."

"Yes."

"Possibly from his superiors. They are at the coast, not in the desert. He is driving away from them; he is joining Bennett's sister."

"Yes."

"I don't like the fact that they have gone to such lengths to protect them. That means they are suspicious. I did not want them to be suspicious. I wanted them to close the case, forget about David Bennett, and move on."

"I understand."

"Continue to follow him and continue to check in with me."

"I will."

"I have just passed Banning."

"He is going to Palm Springs."

"Yes, unless there is some isolated place in the desert."

"He would have turned off and driven up into the mountains. There are many more locations in which to hide there. A single place in the desert would make too fine a target."

"That is true."

"Whatever you do, do not lose him."

"I won't."

"He is in Palm Springs. He just passed the road for the tram."

"That would have made a nice rallying point. Apparently he's going somewhere else."

"The traffic is light. I am two blocks behind him."

"There are many hotels there where they could be hiding. False names are not uncommon in Palm Springs hotels."

"I understand."

"What will you do if you find them all there?"

"I could kill them promptly but that would draw a great deal of attention."

"We do not want any more attention. If you find them we will arrange for some sort of accident. They have to leave sometime. The detective cannot know anything, but the sister might. Her brother might have said something, something that she did not understand at the time, but something that could come out later. It is essential that she be removed."

"Yes."

"I have passed through Cathedral City and am coming into Rancho Mirage."

"Yes . . ."

"I am a block behind him now. Wait . . . he is turning right, driving up into the mountains. There is a resort there."

"A resort? The police would not pay for a resort. Bennett's sister must be paying."

"This will be difficult . . ."

"What? What is wrong?"

"There is a long driveway into the resort, with a prominent porte-cochère There are several bellmen walking around. They will see me if I drive up behind him."

"Park at a distance and continue to speak on your cell phone. Make it obvious that you are involved in a call. They will think you are there to pick someone up."

"I will. Wait . . ."

"What is it?"

"They have taken his car to valet-park it. A woman is coming out of the hotel to greet him."

"Is it Bennett's sister?"

"I don't think so. She is dressed in a swimsuit, with sunglasses and a short robe."

"How can you be so sure that that is not Bennett's sister?"

"The woman is very beautiful. She is kissing him."
"Damn."
"It could be a diversion of some sort."
"Damn."
"This could all have been arranged as part of their plan."
"It was all arranged to make you look like a fool."

CHAPTER SIXTEEN
The 101 at Isla Vista, Santa Barbara
Thursday, 7:30 p.m.

The glimmer of lights on the waves was punctuated by the motions of an occasional pelican gliding in search of a late dinner. "You can see the oilrigs in the distance," Chris Dietrich said, trying to talk her awake. "It looks idyllic, but you can still pick up some tar on a moonlight walk if you don't watch your step."

"I appreciate your driving me here," Diana said. She had slept for most of the drive and her head was beginning to clear as Chris merged and slowed for the off-ramp. She shifted in her seat, stretching her legs and working out the cramps in her ankles. "When will I connect with Tom?"

"Passenger lists are easy to crack, even with phony names, but we'll add some static to the system," Chris said. "We'll fly you to Washington by way of Santa Barbara and Oakland. Tom will leave from Ontario and meet you there two days later. The pictures of you we took in Temecula have been Fed-Exed to a P.O. Box in Falls Church, Virginia. New passports will be ready when you arrive. They'll put the pictures in old folders and date-stamp some of the pages so the passports won't draw any attention. Your British Air ticket will have an Edinburgh leg attached, but the Brits will send two stand-ins to Scotland for you, while you change terminals at Heathrow and fly to Bordeaux with separate tickets on Air France. Complicated for anyone trying to follow, but not complicated for us. How much time do you think you'll need in France?"

"That depends on what we find. There are so many questions and so little time. The longer we wait the harder it will be to retrace David's steps. That's what Tom said and I agree with him."

Tom. Twice now, Chris thought.

"How do you feel now?" Dr. Whelan asked.

"Better than I did an hour ago," Tom said.

"Maybe you're pushing yourself too hard. You've just had major surgery."

"I understand. I was afraid that the headache might be a symptom of something serious."

"I don't see any indication of that," Whelan said, "but you shouldn't press yourself just yet. It takes time to heal. Think about when you go to the dentist . . ."

"I don't understand . . ."

"When you go to the dentist there's something wrong with your mouth. You know it instantly. And whatever it is—a cracked tooth, a loose filling, an abnormal sensitivity—you're constantly aware of it. You keep exploring it with the tip of your tongue. You know there's a problem and you can't stay away from it. Even after you've identified it and know what needs to be done to solve it, your tongue keeps going there."

"Right."

"It's as if there's an intruder there; something's wrong; the problem has to be solved. *Now.*"

"Yes."

"Then as soon as it's fixed you have similar feelings. The new filling or crown . . . and especially an extraction . . . it's an affront to the system. There's something *new* going on and your mouth feels out of kilter. It's not used to the new thing there or the old thing gone, even if it means you're cured. It takes awhile until your mouth starts telling your brain that everything's OK. You've found a new *normal*, as it were."

"I understand."

"Your whole body's like that, Tom. It's a highly integrated organism. It notices disruptions. It tries to get used to them and accommodate itself to them and eventually it does, usually. But it takes awhile. The body is both incredibly hearty and incredibly sensitive."

"I'll try not to think too much for awhile; maybe that'll help."

Whelan smiled. "That's easier said than done. The brain has its own ways of keeping itself in order. Why do you think we dream?"

"I don't know . . . to sort back through the problems of the previous day?"

"There's some of that, but the brain is exploring patterns, coherent patterns. It's exercising; it's doing what it always does . . . finding facts and forms and integrating them through the use of stories. That's one way of putting it anyway. And it's only a theory . . . but it's a theory that makes sense to me."

Tom suddenly noticed that while every feature and object in Whelan's examining room was either white or silver, everything in his office was brown, including Whelan's hair and eyes. He felt better there. Or his eyes and brain did. He hadn't thought of his brain as separate from the rest of his body before the identification and removal of the astrocytoma.

"So what should I do now, Doctor?"

"Just what you would normally do, but don't push," Whelan said.

"Get good sleep."

"Yes."

"Don't overextend."

"Right."

"Try to avoid violence."

"Absolutely, especially trauma to the head."

"How about exercise?"

"Of course, but in moderation."

"I'll do my best, under the circumstances," Tom said.

"That's all we can ever do," Whelan said. "You're fortunate in the fact that your general physical condition is very good. Just take it easy. You know what would be good for you now?"

"What's that?"

"You should sit back in a chair, raise your feet a little, try to clear your head, and just rest."

"For how long?"

"Not for five minutes. Five hours would be better. Ten would be better still."

"I think I can actually do that," Tom said.

"And when you get up . . ."

"Yes?"

"Everything in moderation."

"I'll try," Tom said.

CHAPTER SEVENTEEN
Dominion Conference Center, Chantilly, Virginia
Saturday, 9:40 p.m.

Diana turned off the air conditioner and slid back the window in her second-floor room. The evening air coming off the Blue Ridge was warm and moist. She sat down in the armchair nearest the window and let the warm air engulf her head and neck and shoulders. The room was a combination of generic luxury and conference-room efficiency. She had a simple coffee maker with a tray of foil packets, some pouches of whitener and a selection of teas, sweeteners, and powdered soups. The soap, shampoo, and conditioner came in plastic bottles with an ornate, English-looking design and a Hartford, Connecticut manufacturing address. The shoeshine "cloth" was paper, not cotton, and the heavily-laundered, single bathrobe had no logo. The flat-screen TV offered 120 cable channels along with the principal networks and PBS. Next to it, on an imitation mahogany desk, was a standup, cardboard card detailing the hotel's business-center services and facilities. There was also a card entitling her to a free drink with any entrée in the Commonwealth Room. It had been there when she arrived, nearly two days ago now.

The room next door was actually the security headquarters for the hotel. With all the Washington muck-a-mucks and wannabe muck-a-mucks seeking shelter beyond the beltway, the facility built its market niche on an array of special security services. In the private wing there was a bank of rooms with ingress and egress by separate, locked staircase. The central kitchen made room-service deliveries to the security headquarters and the food was then brought to individual rooms by armed officers. No one from the regular staff knew which guest was in which room. The entrance to the principal section of the private wing from the main hallway was through a locked, dummy door labelled the *Jefferson Suite*. Calls were screened through a separate switchboard and electronic messages on the TV's came through a line serving only the security headquarters and the rooms in the private wing.

There were also adjoining pooled-space rooms for aides, assistants, and gofers; soundproof meeting rooms, laptops for PowerPoint dog and pony shows, multi-tipped power cords for Androids, iPhones, and Bluetooth accessories, heavily-encrypted wireless setups and other mover-shaker emoluments. The windows overlooked a stand of dense spruce surrounded by a twelve-foot security fence. The Blue Ridge and piedmont were visible in the distance, rippling across the horizon like a series of leap-frogging clouds.

At twelve minutes before 10:00 there was a knock at the door. Diana looked through the fisheye peephole and saw the guard's identification tag. They always held it at eye level. She opened the door and the guard, a tall, stocky man named Alan, said, "Someone to see you." He stepped aside and Tom stepped forward. "Hi," he said. He was carrying a brown paper bag.

"Hi," she answered. "Come on in." The guard turned and she closed the door behind Tom. She gave him a hug that was half affection, half relief. "You look so much better," she said. "How do you feel?"

"Good, even after two flights and a stopover in Denver. Actually, *because of* the two flights and the stopover. My doc told me to sit down and kick back, so that's exactly what I did."

"Where's your room?"

"Two doors down the hall, just on the other side of your gofer room. How do you like this place? The city is ringed with them. The goal is to offer just enough luxury to attract the private sector and just enough simplicity to keep the price under the government per diem rate."

She smiled. "What's in the bag?"

"Something to inaugurate our trip. He slid a second chair next to hers, opened the window all the way, and took a bottle of wine, a corkscrew, and two glasses from the bag, placing them on the table in front of them. "French," he said. "I thought we should practice before we do it with the natives." She smiled.

"I wasn't sure what they were serving you here, but I figured it could always stand to be improved," Tom said, taking the dark blue, lead foil from the top of the bottle and going to work on the cork. He eased it out slowly, deliberately. "Try this," he said, pouring her half a glass of the wine. "It should be worth drinking. That's what the guy at the wine store said. I told him I didn't want anything playful or overly assertive. He said this might be a little forward, but I said that that was OK, I could do forward."

She took a sip, put the glass back on the table, and took his hands in hers, clutching him like a lifeline. "It can't be that good," he said. He squeezed her hands gently, released them and picked up his glass, sipping the red wine. "This is very good," he said, "and did I happen to mention how nice it is to see you again?" He tilted his head toward her but her face was turned and her eyes were closed.

He felt awkward and looked around the room, searching for some indication of why she might be feeling this way. On the desk were pictures of her and her brother. He couldn't see them all, but it appeared that there was also a picture of David and Diana with their parents. She and her brother were very young, David no more than twelve, Diana no more than six or seven. There was a snow-covered mountain behind them. They were dressed warmly, the sun in their faces. The parents held ski poles; the children had been brought in for the picture, their parents' hands on their shoulders. A happy and loving family. All of them gone now, but her.

CHAPTER EIGHTEEN

Dominion Conference Center, Chantilly, Virginia
Sunday, 8:15 a.m.

When her phone rang she picked it up without speaking. "How about some breakfast?" Tom asked. "Fine," she said, "just something simple." She sounded better, rested.

"I'll call it in," he said. He ordered toast and breakfast rolls, fresh fruit, and coffee. He thought about where they were going and added two bagels with cream cheese. He told them to bring it to Diana's room. They said it would be there in twenty to thirty minutes. He waited fifteen and then walked down the hall to her door. He knocked and bent down so she could see his face in the peephole. When he heard her hand brush against the door he smiled.

She opened the door and stepped back. She was wearing a knee-length robe. Her hair was pinned up, her eyes were clear and her lips were a deep pink. As he entered the room he saw that she had put the spread back over the bed, covering the sheet and pillows.

"Breakfast should be here in five minutes or so. How did you sleep?"

"Pretty well," she said. "The wine helped. How about you?"

"Fine."

"When do we fly out?"

"The first flight is at 7:50. There's a second a half hour later. We booked the first in case there were any problems with it. If there are problems with the second you have to wait until the next day to fly."

"What about the tickets and passports?"

"I'm picking them up at noon."

"Let me see your incision scar."

"You want to see my scalp . . . before breakfast?"

"I was thinking, here you are running around, buying wine, ordering breakfast, looking after me and all, and I haven't even said anything about you and how you're doing."

"You asked me how I felt when I came in last night."

"That was like saying hi. We never really talked about how you were healing and whether or not you were in pain."

"Have a look," he said, pulling his hair back from the entry site, "still intact. I'm sure it looks sufficiently bad to threaten your appetite but it actually feels pretty good."

"I'm glad," she said, "how about your general strength?"

"Getting better by the hour. I had a little headache a couple days ago, but my surgeon thought it was unrelated to the procedure. Just a standard, run-of-the-mill throb."

"Any dizziness?"

"No, not really. I was a little lightheaded yesterday, but that was after I had been sitting for awhile with my legs locked and I hadn't eaten for about six hours."

She took him through some basic exercises, touching his nose with his fingertips with his eyes closed, keeping his own head rigid, but following her moving fingertip with his eyes. She then took his wrist in her hand and checked his pulse.

"So what's the verdict?" he asked.

"I don't see anything irregular. The pulse is lower than normal, but that's good. So long as it's not irregular and . . . "

"And it doesn't suddenly stop."

"Right," she said.

"You see," he said. "Completely serviceable. Or at least 90 percent so. How about some breakfast?"

Total Wine & More is a successful discount store, the successor to the Hafts' *Total Beverage* outlets. The Chantilly version sits on the south side of route 50, in the back of a long strip mall. What used to be a quiet road to the hunt country is now a clogged, divided highway through an endless line of housing developments, with subdivision signs, nurseries, gas stations, fast food chains, and ersatz town centers as roadmarks. The clientele at *Total* is a cross-section of Northern Virginia, with upscale wine buyers checking Parker ratings, beer-by-the-case natives loading their RV's and pickups, Evian and flavored-Perrier yuppies searching for small-bottle six packs, and suburban hostesses loading up on imported crackers and Riedel glassware.

Tom pulled in at 11:55 and parked between a maroon Toyota Land Cruiser and a leprous '56 Ford Fairlane with the trunk lid removed to create a mini- pickup. The rusty hinges were still in place. He walked through the beer section and on toward the aisles of French wines, stacked on skids in their marked, wooden cases. A man in work clothes was holding a bottle of red Bordeaux and shaking his head from side to side.

He was wearing faded jeans, workman's shoes with thick soles to protect against rocks and nails, and a stained tee-shirt with a Harley logo on the front and patriotic slogan on the back. His forehead was furrowed with lines of sawdust and dried sweat and his unkempt moustache was spackled with droplets of dry wall mud. His shopping cart contained two cases of Bud, a six pack of Michelob, and a cardboard box of Almaden Rhine Blend. Tom approached him from the opposite side of the display.

"Can you believe this?" the man said. "The wife makes me buy wine for her and her friends. Look at this one here: $67.95 a bottle. Who in the hell would pay that for just one bottle?" He returned the bottle to its wooden box; Jack noticed a large mole on his left wrist. His nails were lined with grime.

"And such a small bottle," Tom said.

"Damned right," the man said, shaking his head, nodding and walking away. He pushed his cart toward the opposite end of the store, where the Coke and Pepsi were stacked, paused, picked up another nearby bottle of wine, shook his head, mumbled something under his breath, and moved on.

Tom stayed where he was, inspecting various bottles and checking prices. Finally he walked over to the aisle where the man had stopped on his way to the soda. The bottle he had checked was a split of 2016 Sauternes with a discount price of $39.50, a card carrying a rave notice from Parker, and, now, a set of passports and two tickets to London, two to Edinburgh and, in a second folder, two to Bordeaux.

Tom slid the envelope inside his jacket and took out his wallet in a single motion. He opened the wallet, slipped out two twenties and a five, paused for a moment, picked up the Sauternes and headed toward the checkout. He looked down the long aisle toward the soda. The man in the Harley tee-shirt was nowhere in sight.

CHAPTER NINETEEN
Over New England
Sunday, 8:50 p.m.

The pilot headed up the seaboard before turning to cross the North Atlantic. Twenty minutes past New York Tom got up to stretch his legs and wash his hands before dinner. The toilets in Business class were occupied so he turned around and started down the aisle toward the one at the front of tourist class. Two rows behind him on the opposite side of the aisle was a man in a beige Armani suit, starched white shirt and muted Armani tie; the gold and diamonds of his Rolex were visible at the edge of his French-cuffed sleeve and he was wearing a gold wedding band with a Florentine finish and split-lens reading glasses. His brief case was open and he was going through some papers. Tom looked more closely this time. Something about him looked vaguely familiar, something around the eyes and nose.

Once in the toilet Tom pulled back his hair, touched his incision, combed his hair carefully—the site was still tender—then opened his belt and tucked in his shirt. The scent of the airline cologne was already thick in the air. As he rebuckled his belt he thought about the man in 12C. Suddenly something sparked. He rinsed his face in cold water, washed his hands with the almond-scented liquid soap, combed his hair a second time, and left the toilet, closing the door behind him as quietly as he could.

As he walked back up the aisle toward his seat in row 10 he looked at the man's left wrist. There was the mole. This time the hands were scrubbed cleaner than a surgeon's and the nails were trimmed and filed. They even looked as if they might have had a coat of clear polish. No work shoes, no greasy jeans, no Harley shirt this time. No moustache and no shaving nicks. Nice work, at least in the makeup department.

"Guess what," Tom said, as he eased himself back into his seat.

"What's that?" Diana answered.

"Two rows behind us is the guy who slipped me our passports and tickets back in Virginia. He's in disguise, if that's not too strong a term to use to describe an Armani suit."

"Maybe he's our chaperone."

"Maybe he's watching us to find out what we can learn and who we can locate. If he's on our side, why didn't he make contact? There were no plans for a chaperone. Someone suspicious might assume that he was part of another club, that he had bumped our contact in Chantilly, and now has other plans for us."

"He can't follow us too far. By now we've had the chance to notice him. He should peel off when we get to Heathrow and either go home—mission accomplished—or let someone else pick us up for awhile."

"Right. But if he stays with us we have to take him out. We can't be sure what side he's on and we can't take a chance in the interest of professional courtesy."

"I'll take him. He won't be expecting that," Diana said.

"What do you mean?"

"When we get to Heathrow we'll have a long walk through the airport. The place is bigger than O'Hare. It's not hard to break free of your group. We'll take our time getting off, then we'll let the rest of the passengers from this flight get ahead of us. We'll futz around with our carry-ons, walk a little further, and then go into one of the bathrooms out by the distant gates. We'll take our time, stay in the bathroom for a full ten minutes. If he's still with us when we come out, I'll take care of him. Everybody else will be making their way toward the arrivals hall or the connecting corridors to other terminals."

"What do you mean, 'take care of him'?"

"You'll see."

"I'd like to know first."

"Then it wouldn't be a surprise."

"I don't like surprises. Let me handle him."

She shrugged and nodded in reluctant agreement.

His legs were stiff as they got off the plane and he balanced himself with the handrail in the jetway. Diana noticed but didn't say anything. The jetway led to a quiet set of hallways with steps leading to the upper level. It was the middle of the night on their body clocks but early morning in London, with leaden skies, gray haze hanging in the air from Kent to Berkshire and heavy dew on the dark green grasses lining the highways and runways.

They were in the middle of the crowd when they came into the terminal corridor. Again it was quiet, with an occasional workman buttoning his coveralls and preparing for the day. The walls were bright, the directional signs a garish black and yellow, the gray and red carpeting clean but bland, contrasting with the rubberfaced expressions on the models in the advertisements. *Harvey's Bristol Cream! Schweppes, Ah! Blood Brothers-Still! The Mousetrap! Simply Harrods! Burberry'sBurberry'sBurberry's!*

Diana stopped at a bench at the side of the corridor. She changed the strap on her purse, lengthening it, and slipped it over her head and under her arm. Then she opened the bottom of her carry-on bag, took out a handful of kleenex, folded them, and slipped them into her pocket. By then all but a handful of the passengers from their flight had passed them. They merged into a blur of hats and jackets and carry-ons, working their way toward the Arrivals Hall like a sleepless, aging army.

She and Tom made small talk in the corridor, walking at a leisurely pace. She bumped him gently with her arm—joking, relaxed. When they got to the second set of toilets she stopped, said something to him, waited for his nod, and then turned off to go to the women's. He walked a few steps further and went into the men's. The disinfectant smells hit him the moment he stepped on the tile floor and he remembered his first trip to England in the late nineties: the cologne dispensers at face level on the walls, the urinals with *Armitage Shanks* logos, the white *Durex* machines, the electric rent-a-razors in Victoria Station which people actually used, backpacking tourists huddled with the remnants of the empire and pinstriped businessmen . . . the acrid smell of *Rothman's* . . . . He had to stay focused, keep the memories from rushing in and distracting him from what he had to do. His head was throbbing slightly now, probably from lack of sleep and the skimpy airline meal. He had passed on any alcohol and tried to drink more water than he craved, but he was still lightheaded.

The women's toilet was deserted. Diana checked her lipstick, combed her hair, and rinsed off her hands, patting them dry with a paper towel. If someone *was* waiting for her in the corridor she didn't want him to hear the masking sounds of an electric hand dryer. It might tempt him to make an opportunistic move. She checked her watch. Four minutes. She walked out into the corridor. The man in the Armani suit was standing against the wall, pretending to check his ticket. His attaché case was between his feet.

Diana approached him. "Excuse me," she said. "Do you have any change in British sterling?"

"What do you need?" he asked. His head was turned slightly away from her's.

"I need 50p, but the machine will take 20p and 10p pieces."

He went through the motions of checking the change in his pocket, put it back, and said, "Sorry."

The crisp dollar in her hand slipped through her fingers. She bent over to pick it up. He leaned down in a halfhearted attempt to help as she grabbed the handle of his attaché case and swung it upward, catching him directly on the center of his chin with the steel-reinforced corner.

His head exploded in a flash of silver and black as the circuits crossed and popped. As his legs went limp she gave him a second thump for insurance, this one across the base of his neck. He fell toward the women's toilet, tried to find his footing, and lurched against the doorframe, collapsing at the entrance. She dragged him the rest of the way, propped him in the corner of the wheelchair stall, checked for his wallet, found none, and left him there.

When she returned to the corridor she picked up his attaché case in the doorway as Tom walked out of the men's. "Where did you get that?" he asked.

"From our friend. I thought we might find something interesting inside."

"Where is he?"

"Resting comfortably. Let's get out of here."

The case was locked but Tom worked the catch with the tip of the nail file that had past unnoticed in his carry-on. Inside was a change of shirt, socks, and underwear and a passport in a matching ostrich case. "Very nicely coordinated," he said, slipping the passport into his pocket and sliding the attaché case behind a janitor's cart and leading her down the corridor past the parallel gates.

"Will you do me a favor?" Tom asked.

"Of course. What?"

"Don't ever do that again."

"Do what?"

"Play the Lone Ranger."

"You weren't feeling well," she said. "Your legs were stiff and you kept touching your head with your fingertips. You didn't want to say anything about it, but I knew."

"I mean it," Tom said.

"I had the advantage of surprise."

"The Chief told me you played on college teams."

"Yes, I did."

"They don't use guns or razors in college sports. Out here they do."

"You were walking unsteadily," she said, as they made their way down the corridor. "Circumstances change. Don't you expect me to adjust to them?"

"At the least you should have waited. I could have been there as backup."

"Right," she said. "I just . . . I didn't want you to get hurt."

"I don't want you hurt either," he said, his eyes searching hers as she held her expression. "I work for you."

"We work together," she answered.

CHAPTER TWENTY
Aeroport de Bordeaux
Monday, 12:15 p.m.

She could hear the mock "Merci" just before he put away his phone. She was standing behind a pillar with their carry-ons, looking at the winery posters which blanketed the walls of the airport, a wide-eyed tourist off for a romantic weekend. Her eyes lighted on Chateau *Brane-Cantenac's*. The four-foot bottle floated above the plane of the poster, the gold script below recounting the glories of the Margaux appelation and the special glories of this particular example. Watching the people in the airport she noticed how careful they were in protecting their luggage and handbags.

Tom returned, picked up most of their carry-ons, smiled, and put his arm around her. Together they began walking toward the car rental desk. He was smiling and trying to exude a sense of release, a vacationing American thinking of the sunshine and the wine, anticipating a long drive through the French countryside. Diana was tossing back her hair and straightening the knot on her scarf. Outside, the sun was bright, the sky dotted with scattered clouds. The poplars in the distance were visible through the large airport windows, swaying silently in the midday winds, marking the horizon.

"Interesting news," he said, maintaining his smile. "For starters, our friend, one William Church, is an employee of the United States Government, not a murderous representative of a crime family or some hostile foreign power."

"I'm sorry I hit him so hard," Diana said.

"There's more," Tom said.

"Oh?"

They got in line at the rental desk. He took her by the hand and leaned forward. To any observer he was thinking of her, thinking of their trip together, wondering what it might bring.

"We were working with the FBI," he said, still smiling, "but William Church does not work for the Department of Justice; he works for the Treasury Department."

"Secret Service?" she asked, her eyes probing, searching.

"Yes, Secret Service," he answered, his look responding to hers.

She thought for a moment and then answered her own question. "Assigned to the White House."

"Yes, as a matter of fact. The presidential protection unit, though that's a large group and people rotate in and out of actual service. It could be someone on special assignment."

"What is a Secret Service agent doing following us to London?"

"Exactly the question I asked," Tom said, holding his lips close. "The president is not scheduled to make any trips to Europe so Church wouldn't be here as part of an advance party. And in any case he wouldn't be dressed like a Beverly Hills lawyer."

"He must have been sent by the president."

"Or by somebody who wanted to avoid attention by keeping this in the family. The politics among the intelligence agencies is worse than that in a prep school English department."

"That means that David's death is a part of something much larger."

"Possibly, but not necessarily," Tom said.

"Possibly?"

"Possibly," he said.

They stopped at a winery at 1:20 and pulled over a second time to pick up some bread, fruit, cheese and bottled water at a village store.

They were driving west toward Les Eyzies. The sun was still bright in the afternoon sky, the vines tightly grouped in orderly lines abutting the highway. At 3:00 they drove into Bergerac. "How about a bathroom break?" Tom asked.

"You go ahead," she answered. "I'm fine."

He pulled into the railway station parking lot and entered the toilet at the west end of the building. The room was deserted. He splashed his face and rinsed his hands with tepid water, passing up the communal ball of soap on the steel post, and dried his hands on the driest corner of a revolving towel. Then he combed his hair and walked over to the china urinal. A moment after he got settled a man in a green shirt and black jeans walked in and stood beside him. His hair was dark brown, flecked with gray. "Nice day for a drive through the Dordogne," the man said. "A lot more fun in a red convertible than in a tiny Ford sedan."

He was medium height, but thick, with worry lines around the eyes and mouth that were accented by a recent tan. He looked like a bureaucrat who moonlighted as a bouncer.

"I take it that you're Walt," Tom said. "And by the way, what is actually going on here?"

"Not much," the man said. "We had a friend along to keep an eye on you and your girl friend but she decided to take him out. Left him to cool off in a Heathrow toilet. That's not what I call interagency cooperation."

"How were we supposed to know he was on our side?"

"Fair question."

"He's with the Secret Service."

"Yes . . . well, they wanted to keep tabs on this one."

"Why?"

"If I knew I'd tell you."

"Come on Walt, let's not dance around. This is your plan and setup. They'd tell you *something*."

"I mean it, Detective. I don't know. All I can do is guess."

"Go ahead then, guess."

"Maybe this is bigger than you thought."

"We've already figured that out, Walt. And call me Tom."

"I said *maybe*. I wouldn't draw any heavy conclusions from this. It probably doesn't mean anything. Those people are so jumpy these days they run after everything. When you requested special passports through your PD it set off bells and whistles. With the current level of trust in Washington we're lucky we didn't have to deal with three or four other agencies as well. The moment we cleared our own operation with the Director we found out that the White House was planning to intervene. Bureaucratic ESP."

"You mean bugs and wiretaps."

"And probably some overt leaks."

"Well they aren't intervening now. Listen Walt, do me a favor."

"What's that?"

"Tell the government that whenever they want to bring in a backup they should bring in the first team. We may need them."

Five minutes later they were back on the road. "It'll only be another hour or so," Tom said. Diana just smiled.

"There's something else I need to tell you."

"What's that?"

"I made contact back there."

"In the toilet?"

"Yes."

"Men . . ."

"Where else would you propose we make contact?"

"Nowhere. It's just so . . . fifties."

"I'm sorry, that's our favorite decade."

She smiled. "Was it the man you were expecting?"

"Yes. His name is Walt McNeice. He and Chris Dietrich were in the service together. Afterwards he went into the FBI and Chris enrolled in the police academy."

"I thought the FBI was only supposed to do its thing inside our borders."

"He's on special assignment."

"What does that mean?"

"It means the Chief requested him. He wanted someone he knew and could trust."

"Were they in combat together?"

"Yes. McNeise carried Dietrich over three miles to an unofficial installation in some dusty mountains. His leg was pointing in three or four different directions at the time. McNeise helped save the leg and also kept him from bleeding to death."

"That would take considerable strength as well as knowledge and determination."

"The Chief said he could vouch for him, especially if we got into something tight."

"Did he say why the Secret Service guy was following us?"

"Not really. He speculated that the case could be bigger than any of us are aware of. He also said that paranoia levels are always high in Washington and that our request for doctored passports could simply have tripped a signal that brought an automatic response."

"Shouldn't it have been an FBI agent who gave you the papers, with this guy intervening later? And unexpectedly?"

"Yes, but perhaps the agencies were simply cooperating in a bona fide spirit of openness. Or maybe the FBI guy had to go to his son's soccer game that day."

"Or maybe McNeise is holding something back."

"Maybe that too. We're still not at the point of total interdepartmental unity and integration."

"Better then that I took him out. If they don't have their act together we have to be ready to fend for ourselves."

"You're right," Tom said.

"Thanks," Diana said.

CHAPTER TWENTY-ONE
Hotel de Cro-Magnon, Les Eyzies de Tayac
Monday, 7:55 p.m.

"How was that recently-departed goose's liver?" Diana asked, towelling off her hair and combing it into place. "I noticed that you made short work of it. Most of the things around it too."

She was playing her part as wife or girlfriend. He was surprised that she did it with so little effort.

"It was fantastic and I wasn't surprised, since this is the best place on earth for it. How was all that goat cheese and lettuce and asparagus?" He was talking about food but he was thinking about the smell of her hair and the scent of soap on her arms and legs.

"Great."

"I was reading the desk brochure when you were in the shower. They built the hotel in the late nineteenth century for British tourists. After they discovered the remains of Cro-Magnon man in his rock shelter (just on the other end of the hotel, by the way, right by where we parked) the rich and famous from the other side of the channel made regular pilgrimages here. When you're finished there you should look at the pictures of them with their little maps, walking sticks, long dresses, and heavy wool suits. That may be why the place looks like an English country inn with the pastels and the chintz and the flowers everywhere—to make them feel at home."

"But with French food. It's perfect."

"Yes. I have to keep reminding myself that there are probably people around us who would like to cut our visit short."

"Where's your friend?"

"Next door, to the right." He gestured with his thumb.

"I still haven't seen him."

"Good. You're not supposed to."

"Is anyone with him?"

"Two locals and one assistant."

"And they're . . ."

"One on our other side, one above us and one below us."

"And when did you learn this?"

"Right after we finished that thing with the white nectarines and sorbet but before we started on the coffee and cognac."

"Meeting in the men's room again?"

"Think of it as our special place."

"What time do we leave tomorrow?"

"When I checked the website for the cave it said that they open at 10:00. I thought we'd leave at 8:45. I told Walt where we're going."

"He didn't know before?"

"He knew that we were here to look at ice-age cave art and that some of the art was somehow connected with the death of your brother. I didn't say anything else. I know him a little now and I think I can trust him but I don't know the people with him."

"Tom . . ." She was opening the twin bed that paralleled his.

"What?"

"Dinner was nice. I enjoyed it, even if we were forcing the smiles and worrying about who might be watching or listening."

"I did too," he said.

"The investigator remains alive, as does the sister." The voice was sharp, the tone abrupt.

"Yes, we know that."

"You assured me that these problems would be eliminated."

"I take full responsibility for that; we did the best that we could."

"I would be a little less ready to admit your incompetence if I were you. Incompetence can lead to results that you might find quite unpleasant."

"I understand. Rest assured that we will find them. We have already tracked the two of them to London. They were scheduled to fly to Edinburgh together, but substitutes were sent in their place. The government is clearly involved."

"The government is irrelevant. If their agents are in our way we will simply remove them. Where have they gone from London?"

"We haven't determined that yet. We will."

"Could they have learned about Tenedos?"

"No. At this point it wouldn't be anything to them but a word."

"They couldn't know about our other activities yet, so they must be in France. The brother must have left something, something you failed to find. If they discover what has happened there they will quickly learn of Tenedos. That cannot happen yet. The timing is very important. The connections between the events must be plausible, not suspicious. Do you understand?"

"I will go there tomorrow myself."

"Eliminate them at once by whatever means necessary. They are getting too close. They should never have been permitted to leave the country."

"They will not return to it."

"See that they don't. Where are you now?"

"In a hotel at Heathrow airport."

"And you will fly to Bordeaux tomorrow?"

"Yes.

"And then you will drive directly to Cahors?"

"Yes, and then to Les Eyzies. They will be dead tomorrow evening."

She said good night as he turned on his side, his head against the edge of the twin bed, watching the moonlight filter through the vines beyond the window. He had left the shutters open and the light pulled up a succession of distant memories—images of European villages in cloudy moonlight. Remakes of old Universal horror pictures. Villages with vampires and werewolves, dusky skies painted on soundstage plywood, looming above toy cities with steeples and cobblestones, timbered walls and dark, crooked alleyways. Everything old and magic and frightening. Grave robbers with rusty shovels and picks, ragged clothes and hungry dogs, making their way across the looming sky with leaves blowing over their shoes and nightbirds calling in the distance.

And all of it unreal, straight from the imaginations of the German expressionists to the sets of Universal City and on to the local theatres of his father's day, with cartoon carnivals, previews, newsreels and a second, 70 minute feature. Europe for Americans: quaint and small, with village clockmakers, bakers, and jewelers, woodworkers, toymakers, and tailors. And just down the road, just beyond the torches and pitchforks of the villagers, there, on the hill, on the edge of the forest, castles with histories of monstrous evil.

Every Saturday his grandparents dropped off his father at noon at the local theatre and picked him up at four. On horror-movie days, he said, he left his bedroom door open so that he could hear his parents' voices, see the light from the living room find its way to the back of the house and down the hall, linking him to them.

At 7:45 the next morning there was a knock at the door. An accented voice said, "Service." Diana looked at Tom. He opened his luggage, slipped out a lead-lined box, and removed a large automatic. She looked at him, waiting for his signal. He motioned her behind him and opened the door without speaking. Then he opened it wider.

A man entered with a white jacket with black tie and gold epaulets. He was carrying a tray with coffee, cream, croissants, and preserves. Tom closed the door behind him and the man put the tray on the table. "Diana Bennett," Tom said, "Walt McNeise."

"How do you do," she said. "We weren't expecting you." She tightened the belt on her robe and pulled the lapels close.

"I know. I had to see you. They've closed the cave. It's been closed for three days."

"What do you mean?" Tom asked.

"I had one of my people drive down this morning, just to take a look. They've closed it. No visitors allowed. We got people from the government out of bed. The official word is that this happens all the time. Lascaux has been closed for over fifty years. The Chauvet Cave—the one they found in the 90's—is never going to be opened to the public. If you want to see it you have to either buy a book or go to their website."

"The cave at Pech-Merle has been open since 1924," Diana said. "My brother is dead and now, suddenly, it's closed. I don't believe in coincidences like that."

McNeise's expression didn't change.

"We've got to get in there," Tom said.

"I know," McNeise answered. "We're working on it. The cave is controlled by the Culture Ministry. We have to work through the National Heritage Department. That's what it is in English anyway. Have you ever tried to work with a French bureaucracy when their culture is at stake?"

"I think we helped save some of France's culture in the 1940's," Tom said. "We're not here to do any harm to their culture or to their cave."

"The harm's already done, Tom. It's green disease. That's what they call it. Too many tourists, too much carbon dioxide, too much heat from the cave lights, too much pollen carried in from the outside. When the moss forms, the paintings and drawings are destroyed. It happened to Lascaux. They don't want it to happen to Pech-Merle."

"I'm with Diana, Walt. This is too coincidental."

"Like I said, we're doing what we can, but this is serious, Tom. They've closed the grounds, the food service, the museum, everything. This is one of the greatest caves in Europe. The paintings inside are 20,000 years old. They can't jeopardize it further. They already have the makings of a major scandal. They're trying to keep it quiet but we found out that right after they discovered the green disease the director took his own life."

"He *what*?" Tom said.

"He poisoned himself. He couldn't stand to see the cave die on his watch."

Tom looked at Diana, then back at McNeise. "We're leaving in ten minutes, Walt."

CHAPTER TWENTY-TWO
Grotte du Pech-Merle
Tuesday, 9:20 a.m.

Driving southwest from Les Eyzies the 70 kilometers slipped by quickly until they reached the Lot and the rock formations above it. The curls of limestone formed low arches over the highway, cut away by the river hundreds of thousands of years before. Buses filled with disgruntled tourists inched their way along the road, dodging the overhanging rock while leaving enough room for cars and vans in the opposite lane to pass. As the road turned away from the river and into the woods above, the warning signs began. Tom drove past them. A hundred yards ahead he could see the chains stretched across the road. He pulled off the asphalt and eased into the grass and trees.

"I just thought of something," he said. "Whoever we're up against has a vicious sense of humor—having a man surrounded by the food from Dordogne-Périgord poison himself."

"He knew something that they wanted to die with him," Diana said.

On the other side of the chain there was an open stretch of road nearly two hundred yards in length. To the right of a slight bend they saw the heavy equipment: bulldozers, generators, flatbeds, cranes, all of it parked in a straight line, ready to be hauled away. On the back of an open truck there was a large fan in a steel frame. The wires projecting from the back of it were withered and bent.

"The ventilation system for the cave," Diana said. "They probably checked it and then rebuilt it immediately to stop the spread of the moss."

"Let's have a closer look," Tom said. There was no one in the area as they walked along the road. The only sign of life was a workman's cap and a single abandoned shoe. Tom lifted the cap with the end of a pen. No obvious blood stains on it. He poked at the shoe. It looked as if something had been chewing on its edges.

When they came into the parking lot across from the museum, just above the entrance to the cave, they heard voices. Tom put his finger to his lips and they slowly worked their way down the slope and through the trees.

He saw McNeise standing with four uniformed Frenchmen and a younger man with a flashlight. He looked like a tour guide. All of the men seemed agitated. As Tom and Diana walked out of the trees one of the uniforms approached them, extending his upright palms and telling them that they would have to leave. McNeise said something to him in French and the man stopped gesturing. He looked frustrated and confused.

McNeise took Tom and Diana aside. "They're ready to lose it," he said. "First the green disease and now the death of the director."

"They believe it was suicide?" Tom asked.

"Yes. I haven't said anything that might change their minds."

"How long ago was the green disease noticed?"

"A little over a week, I think. An Englishman saw it first. The security chief told me that the director immediately called in a crew to spray the walls with antibiotics and formol and to check the ventilation system. They worked through the night spraying solution and making repairs."

"Can we go inside?"

"Give me some time on that. A full delegation from the Culture Ministry is arriving at noon and they're nervous about letting anyone else in first."

"They let all the repairmen in," Tom said.

"I know, but they had to do that."

"Tell them we only need a few minutes."

Diana put up her hand. "Tell them my brother was a famous artist and that he died studying the *Chevaux Ponctués*. Tell them his name."

McNeise's expression said that he thought this was a long shot but he told them that he'd try it. He told Tom and Diana to stay where they were and walked back over to the Frenchmen. As he spoke to them they each turned and looked at her. The senior officer stepped aside and walked toward them. She could hear his leather-soled shoes on the gravel, see him bracing his chest and preparing to speak. His nameplate read *Cossard*. He presented himself and told her, in slow, halting English, of his great respect for her brother. He told her he had seen his paintings in Paris, in Rome, and in Madrid. Then he kissed her hand.

She looked toward the entrance to the cave. "Pour dix minutes?" she asked.

"Certainement," he answered, his head cocked and bowed.

He summoned the man with the flashlight and they hurried toward the wooden structure enclosing the entrance.

When the heavy oak doors were opened they felt the cold air rush against their faces. The guide turned on the light in the passageway to the cave and they started their way down into the earth. "There are two main chambers," McNeise said. "The one on the right is small; it has some bear bones and artifacts. The main chamber is to the left. That's the one with the paintings."

As they entered the cave they could feel air currents and they sensed that they were in a natural corridor. The guide turned on the first bank of lights and they saw the stone wall before them and the path to the ossuaire on the right. "This way," the guide said, in a heavy accent. He led them to the left along a path into the main chamber. "The *Frise Noire*," he said, indicating the paintings of the mammoths off in the distance. They stared at them, struck by the very fact of their presence as well as the skill in their execution. Tom's eyes were wandering, taking in as much of the cave as he could through the light and shadows.

"My god," he suddenly said, "look."

To the right, thirty or forty yards below them, were the horses.

"The *Chevaux Ponctués* we see last," the guide said.

The route of the tour began with the mammoths and then wound around to the rear of the chamber, near the original entrance to the cave, past the cave pearls and what were claimed to be ice-age human footprints. The real tour ended at the frieze of the horses and then a few anticlimactic minutes in the ossuaire before ascending back to the surface. The drama of it was clear. You saw the high point at the beginning of the show but you had to wait until the end to see it at close range, to study it, to absorb it. It loomed there in the distance, teasing and inviting.

"You can't take your eyes off of them," Diana said. "That's why they picked that stone to paint. Imagine it in torchlight—the centerpiece of the hall—visited perhaps once in a generation. The paintings are magnificent, but in their setting they're breathtaking."

"Walt," Tom said in a whisper, "we can't spend our time going through the whole tour. We've got to get down to the horses now." McNeise spoke to the officers and the guide, who looked perturbed. He directed them to a path and they made their way down to the frieze. Surrounded by yellow rock formations glistening in the direct and reflected light, Tom looked up toward the ceiling from which the stone on which the horses were painted had fallen. He looked over at Diana. She had taken her brother's pictures from her jacket and she was studying them intently.

The guide went into his full presentation, pointing out the red fish behind the horses, telling them that it was drawn first, then talking about the horses themselves and their possible dates. The hand negatives were described as parts of prehistoric rituals, as were the large spots (which he called 'dots') inside the horses and along their backs, highlighting and outlining them. He was very sure of himself with regard to dates and purposes; he was not the sort of man who would welcome being questioned. "Les '*Chevaux Ponctués*'," he said, in summary. "They are fantastic, are they not? So very beautiful."

Tom nodded in agreement. Diana was looking up and down, from the frieze to her brother's pictures. She whispered something to Tom and he struggled to hold his expression. He whispered something in return. She answered, he nodded, and then walked around to the side of the stone and looked at the point where it met the floor. He squatted down and got closer to it. "Please, you may not touch it," the guide said.

Tom signalled to McNeise and the senior officer, Cossard. "What is it?" McNeise said. "Look," Tom answered. "It's green."

Cossard became agitated. "Vert?" he said. "Sur les Chevaux Ponctués?"

"Not moss, not disease," Tom said. Cossard was confused. McNeise translated for him and he suddenly looked relieved.

"No, not green moss," Tom said. "It's green cement. The paintings are forged. The substitute stone was attached to the floor and the cement hasn't dried yet."

McNeise translated and the Frenchmen looked at him as if he had just told them that their children had been killed. "No, no," the tour guide said. "That cannot be."

"Look," Diana said. She showed them the photographs of David's work, then pictures of the original paintings. "He left out one of the red dots. Count them." She traced her finger along the painting of the horse on the left. "There should be a triangle of dots . . . *there*. The bottom one is missing."

"But why would he do such a thing?" the guide asked.

"He wanted to tell us that he could never copy the original, no matter how expert the work," Diana said.

"No," the guide said again. "It cannot be. These are the horses of Pech-Merle, these!"

"They are very beautiful," Diana said, "but they are not the *Chevaux Ponctués*."

Cossard was shaking his head. "Impossible, impossible," he said.

"No, it was very easy," Tom said. "With the cave sealed and the heavy equipment they brought in they could have made the switch easily. David Bennett's work was difficult; this wasn't."

"We should go outside now," the guide said. "The lights, the gas."

"There was no green disease," Tom said, as McNeise translated. "Someone left some lights on, probably brought in some pollen and a tank or two of carbon dioxide, and then called the director and showed him the results. The director panicked and closed the cave. At that point he was probably held incommunicado until the ventilation men could come in and switch the stones. His murder was faked to look like a suicide and the government officials organized a delegation to drive to Pech-Merle and pick up the pieces. By then the real paintings were long gone."

"No, no, why here? Why?" the guide said, his voice shaking.

"Because the paintings are so wonderful and because they're portable," Diana said. McNeise was translating and the officers were hanging on every word. "You cannot carve the bulls from the walls of Lascaux or the mammoths from Rouffignac or the polychrome bison from Font-de-Gaume without destroying them. The *Chevaux Ponctués* *could* be stolen."

"This is the theft of our soul," the guide said.

"That's exactly what it is," Tom said. "The planning had to be equal to the stakes."

"The planning? But you said this was easy," the guide said.

"The switch was easy. Having the forgery ready and coordinating the substitution for the original with the movement of the equipment and the murder of the director was very difficult."

He looked at Diana. She was staring at the stone, the tears welling in her eyes. "This was his last work," she said, "and so beautiful."

CHAPTER TWENTY-THREE
Le Bugue
Tuesday, 5:48 p.m.

"They'll try to find out the name of the Englishman who first spotted the moss and get back to us," McNeise said. "The director's secretary may have made a note of the meeting. Her name is Hélène Scaviner; she lives in Cahors but she's in Cherbourg visiting her sister and they haven't been able to reach her yet. They say she was close to the director, a man named Ponge. They *have* learned that the heavy equipment was rented. No big surprise there. They're trying to trace the identity of the contractor, but there was nothing in Ponge's records and no notes or chits or letterhead left in any of the equipment itself. None of the guides or museum employees remember seeing any names on the cars or shirts of the contractors and none of the workmen paid for anything with credit cards. They'll try other sources, but since the bureaus are all closed by now it will take some time."

They were sitting in an Italian restaurant called *La Pergola*, a block from the Vézère in a village called Le Bugue. The sky was steel gray, the river brown. They were drinking Lacryma Christi rosso, absorbing the impact of the day. They talked about the paintings and about the cave, about David and about his work. Diana was eating small pieces of bread and some broth. There was no street traffic except for an occasional bicycle. They could hear the sound of the river in the distance.

"Quite a feat," McNeise said. "How do you bring a section of rock that size six or seven thousand miles?"

"By private aircraft," Tom said. "The window of opportunity was too tight for anything but a plane and the stone slab was too big for a common carrier. Besides, it would have attracted too much attention; it would have been like a grand piano crate with the weight of a tank. We're talking more than organization to pull this off. We're talking very big money."

"Not as a return on investment," McNeise said. "The paintings would be priceless."

"But who would front the money?"

"No one connected. They prefer sure things like numbers or dope; they wouldn't invest in ice-age cave paintings."

"It has to be a single-source contract," Tom said. "A rich collector who wanted something unique and who had the means to buy it."

"Along with two murders."

"Two that we know of," Tom said.

"True. There's something else we can say about the person who wanted the paintings of the horses," McNeise added. "He's somebody who doesn't feel the need to share. No one's ever going to see the paintings except for him. He left the copy for everyone else. That tells you something too. He doesn't want just art—the copy's beautiful—he wants the object. And he doesn't want anybody else to have it."

"David would never have done that for money," Diana said, breaking her silence. She paused for a moment before speaking again. "Tom's right. He must have been threatened or coerced in some way."

"They probably threatened to hurt you," Tom said. "I didn't want to say anything earlier, but it's pretty obvious, don't you think? Your parents are gone. There was no one with whom your brother was involved. The two of you were extremely close. What else would they threaten him with? What else could they take away? This was big. It wasn't just a simple favor. The project would have taken weeks, probably months. The way he would have gone about it it could have taken even longer. Did you ever feel as if you were being watched or followed—I mean months before his death."

"I don't know. Nothing specific. I live alone and spend a lot of time in the worst parts of the city. I sometimes feel as if someone might be watching. We all feel that way sometimes, don't we?"

"Yes, but it's usually not true," Tom said. "Did anyone contact you, anyone suspicious?"

She shook her head and didn't respond further; her thoughts were on her brother and the things he must have suffered in trying to protect her. The silence would have been the worst—keeping it all to himself, not being able to tell her what he was going through. Dealing with thieves and murderers. Being forced to use his talents for terrible people and terrible purposes.

"I'll call the Chief," Tom said. "I'll bring him up to date and ask him to check your brother's client list. Most of them would be wealthy but not in the league to pull off something like this. Obviously whoever's behind this admired your brother's work. Perhaps he had purchased something else earlier."

"I can make a discreet run through our data bases," McNeise said. "Art collecting and homicide are an unusual mix; we'll see if we can turn anything. We can also take some shots in the dark. We can ask the IRS to check on big tax write-offs for gifts to museums or art schools and see what names fall out. We'll check on calls to and from all the heavy equipment contractors in France. We can check the rentals of private aircraft and registered flight plans in California and France."

"What was the poison used to kill the director?" Tom asked.

"Arsenic," McNeise answered.

"Too many industrial applications. That could have come from anywhere. How about car and truck rentals in France? They had to get around somehow."

"The French are checking on that," McNeise said. "They're also checking credit card chits from all restaurants and service stations within a fifty-mile radius of the area."

"Good," Tom said.

"That's what it comes down to, isn't it?" Diana said, taking a drink of her wine and then putting down the glass.

"What's that?" Tom asked.

"They kill and steal and we have to study records, work our way through lists, check and cross check, ask questions, jog memories."

"Unless they show themselves," Tom said. "Then it can happen much more quickly. There's only one problem . . ."

"They already have what they wanted here. Their only reason for showing themselves now would be if they wanted to kill a few more of us," Diana said.

Tom nodded as McNeise got up from the table. "I'm going to check in with Jeff and see what's happening."

He returned in three minutes. "That's odd," he said. "I asked him to stay in your room, to wait for calls, turn the lights off and on, run the television set, and generally make people think you were there. He's not answering."

CHAPTER TWENTY-FOUR

Les Eyzies de Tayac
Tuesday, 7:40 p.m.

They stopped in the lot of the *Centenaire* at the south end of the village and talked their way through possible scenarios. "If something *has* happened and they're waiting for us, we'll be walking down a tunnel like silhouetted targets," Tom said. "There's only one road to the hotel, straight through the village, with shops on either side, open parking lots below and sloping rock shelters above. Think about it from their point of view. Your victims are coming toward you along a single path. Where would you position your people if you wanted to do maximum damage? In cars in the hotel parking lot or in the shrubs and trees along the lot's perimeter? In the stairwells of the hotel? In the woods above the hotel in case we were suspicious and tried to circle around and come in through the rear?"

"Possibly somewhere along the street," Diana said. "Sitting at that pizza and ice cream place, watching the traffic, or just on the edge of one of the buildings, smoking cigarettes and checking faces and license plates. They'd want to know when we were approaching the hotel and how many of us there were. They could call ahead to people waiting at the hotel or direct fire from snipers in the woods or in second-floor windows. It's only a few minutes' walk from one end of the village to the other. Even with the pedestrian traffic, you're exposed. They can see you coming and pick their opportunity."

"They could have explosives in the room and a sensor device," McNeise said, "first-day-of-school technique. Or they could have a shooter out in the trees waiting for one of you to come to the window to close the shutters. Hell, they could lob in a grenade. Your window is no more than ten or eleven feet from the ground. They've got plenty of choices."

"Let's try this," Tom said. "Diana can stay here with the car. I'll climb up to the path on the level above the street, the walkway the tourists use to visit the rock shelters. I'll start down by the Prehistory Museum and then work my way up into the woods above the shelters, then circle around to the edge of the treeline behind the hotel. I'll take my time and play cautious. You swing around to the left, down by the parking lots and the kiddie railroad, behind the shops on the main street. What time is it now?"

"Ten of eight," McNeise said.

"It'll be dark by 8:30. We'll converge then on the rear of the hotel parking lot from opposite sides. I'll be watching the trees and shrubs; I'll have better visibility from above. You watch the cars and the areas at the edge of the building. If the lot's clear we'll go into the building, through the hotel kitchen and up the back stairs to the top level, then work our way down to the second floor and find out why your man's not answering the phone."

"I'm not going to stay here," Diana said. "What good will that do?"

"It will be one less target if they try to kill us," Tom said.

"That means more bullets for the two of you," she answered.

"Look, I work for *you*," Tom said, "not the other way around. I can't afford to start losing cooperative citizens; it'll kill the reputation of the department. Just sit tight here. We'll be back at 9:00 or earlier."

"How do you feel?" she asked.

"I'm fine, don't worry," he answered.

"You have your automatic?"

"Yes," he said.

Diana sat back in her seat and turned her head away. She cupped her face in her left hand and stared out the window. "Be careful," she said, as they got out of the car.

Tom climbed the steps to the rock shelter path above the village and passed the larger-than-life statue of Neanderthal Man, a tourist magnet. The sculpture was standing next to the railing, looking across the valley of the Vézère, the reason for his presence there (in lieu of Cro-Magnon man) not entirely clear. With his thick brow and hunched body he seemed tired and uncomprehending. Fifteen minutes later Tom was in the woods above the hotel. Crawling among the rocks, leaves, and pine needles, he was beginning to feel lightheaded. He checked his watch: 8:18. He surveyed the parking lot and the surrounding trees and shrubs. Except for a well-dressed elderly couple arriving for dinner the area was quiet.

By 8:25 he had changed positions twice, each time trying for a better field of vision on the area below. He looked for McNeise in the distance but couldn't see him. At 8:27 another car entered the lot, this one with a younger man and woman. They got out of their car, looked around the edge of the building, checked the lot a second time, locked their car, and left. With every parking place on the street occupied they were using the lot of the hotel illegally rather than driving to the more remote public lots below the village.

At 8:30 Tom came out of the treeline and slipped down to the rear of the lot. He stepped on some dried leaves, froze, and then saw movement twenty yards ahead. It was McNeise, rising from a prone position. A few seconds later he was walking toward him. When they approached one another neither spoke. Tom pointed to the entrance to the kitchen at the rear of the building, they walked in, said their *excusez-moi's* to the apprehensive staff and hurried to the rear stairs.

The stairwell was empty. On the third floor Walt listened at the door of the man posted above Tom and Diana's room. His name was Alain.

Silence. They went back to the rear stairwell and walked down to the second floor. Walt put up his hand, signaling Tom to wait. He went into the linen closet at the end of the hall, slipped on a starched, white jacket, and put a freshly-folded towel over his right arm. In his left hand he held some miniature rosettes of soap; in his right he held a 9mm automatic.

He knocked on the door and said, "Service." There was no answer. He tried the knob and the door opened. The room was dark. He turned on the light and saw Jeff. He was sitting in a chair in the corner nearest the window. It was an overstuffed wing chair with flowered upholstery. It looked as if it might have been comfortable. Jeff was sitting upright, fully clothed, his hands on the armrests. There was a red and black bullet hole in the center of his forehead, his face webbed with tiny rivulets of blood. His mouth was distended by a salmon-colored napkin that had muffled any attempted cries. By then Tom was in the room, his weapon drawn. "His fingers have all been broken," Walt said.

Before Tom could respond, the door across the hallway flew open and two figures with ski masks and automatic pistols rushed toward them, spraying the room with fire. McNeise's body contorted with the impact of multiple rounds. He fired back as he hit the wall. The wall lamp next to Tom was shattered by a burst of automatic fire and shards of glass tore into his neck and cheek. The figure at the edge of the doorway dove into the hall as Tom shot the other, standing under the light at the edge of the room. He lurched, fired four rounds in Tom's direction, and stumbled back into the hallway. The other figure was already gone. The wounded man braced his arm against the wall and limped toward the stairwell, blurry and disoriented. Just then Diana appeared before him. He started to raise his pistol toward her and she leaped forward, driving her right fist into the center of his throat. His body jerked in pain and his neck and chest throbbed with spasmodic heaves as he fell to the floor. She ground the full weight of her right heel into his wrist and the pistol slid over his fingertips, a joint at a time.

Tom kicked it away and hurried down the steps in pursuit of the other figure. A group had formed in the lobby, still holding newspapers and cigarettes, and staring out the windows and door as a late-model Mercedes drove off, its tires spinning and squealing in the dusty street. Tom shoved them aside and ran out. The lights of the car were off, the license plate illegible. He saw pedestrians diving out of the way of the car, gesturing at it angrily. Tom looked around at the faces of the hotel guests. They looked back at him, hoping he might somehow have answers to their half-formed questions.

CHAPTER TWENTY-FIVE
Hôtel Le Cro-Magnon, **Les Eyzies de Tayac**
Tuesday, 8:58 p.m.

Diana met Tom at the top of the stairs. She was holding the gun of the man in the hallway. "How is Walt?" he asked, his breath thin. She shook her head. "His blood was everywhere and there was no pulse. There was nothing that could be done," she said.

The man in the hallway was still breathing but the rug was wet with his blood and urine. Tom turned him over. He could hear the sucking chest wound and see the fluttering movement of the stained and torn fabric just below his heart. Tom pulled off the mask. The man had dark brown hair and brown eyes. The eyes were rolling and unfocused. Tom grabbed the towel that Walt had been carrying and pressed it against the man's chest. "Who are you?" he asked. "Who are you working for?"

The man's mouth closed and his eyes filled with contempt. "You'll survive this," Tom said. "Then you can start thinking about French prisons and French guillotines." The man forced his lips into the beginnings of a smile. "She'll . . . die . . . first," the man said, the words seeping out slowly.

Tom looked up at Diana. She was holding herself back. There was no fear in her eyes and no pity. "Did you kill my brother?" she asked, her voice tight with restraint. The man stared at her in cold silence. She took a step forward, her anger palpable. "Don't," Tom said.

"Don't what?"

"Don't go to work on him with that heel again."

"Why not?"

"Because his heart just stopped beating and it wouldn't do any good."

"He wasn't French," Tom said, "or if he was he spoke perfect English. I asked the hotel manager to try to reach Cossard. He could be of help with the local police."

"I'm very sorry about Walt's death," Diana said, searching his eyes for responses.

"Thanks," Tom said. "There's not really very much to say anyway. He tried to save someone else again. This time he didn't make it out himself."

"They were waiting for you, weren't they?"

"Yes. Walt's man wouldn't tell them where we were so they waited for us here. The two other men were killed as well, the one in the room above us and the one in the room just below. Neither of them had been tortured."

"Perhaps because they could only speak French."

"Good point. Let me ask you something."

"What's that?"

"Why didn't you stay in the car?"

"Do you wish I had now?"

"Now's easy. What if you had ended up in the hallway with a bullet in your head or sitting in a room with them where they could break your fingers one at a time?"

"I wanted to help."

"You *did* help. You flattened the son-of-a-bitch, disarmed him, and then kept him from getting away."

"Thanks."

"The question still stands. What if it was you on the floor instead of him or you in the chair instead of Jeff?"

"Then it would have been me. And you would have had to find

them on your own . . . and secure the revenge for David's and my deaths. That's what you would have done, isn't it?"

"Yes, that's what I would have done."

"Is protecting women something you've always felt you had to do?"

"Does it bother you?"

"You don't see me leaving, do you? Does it bother you that I might want to protect you too?"

"No, I need all the protection I can get."

"Don't be flip. I'm serious."

"So am I," Tom said.

A few moments later there was a knock at the door. It was the concierge, Monsieur Bonnard. "They have found the other man," he said. "I thought you might want to come and see him."

Tom looked at Diana, she got up, and the three of them left together, the concierge driving. "It is just beyond the village, a few hundred meters past Les Combarelles."

They were there in less than five minutes. On the east side of the road they saw the sign and the wooden building at the entrance to the Combarelles cave. Ahead in the darkness they could see blinking lights. The Mercedes was in a culvert, its headlights and taillights still burning. The driver was visible from the road, his head and upper body illuminated by half a dozen flashlights. His ski mask had been removed and the left side of his face was gone.

The concierge told Tom and Diana to wait by the car while he spoke with one of the policemen. He approached him and offered him a cigarette. They appeared to know one another well. After five or six minutes he walked back to his car. "There is no identification on the driver and the car is rented," he said, "probably with false credentials. A man from Lyons driving with his family told the police that he thought he saw the car leaving the Combarelles car park and a second car following, but he could not identify the second car." He looked up and down the highway and ran his fingers over his forehead and through his hair. "I feel very bad for the village. These things do not happen here. Now no one will come to the caves for many weeks."

"Don't worry, they'll still come," Tom said.

The man nodded appreciatively, trying to convince himself.

"Thank you for bringing us," Tom added.

When they returned to the hotel they told Monsieur Bonnard that they would have to leave. "I understand," he said. "Whoever tried to hurt you and your wife could return again. Here, I want you to have something . . ." He walked around from the side of the front desk and opened up a cabinet at the entrance to the restaurant, a few feet away. He reached inside and took out a white porcelain dish with a drawing of a prehistoric reindeer and the name of the hotel. "We sell them to those who dine with us. Keep it please. It is just a token."

"Thanks very much, it's lovely," Tom said.

Ten minutes later they had loaded the car and returned to the highway where the Mercedes was found. The body had been removed and the car was being towed. "It must have been their rendezvous point. He reported their failure to kill us to whoever was in charge and the person followed him out of the lot, drove up beside him, and blew away the side of his head."

Tom could hear Diana exhale. "Now we face the killer who survived," she said.

CHAPTER TWENTY-SIX
Hotel Le Cygne, **Le Bugue**
Tuesday, 10:27 p.m.

More an inn than a hotel, Tom had suggested *Le Cygne* because it was on the edge of Le Bugue, beneath the Bara Bahau cave, with sufficient shadow and foliage to both conceal their car and provide an opportunity for escape if that proved necessary. The room was clean and simple, more French than English, with yellows and slate blues and a small clear-glass vase of freshly-cut purple wildflowers on a polished pine stand.

The room was on the second floor in the rear. There were two windows, each with bolted shutters, and a single bed. Tom took the seat and back cushions from the largest chair, spread them on the floor, and took the spare blanket from the cupboard next to the bathroom.

"Why don't you take the bed? You'll sleep much better," Diana said.

"I'll be fine. After the trees and rocks above the *Cro-Magnon* this won't be any problem."

"How's your incision?"

"It's fine, really. Don't worry about it. Get some rest."

She handed him one of the pillows. "In the morning we'll check with Cossard," he said. "We'll see if he's reached Ponge's secretary in Cherbourg. Maybe we'll even get lucky and the two men from the *Cro-Magnon* will have fingerprints on file."

"Good night," she said. "And thanks."

"For what?"

"For worrying about me."

He slept fitfully. In the past he often had anxiety dreams, confronting tasks for which he was ill-equipped or faced with questions for which there were no real answers or processes for which there were no logical endpoints. Sometimes he was standing in the shadows, watching himself within the framework of the dream, as if he were a ghostly bystander, wondering why he was conscious of the things he was unable to control or even fully understand. Sometimes the spaces were dark, sometimes starkly white. This night he woke up from a dream of limestone cliffs and silhouetted hands on the sides of cave walls. There were no tasks or challenges, no dark spaces or white rooms, no sudden confusion and equally sudden release, just unanswered questions and unexplained images.

He couldn't remember when it was that he was supposed to dream—right after he fell asleep or right before he was about to awake? And was the dreaming part of REM sleep? Was that when you dreamed most deeply, the times when you rolled your eyes and kicked your legs like a restless puppy? And why should he care about textbook predictions or diagnoses, since his personal mode was either to dream for a few moments or to dream constantly. Tonight he fell asleep and dreamed, awoke, fell back asleep and dreamed, awoke again and dreamed again, all in a series of steps like a Hogarth progress piece or a walk through a mist-filled museum with pictures from his recent life arrayed along an endless hall.

First there were the silhouetted hands and the limestone, then the restlessness caused by the awareness of pain in the back of his head and the sight of moonlight illuminating the edges of the shutters, then dreams again, this time of city squares and parades through them: children with tin kazoos in clown suits with bent hats and dirty knees, proud parents, restive dogs, food waste spilling out of barrels in the small city park. Suddenly the awareness of Diana's breathing and the tick of the wall clock, then dreams of highways that led to bridges that led to more highways that led to more bridges that led to mountain passes and valley floors and alleyways and boulevards and skyways and lanes and streets and roads and finally tire tracks through high grass leading to open meadows and gravelly beaches along deserted seas.

No beaches with green mats and palm trees, the taste of long drinks in chilled glasses and the smell of banana and coconut oil; the feeling that the task was done, the case wrapped, the file closed; the rest of your life ahead, but all in good time, not now. Not with the Trades cooling your body in the warm summer air and the clouds slowly making their way east across a sky of the purest blue.

Again, Diana's breathing, and all of the memories of the last few days and all of the threats and uncertainties of the days to come. Silent, faceless enemies with ropes and bombs and automatic pistols, with images of David's death and promises of Diana's. The only figure in between a tall man with a split head held together by fraying sutures and scar tissue.

The light was brighter now. He had overslept. His face was damp with anticipation. He rose to his feet and saw Diana laying diagonally across the bed, on her belly, the blanket down around her waist. Where was the phone? And where was Cossard's number? He took out his wallet, checked the partition between his cards and his money, removed the note, stared at it, refocused his eyes, verified it, then reached for the phone. He refocused again and checked the wall clock. It was only 6:18. He walked over to the desk and checked his watch: 6:19.

"What is it?" Diana asked, sitting up and covering herself with the blanket.

"It's nothing. I'm sorry, I thought it was later."

"Are you all right?"

"Yes, I'm fine."

"Did you hear something?"

"No, I'm just jet-lagged."

"Lay back down," she said. "We'll face it as it comes."

She turned over, stretched her legs, and pulled the corner of the blanket up to her face. The room was beginning to warm from the morning sun and she fell back to sleep, dreaming of southern California, of freeways and boulevards, shops, restaurants, signs, lights, studios, museums, and galleries. Then she was in Brighton's car, facing the oncoming headlights, but no one was driving. She was alone in the passenger seat, the radio a quiet hum, the car on autopilot, taking her to her parents' home in the canyon, the road empty, the moss on the pine trees visible in the headlights.

Suddenly she was with David and it was autumn; they were trying to see through the bare limbs of the oaks and maples to the sea beyond. David's mouth was moving but she couldn't hear him; it was like an old 8mm home movie, the colors bleached, the action jerky and forced. He was smiling and waving his arms and calling to her. He had found something, seen something, something wonderful that he wanted to share with her. She ran toward him but her feet sank in the loamy soil and her legs grew heavy. David motioned her on, smiling, waving, and encouraging her. She moved her arms in a swimming motion, trying to pull herself from the ground and toward her brother.

A moment later she awoke, feeling a draft on her shoulder. The room was warm but her body was chilled. She reached for the edge of the blanket and saw Tom sitting in the chair. He had put away the blanket and replaced the cushions. He was sitting quietly, oiling his automatic and checking his clips of ammunition.

"Hi," he said, "how about something to eat?"

"You order; I'll put on some clothes," she said, slipping on the robe on the corner of the bed and going into the bathroom. He ordered coffee, croissants, and brioche, with butter and preserves. The hotel also had melon and smoked ham and he ordered two portions. Diana came out of the bathroom for a few seconds, took some clothes from her luggage, and then went back in. She came out a few minutes before the breakfast arrived. She was dressed in dark slacks and a dark blouse, her chestnut hair turning to gold in the bright morning light.

"You finished with your gun," she said.

"Yes."

"I was watching you clean it."

"Old habit," he said.

"In the movies they do it mechanically—step by step, item by item, timing themselves."

"They teach you to do it mechanically so that you can do it in the dark or with your hands under an oilcloth cover in the rain. I like to clean the wooden grip, keep it oiled and polished. Strange hobby. Some people refinish picnic benches . . ."

"I can't imagine you doing that—down in a basement shop, firing up your SkilSaw, planing down the edges of a piece of plywood, routing with your router and grinding with your grinder or whatever."

"No, that was never me," Tom said. "My father did all those things. During the day he worked with his head and at night with his hands. I've always had to do a little bit of both."

"So what do you do at night?"

"Mostly read or drive along the coast. Enjoy the night air, smell the orange blossoms and the magnolias. Sometimes I get together with Hector and we drive out to the forest and check out the trails. We don't do much."

"Is Hector married?"

"He was. She's a nurse."

"And you've never been married?"

"No. I came close once but in the end it didn't happen."

She looked at him but didn't press.

"Sometimes it's a matter of the relationship between the people," he said. "Sometimes it's a matter of timing. Sometimes it's both."

"I never really had the time," Diana said. "Medical school is all-consuming; so is the internship and residency. By the time I emerged on the other side David had achieved great success and needed me."

"He still does," Tom said.

"Yes, I know he does."

CHAPTER TWENTY-SEVEN
Route N. 710, North of Le Bugue
Wednesday, 11:05 a.m.

"Where are we headed?"

"Just around the countryside for a few minutes; I want to make sure there's no one following us. I called Cossard and he's arranged a meeting at 2:30 in St. Emilion. We're going to a winery called *Chateau Bison*. Prime real estate, on D245, between Figeac and Cheval Blanc. They have a private facility for special tastings, with its own entrance. We'll be able to park and walk around without worrying about who might be watching. Cossard and his people will be there and they'll brief us on what they've learned so far. He did say that they've found Ponge's secretary in Cherbourg, but they haven't been able to interview her yet. They should know more by the time we meet."

"What was her name—Scaviner?"

"Hélène Scaviner."

"What about the two men who tried to kill us?"

"He didn't say anything over the phone. We were working through a translator and he wanted to keep everything to a minimum. He *did* ask how you were."

"What did you say?"

"I said that you looked as if you'd been on vacation for weeks and that I hoped you felt half as good as you looked."

"I wish," she said, noticing that Tom seemed to be watching the road behind them more often. "What do you see in your rear-view mirror?"

"Nothing except for that sign inviting tourists to the farm where they can see the breeders feed their geese in authentic local fashion."

"I'll pass," Diana said. "I don't need to see that. The French *are* cruel, aren't they?"

"What do you mean?"

"Shoving food down a goose's neck, forcing it to overeat so its liver distends. That's cruel. I mean, I know the foie gras is wonderful, but what about the goose?"

"How many geese would there be if there was no appetite for them? They wouldn't be bred. Those that remained would have to fend for themselves in the wild. Besides, they're practically worshipped. Have you ever had ortelans?"

"No, what are they?"

"They're what we call garden buntings. The French catch them with traps; they don't want to damage them in any way. Then they twist their necks, fry them in their own grease, and eat them under a miniature tent so that they can savor the aroma and taste."

"Under a tent?"

"Yes. They make the tent out of their napkins. They put the napkins around the backs of their necks and then flip them over their heads and over their plates. They eat everything on the ortelan but the beak."

"That's disgusting."

"Not to the ortelan eaters, many of whom are British. They come over when the ortelans are in season and scarf them down. You see, the French are violent but they have a whole world of unindicted co-conspirators."

"Would you eat one of them?"

"Not if I had to wear the tent."

"Seriously."

"I am serious. Throwing napkins around like that . . . you could knock over the wine glasses."

"Where did you learn about all that?"

"From my French teacher, at Irvine."

"Sounds like a bad influence."

"Sometimes. As eighteen year-olds we loved it."

"You're looking at the mirror again. Why?"

"I'm sorry; I'm just naturally suspicious. Don't worry, there's no one behind us."

A minute later she noticed him check the mirror again. He was doing it without turning his head. He was talking to comfort her, to distract her from the fact that something violent and unexpected might happen at any moment.

Chateau Bison had a brown metal medallion over its entryway: a carved silhouette of a prehistoric bison, floating in the air against the blue-gray sky in the same way it might float against a wall in an ice-age cave painting. The winery was closed for tastings and the public parking lot had emptied. After Tom drove through the gate an elderly man appeared from behind the stone supporting pillar on the right and carried a heavy chain across the road, securing it at bumper level on the other side. It was 2:25. The afternoon sun was still warm and the gathering clouds were threatening rain. The air was close, the breeze light.

They drove behind the chateau—largely a facade housing the corporate offices of the winery—and parked behind a single-story stone structure whose public entrance was on the east end of the building. On the west end in the rear was a highly-polished oak door. They entered, the door was closed behind them, and locked.

"Bon jour, Mademoiselle Bennett et Inspecteur Deaton," Cossard said. "Asseyez vous."

They sat down around a hand-carved rectangular table with 14 chairs. The room was dark, with curtained windows, baroque furniture, and heavy tapestries. Tom whispered to Diana that it looked like an upper room in a Moorish castle. Cossard was sitting in the center of the table. He turned to an associate in a business suit and nodded. The man sat up straight in his chair and greeted them. "Good afternoon, my name is Derieux. The chief investigator has asked me to brief you on the results of our work."

"We appreciate your help and your courtesy," Tom said. Derieux cocked his head and smiled briefly.

"Neither of the men who killed your friends from the American Federal Bureau of Investigation has been identified. There is no positive fingerprint match and no identifying marks sufficient to conduct a successful computer search. There were no tattoos, though one of the men appears to have had one that was removed. We are circulating pictures, of course, but that can take a great deal of time. DNA tests will also take quite some time. Their weapons were unregistered; both were of German manufacture. The car found outside Les Eyzies was registered to a fictitious person; the passport and credit card were forged. Since such documents require some effort to obtain, it is clear that your friends were not the victims of random violence. No one suspected that, of course, but the forged documents and the evidence of advance planning suggest that this operation was conducted by professionals."

"Hired, do you think?" Diana asked.

"Ultimately, of course," Derieux said, "but not necessarily for this particular operation."

"What about their dental work?" Tom asked.

"Of high quality, probably American," Derieux said. "Both had porcelain fillings; one had two crowns, the second a bridge of recent manufacture. All expert work. One of the men had had an appendectomy and the second—the one murdered outside Les Eyzies—was wearing orthotic supports in his shoes. The identifying marks on the orthotic supports had been melted out. We can cross-check the dental work with that of possible suspects, but again, it will take a great deal of time."

"Clothing?" Tom said.

"Generally of American manufacture, though the man you shot at the *Cro-Magnon* was wearing Italian shoes. Expensive shoes. Perhaps 250 euros for the pair."

"But available everywhere?" Tom asked.

"Yes. The bottom line, as you would say, is that the men were probably from America. They were here specifically to kill the Federal Bureau men or to kill you, probably the latter. At this point we cannot say when they arrived in France. In all likelihood the murderer of the second man was a confederate, one who wished to both punish the man for his failure and insure his silence."

"Can you tell us about the director's secretary, Madame Scaviner?"

"Yes. That is quite interesting. *Quite* interesting."

CHAPTER TWENTY-EIGHT
Chateau Bison, St. Emilion
Wednesday, 2:52 p.m.

Before Derieux could continue, a representative of the winery entered the room and put two bottles of red wine on the table along with two plates of fruit, cheese, and bread. The plates were hand-painted country porcelain. The wines and food were exquisite. Tom tasted the wine and said, "Excellent." The server smiled, said "Merci, Monsieur," and promptly left. The Frenchmen responded to the wine the way most American businessmen would respond to a pitcher of ice water accompanied by a stack of scuffed, plastic glasses.

"Madame Scaviner has been quite helpful," Derieux said. "It seems that Monsieur Ponge's personal appointment book has been lost. Stolen, we assume. However, Madame Scaviner has kept her own book for many years. She has also had the foresight to keep her book in her own possession and not leave it on her desk. It seems that she was devoted to Monsieur Ponge and sought to protect him and his activities from the eyes of curious visitors."

"Do you have the name of the contractor?" Diana asked.

"No, Mademoiselle Bennett. You see, there was no contractor. There was what you would call a 'consultant.' This person appears to have secured the workmen who entered the cave and stole the *Chevaux Ponctués*. We believe that this man was recommended to Monsieur Ponge. The firm was not a local one. Thus, we are assuming that Monsieur Ponge contracted with the consultant in order to conceal the existence of what he believed to be the green disease. He wished to avoid embarrassment. That, at least, is what we are expected to believe."

"And you have his name?" Tom asked.

"We have the name of his company," Derieux said. "It is a British organization. Does that surprise you?"

"There was an Englishman who claimed to have discovered the green disease," Tom said.

"Yes. This individual was probably the person who referred Monsieur Ponge to the British organization. If that is the case (and we believe it to be so) the Englishman and the consultant conspired to steal the *Chevaux Ponctués*. Madame Scaviner's memory was quite acute. She told us that the Englishman was young, perhaps twenty five or thirty years of age. He feigned nervousness and concern, as if he had discovered some great evil. You realize, of course, that at that time Madame had no knowledge of the green disease. She was simply confronted with a man demanding to see Monsieur Ponge. Madame tells us that he was tall and blonde and wore the clothes of a businessman rather than those of a tourist or scholar. He carried an attaché case when he presented himself to Monsieur Ponge. He used the name Hayward; we are checking with British authorities, but we assume that the name is fictitious."

Derieux sat comfortably in his chair, bridging his fingers as he told his story. Cossard, on the other hand, was tense and frustrated. His English was inadequate but he was anxious to participate in the discussion. Occasionally he nodded insistently or cocked his head like an attentive terrier. His fingers were inverted and interlaced, as if they were holding in the pressure building in his chest and temples. Tom thought of the children's game 'This is the church and this is the steeple,' but Cossard kept his fingers together, squeezing them tighter and tighter as his knuckles whitened.

Derieux's brown eyes were warm, his expression easy. His hair was neatly combed. He wore an intricate gold ring on his left hand and a muted tie to complement his brown suit and shoes. Cossard was his polar opposite, his gray eyes darting from side to side, his hair neatly trimmed but his face darkening with whisker stubble. He had worked around the clock and now that they were making progress he was consigned to the sidelines. Finally he blurted out the words, "English, Inspecteur Deaton, Englishman."

"Yes," Tom said. "And the consultant as well."

Cossard shook his head in frustration.

"This is the benefit of an excellent secretary," Derieux said. "She is scrupulous with details and absolutely loyal to her supervisor. She serves him even after his death."

"The consultant," Tom said. "You were going to tell us the name of his organization."

"That is what I mean," Derieux said. "Such precision, such accuracy. It is so rare these days."

"Yes," Diana said. "And the name?"

Derieux took a sip of his wine and picked up an apple and a paring knife. "That is what is so fascinating," he said, as he peeled the skin from the apple in a single, long strip. "From Normandy," he said. "Quite nice. You should try one."

Tom and Diana waited. Cossard was lifting his chin and turning it from left to right as if his starched collar was choking him. Derieux took a bite of his apple. "Yes, excellent," he said. "Now . . . Madame Scaviner. A woman of great observation. Monsieur Ponge must have given her a business card of the consultant's or, perhaps, he wrote her a note so that she might record his telephone number in her file. She remembered it precisely when we asked. She did not even have to look in her book. The firm was called . . . here, let me write it for you."

He took out a pad, removed his fountain pen from the inside of his jacket, wrote down seven letters, tore off the sheet, and handed it to Tom and Diana. It read:

Tévedos

"*Tenedos*," Tom said.

"Very good," Derieux answered. "Madame reproduced the nu. When we asked her about it, she pronounced it *Tevedos*. That is what I mean by precision and attention to detail. That is what she was given and that is what she remembered. Quite remarkable in these days. You must be a Greek scholar, Inspecteur Deaton."

"Catholic High School graduate," Tom responded. "My father insisted on it. *Tenedos* is an odd name for a consulting firm."

"Yes, I agree, but Madame Scaviner was quite specific."

"And you said that it's British," Diana said.

"Yes, Mademoiselle. We even have the telephone number. We have called them, of course, but there was no answer."

"Was there a recorded message?" Tom asked.

"No, as a matter of fact there was not," Derieux answered. "Would you expect one?"

"Most people who are self-employed rely on them. Did the phone number carry a London city code?"

"Yes, we expected that, of course."

"I'd appreciate the number."

"We can do that for you. Presumably it is public knowledge. Do you intend to go there?"

"Yes," Tom said, looking at Diana. "We'll leave as soon as possible."

"May I make a suggestion?" Derieux asked.

"Certainly," Diana answered, Tom deferring to her.

"These people have been responsible for six deaths on French soil. So, at least, we believe. If you intend to seek them you should be very careful. When we are finished here I would like to speak with you further."

"Of course, Monsieur Derieux," Diana said. "Thank you."

Derieux turned to Cossard and whispered something to him. Cossard stood up immediately, nodded to Tom and Diana, and walked toward the door. The rest of the men followed him out of the room.

Derieux rose, gestured to Tom and Diana and took them to the far west corner of the room, where they could stand under a vent fan whose vibrations would mask the sounds of their voices.

"I would trust all of these men with my life," he said quietly, "but that does not mean that one cannot still be careful." He handed them a large brown envelope. "This contains additional automobile plates if you need them," he said. "We will return the vehicle which you rented. If anyone attempts to follow it they will find four armed men. At the rear of the car park is a private vehicle from the Culture Ministry for your use. After you have driven it a safe distance you can change the plates if you so choose. They will provide an added precaution, one that is probably unnecessary, but I prefer to err on the side of safety and I suspect that you do as well. Take whatever route you wish and whatever means of travel you choose. Park the car, lock the keys in the glove box and call me after you have arrived in Britain. I will arrange to have it picked up. You should know that these plans have been made by Monsieur Cossard. He has asked me to explain them to you."

"You have both been very helpful and very kind," Tom said. "Please convey our thanks to him."

Derieux nodded. "We will do what we can with the authorities in Britain," he said, "but you may have better luck than they. I wish you well. Mademoiselle's brother *must* be avenged . . . and the horses *must* be returned to Pech-Merle."

"*Avenged?*" Tom asked.

"But of course," Derieux responded. "Hopefully the courts will do this, but if they are unable to, we must still have justice. Otherwise, what is the point?"

"Policemen are not permitted to speak that way in America," Tom said.

"Of course not. But you see, I am not a policeman. I am a student of art. We are far less forgiving."

CHAPTER TWENTY-NINE
Cherbourg
Thursday, 1:22 a.m.

They checked into the Marine Hotel at the harbor. Their room was at the north end of the building, overlooking the marina. The moonlight illuminated the walls and windows of the surrounding city and the light from the docks and boats was glistening in the swaying water. "This is lovely," Diana said, as she opened the drapes, took in the view, and let in the late night air.

Tom put down their bags and walked across the room. "Yes," he said. He was standing next to her. She turned her head and smiled at him; her shoulder brushed against his arm. "So far so good," she said.

"So far so good," he answered.

"I'll take that couch," she said, "and I don't want any arguments."

"It looks softer than the bed," he answered. "It's yours."

"In that case . . ."

"No, no arguments," Tom said.

"All right, no arguments."

The harbor bell sounded at 2:00 a.m. as Tom shifted position. He was still unable to sleep. For the last hour and a half of the drive his eyes had been heavy and burning around the edges. When he blinked to focus them they sometimes continued to blur. He had forced his fingernails into his thumbs and palms to keep himself alert. Once they arrived at the hotel he had unwrapped some of the food that Derieux had persuaded him to take along: Normandy apples, Isigny brie, and still-fresh slices of French bread. He had also included a spare bottle of the St. Emilion. Diana had gone right to sleep while Tom had stayed awake, eating, thinking, and absorbing the events of the past few days. He had hoped to fall asleep quickly, but the food revitalized him and as he lay in bed he listened to the sounds of the harbor: boats rocking against their moorings, members of the harbor master's staff making late-night rounds, the pop of a welding torch off in the distance and the occasional cries of gulls fighting over scraps.

At 2:30 he reached for his watch on the nightstand, raising it in the air to catch the moonlight on the dial. His eyes were heavy and his knees and ankles were cramping but the circuits in his brain were still overloaded with plans, contingencies, repeating melodies, and the fragments of dreams and random thoughts.

In the shadows between sleep and consciousness. Thinking he was talking about his girlfriend Sarah, explaining to Diana the circumstances of their breakup. No real need to explain. Nothing to say, actually.

Suddenly a noise. Broken glass, a barking dog, shouts. Tom was out of bed instantly, his gun in his hand, poised at the side of the window, not offering a target. Diana cried out, "What was that?" and ran to his side. "Stay back," he whispered, pinning her to the wall with his left arm, his pistol next to his cheek.

More noise. Footsteps, the sounds of a scuffle. Finally coming into view: the harbor police bracing a teenager. Tom at the window now, seeing the broken glass from the stolen liquor bottles. A tall boy with a guard on either side, each twisting one of his arms. "It's all right," he said. "Just a kid trying to steal from one of the motor yachts. The guards caught him."

She didn't move. He turned to look at her. Her back was against the wall and she was breathing heavily. "It's OK," he said. "It was nothing."

She was wearing a long tee-shirt and as her chest rose with her breathing he could see the outlines of her body. He put his pistol down on the nightstand, put his arm around her and walked her back to the couch. "Go back to sleep," he said. "It's still the middle of the night." She put her arms around his waist as her head fell against his shoulder. She was still warm from the bedclothes and her breath smelled of sleep. She kissed him on the cheek, said "Thank you," and slowly separated from him.

He felt as empty as he had when he saw Walt McNeise's body hurled against the wall, his chest exploding in a mist of smoke and blood and shredded fabric. He reached out to pull her back and she suddenly froze, looking up at him. He dropped his arms to his sides.

"Why did you do that?" she asked.

"I don't know. I just, somehow, wanted to hold you. I'm sorry."

"No, I mean why did you stop?"

"I didn't want to take advantage of the circumstance."

"The circumstance," she said, "is that I was asleep, you heard a sound, and you leaped out of bed to protect me. Why shouldn't you hold me?"

He put his arms around her. Her cheek was against his neck, cooler now, as the breeze from across the harbor filled their room. His hands fell to the small of her back and he felt her breasts pressed against his chest, full and separate. He kissed her cheek as she had kissed his and she turned her face toward his, trying to search the depths of his eyes in the dark. Her hands were on his shoulders, her arms in parallel, her elbows above his waist. He felt the pressure of her fingertips as he offered more words of reassurance.

CHAPTER THIRTY
The Channel
Thursday, 1:47 p.m.

The sky was gray, the cloud cover thick, the waters of the channel nearly flat. There were no storms predicted for the next twelve hours, but the uncertainties of the channel were always there. Even with its great bulk and with swells no greater than one to two feet, the ferry seemed to slap the water, keeping legs unsteady and stomachs on edge. The heads did a good business as passengers lost their breakfasts and lunches and washed their green faces with unpotable sink water. Too much motion; too little sleep; too much rich food. The vacations were over. The gulls followed them for the first few miles and then returned to land.

Tom and Diana sat on the top deck, turning their faces toward the wind. The air was cool and moist. Tom had slipped his jacket around her shoulders.

"I want to tell you something," he said.

"What's that?" she responded.

"When I told you that you should have stayed in the car . . . "

"Yes?"

"Don't think for a second that I wasn't grateful."

"I know that."

"I just think you've been hurt enough."

"Yes?" She knew there was more.

"And I wanted you to know that I never doubted you."

"What do you mean?"

"That you could hold up your end."

"I couldn't if I had stayed in the car," she answered.

"I just wanted to protect you," he said.

"I know," she said, putting her hand over his. "Are you hungry?"

"I could eat something," he answered. "Let's take a look and see what they have."

The cafeteria offered four different types of sandwich: ham, salmon, cucumber, and cheddar. The cheese was grated rather than sliced and each of the sandwiches was principally discernible by its color, the filling consisting of a thin line of vague substance bookended by two pieces of processed white bread. Each was packaged in thick plastic and all were wedged together in a glass case next to the beer tap. The case was illuminated and heated by a large white light bulb. There were droplets of moisture along its edge.

"Lovely selection," one of the British travelers said. After seeing the *Courage* tap, he added, "I haven't had a proper pint in two weeks."

"Island cuisine rather than continental. One of the fringe benefits of a British ship," Tom said. Diana smiled. They bought cheese sandwiches and tea and found an open table in the aft portion of the deck.

"You were saying that you wanted to protect me," Diana said.

"Yes," Tom answered.

"You didn't want me to take out the secret service agent in Heathrow either."

"No, I didn't. The risk was unnecessary."

"But if you didn't doubt me . . . ?"

"I don't now."

"But you did then?" Her eyes were bright and searching.

"You're talking like a wife," he said, "not like a citizen."

"I am? I thought I was talking like someone in pretty decent physical condition who knows where the soft points are on the human body."

"I didn't say that I didn't like you talking like a wife . . . "

"Good answer," she said. "You know what?"

"What?"

"We've got the limestone bluffs of France behind us and the cliffs of England in front of us. You know where that puts us?"

"How about . . . between a rock and a hard place?"

"Right, and to me that says that we'll need each other more and more before this is over."

"In what sense?"

"Wait, now you're doing it," she said.

"I thought it was my turn," Tom answered.

"You're good," she said. "I like someone who stays on task."

"So are you," he answered. "When this is all over . . . "

"Yes?"

"And if we're both still standing . . . "

"Don't say that," she said.

"Always a possibility."

"OK, and if we're both still standing . . . "

"I'll take you out for a real sandwich."

"Deal," she said, looking at him closely and not blinking.

III

TENEDOS

CHAPTER THIRTY-ONE
Friday 12:05 a.m.
Waterloo Station, London

"We're set at the *Grosvenor House*," Tom said. They were standing at a bank of phones in Waterloo station, their luggage at their feet. The adjacent W. H. Smith bookshop with its bright yellow sign had just closed for the evening, but the pub and the chemist were still open. Families were gathered in small groups to catch late-night trains and individuals were pacing the platforms, sipping coffee from stained cardboard cups and checking their wrist watches, waiting impatiently for arriving passengers.

"The *Grosvenor House* is in Park Lane, isn't it?"

"Right, but with an exit at the rear. If we need to, we can go into the streets on the east or the park on the west. The hotel itself is also fairly formidable. It's used for business meetings and conventions. There are large public rooms as well as corners and cubbyholes. One room is so large it used to be used as a skating rink. I think it's the perfect place for our purposes."

"Fine," Diana said. "Let's get a taxi."

The smells of York Road were the smells of London: aged earth, diesel fumes, the hint of vats from distant breweries; the smell of whiskey, stout, and cigarette smoke, of fried fish and vinegar, unwashed clothes, wildflowers, and coal smoke hanging in the leaves of giant planes and oaks; the gravel, wood, and stone washed by a tidal river; the smell of black and gold paint, of brass polish, sawdust, and window cleaner, of unrinsed milk bottles resting untouched on porches and steps; and everywhere the steam from damp streets with ground-in dust and grit drying in the wake of taxis and lorries hurtling through the swirling air.

Southwark was quiet except for the street traffic. The Royal Festival Hall and National Theatre were closed for the night, the County Hall still dark—undergoing massive renovation at the expense of yet another new owner. The Old Vic had let out an hour and a quarter earlier and the pedestrian traffic near the bridge was reduced to a handful of couples returning from the west end and a lone drunk, humming happily to himself and cradling a brown-bagged bottle as he lurched toward an open bench along the Thames.

The air was heavy but cool, the streets still glistening from an earlier shower. The sidewalk stones were covered with an oily black sheen of city damp. A single patrol boat was cruising the river, shining a searchlight along the Southwark shore and making its way toward the Embankment to check the shoreline and the row of commercial vessels moored there.

They had gotten the last car in the taxi queue, headed across Westminster Bridge, travelled north up Whitehall, west past the palace, and north into Mayfair. The streets were quiet except for the remaining late diners making their way to their Jaguars and Mercedes. Row houses and mews houses were accented with the colors of blooming cyclamen in window and porch boxes amid glass-globed lights. Gray stone contrasted with sandstone, white marble, brickwork, glass, and flowers. A rich village in the center of a rich city, Mayfair was dotted with antique shops, styling salons, boutiques, brasseries, and small hotels, all neatly separated by grand townhomes, expensive flats, and small parks.

The back of the *Grosvenor House* was an open rectangle of upscale shops. Two doormen greeted the taxi as it arrived; the younger of the two took Tom and Diana's luggage and handed Tom a numbered ticket. Except for an elderly man reading a hardcover book and two women talking quietly on the opposite couch, the lobby was empty. The clerk at the reception desk, a young woman named Emma, checked them in. Her smile was bright and her eyes alert, given the hour. Tom handed her a VISA card with the simple 'W. Justice' stamped on it and she put it in the electric imprinter, printed a blank chit, removed them, and returned the card to him. She seemed to do it all in a single motion, taking some pride in her efficiency.

He thought about the fact that the better the hotel the quicker they returned your credit card. It was a point of honor somehow. They didn't need the money. They didn't doubt the probity of their clientele. Besides, they could find you anyway, since they had your name, address, phone number, travel agent's number, credit card number, frequent flier number, hotel honors number, blood type, fingerprints, and DNA profile. Except with Tom they didn't have any of those things. He signed the register as Wayne Justice, 5005 N. Harbor Drive, San Diego, California 92106, USA. Which made his happy hearth and home one of the 111 rooms of the *Best Western-Posada Inn*, just a short hop, skip, and jump from the Zoo and Sea World. Centrally located and always ready to provide the friendliest of service.

Their room was on the fourth floor, overlooking the park: a mini-suite with an additional three-quarter bath adjoining the sitting area at the base of the twin beds. Tom took the shower and offered Diana the tub. He unpacked his bag as she turned on the water for her bath. She added some lavender fragrance, pouring it directly into the faucet stream, and watched the bubbles spread across the surface of the warm water. After checking the temperature she returned, opened her bag, took out her cosmetics, and put them on the shelf above the bathroom sink. When the tub was full she turned off the blue and red faucets, returned to the bedroom, and looked inside her bag. She took out a silk gown cut like a tee shirt and a fresh set of underwear, returned to the bathroom, and set them on the sink. She closed the door but didn't shut it tight. He could still see the light and hear her voice.

Halfway through his shower the lights and shadows in the room changed as Diana walked from the doorway to the heated towel bar, her body momentarily interrupting the glow from the fixture above the sink. He turned and wiped some of the condensation off of the door. He saw the outline of her body as she put the heavy cotton towel on the aluminum shower door handle. She turned and he changed position, leaning closer to the glass, so that he was able to see her walking back into the bedroom. She was barefoot, her hair was wet, her body covered by a white hotel robe. She had been thinking of him, wondering if he needed anything. And then, without hesitation, she had simply walked into the room where he was showering. Did she know that the glass was fogged?

He dried himself, slipped on his underwear, and walked into the bedroom. She was in bed, on the far side, her nightstand light turned on, but dim. He switched it off and she suddenly moved, turning toward him.

"Good night," he said. "Thanks for the towel."

She smiled, said, "You're welcome," and closed her eyes.

CHAPTER THIRTY-TWO

Grosvenor House, **Park Lane**
Friday, 8:57 a.m.

As he arranged the breakfasts on the coffee table Tom considered the changes in his life in the last week and a half. His incision was healing ahead of schedule and what pain there was could be masked by a few over-the-counter pills. There was a new person in his life whose interest in him could be personal as well as professional. He was hunting the killer of the most important artist in California and he was doing it with a civilian who was also the victim's sister. The fact that a number of well-armed men were trying to kill the two of them in violent and unexpected ways somehow seemed peripheral.

Things were turning, doubts diminishing. For a time he had wondered if he would come out of the hospital on his feet or on his back. Assuming the brighter possibility, he wondered if he would slip effortlessly into his former role or instead nurse a series of constant, perhaps unending uncertainties. Sarah had become more of a nurse than a lover. That part of his life had changed, perhaps irrevocably. She had visited him out of a sense of duty and he wondered if her prayers for his recovery centered on her desire to be free of that responsibility rather than on any hope that they might be able to somehow recover whatever it was that they had shared in the past. It all seemed less important now. He *had* recovered, he *had* been able to call on skills and instincts that had not been lost, and he was working a case of great importance with commensurate challenges. Most of the time he now felt that he was equal to them. Moreover, there was someone else along who seemed to agree.

Or so she said. There were risks on that front as well, risks of self-delusion, risks of loss. But risks were the one thing he had missed and when he was able to handle them he felt as if everything in his life that had nearly trickled off and evaporated in the dust and gravel had come together again in a broad, fresh stream.

Seeing Diana moving between the bedroom and the bathroom, adjusting her clothes and applying her makeup, he dropped the thoughts of cold hospital rooms with starched cotton sheets, monitoring equipment with electronic displays and monotonous beeps, of food designed by dietitians rather than chefs. He also forgot the gunshots and the broken fingers, the lingering smell of cordite, and the vision of Walt McNeise sprawled like a broken mannequin, his blood spreading into the carpet.

"Marmalade or preserves?" he asked, trying to focus.

"Marmalade," she said. "Thanks."

"Cream or sugar?"

"A little cream, thanks."

"Bananas or strawberries?"

"Let's split them."

"Sugar on yours?"

"Just a little."

"Done," he said.

"You're spoiling me," she said.

"My job," he answered. "By the way, we should be leaving in twenty minutes."

"I'll be ready," she said, picking up a piece of toast on her way through the bedroom. She was wearing light wool slacks and a cream-colored silk blouse, loosely buttoned at the wrists. She was trying to look relaxed, ready to hit the aisles at *Harvey Nichols* and the halls at *Harrods*, but she was also unencumbered, ready to climb, kick, or run. "How far away is the Tenedos office?" she asked.

"A twenty- or twenty-five minute walk or an eight-minute taxi ride, unless we hit traffic."

She leaned out from the bathroom and looked at Tom, standing near the window. "Aren't you eating anything?"

"I put cream in my coffee," he said.

"Lean and hungry, eh?"

"Yes," he said, slipping his arm around her waist as she walked past.

"Let's go get them," she said.

"How did you learn so much about England?" she asked, as he hit the lift button for the ground floor.

"Two years ago I was the Department representative for a set of Interpol meetings in London. The Chief was otherwise occupied and the lieutenants passed on it. The meetings themselves were sometimes interesting and I had enough spare time to explore the city and any place I could get to on the weekend, which was practically *every* place."

"That sounds like a good job."

"I thought so. It was a nice opportunity. The Department is small, but in a key location. Given the problems that we deal with regularly, particularly those involving drugs, illegal immigration, and the protection of high-profile terrorism targets, we get involved in issues that a comparably-sized department in a rural location would not. I think there may also be a hope for reciprocity in the scheduling of future meetings, regardless of the international organization. Everyone wants to come to Laguna."

"Don't sell yourself short," she said. "You'd be a good spokesman for your Department; people would assume that it was a skilled one if you were a representative member of it."

"Thanks," he said. "That's very kind. This is our floor."

The elevator door had opened, but Diana's attention was focused on Tom. "Let's walk," he said, as they approached the revolving door beyond the concierge's desk at the rear of the hotel. "Stop for a second and check out the clothing in the window of the store on the right. Remember, we're supposed to be here for some personal time and some serious shopping."

"Right," she said, pausing at the second window and looking at a pink Chanel suit with large, black and gold buttons. "A little over the top for me," she said. The price was in four figures.

"Too old for you," Tom said. "I see you in something less garish."

He put his arm around her waist and they strolled down Park Street as if they had all the time in the world. "By the way, look at those decorative pieces." He pointed to two four-foot, matched Chinese vases in the window of an antiquities dealer named Rostof. Each was heavily ornamented with emperor dragons chasing each other's golden tails.

Diana smiled and took Tom's hand in hers when he extended it. They passed the restaurants, galleries, and styling salons on Mount Street and entered the northwest corner of Berkeley Square. "Tenedos is on Dover Street. We're only five minutes away," Tom said. I've got 9:35. We may be a little early, but that's OK. I'd like to take a look first before we actually go in."

The traffic around the square was heavy and every metered space was filled, even at £1 for a bare fifteen minutes of parking time. They crossed at the zebra on Charles and headed east toward Berkeley Street, then south past the *Mayfair Hotel*. "There's an alleyway behind the *Holiday Inn*," Tom said. "Right over there," he said, pointing. "It's like a tunnel. It's called Dover Yard."

The passage way was dark and narrow but the link with Dover Street was convenient and the pedestrian traffic steady. Emerging on the other side Tom checked the address in his notebook and decided to turn left. He took two or three steps and stopped abruptly. "It's right here," he said, "just one door above the tunnel."

At the ground level was a gallery display window with three large oils, the most prominent an impressionist landscape of brooks, cottages and distant pastures in late autumn light. Tom studied it for a second or two. "Your brother would have added something," he said, "there would have been more than simple technique."

Diana nodded and squeezed his hand. "There," she said, indicating the door to the above floors and the list of occupants on the adjacent plate. "Second floor. What we call third." They looked up but the windows were all curtained. "Just a second," Tom said, taking her back through Dover Yard and checking the back of the building. The windows were dark and there was no rear exit. There was a door on the Yard from the building that abutted Tenedos' but it looked as if it hadn't been opened for years. "OK," Tom said, "let's go in."

They walked up the steps and opened the main door, then climbed the stairs to the first floor. The stairs were narrow; the bannister had been repainted recently in shiny black lacquer. The single resident of the first floor was an insurer of fine art called *Carstairs Ltd.,* the single resident of the second, *Tenedos.* Not the Tenedos Corporation. Not the Tenedos Society. Not Tenedos, Inc. or Tenedos, Ltd. Just the single, anglicized word: *Tenedos.* The name was carved in the center of a windowless, solid-oak door, with a heavy brass knob. Tom looked at Diana and then raised his hand and knocked.

CHAPTER THIRTY-THREE
Dover Street, Mayfair
Friday, 9:51 a.m.

There was no answer after the first knock and none after the second. Tom walked over to the edge of the staircase, looking up and down and listening patiently. Then he returned, slipped on a pair of plastic gloves, took out his pocket knife, and quietly slipped the bolt. He extended his hand toward Diana, indicating that she should come around behind him. He handed Diana a pair of gloves, turned the knob slowly and quietly opened the door.

Nothing. The room looked like an abandoned Dickensian counting house, with unpadded, dark brown chairs, mahogany desks and library tables stacked with papers and photographs. Tom closed the door behind them and locked it.

The art on the wall was of high quality, with discreet but alarmed security wires. Early twentieth-century mostly, but with an occasional later piece. There was no sculpture and no antiques, except for the functioning office furniture. Diana started through the material on the tables and Tom checked the desk drawers. Most of the correspondence concerned appraisals and restoration estimates. The principal clients were European collectors, galleries, and insurance agencies. The file cabinets contained more of the same, with correspondence dating back to the 1940's. Diana showed Tom an invoice dated 1947.

There were bills for paints and chemicals but no such substances in evidence and no room for restoration work within that office. There was no safe, either wall or walk-in, and no special lights, tools, or imaging equipment beyond simple magnifying glasses. The restoration work was either done off site or *in situ*.

The appraisals were short and precise, the language terse and to the point, with straightforward figures in local currencies. Restoration estimates were equally brief, with a minimum of information and explanation. The letterhead read, simply, **TENEDOS** and all correspondence was signed 'Walter Kepler.' Diana showed one of the letters to Tom, pointing silently at the signature. The letterhead was printed in black ink and the samples adduced by Diana suggested that its design had not changed in fifty years.

The drawers of Kepler's desk were filled with pen nibs and pencil stubs, staples, simple metal paperclips, and rubber stamps with black-ink pads. There was even a box of carbon paper. No rolodex, post-it pads or flash drives; no cd's, mouse pads, indeed, no computer. And no copying machine, fax machine, or portable phone. Kepler's rotary-dial relic sat at the side of his desk, next to a Royal manual typewriter—top-of-the-line and state-of-the-art in 1954.

Tom turned to the oak filing cabinet behind the desk. It was unlocked. Inside were personal bills of Kepler's, some addressed to the Tenedos office address, some to an address in Cobham, Surrey. Tom wrote down the number and street in his pocket notebook. Except for utility charges the bills were widely spaced. Most were from repairmen, a few from grocers and department stores. Mr. Kepler had purchased a new suit in 1992 and two pairs of shoes in 1996. He had had the collars of his shirts turned in 1997.

Twenty minutes later they stood at the door, ready to leave. Tom listened for a moment, turned the bolt, and opened the door. They slipped into the hallway, down into the street, and through Dover Yard. "Welcome to the 1950's," he said.

"Remarkable," Diana answered. "Every appraiser, restorer, insurer, and art historian has a computer now. They work from flash drives or images on the Web. Kepler doesn't even have slides or reference books."

"He doesn't need them," Tom said. "He carries it all in his head. That's why his invoices and estimates are so short and sweet. He's saying take it or leave it. I'm the best and this is what I charge. There's no persuasion, no justification, just the bottom line. He's been in that office forever and he doesn't care to change."

"Or increase his business," Diana said.

"No. He does what he does, discreetly and well. That's why the French would have called him in, or why someone would want us to think that the French called him in. Quiet, conservative, old-fashioned, and no doubt highly competent."

"Also no paper trail, at least not on Pech-Merle."

"Was there any paperwork on any other French cave art?" Tom asked.

"None that I could find," Diana answered.

"Spanish or Australian?"

"No."

"I take it his name doesn't ring any bells."

"Not with me, but I'm hardly an expert. His only work with the U.S. was with old master paintings in a small handful of museums, some of it from twenty and thirty years ago."

They slipped into the restaurant at the *May Fair Hotel*, now a part of *Radisson*, and ordered coffee. They had been greeted by a British woman, served by a younger, German woman.

"No biscuits or sweets?" the waitress asked.

"No thank you," Tom answered. She looked at Diana, who smiled and shook her head *no*. The waitress smiled politely, turned, and whispered something to the other woman, who was now checking the cash register.

"Most of his work consisted of large commissions," Diana said. "His client list was small, but his prices high. And probably worth every penny."

"He can't be very young," Tom said. "If he had sufficient reputation to attract that kind of business fifty years ago he must be semi-retired by now. He may only come in a few days a month." Tom checked his watch. "I'll call the Tenedos number in a little while and see if he's there. If there's no answer, let's go to his home."

"What was the name of the Englishman at Pech-Merle who warned them about the green disease?"

"Something like Hayman," Tom said. "Just a second." He checked his notebook. "Not quite. His name was Hayward."

"And he was young."

"Yes, mid-twenties to early thirties," Tom said, going over his notes. "Tall, blonde, business dress. He was carrying an attaché case."

"Not Walter Kepler. Perhaps his assistant or grandson?"

"Could be," Tom answered.

Tom called Tenedos at 11:00 and again at 11:30. No answer. Rather than negotiate London traffic, they took a taxi to Heathrow, rented a car, drove west on the circle road and picked up the M25. The traffic was heavy but it was moving briskly. It took them twenty-five minutes to reach the A3 and, shortly thereafter, the Cobham exit.

An overgrown Surrey village between Woking and Esher, Cobham was bisected by its High Street and anchored by lanes of freestanding, brick two-stories for well-heeled London commuters. Walter Kepler's home stood alone in a copse of planes and chestnuts near the A3, opposite the river Mole. The stucco and beam elevation was vaguely Tudor. The roof was spotted with gray-green moss, the gravel driveway dotted with scattered patches of weeds. Some were beginning to flower. There was no car parked there. A shed was visible in the rear of the property. The curtains of the main house were partially drawn and the bright midday light reflected off the central windows.

Tom parked the rental car off the road, beneath the line of sight, and he and Diana walked back to the house, the sound of the gravel under their feet barely audible. A dog began to bark; Tom could hear its paws rattling loudly against the sides of its pen. They walked toward the house as if they were invited guests. There was a small cement apron in front of the main door. Tom knocked and they waited for a response.

Fifteen seconds later he knocked again but there was still no answer. They walked around to the back where Tom could see the neighbor's dog, its paws pressed against the top bar of its pen. It was a bull mastiff, large and brown, with drool along its jaws and anger in its eyes. Diana knocked on the window of the back door. The dog matched each knock with a loud bark. Inside she could see a kitchen. There were no lights on and no dishes stacked in the sink. The cupboards were closed, the table empty and both of its two chairs neatly in place.

There was no response when she knocked a second time. Tom slipped out his knife, opened the door, and let them in. The dog continued to bark, even after Tom closed the door. The house was still. There was a slight musty smell. Tom cracked a door off the kitchen and smelled the rising damp from the walls of the cellar below. They walked into the living room and found themselves again in another era. The room was filled with faded velvet couches, overstuffed chairs with antimacassars covering the arms and backs, ornate glass lamps, and hand-carved chests and tables, the corners reinforced with polished steel plates. The grandfather's clock on the far wall was made of walnut, with elaborate claw feet and swirled finials. Tom pointed at the weights; the clock had been rewound recently. As it chimed 2:00 Tom checked his watch. Then came the voice.

"Do not move. Raise your hands very slowly." When they did, the voice told them to turn around.

She was young, no more than thirty-five, dressed in plain black slacks and a white cotton blouse. She was wearing black leather shoes with low heels. Her hair was light brown, her eyes blue. She was wearing rimless glasses and holding a large, double-barreled shotgun. Tom thought it was

Italian. The workmanship was exquisite, from the inlays on the stock down to the fine metal fretwork surrounding the trigger housing. It was pointed at their eyes.

CHAPTER THIRTY-FOUR

Cobham, Surrey

Friday, 2:01 p.m.

"Who are you?" she asked. "Why are you here?"

"We're looking for Mr. Kepler," Tom said. "We believe he's been falsely implicated in a crime."

"What crime?"

"I'd prefer to speak with him," Tom answered.

"Who are you?"

"My name is Deaton; I'm a police detective from California. This is Diana Bennett."

"Diana Bennett . . . David Bennett's wife?"

"I'm David's sister," Diana said.

"I was sorry to hear about your brother, truly sorry."

"Thank you," Diana said. "Please put down that gun. We don't mean you any harm."

"Does this have anything to do with the death of your brother?"

"We think that it does," Tom said. "Has Mr. Kepler been in France in the last several weeks?"

"He hasn't been in France since last March," the woman answered. "Is that where the crime was committed?"

"Yes."

"How was Mr. Kepler implicated?"

"There was a fraudulent restoration project that actually involved the theft of a major art object. Tenedos was represented as the restoration agency."

"What art object?"

"Please, we need to discuss that with Mr. Kepler."

She paused, stared into Tom's eyes and then Diana's, and said, "Mr. Kepler is upstairs."

She pointed toward the stairs with the barrels of the shotgun and tipped her forehead in their direction, the shotgun now held at the level of Tom's and Diana's waists.

"Is he all right?" Diana asked. "We knocked but there was no response."

"He's upstairs, go ahead and see."

Tom put his hand on Diana's back, signaling her to go ahead. Following closely behind her, he shielded all but the top of her head from the shotgun's line of fire. The woman followed closely behind but with enough room to prevent Tom from striking or kicking her.

"He's in the room at the end of the hall," she said.

The upstairs was dark. The doors had all been closed and the small pane of rose-colored glass in the center of the hall was shaded by one of the chestnut trees. The hallway was free of furniture except for a single Austrian chest with flowered patterns that had been hand-painted in four colors. There was a small arrangement of family photographs on the walls, all in sepia and all at least seventy or eighty years old. The frame of the door at the end of the hall was outlined in light.

"Go on in," the woman said, as they got closer.

Tom put his hand on the door, pressed slowly, and saw the bathroom tile beneath the door. He opened the door, caught a glimpse inside, and then asked Diana to stay in the hallway.

"Why?" she asked. "What's wrong?"

"Please," he said.

Walter Kepler was sitting upright in his bathtub. The water, which came up to just below his armpits, had long since cooled. The blood on his left wrist was now dark and crusted. A pool of dried blood covered the floor beneath his wrist and the side of the tub was streaked with red stains. His right hand was in the water, resting in his lap, and the water was a light magenta. The afternoon sun cast a glow on the right side of his face. The lace curtains swayed with the west wind. Two flies and a small bee had come in through the open window and were inspecting the body.

Tom walked closer and saw the razor on the side of the tub, next to the red, hot water handle. It was an antique, with an ivory handle with black inlays forming a compass pattern. The side of the blade was inscribed with another compass pattern, this one elongated. The edge of the blade was streaked with dried blood. On the wall next to Kepler's right arm was a succession of spurt marks. One of the flies was fluttering above it, like a small boy leaping across the stones of a rushing brook.

Tom felt Diana's hand on his shoulder and when he turned toward her he saw that the woman was now holding the gun at her side.

"Did you find him?" Tom asked.

"Yes, this morning."

"Was his body still warm?"

"No. I think he must have died sometime during the night. I talked to him in late afternoon."

"And you're certain it was him on the phone."

"I've worked with him every day for the last twelve years, Mr. Deaton. I would recognize his voice."

"You were his assistant?" Diana asked.

"I am his student," she answered. "My name is Margaret Harrell."

"Was there any reason to suspect that Mr. Kepler was considering suicide?" Tom asked.

"None whatsoever. He was murdered," she answered. There was no doubt in her voice and none in her eyes.

"How can you be so sure?"

"He told me he would meet me this morning. We were working on an appraisal. The piece was Etruscan. I had made some enquiries at the Ashmolean and at the British Museum. I was ready to make my report. He would not have deceived me. He would never have deceived me."

"This must have been a great shock to you," Diana said.

"He would never have willingly inflicted this upon me. He was a kind man, an understanding and sensitive man. He knew that I was coming. He would never have wanted me to find him like this."

"My brother's death was also presented as a suicide," Diana said.

"Your brother was murdered?"

"Yes."

"The London papers merely reported his death. I'm so sorry."

Diana nodded.

"Have you called the police?" Tom asked.

"No. I am still trying . . . to accept . . . this. I was upstairs when I heard your knock. I thought you were his murderers and had returned for some reason."

"You should call the police," Tom said, closing the door to the bathroom.

They went back downstairs; she phoned the local police, explained that she had found his body, and answered three or four questions. The police promised to send someone promptly. She took them into the living room and poured three glasses of whiskey and unchilled soda.

"Tell me about the crime," she said.

Tom paused for a moment and then asked, "Do you know the horses of Pech-Merle?"

"The *Chevaux Ponctués*? Of course."

"They have been stolen."

"That's impossible," she said. "They're painted on a slab that weighs several tons. How could one remove it? Besides, the cave is visited by hundreds of people every day. Where would you find the opportunity to even try to steal it?"

"The director was told that the cave had green disease. He closed the cave immediately. Heavy equipment was brought in to replace what they thought was a faulty ventilation system. They replaced a piece or two and then used the equipment to remove the stone and put a copy in its place."

"My God," she said.

"And Tenedos was represented as the agent."

"By whom?"

"By a young man with a British accent. He hasn't been identified as yet," Tom said.

"Everyone in the world of European art knows Tenedos," she replied. "Mr. Kepler's reputation was beyond question. He would have been the person to call. Now that they have murdered him he cannot defend himself."

"The further implication, of course, would be that he was complicit in the act and took his life out of guilt or remorse," Tom said.

"Yes, I see," she said. "Such lies. Such filth."

"They murdered my brother for the same reason," Diana said. "I'm certain of it."

"How was your brother involved in this, Miss Bennett?"

"We believe that he prepared the copy that was substituted for the original paintings."

"Why would he do such a thing? Your brother was a man of honor, just like Mr. Kepler."

"We don't know," Diana said. "He was probably forced to do it because of some threat."

There was a knock at the door. Tom could see the man through the drawing room window. He was in plainclothes. A small blue sedan was parked in the driveway. Margaret opened the door and he introduced himself as Detective Chief Inspector Charles Baker. When he entered the room he acknowledged Tom and Diana but his eyes immediately ran to the shotgun resting on the sideboard.

He asked a series of questions, told all of them to relax and stay where they were while he inspected the body. During the time that he was upstairs alone his team of medical technicians arrived at the door; Margaret directed them to the stairway and told them that the body was in the room at the end of the hall.

They worked for an hour and fifteen minutes before removing the remains of Walter Kepler in a zippered vinyl bag. Baker followed them down the stairs. He removed his rubber gloves, turning them inside out in the process, and slipped them into his right jacket pocket. Margaret invited him to sit down. She offered him a drink of whiskey or tea, both of which he politely declined. He removed a notebook from his inside jacket pocket, took out a fountain pen, and recorded Tom's and Diana's names and addresses. Then he turned toward Margaret Harrell.

"May I ask you why you waited so long to call us in, Miss Harrell?"

"Mr. Kepler was my friend as well as my teacher, DCI Baker. We were very close. It has been very difficult for me to recover from the shock of finding him that way."

"Yes, quite," he responded. "Not the sort of man you'd expect to find in that state. You *did* find him just like that?"

"Yes. I didn't touch him, if that's what you're asking."

"And you said you spoke with him yesterday."

"I did. Late yesterday afternoon."

"You would recognize his voice of course."

"Yes, I would."

"And is that your shotgun, Miss Harrell?"

"Of course not. It was Mr. Kepler's."

"And was Mr. Kepler a sportsman, Miss Harrell?"

"No, Inspector. The shotgun was a gift to him. He did some work for the Uffizi. The directors were very grateful."

Baker rose and walked over to the sideboard to inspect the gun. "Do you mind, Miss Harrell?"

"Of course not," she said.

"It's not loaded," he said. "Were you aware of that?"

"No, I wasn't," she said.

"It would still make a lovely bludgeon. Good balance," he said, hefting it and passing it from hand to hand. "Did you notice the bump on the right side of Mr. Kepler's head?"

"No, I didn't," she answered.

Diana looked at Tom, who held his expression.

"Neither did we at first; it was very slight."

"Do you believe there was a struggle?" Tom asked.

"A struggle? Not much of one, I should think," Baker answered. "He *was* murdered, of course. That's clear."

"How can you be sure?" Margaret asked.

"Weren't *you* sure, Miss Harrell?"

"Yes, I told you I was."

"And why were you sure, Miss Harrell?"

"Because I knew him; there was no reason for him to take his own life."

"We believed you. Shouldn't we have done so?"

"Is that all you have?"

"No, Miss Harrell. There is more. Mr. Kepler was right-handed, was he not?"

"Yes, how did you know that?"

"From the position of his toothbrush and safety razor in the bathroom cupboard. The handles were to the right. One does not reverse the handles when replacing them. Now consider the state of Mr. Kepler's body. The right wrist was nearly severed, while the cuts on the left wrist were relatively superficial. A right-handed suicide will cut more surely with his right hand. I'm sorry to say this, Miss Harrell; I know of your feelings for Mr. Kepler, but it appears that one of two things probably happened. Either there was a struggle and his assailants were not able to make a clean, deep cut on the left wrist or they began with the right wrist, cut it through, and then added the slices on the left wrist for the purpose of symmetry. This was part of their attempt to persuade us that the wounds were self-inflicted.

"Odd, isn't it? No one ever says, 'He cut his wrist.' Suicides cut their wrist*s*. Or rather, they *slash* them. But there's always a pair. It seems more orderly that way, more tidy. Even with one wrist nearly hacked in two and blood splashed here and about, there's that need for symmetry. Quite fascinating really, don't you think? There's also the matter of the bump. It was fresh and recent. Warm-bath suicides seek to relax. They wish to leave this vale in peace, particularly when it's become a vale of tears. It's quite interesting really. The violence of the cuts is balanced by the soothing water. They're familiar with pain and it becomes their road to peace. Back to the amniotic fluid and all that.

"Mr. Kepler's head was bumped but his body was upright. If he had fallen against the rim of the tub or the sill of the window (or indeed, been struck) the position of his body would have suggested that fact. Instead, his body was arranged just as they wished us to find it, positioned to deflect our attention from the bump on his head, positioned to reinforce the initial impression that he had calmly entered his bath, stretched out his legs, rested his arms and then quietly opened the veins of his wrists. I'm sure you have anticipated my next question . . . ladies . . . and Detective Deaton: who did this thing?"

CHAPTER THIRTY-FIVE
Cobham, Surrey
Friday, 3:12 p.m.

"Perhaps it would help if I gave you the short version," Tom said.

"Please do," Baker answered.

"Dr. Bennett's brother was a distinguished California painter whose body was found a little over a week ago. We are certain that he was murdered, but the scene arranged by his murderer was intended to persuade the authorities that he died by his own hand. We believe that he was coerced into preparing a copy of a famous work of art which was then stolen and replaced with the copy. The murderers deflected attention from their actions by bringing forward an individual whose statements associated Mr. Kepler's appraisal and restoration agency with the project. He is now implicated in the object's theft, while the actual perpetrator has disappeared."

"Fascinating. How long has it taken you to deduce all of this?"

"A few days, why?"

"That's very good."

"Thank you. You should also know that we are not working from inference and circumstantial evidence, DCI Baker. A friend of mine along with the members of his team was killed and one of his attackers was later found murdered. The murderers are real and they know we are trying to find them."

"They killed their own chap."

"Yes."

"To maintain his silence, of course."

"Yes."

"There's a great deal of silence here, isn't there?" Baker said.

"Yes, there is," Tom answered.

"Also a great deal of tidiness and planning."

"Yes."

"Might I have that whiskey now, Miss Harrell?" Baker asked.

"Of course," she said, filling his glass half-full with whiskey and soda and freshening the other three drinks.

"Where did all of this occur?" Baker asked.

"My brother died in California. The theft occurred in France," Diana said. "Detective Deaton's associates were killed in France as well."

"And what did they take? Wait, don't tell me, I'm game to guess. Not the Da Vinci?"

"No," Diana answered. "That would have been easier."

"Easier?" Baker said, raising his eyebrows.

"They stole the *Chevaux Ponctués* of Pech-Merle."

"I don't know that piece," Baker said.

"Upper paleolithic, probably at least eighteen-thousand years old," she answered.

"A cave painting?"

"Yes. Actually a set of paintings. On a slab in an exceptionally large cave next to the river Lot, near Cahors. The entire slab was removed."

"What cheek. But at least that narrows it. The thief either loved art or he loved horses, what?"

They were all staring at him.

"Sorry," he said.

"Now you know what we know," Tom said.

"Quite interesting, but it doesn't answer my first question: who did this thing?"

Again there was silence as Baker took a sip of his whiskey.

"We had hoped for help from Miss Harrell," Tom said.

"And can you provide it, Miss Harrell?" Baker asked.

"I don't know who killed Mr. Kepler or Dr. Bennett's brother, if that's what you're asking," she said.

"Of course you can't," Baker said, "or you would have already done so, what? Tell us whatever you can. Paint in the background, as it were. By the way, this is excellent whiskey. I appreciate your hospitality. Might one . . ."

"Certainly," Margaret said, pouring more into his glass.

"Cheers," he said, nodding toward her and taking a deep drink.

"I'm not sure where to begin."

"Begin anywhere."

"All right," she said, taking a sip of her drink. "Let me tell you about the origin of Tenedos." She put her glass on a doily on a side table and continued. "Early in the last century the German art market was in chaos. Many aspiring collectors were finding difficulty acquiring impressionist pieces because of their rising cost and since they were often skeptical of the modernist pieces coming from other parts of Europe an opportunity presented itself for a group of enterprising young men. In effect, these young men determined to avoid problems in the art market by changing the nature of that market.

"Many of the collectors, like most members of the German public, were fascinated with antiquities, particularly antiquities concerning Troy. Schliemann had been dead for a generation but there was still great interest in his digs at Hissarlik. He was a most interesting man, of course. He had made an early fortune from trading indigo and still another fortune as a contractor during the Crimean War. He was even in California in the middle of the nineteenth century when it became a state and he vowed to become an American citizen. Did you know that Detective Deaton?"

Tom nodded no.

"Later, with the fruits of his industry, he was able to finance his digs at Hissarlik. He sent to Germany over 250 silver and gold objects which he called 'the Treasure of Priam.' These were confiscated by the Russians during the war. As a matter of fact they have recently resurfaced."

"Quite right, quite right," Baker said. "Go on Miss Harrell."

"Schliemann was wrong, of course, about the treasure. Troy had been rebuilt many times and the structure from which the so-called 'Treasure of Priam' came was actually pre-Homeric. He was digging too deep; the real Troy—Homer's Troy that is—was above him. Nevertheless, there was a great interest in Troy and the Trojan War in Germany, but artefacts were very rare. On the other hand, there were a great number of Mycenaean pieces available. Mr. Kepler and a number of his associates formed a consortium . . ."

"Tenedos," Tom said.

"Yes," Margaret answered.

"I don't know why it took me so long to remember it."

"Remember what?" Diana asked.

"Tenedos is the island on which the Greeks camped before they sacked Troy."

"Yes," Margaret said. "The Trojans thought they had left, but they had not. Odysseus and his men were on Tenedos, making their preparations."

"So," Tom said, "while other dealers were confused or overconfident the Tenedos group waited and planned and positioned themselves to corner the art market for Homeric antiquities."

"I'm not sure it was that melodramatic, but, yes, that's what they did," Margaret said.

"Go on," Baker said.

"There's not much more to tell. After the Nazis came into power Mr. Kepler left Berlin and came to England."

"He was Jewish?" Tom asked.

"His maternal grandmother was Jewish and that would have been enough for Hitler. The Gestapo broke into his offices, seized his papers, and arrested his personal assistant. The assistant was held incommunicado for four days. After his release Mr. Kepler decided to leave. The Nazis forced him to turn over a quarter of his assets before they would permit him to depart. He was protected by his notoriety. If he had not been so widely known and respected they would have simply arrested him. His associates stayed on but the business soon died. As Europe was plunged into war the art market evaporated. Pieces were lost, stolen, and confiscated."

"And what happened to Mr. Kepler's associates?" Tom asked.

"I have no idea," Margaret answered. "Why do you ask? You can't believe that one or more of them could be connected with Mr. Kepler's death."

"Someone used the name of his organization," Tom said.

"Yes, but as I told you, everyone connected with the art world was aware of Tenedos."

"But only one killed Walter Kepler," Tom said.

"Why would it possibly be someone who knew him so long ago, someone who had disappeared from his life for decades? When I asked him about the origin of Tenedos he explained it in the most offhand of fashions. It meant nothing to him any longer. He didn't even mention the names of his associates."

"Consider it syllogistic," Baker said.

"I don't understand," Margaret answered.

"Do you know of anyone with a motive to kill Walter Kepler?" he asked.

"No, DCI Baker. I told you I didn't."

"Well, there you have it," he answered.

"There you have *what*?" she said, her patience fraying.

"The majority of murders are committed by individuals who know their victims," Tom said. "None of Walter Kepler's current acquaintances would kill him. You just reiterated that fact. Therefore . . ."

"Therefore, one of his *past* acquaintances killed him," Baker said, "or, at least, is likely to have done."

"You're forgetting about the horses of Pech-Merle," Margaret said. "The criminal act was an art theft. David Bennett was an artist; Walter Kepler was an appraiser and restorer. They may have been used; they may have fallen in the murderer's way, but this is not a question of human relationships. It has to do with something else entirely—with money or art or material possessions. This was *not* a crime of passion."

"Forgive me, but I very much doubt that, Miss Harrell," Baker said. "All murders are crimes of passion. The trick lies in determining that passion's object."

CHAPTER THIRTY-SIX
Jermyn Street, London
Friday, 10:57 p.m.

"I've been worried about you," Diana said. "I expected you sooner."

"Sorry. I had a lot to do," Tom answered, "and I didn't want to draw any attention to you by calling here." They were sitting in the basement of a trattoria called *Marco's*. The theatre crowd had filled the main floor dining area and Diana was seated in a corner booth next to the wine cellar, grateful for the privacy. When Tom arrived she had been waiting for him for forty minutes. Baker had taken both Diana and Margaret from Kepler's house and left Tom to drop off his rental car. Margaret was sequestered in a safe house in Chiswick and Diana had waited with her there, under guard, until another officer brought her a new hotel key and drove her into central London at 10:00. Baker had arranged the rendezvous at *Marco's*. He had also arranged to have their luggage discreetly removed from the *Grosvenor House* and transferred to the *May Fair*.

"I'm glad you got here OK," Tom said. "Baker's very good, isn't he?"

"Yes."

"What are you drinking?"

"Still mineral water."

"We can do better than that," Tom said. He signaled the waiter, who was serving a couple at the only other occupied table in the basement room. "What do you want to eat?"

"Anything . . . something simple."

Tom ordered tricolor salads, angel hair pasta, and a bottle of Barolo. "Aperitifs?" the waiter asked. Tom turned to Diana. She said, "Maybe just some coffee. White."

Tom ordered a bottle of Peroni. "Now, where should I start?" he said. "I left just as you did and followed Baker for a mile or so to make sure you weren't being followed."

"Yes, he commented on that," Diana said. "He seemed amused by it."

"After I was sure that you were all right I drove back to Kepler's house and waited outside in the road. No one came by."

"You shouldn't have done that."

"Why?"

"Without backup? Someone could have been following you. They could have followed you here."

"I stayed in the shadows. Anyway, I waited about thirty minutes and then left, but instead of getting back on the M25 I drove toward the city. I puttered around on the A3, turned off into Wimbledon and started driving back streets. From Wimbledon I cut over to Kingston, crossed the river, passed Hampton Court, and came into Heathrow from the back door, picking up the circle road from inside the M25 and avoiding the main traffic flow. The Hertz driver took me back to Terminal 3 and I stepped out of the van and into a taxi. I was in central London in twenty-five minutes."

"Did you go by the *Grosvenor House?*"

"No."

"Good."

"I got off the beaten track and spent most of the afternoon and early evening in Hampstead. I found a pub in Finchley Road called the *Dog and Sparrow* that had good food, good beer and a quiet room on the second floor. I called the Chief three times before I connected with him. We talked for nearly an hour. I brought him up to speed on everything that's happened here and I told him what we needed. He's conveying my wish-list to the feds."

"What are they doing?"

The waiter brought Diana's coffee and Tom's beer. The coffee was steaming hot, as was the milk. Tom took a drink of the Peroni. "First they're checking with the art history and German history people at UCLA. There's always a chance that we might get lucky. Then they'll run through European art magazines and German newspapers between the wars and see what they can find out about Tenedos. Basically I said that what we need are the names of all of Kepler's Tenedos associates as well as their current whereabouts. If any of them are dead I said that we'd like information on the circumstances surrounding their deaths. I also said that we're particularly interested in any individuals in London or southern California.

"It's probably a long shot, but Baker is checking on recent homicides and supposed suicides in the greater London area. There may be another victim or victims connected with the case. He's also checking on any reports of art thefts. If he can find the staff he'll also check on passengers travelling between London and Bordeaux, Bordeaux and Paris, and London and Paris over the last several days. Again, we could get lucky. If we *don't* check we *know* we won't find anything.

"I've also asked the Chief to ask the feds to check with art dealers, particularly the very rich and the somewhat shady, to see if there's any buzz on the street about this. This doesn't look like spec work, but you can never be sure. There's also the possibility that with a score this big one of the people involved will have trouble holding his tongue."

"Is there anything new on David?"

"No. The Chief has asked Hector to keep an eye out. No change yet. Both the home and studio have been staked out, but except for some curiosity seekers there's been nothing worth reporting. They've checked on Sandra Harkin—the woman who works at his gallery in Santa Monica . . ."

"Yes?"

"Nothing there. She was sick for awhile but she's back at work now. There's nothing suspicious in her background and nothing unusual in her behavior immediately prior to your brother's death. She was never considered a suspect, but there's always a chance that she could have been used in some way. If she was, there's no evidence to that effect."

"What about Margaret Harrell?"

"Baker's investigating her. I talked to him about an hour ago. She seems OK. She grew up in Plymouth and worked as an assistant at the Plymouth library. Baker talked to her supervisor there, who's now retired—a woman named Pauling. Plymouth is Reynolds country and they have a number of his portraits at the library. Margaret got hooked on eighteenth-century painting as a teenager and later studied art history at the University of London. She worked with Kepler as an intern on a special project while she was still in college and then went to work for him full time after she graduated. He was starting to wind down and she was covering the office for him more and more as the years passed."

"How long was she with him?"

"Eleven years full time and a year and a half as an intern."

"And that's her whole life?"

"So it seems. She lives in a two-room flat in Cobham, drives a used Mini, when it's running, and stops into the local for a drink once every two or three weeks. From all appearances she spent most of her waking hours working for Walter Kepler."

"It sounds like a father-daughter thing."

"She says 'teacher-student' but there was a strong personal attachment too. Nothing suspicious, just old-fashioned affection."

"That's a nice switch."

The waiter brought the salads. The lettuce base was crisp and fresh, the olive oil, avocado, tomato, and mozzarella up to expectations. The waiter ground some fresh pepper on each and hurried back up the stairs to get their wine. The cellar was kept locked and loose bottles were displayed in the main dining area on shelves surrounding the rear tables.

"So that's about it," Tom said. "Now we wait."

"Baker's assistant gave me our hotel key. It's an unmarked Vingcard."

"In the *May Fair*?"

"Yes, room 218."

"Good. That's only a few blocks away."

"A block and a half from Tenedos," Diana said.

"We can walk by on our way back to the hotel."

"What do you expect to find?"

"I don't know. Margaret Harrell's still alive and Walter Kepler was alive until last evening at approximately 11:30 p.m. That's the time of death according to Baker's med tech. They always seem more certain of it here than the people back home. We were in the Tenedos office yesterday and there were no obvious signs that the office had been searched. If it had been, we might have noticed and Margaret certainly would have. If they had walked in on her while she was there they would have killed her, but that didn't happen. They didn't walk in on us either. Now that Kepler's gone, Margaret's incommunicado, and we've dropped out of sight, they might make a move."

The waiter cleared the salad plates and replaced them with their pasta. He also refilled their wine glasses. Tom asked for some mineral water and the waiter brought it with ice and a see-through sliver of sliced lemon.

"The Tenedos connection is real," he said. "We're not sure what the nature of the connection is, but we know there's a connection. Walter Kepler died because of it. If I were his murderer I'd wonder what was sitting there in his files. I'd wonder if anything was there that had my name on it. Wouldn't you?"

"Yes," Diana said, digging into her pasta. "Let's pass on dessert."

CHAPTER THIRTY-SEVEN
Dover Street, London
Friday, 11:58 p.m.

Piccadilly was nearly deserted except for three tipsy French teenagers, standing with their arms around each other's shoulders, waiting for the *Fortnum & Mason* clock to sound, and a group of middle-aged, middle-eastern men filing into a dance club at a B-list hotel. The last trickle of taxis was heading east, looking for theatre and movie stragglers. The streets were dry and the dust in the air was light. The slightest hint of coal smoke and diesel fumes was blowing in from the west. Stars were visible beyond the streaks of clouds in the northern sky.

The basement wine bar across from the Tenedos office was still open, the sounds of music and loud conversation seeping through the glass doors and into the street, and an elderly man with a heavy coat and cane was just emerging from Dover Yard.

"Here," Tom said, stepping into a doorway on the east side of the street. "Let's take a look." The moonlight reflecting against the Tenedos windows blinked and faded with the movement of the clouds. "There," Tom said, as the moonlight briefly dimmed. "The office is dark; let's go in."

The front door was heavy, with an oversized handle, but Tom slipped the lock quickly. After pausing to listen for a moment, they hurried up the stairs. Listening again at the Tenedos door, he slipped that lock and they walked inside. "Stay back from the windows," he whispered. "There's a light in the clothes closet. We can take stacks of documents in there if we need to check them closely. That way we won't draw any attention from the street.

"It looks the same," Diana answered, "but I'd expect that. I'll do the desk and tables; you take the file cabinets, OK?"

"Fine," Tom answered.

It only took eight minutes. "Look at this," Diana said. "I haven't touched them, though I'm sure they've been wiped clean." Tom walked behind the desk. As Diana had worked her way through the pile of documents on the left side of Kepler's desk she had found them: two photographs of the Pech-Merle horses. The first was a full view, taken approximately eight to ten feet from the slab with a view of the cavernous background in which the slab was situated; the second was an enlargement of the first, focusing specifically on the horses.

"Which is it, the original or the copy?" Tom asked.

The moonlight was dim but bright enough for Diana to be able to see the triangle of dots on the left horse's side. "It's the original," she said.

"They didn't need to plant a picture of the copy. All they needed to do was establish a connection between Kepler and the theft. I wonder if they planted anything else."

"Let's see," she said, checking the rest of the documents on the desk and then working her way through the materials on the tables. She didn't expect them to be too obvious about it, but neither did she expect them to bury something in the bowels of an ancient file cabinet.

They worked for two hours and a half. "Anything?" Diana asked. "I think this is new," Tom said. "At least I don't remember seeing it earlier."

"Where did you find it?"

"In the cupboard, stuffed in Kepler's sweater pocket."

"Let's see," she said. Tom was holding it by the edges: a small slip of paper with a handwritten note:

For value received. St. P project.

"A payoff note," Tom said. "At least that's what we're supposed to believe. It looks unofficial and off the books, the kind of thing you'd stick inside a rubber band wrapped around a roll of bills."

"Who is St. P?" Diana asked.

"Hard to say. There are a lot of saints whose names start with the letter P: Peter? Paul? . . . Saint Patrick? Try this: the abbey in Westminster is actually Saint Peter's and the cathedral in the City is Saint Paul's. The royalty are in Westminster, the money in the City. In the old days the king had to ask permission of the Lord Mayor to cross Temple Bar and enter the City of London. The two are traditionally in competition, with the fear that one is subsidizing the other. That's where we get the saying 'robbing Peter to pay Paul.' If these people would steal prehistoric cave drawings they'd certainly rob Peter. Think of the possibilities in the abbey. Where would you start, with the Coronation Chair or the body of Edward the Confessor?"

"*If* the P stands for Peter."

"Right," Tom said. "The point is—*if* this note was planted—there's been more than one theft. There were no saints at Pech-Merle, not sixteen or eighteen thousand years before Christ. We'll get Baker involved first thing in the morning. He can check on cathedrals and major churches and see if there have been any closings or suspicious activities."

"How long were they inside?"

"Nearly three hours. It's five minutes before three o'clock."

"Very diligent. They must have found the note and pictures."

"Yes."

"Kepler is implicated then."

"If they believe it."

"They have nothing else. What of the assistant?"

"The police must have her in custody. She has not returned to her flat."

"They will only protect her for a short while. She can be removed at any time. A young fool fawning over an old fool."

"We don't know what he might have told her."

"He could only tell her what he knew."

"Yes."

"Where have Deaton and the sister gone?"

"Back to their hotel."

"And are they now intimate?"

"They appear so."

"Good. That will make it easier."

Diana walked into the bedroom, the oversized white towel encircling her body. Tom was dressed, sitting on the bed, his back leaning against the headboard. "What are you thinking?" she asked.

He looked up at her and said, "Nothing, really."

"Tell me."

"I wasn't thinking of anything. Just old stories, from long ago."

"Tell me, I'm interested."

"OK. Just now I was thinking about a television program. It must be at least twenty years since I saw it on a rerun channel. It fascinated me at the time. If I saw it now it would probably look simple and crude, but I've never forgotten the story. It was like a locked-room mystery, except that there was no room and everything was in motion. Beautifully simple too."

"Tell me about it." She sat down, drying the back of her neck with the corner of the towel.

"OK. The authorities are anxious to protect some very special cargo from a group of highly skilled thieves. They put the cargo on a car in the center of a train and send it hurtling across the country at night. The train is not permitted to stop at any point. Who, the authorities reason, could steal a cargo weighing many tons, particularly when that cargo is in motion, travelling in darkness at sixty or seventy miles an hour? When the train pulls into the station the authorities breathe a sigh of relief and enjoy a short moment of self-congratulation, until they discover the fact that the car has disappeared, even though the train has never stopped."

"Good story," she said. "How did they do it?"

"It was easy or at least they made it seem easy. They ran a cable attached to a heavy winch between the cars above and beyond the car in question. As they approached a siding they uncoupled the car in between and let the train space out. The car they wanted to steal went off on the siding; the tracks were realigned, and they pulled the train back together using the cable and winch."

"It suddenly seems obvious, doesn't it?"

"Once you hear the explanation."

"And you were thinking about the theft of the horses, how easy it seems once you see how they did it." She had finished drying her hair. Tom could smell the twin scents of the shampoo and bath essence.

"I was thinking about the train," he said. "I don't remember what it was that was actually stolen. It doesn't really matter. The method was the whole point; the object of the theft was quickly forgotten. It was a television show: entertainment. This is different. We know *what* was stolen and we can't forget it. We think about what else they might steal, never mind the method. The story here is the thief. The mystery is the darkness at the center, the ravenous greed, the towering ego. What happened to your brother and to Walt McNeise and to Walter Kepler was terrible, but I have the feeling that their deaths are only footnotes. Something horrible stands behind this."

She had wrapped the towel around her tightly again, as if it might somehow protect her. Her eyes were moist with tears.

"I'm sorry," Tom said.

"I asked."

"I didn't mean to minimize the importance of your brother's death. What I meant was that . . ."

"That it wasn't at all important to whoever killed him."

"Yes."

"Then what we have to do is forget the cargo because the number of possible objects is endless."

"Right."

"And forget the method, because this thief will always find a method, no matter what the cost."

"Yes."

"The key is in his heart, in his nightmares and obsessions."

"Yes, or in her's."

"And if we know those we know him or her."

"Yes, I think we would."

As she stood up and walked toward the far wall the room seemed to fill with the mix of fragrances. "Can I get you anything?" she asked. "There's juice and mineral water in the minibar."

"No thanks," he said. "I'm going to get some sleep."

When she returned from the bathroom she was wearing a silk nightgown. She saw that he was still awake. "Tom . . . " she said.

"What?" he answered.

"Nothing really. I just wanted to thank you for all that you're doing for me."

"Forget it," he said, "get some rest."

"I'll never forget it," she answered, standing beside her bed and looking toward him. "Never."

CHAPTER THIRTY-EIGHT
The *May Fair Hotel*, Stratton Street
Saturday, 9:17 a.m.

"You do know that it's a little after one in the morning here, don't you Tom?"

"Yes, Chief. Isn't that about the time you used to get up at Ranger School?"

"Actually a little earlier," Dietrich answered. "Anyway, I've got some information for you. The feds are still in Westwood. They've got a couple of sleepy professors on their hands but they've been able to piece together part of the story."

Tom was using a public phone in a hallway a few dozen yards off of the *May Fair* lobby. It was too early in the morning for heavy traffic to and from the hall toilets and even though the phone was not enclosed someone had been kind enough to place an overstuffed wing chair next to the stand on which it sat. He took out his notepad and a *May Fair* ballpoint. "What have we got, Chief?"

"I'm not sure what it all means, but it's anything but dull."

"Run it down for me."

They met at Westminster Pier at 12:30 and boarded the boat for Greenwich. Baker was in tourist dress, with a striped rugby shirt under an open, poplin jacket. There was a .35 mm Nikon camera hanging from a black leather strap around his neck. Tom and Diana were wearing light sweaters over casual slacks. "Let's go below and have a drink," Baker said.

"There's a bar on board?" Diana asked.

"Of course. Who would come aboard without a bar?" Baker said. "We'll be less conspicuous there. I have some of my people above us to keep an eye on the stairs."

There were two men on the bridge, one at the wheel, one at the microphone, announcing sites along the Thames. Neither was wearing a formal uniform. The man with the mike was sprinkling his commentary with double entendres and cockney slang. It was cool on the river and the wind was beginning to pick up. The midday cloud cover brought a chill and the glassed-in bar deck was warm and comfortable.

"Courtesy of the Yard," Baker said, as he distributed whiskeys and soda. "Have a taste and tell me how they are."

"Good," Tom said, after taking a sip. Diana also nodded her approval.

"I know you yanks are discovering more and more of our whiskeys. This one is particularly good. Very peaty, don't you think?"

"Yes," Tom said. "It's very nice. Tell me, what have you learned?"

"A great deal, actually. At least we think so."

"So have we. Why don't you start."

"Very well," Baker said. "We've been checking for suspicious suicides as you know and we've managed to come up with one. A man by the name of Michael Sechrist. He was found in his garage with the motor of his Rover running. Sechrist was an expert on writing and manuscripts, an appraiser and dealer as well. Far younger than your Mr. Kepler, I'm afraid, a mere 38 at the time of his death.

"His wife said that there was no reason for him to want to take his own life. He was quite happy. *They* were quite happy. At first we were a bit suspicious. The problem, you see, is that this sort of thing happens all the time. The wives have no idea what their other half is up to. Infidelity, dressing up in women's clothing . . . the whole lot. Sometimes, of course, they're trying to protect them. Disease, embezzlement, that sort of thing.

In Mr. Sechrist's case there was no evidence of anything untoward. Unfortunately there was also no evidence of any foul play."

"Where were his offices?"

"Why do you ask? They were nowhere near Mr. Kepler's."

"Where were they?" Tom asked.

"Just off Ludgate Circus."

"Near St. Paul's."

"Yes, just down the hill. Is that important?"

"I don't know," Tom said. "Last night we went back to the Tenedos offices."

"Really? That's quite dangerous, you know. I wish you had said something first."

"Yes," Diana said, "we know." She was beginning to lose her patience.

"How about another round?" Baker asked.

"Not for me," Diana said.

"All right," Tom said.

"Jolly good," Baker said, and got up to fetch the refills. "Coffee, Dr. Bennett? Tea?"

"No thank you."

"You'll ask if you change your mind?"

"Yes, Inspector."

"I'll be back in a jiff."

"Now, where were we?"

"The Tenedos offices," Diana said. "We found some photographs of the spotted horses. They were not there when we checked the first time."

"Planted, eh? Very interesting," Baker said.

"We also found a note that referred to a project called 'St. P'. It said 'For value received.'"

"Some sort of payoff, then."

"So it appears," Diana said.

"I'm afraid we have a great many St. P's in England, Dr. Bennett."

"But only a few obvious ones."

"Yes, quite. Sechrist was in Ludgate Circus for a reason, of course. In London we take these historical things quite seriously. For many years the booksellers set up shop in St. Paul's Churchyard, just next to the cathedral. The printers, of course, were in Fleet Street long before the modern newspapermen arrived, though most of them are gone now as well . . ."

"Ludgate Circus is right in between," Tom said.

"Yes, of course. A nice compromise in a way. There's very little business in the churchyard just now and Fleet Street is all sandwich shops and bustle."

"Is it possible that something could have been stolen from St. Paul's?" Tom asked.

"What a horrid thought," Baker answered, "what a perfectly horrid thought."

"But possible," Diana said.

"Certainly. If this lot could steal a stone slab from a French cave they could steal something from an English cathedral."

"But Sechrist was an expert on manuscripts."

"Yes, but on many other things as well, I'm afraid. Ancient lettering, carving, scripts, that sort of thing. He was an expert on, how would you say . . . *texts*. Texts on paper, texts on papyrus, texts on stone. He sold autographs as well as manuscripts, for example, and he authenticated them as well. He was a man to whom one would go for verification of the authenticity of some form of writing."

"Or for the fabrication of some form of writing," Tom said.

"Quite possibly. He had no criminal record, however. I checked on that myself."

"He would have been familiar with the contents of the cathedral," Tom said.

"Oh my, yes," Baker answered. "St. Paul's is more than a cathedral. It's a . . ."

"A museum," Diana said.

"Quite," Baker said. "The crypt is filled with graves and busts and statuary. And it has Wren's original model for the church. All in miniature, of course, but quite spectacular. St. Paul's is filled with treasures. But there are people there constantly, either touring or worshipping."

"There were people in Pech-Merle as well," Diana said.

"Look," Tom said, as the black dome of St. Paul's came into view through the boat's windows, looming above the Thames.

"Good God," Baker said. "We'll have to get right on this."

CHAPTER THIRTY-NINE
The Thames, off Limehouse
Saturday, 12:58 p.m.

Baker put his cell phone back inside his camera bag. "I very much hope you're wrong," he said.

"So do I," Tom said. "Let me tell you what *we've* learned."

"Yes, please do." Baker crossed his legs and picked up his glass of whiskey, cradling it in his hands as if it were a small child.

Tom opened his notebook, flipped through several pages, took a sip of his whiskey, and then began: "Kepler left Germany in 1938. He, of course, was not the only one to leave. His departure was overshadowed by Freud's but it still made the papers. Like Freud he went to London, but Kepler survived nearly eighty years. Freud lasted a little more than one. Apparently they were friends. Freud was a great collector of antiquities and Kepler helped him acquire part of his collection. They both lived in Hampstead initially but after Freud's death Kepler moved to Surrey."

"Margaret Harrell never mentioned Freud," Diana said.

"Curious," Baker said. "Please go on."

"Kepler left behind four partners." Tom checked his notepad. "Karl Bachmann, Heinz Berthold, Rainer Erhard, and Klaus Driessen. Kepler continued to use the Tenedos name when he established his business in London. An acquaintance of Kepler's was interviewed by the *Times* in 1939 and said that Goering had personally gone to Kepler's office just before his departure the previous year and told him that he would see him again in London."

"What did he answer?" Baker asked.

"He asked Goering if he would be so kind as to send him Nazi artefacts. 'They will be of considerable value to collectors,' he said."

"Jolly good," Baker said. "Just what that great fat bastard deserved." He took a drink of his whiskey, suddenly realized what he had said, and turned to Diana. "Sorry, Dr. Bennett."

"That's quite all right," she said.

"The other Tenedos partners chose to remain in Berlin," Tom continued. "There's no way of knowing what they were thinking. Perhaps they expected Hitler to win the war. That, of course, was not to be. After Normandy things moved quickly. The Air Corps had already been bombing Germany in January of 1943. A year and a half later we were in France. Paris was liberated in August. On December 16 Germany counterattacked in the Ardennes, but the 4th Armored Division relieved Bastogne the day after Christmas. By late February the flag went up on Mount Suribachi. Two weeks later the First Army crossed the Rhine at Remagen and three weeks after that we were on Okinawa. In April the GI's liberated Buchenwald and the Tommies liberated Bergen-Belsen. Hitler killed himself in late April as the Russians approached Berlin. The Tenedos partners had waited too long to leave.

"At this point everything becomes murky. Bachmann and Erhard are mentioned in a story in 1947 about *entartete kunst*—the modern art which the Nazis labelled *degenerate*. Driessen was photographed at a conference in Zurich in 1948 and Berthold published an article in a French art magazine in 1949. They appear to have been bankrupted by the war since they were never again able to mount any serious business ventures. Either they were destroyed financially or their property was confiscated by the Russians after they took Berlin, possibly both.

"They surface again briefly in the 50's and 60's and they were photographed together in 1972. I haven't seen the picture, but I'm told that they all appear broken and old beyond their years. Erhard was working as a restorer; Driessen was teaching in a polytechnic; Bachmann was arrested twice for public drunkenness; and Berthold was working as a factory watchman."

"I don't understand," Baker said. "Even if they had lost their fortunes they hadn't lost their knowledge. Surely they could have found something."

"True," Tom said, "but they didn't. Maybe they were dead inside."

"What finally happened to them?" Baker asked.

"This is where it starts to get interesting. No one knows."

"You mean there were no more notices?"

"No, there were notices on each of them. Each of them disappeared. The time span was broad: from 1975 to 1989. One by one they simply fell off the edge of the earth. The Berlin papers are quite explicit. Erhard took a trip to visit a sister in Austria and never reached his destination; his rental car was found abandoned on the side of the road. There was no blood, no sign of violence, nothing. Berthold simply failed to report for work one day; his apartment was searched; everything was in its place except for its owner. Bachmann was seen in an alley in Leipzig, drunk and disorderly. He had accosted an elderly couple, demanding money. When the police came to arrest him he was gone. Driessen told his cousin that he would meet him for dinner. It was a holiday weekend and they had travelled together to Bavaria. The man waited for two hours; Driessen never appeared. They looked for him but found nothing. The bed in his hotel room was made. His clothes were hanging in the closet; his toiletries were in the bathroom; his travel clock was ticking on his nightstand. He was gone without a trace."

"And where was Kepler when all of these crimes were being committed?"

"In the U.K. apparently. He was interviewed when Erhard disappeared and again when Driessen did. There was no suggestion in the press that he was suspected of involvement in their deaths. From the dates of the reports and the interviews it appears that he was in London and Edinburgh when his former partners died, assuming, of course, that they did die."

"They must have died; they've never been seen again," Diana said.

"That would seem to be a reasonable conclusion," Baker said.

"But then who killed them?" Diana asked.

"A very good question," Tom answered. "Assuming that it was not Kepler (who had no apparent motive in any case), there are three possibilities . . ."

Baker interrupted him. "Either another party or parties killed one or more of them or one of the Tenedos partners was the murderer," he said. "Or, of course, some combination of the two, though that is unlikely. Which one was the last to disappear?"

"Driessen."

"The one in Bavaria."

"Yes, in Garmisch."

"It doesn't have to have been him," Diana said. "Driessen might have tried to kill one of the others. That man escaped, hid out, and then returned to take vengeance on Driessen."

"Possibly," Baker said, "but there is one very large problem here. Where is the motive? These men were partners; they were photographed together years after the war. Why would they wait so long to take vengeance if there were some kind of problem between them?"

"There could be any number of reasons," Diana said. "Perhaps it took them years before they discovered what one or more of them had done to the others. Perhaps the killer enjoyed seeing his victims fall farther and farther into the pit. Perhaps they expected to be murdered and were on their guard; it could have taken months or years for the right opportunity to present itself. Who knows what happened? These people go back at least fifty years together. Their lives and business were intertwined. Besides their endless dealings with one another there were two very large problems with which they had to cope: the Third Reich and the Red Army."

The boat lurched as it turned in to dock at Greenwich. The tourists were already lining up to disembark. "Do we have to get off?" Tom asked.

"No, no," Baker said. "This one's going right out again. Just stay there. I'll get us all another round. Dr. Bennett?"

"All right," Diana said.

He returned and placed the drinks on the table, removing the empty glasses and placing them on an adjoining table. "Now," he said, "if it was only that easy to discover who was responsible for the murder of the Tenedos partners."

"My associates and I are working on a solution," Tom said.

"Really?" Baker said. "I trust that you'll be good enough to tell us about it."

CHAPTER FORTY
The Thames, off the Isle of Dogs
Saturday, 1:32 p.m.

"The Tenedos partners did not begin to disappear until thirty years after the war. They were photographed together in 1972. In 1975 Erhard disappeared. There's no way of knowing one way or the other at this point, but I think it's reasonable to assume that something happened which led to their disappearance. People don't start dying in groups for no apparent reason. If the event which resulted in the murders happened earlier, why did the killer wait so long to act? I believe that we should begin with the assumption that something happened much later, something prior to 1975 and probably later than 1972. If the men could be brought together for a photograph they could be brought together for a murder. Something must have happened after that occasion."

"But what?" Baker asked.

"I have no idea. That's what we have to find out."

"And why were the murders so widely spaced?"

"Perhaps because the victims started to realize that they were being hunted down. Once their friends started to fall the remaining partners made themselves scarce."

"You mean it took him fourteen years to find them all."

"Possibly."

"That's a very long time," Baker said.

"Perhaps not so long to those who were being stalked," Tom answered.

"These were elderly men," Diana said. "They had all but disappeared anyway. Perhaps the killer was just as old. Perhaps he was just as poor. He needed time to secure his weapons, to hire associates, to gather his strength as well as his information."

"I know your feelings on the subject, but I continue to return to Kepler," Baker said.

"It couldn't have been Kepler because Kepler's death is somehow related to David's," Diana said, "and David had nothing to do with these other men."

"Nothing that we know of," Baker said, correcting her gently.

The boat passed Wapping. "Look there," Baker said, changing the subject momentarily. "Wapping Dock. Where the mutineers and pirates were executed. The authorities let their bodies hang in state until three tides had washed over them. A lesson to others who might be contemplating a similar career. Swift and sure justice that. Necessary in those times, of course. No real police in London yet. Made an example of criminals then, they did. Forced the apprentices to attend public executions; kept their hands clean and their minds concentrated. It's all changed now, of course." He took a sip of his whiskey.

"You may have something there," Tom said.

"Swift justice? Not much of that now."

"No, the absence of police."

"What do you mean?" Baker asked.

"There were no police and there were no systems of communication beyond whistles and shouts. No cars, no airplanes, no high-speed trains, no telephones, no fax machines, no computers, no shared records. Nothing."

"I don't take your point," Baker said.

"My point is that our killer should have had some of those things at his disposal. This was not the eighteenth century and yet it took him thirteen or fourteen years to find and murder all of his victims, victims who were all residing in Berlin, victims who had surfaced from time to time over a period of nearly thirty years and who had been seen together as recently as 1972."

"And?" Baker said, curtly.

"Something interrupted the process; something kept him from using the tools and weapons and resources that should have been at his disposal. Perhaps he had no such resources."

"But why should he not use them?"

"Perhaps he didn't have access to them."

"Tom, I'm not following you," Diana said. "Anyone trying to find someone at that time could simply look in a phone book or a deed register. He could have checked a newspaper morgue or an index. Why would a killer *not* do that?"

"Think about it," Tom said. "We've been imagining this situation in conventional terms: five men in Berlin, say, all of them walking the same streets, waiting for the right opportunity. Suddenly one is missing. Then two, then three, then, finally, four. But what if the situation was totally different, as in the eighteenth century?"

"Come now, Deaton," Baker interrupted. "The killer was no bloody time-traveller."

"Of course he wasn't. Try this," Tom said. "You've just had another skirmish over the Falkland Islands. England nearly went to war over the Falklands in the eighteenth century."

"Yes, and?" Baker said, trying to restrain himself.

"There was a great difference between the two situations," Tom said.

"Yes, of course there was a great difference," Baker said. "There were no modern weapons."

"There were also no modern *communications*," Tom said. "Before the government could act it needed intelligence from the Islands themselves. Each communication involved a time lag of approximately six months. A decision was made and then everyone sat on their hands, waiting to hear of the result."

"I still don't take your point," Baker said.

"Perhaps," Diana said, "the Tenedos partners and their killer were separated in space as well as in available resources. Perhaps they were so distant from one another that they couldn't find each other easily or quickly."

"Perhaps they were in some place where communication systems were nonexistent or not in use," Tom said.

"They were in bloody Berlin," Baker said.

"The Tenedos partners appear to have been in Berlin much of the time," Tom said, "but what of their killer?"

"I still don't follow," Baker said.

"Forget weapon and motive for a moment and focus on opportunity," Tom said. "The problem is that we must account for a great lapse of time between events and, possibly, a lack of contact between the killer and victims. Perhaps the killer had fled Germany and gone to some remote area; many did."

"Hitler in the jungles of Bolivia and all that?" Baker said.

"Possibly," Tom answered.

"Very well," Baker said, "but then he somehow returned."

"Yes."

"For what reason?"

"We don't know."

"And then it took him fourteen years to finish the job he started in 1975."

"Yes."

"Why?"

"We don't know."

"Bloody hell. We don't know much at all then, do we?"

"We know a great deal," Tom said. "We've only been looking for a few days. Besides, we have things that your pirates didn't."

"Phones, computers, and bloody fax machines."

"Yes."

"We have something else," Diana said. "We know that the killer or his people have recently been in California, France, and England."

"*If* these cases are connected," Baker said. "That is not at all certain. For one thing there is a break in the killer's method. Your brother, Dr. Bennett, was found dead in his studio. Kepler was left in his bathtub; he did *not* disappear. Michael Sechrist—assuming for the sake of argument that his death is related as well—did not disappear either. His body was found in his garage. And your associates in France were simply gunned down, as was the killer's accomplice. No disappearance there; your friend was assaulted in the hotel and their man was left in his car by the side of the road in plain sight. Either this is a different killer or he's become very sloppy indeed."

"There is another possibility," Tom said.

"And what is that?" Baker asked.

"The killer does not know that we are aware of the connection between those murders and these."

"Assuming that there is such a connection."

"The assumption is becoming more and more plausible," Tom said.

"Give me a possible scenario," Baker said. "I don't mean to challenge, but I would find it quite useful if you could do so."

"All right," Tom said, taking a slow drink of his whiskey and then placing his glass on the table. "I will give you a scenario. Imagine that the Tenedos partners had lost their business and were unable to continue as legitimate dealers. Instead, let us suppose that they began to deal in forgeries. The chaos associated with the war and its aftermath would have made that easier. Pieces were lost. Pieces disappeared and resurfaced later. Pieces were created that could not come on the market at that time. Works were confiscated or destroyed; trade was suspended. Suppose the Tenedos partners marketed forgeries; suppose they shipped them to distant parts of the world, to private collectors with deep pockets and shallow knowledge."

"Yes . . ."

"Years later one of the individuals they had duped discovered what had happened and sought them out. By then they had dispersed and were in semi-retirement. One or more of them were eventually found but each refused to make restitution. When they began to feel threatened, one or more of the remaining partners discovered the outraged buyer, killed him, and arranged their own disappearances. Any other duped buyers would draw the conclusion that they had been killed and assume that justice had been served."

"And now they are back in business, but selling originals and putting forgeries in their place," Diana said.

"Yes, possibly," Tom said.

"Very doubtful," Baker said.

"But not impossible," Tom said, "and not implausible."

"No. Is that what you think happened?"

"I have no idea what happened," Tom answered. "All I am saying is that there are plausible explanations which fit the known facts."

"Yes," Baker said. "We might also consider this. The selling of forgeries is easier in a world where the provenance of the pieces has become clouded. Computers and reference books and curators and bloody art historians change all that. One can only go on so long selling what purport to be lost masterpieces. Tenedos would have had to have changed their line. On the other hand, if they began to sell known masterpieces they would have realized one clear advantage: their purchasers would always remain invisible and silent. They would know that their newly-acquired works of art had been stolen and they could not allow the pieces' existence (or their possession of them) to become known. Second, the remaining Tenedos partners would have what you yanks call a fall-back if they ever decided to return to their old ways. They could sell forgeries of known pieces. If their customers discovered that they had been swindled, they would be unable to go to the police without announcing the fact that they had knowingly purchased stolen goods."

"But a skilled forgery would require a skilled expert for its—what would you say—authentication?" Diana said. "Someone would have to provide assurances that the pieces were good enough to pass muster. Perhaps that is where Kepler came in (or where we are supposed to believe that he came in). The forger or forgers killed him and implicated him in the crime to distract attention from themselves. They've successfully escaped again."

"Right. It would actually work either way," Tom said. "If Kepler detected or, as you say, authenticated a forgery he has now been silenced. At the same time, Tenedos (through Kepler) is associated with the theft of a masterpiece while each of his former partners remain invisible and forgotten, presumed dead. At this point we can't be certain of the killer or killers' precise activities, but we can imagine several scenarios and see how Kepler might have been involved."

"This is quite amusing," Baker said. "You've nearly landed me."

"I was not trying to persuade, I was merely trying to suggest," Tom said.

"I understand. Ah, here's the Tower. They'll let us off here and I can check with the Yard on Sechrist and St. Paul's. Perhaps they've made progress. We'll be back in touch presently."

"Excuse me for a moment; I want to make a call," Tom said.

CHAPTER FORTY-ONE
Tower Hill
Saturday, 2:17 p.m.

"Who did you call, Tom?" Diana asked. They were moving through a crush of people, sidestepping those who were edging their way toward the kiosks to buy tickets for the Tower and doing their best to blend in with those who had completed the tour and were trying to free their hands and elbows to compare the souvenirs they had purchased from the Tower gift shop. Gardeners were trimming the grass on Tower Hill and bartenders from nearby pubs were clearing empty glasses from outside tables as the scent of stale beer mingled with the smells of a working river. The tourists queuing near the Tower entrance were largely couples and families, while isolated individuals and groups stood near the pubs and drink stands with glasses or cups in their hands. Tom heard Dutch, French, and Spanish voices. A group of four German teenagers were standing together, talking loudly. The girls were in black jeans and black tank tops with silver necklaces and workboots; the boys wore bootleg 49ers and Berkeley tee-shirts with earrings and razor stubble. Each of them was holding a cigarette and releasing small puffs of smoke with each word or laugh.

"I was talking to the Chief; he promised to talk again to an old drinking buddy," Tom said.

"From where, Army Intelligence?"

"No, as a matter of fact. I'm not exactly sure what his employer's current designation is."

"Part of the CIA?"

"Uh-huh."

"And he'll give Chief Dietrich information, just like that?"

"No. He'll probably ask one of his assistants to do it. He's busy keeping an eye on the Chinese."

"Is that legal—passing secret information to local law enforcement?"

"The Chief will have to put in a formal request. That will make it kosher. I'm very glad he agreed to do it; we may get an interesting response to a question I posed."

"What information did you ask him to provide?"

"I gave him five names: Bachmann, Berthold, Erhard, Driessen, and Kepler."

"They sound like the accounting firm from hell."

"They do, don't they?"

"What is he supposed to find out about them?"

"He's supposed to do a run on each, checking to see where and when their names surface, particularly in the period between 1972 and 1975. He's also supposed to check on anything suspicious that could involve Germans and/or art pieces."

"During the same period?"

"Yes."

"That's a large order."

"Yes, well, they have a big computer and a lot of programmers."

"How long will it take?"

"For the runs? Once they've asked the questions, a matter of minutes. It will take much longer to analyze what they turn and see whether any of it has any potential significance."

"Will the Chief tell his friend all of the details of our case?"

"He'll give him as much as he needs to know in order to do the job. He and the people in his shop basically answer requests. They aren't in the habit of asking for reasons."

They met for dinner at *Rules*. Baker was late and apologetic. The waiter approached immediately, anxious to take his drink order. "Just some whiskey and soda," he said. "Have you ordered?" he asked.

"We were waiting for you. What would you recommend?" Diana said.

"Contrary to belief, the game is for the tourists. The yanks go home and talk about all of the strange things they've eaten at *Rules*. We get too much of it in school. If I were you I'd have the steak. Aberdeen Angus, you know. You can always eat weasel or whatever, but Scottish beef is something else again."

"Have you learned anything?" Tom asked.

"No, we haven't, but we're really rather relieved after all. Wouldn't you be? There are too many things in our cathedrals that we'd rather not lose. We had one brief start. One of our chaps thought that they might have taken the bust of Blake from the poets' corner in the Abbey. Epstein, you know. A bit piercing for my taste, but that's Blake after all. The bust was authenticated; I don't know who thought it looked off. It turned out to be the lighting and some dust in the eye sockets. When you're looking for something odd you can always find it, what?"

"How about at St. Paul's?" Tom asked.

"Not a thing out of place," Baker said. "We had another thought though. We've begun to check paintings and statuary of every saint with a surname beginning with *P*. Needless to say, that has not been easy, not in a city filled with galleries and museums. The staff of the Courtauld is lending a hand. For example, there's a statue of St. Peter, upside down on a cross. All in gold, mind you, and done by Cellini. Priceless, of course. It's in one of the side chapels at the Brompton Oratory. And it's *still* there I'm happy to say.

"That's the *good* news. The other news is that the Yard is a shambles. They don't have the staff to check the riches of the entire bloody country, but what can they do? They certainly can't let these buggers steal from us the way they've stolen from the French."

"So they're checking the entire country," Tom said.

"Trying to," Baker said. "There's just too much of it." The waiter brought his drink and Baker gulped it. "Perhaps one more of those," he said. "Steaks all around?" Tom and Diana nodded. "And a nice wine. How's the house claret?"

"Not as nice as this one, sir," the waiter said, pointing to an Australian wine on the list at the side of the menu. "This one is quite lovely and good value as well."

"Why not bring two bottles," Baker said, "save you a trip later."

"Very good," the waiter said.

"Now, where was I?"

"The dimensions of the problem," Tom said.

"Yes, quite. Well, I'll give you an example," he said, finishing the rest of his whiskey in the second drink. "Take Plymouth. Hours away. Practically to Land's End and it's filled with things that one might nick. You know the story about Drake and the Armada. He's on the hoe playing at bowls and he gets word of the Spanish ships. Tells them he'll finish his game first and then sail. Quite charming. Rubbish of course."

"He was waiting for the tide; he couldn't leave until then," Tom said.

"Quite," Baker said. "Anyway, the queen was quite grateful for his help on that occasion and others and the local museum is filled with tokens of her appreciation. Navigational instruments and all that. Here . . ." he said, digging his fingernail into the tablecloth and outlining the island. "We're running all round the country. Here's Plymouth, there's Oxford and the Ashmolean, here's Glasgow and the University gallery, here's bloody Edinburgh and the castle and there . . . would be Aberdeen. We did hear of a possible theft at Aberdeen. The University has an old sword in its collection which may or may not have been stolen. Very hard to say. The piece wasn't important, so who knows whether it was authentic to begin with."

"What sword?" Tom asked.

"Not excalibur, if that's what you're thinking," Baker answered, as the waiter removed his whiskey glass and brought a fresh substitute. "It had some scrawls on it and the name Angus."

"Is that all that you've found?" Tom asked.

"That's all that we consider suspicious," Baker said. "It will take weeks to check everything. We can't just make a public announcement, of course. These things must be done quietly. We don't want to alarm the people and we don't want to let the thieves know that we're checking. How about yourself? Any news from your end?"

"It's too early for us as well," Tom said. "The world is filled with art and filled with Germans. Even if we narrow the time frame to a period of three or four years there's a great deal of material to sift through. I'll call in a few minutes and see if they have anything. How about Sechrist?"

"Still checking when I left. I'll call in as well. Let's just give them a little time," Baker said, as the waiter poured the wine. "You won't let them overcook those steaks, will you?" Baker said.

"Certainly not, sir," the waiter answered.

The chilled celery accompanying the stilton looked a bit wilted by the time Tom returned to the table. He had been crunched in a corner of the second floor of the restaurant, just beyond the stairway, balancing his notebook on his knee, listening to Dietrich's voice through a succession of transatlantic crackles and blips and jotting down information quickly and carefully. At times Dietrich's voice broke as if he was using a respirator to speak and the words were stopped in mid-syllable while he caught his breath. The walls above the steps were covered with photographs of famous diners and testimonials from happy tourists. The air was as heavy as the red, flocked wallpaper. When Dietrich had asked where he was calling from, Tom replied that he was in an institution.

"Port?" Baker asked.

Tom hesitated for a second.

"You've certainly earned it. You were gone for nearly thirty minutes."

"All right," Tom said, "thanks." Baker signalled to the waiter.

"There's not much yet," Tom said. "The people in Washington have to work with multiple parallel agencies so we lose a little time with each account. So far most of the reports have to do with thefts from museums and private collections, but many of the works were later recovered and authenticated. We've also found a lot of material on Kepler. Nothing that suggests that he was dirty, but a long list of references to his qualifications. He was *the* art expert in postwar Europe; there's no doubt about that. There are also the usual accounts of Nazis in South America, but no connections with art or Tenedos, at least not yet. There is one interesting thing . . ."

"Yes?" Diana said.

"A man named Bachmann was detained in Chile in 1975."

"Karl Bachmann?" Diana asked.

"They don't have a first name yet. The paper didn't report one. They're checking the Chilean police records."

"What was the charge?" Baker asked.

"It's very vague at this point. There was a fire in a house that contained an art collection. Apparently there was the suspicion of arson. Bachmann's name turned up in a police report, but the details were vague and sketchy."

"Was it Bachmann's collection?" Baker asked.

"Apparently not. Bachmann was found near the scene, taken in, and briefly questioned. The reports make it sound as if he could have been a bystander who was asked routine questions. The curious thing is that the home with the collection was in the Maipo Valley, forty-five minutes outside of Santiago. The house was on a remote road, not the kind of place that would attract bystanders, unless they were lovers or burglars."

"What happened to the collection?" Diana asked.

"Apparently it was saved. There were no details on how it was done, but the article spoke of a near-catastrophe that was luckily averted."

"It sounds *very* lucky to me. There wouldn't have been a fire department down the street," Diana said.

"No, the owner probably had a sprinkler or some other security system," Tom said. "If the collection was valuable the owner would have taken steps to protect it."

"Was this Bachmann alone?" Baker asked.

"Apparently not. He was part of a group of people near the scene. It's not clear that they were linked in any way. They may have been drawn separately, attracted by the fire. There were no other names reported, except Bachmann's."

"Are you thinking what I'm thinking?" Diana asked.

"That the house contained forgeries that had been detected and Bachmann was trying to destroy the evidence?" Tom said.

"Yes."

"It's a distinct possibility, but some things don't fit. For example, why wasn't he prosecuted by the owner? If the owner knew he had been bilked he would have been more interested in bringing Bachmann to justice than in saving a room full of fakes."

"Assuming that he knew Bachmann was the one who cheated him," Baker said.

"Yes. He could have been dealing with one of the other Tenedos partners and Bachmann was sent in because he wouldn't be recognized. Still, it's a bit of a stretch to find a German citizen wandering around on a dirt road above the Maipo River in central Chile. If I were the owner of the collection I'd be suspicious, wouldn't you? The story made the Santiago papers, so the collector would have been aware of Bachmann's presence there. If that were me I'd be on the phone to the police instantly."

"Unless he didn't want the police involved," Baker said. "Perhaps he had something to hide . . . or perhaps he wanted to exact his own punishment."

"Yes. It's certainly worth pursuing. The problem is that there were a lot of Bachmanns in South America in the 1970's."

"Were there any other leads?" Diana asked.

"As a matter of fact there was one. It has to do with Erhard.

Remember—he was the one whose empty car was found by the side of the road. He was on his way to visit his sister in Austria."

"And?" Baker asked.

"We've been hypothesizing that he might have arranged for his own disappearance."

"Yes," Baker said.

"When the car was found and the family was contacted the sister had been waiting for him at the airport."

"That changes everything," Diana said.

"Not necessarily," Tom said. "It only means that the sister wasn't aware of what he was planning to do. It could all just be further mystification for the police. He was using his sister to buttress his story. You could fill in the blanks easily: he knew he was being followed so he arranged to leave Berlin. Then something happened and he had to leave in a hurry. He tried to elude them by flying to the west and renting a car. They followed him, caught up with him, and now he sleeps with the Danube fishes. That is what you're supposed to believe."

"Or it could mean that he *was* taken," Baker said.

"It could mean that as well," Tom said. "From this distance it's very hard to determine what actually happened, but the sister's ignorance could suggest further evidence of foul play. Organized foul play. If he *was* taking a plane directly to Vienna, someone had to take him down and later rent a car and abandon it, unless they had someone else to do that part. My guess is that if he actually was abducted there were almost surely several individuals involved. Taking a man from a crowded airport or intercepting him on a major highway is not simple. Neither is driving a missing car half way across West Germany to Austria without being noticed. It would be much easier if the two were done simultaneously. It doesn't sound like the work of a freelancer with a vendetta. It sounds like something that was carefully organized."

"Like the theft of a major prehistoric artwork from a French cave," Diana said.

"Possibly," Tom said. "It could, of course, simply mean that he was very clever in crafting his story."

"It could also mean that he was the victim instead of the perpetrator," Diana said insistently.

"Or some of both," Tom said. "The Tenedos partners could have betrayed one another."

They paused, letting that sink in.

"I suppose it's my turn to check with the lads," Baker said. "By the way, how is your Port?"

"Very nice," Tom said.

"I won't be long," he said, rising and walking toward the stairs in the southwest corner of the restaurant.

"Was that everything?" Diana asked.

"Yes," Tom answered. "There are endless reports of Erhards and Driessens and Bachmanns and Bertholds, but they don't have anything to do with art and at least so far they don't have anything to do with violence or death, except, of course, for the case in Chile."

"What was the name of the man whose house was burned?"

"It wasn't reported in the paper," Tom said.

"Interesting."

"Maybe," Tom said. "There was a lot to hide in Chile in those days. Pinochet's country house was only fifteen minutes away from the house that burned and a later attempt on his life occurred less than six miles up the river. The fire may not have been accidental but it still may have nothing to do with our case."

"The Chilean wineries are in the Maipo Valley, aren't they?" Diana asked.

"Yes, the best ones."

"It sounds like the kind of place a rich collector might live—outside of the city, away from prying eyes."

"Yes."

"And if I had a valuable collection—or believed that what I possessed was valuable—I'd do all that I could to protect it."

"Yes . . ." Tom said.

"I'd have security systems, weapons, attack dogs . . . there isn't any neighborhood watch in the Maipo Valley. If you're rich you have to look out for yourself."

"Right," Tom said.

"So if someone managed to get in and set fire to my house . . ."

"They'd have to be very skilled and very well organized."

She nodded, holding his glance with her eyes.

"We've got something," Baker said. He stood next to the table, finishing the rest of his Port.

"Sechrist?" Tom said.

"Yes, there's part of a document. They've just found it."

IV

HEATH STEPPER

CHAPTER FORTY-TWO
Ludgate Circus
Saturday, 11: 47 p.m.

Sechrist's office was a small suite of rooms on the southwest side of Ludgate Circus. One flight up from an antiquarian bookshop, the door was marked with a small brass tablet with simple Roman lettering:

M. SECHRIST, LTD.
APPRAISALS

The knob turned in Baker's hand and he, Diana, and Tom entered without knocking. The room was chilly; Baker's men had kept on their raincoats while they worked. There were three of them, all seated around a short, walnut library table.

"What do we have?" Baker asked.

A bald man with bushy brown-and-gray eyebrows slid a clear plastic folder to the center of the table. Inside was a single sheet of thick paper. The paper was scorched, with burn marks around the edges. It was brittle; several of the edges had been taped to the plastic folder to prevent further disintegration.

"There, Guv," the man said, pointing to the bottom section of the sheet. "You can just make out three words." Two of the words were side by side on the same line. A little below and to the right was the third word. The first two words appeared to be in medieval lettering. An h could be seen, then an æ, and finally what appeared to be a letter d with a line through the arm above the circle. The second word began with a long s, followed by the letters t-a-p-a. The third word also began with an s and t but they were followed by an o and a letter which looked like a bent p.

hæð ſtɑpɑ

ſtop

Tom bent over the table for a closer look as one of Baker's men lit his pipe and slid his chair back from the table with an air of authority. The oldest man in the room, his eyes and forehead were heavily lined and his arthritic fingers were pointed in odd directions. "What do you make of it, Leonard?" Baker asked.

He puttered some more before he spoke, toasting the top of the ash a second time. "It looks old, but it's not. We put a piece from the corner under the microscope. It's good stock all right, but it's modern paper. No doubt of that. The fibres are wood, not flax or hemp."

"Which would date it . . . when?" Baker asked.

"Mid to late nineteenth century at the earliest," Leonard answered.

"Oh, I'm terribly sorry," Baker said, "Ralph Leonard . . . Diana Bennett and Tom Deaton." Each offered the other a polite nod.

"And the language?" Baker asked.

"Not my line," Leonard said. "We've rung up an expert. He's on his way."

"An expert?"

"You know him . . . Roberts . . . the language chap."

"From St. John's Wood, the retired don?"

"Yes."

"You awakened him?"

"Yes, he seemed quite game to join us."

Tom lifted the corner of the plastic cover enclosing the sheet of burned paper. "Do you mind?" he asked.

"No, of course not," Leonard said. "Just hold it under the center so that it doesn't flake any further." Tom took the paper to a side table with its own lamp. The man with the bushy eyebrows offered him a magnifying glass. "Thank you," Tom said.

He studied it for several minutes. "It could be Old English. What do you think?" he asked.

"It may be some old Scandinavian language; it looks like Scandinavian writing," Bushy Eyebrows said. Leonard remained silent, not wishing to hazard a guess that might later prove to be wrong. The pipe was in the corner of his mouth now, the smoke escaping from his lips in measured wisps.

"Well then," Baker said, "when is Roberts due to join us?"

"Any time now," Leonard answered.

"Then we don't have time for a drink," Baker said. Tom caught Diana's expression of surprise out of the corner of his eye but he quickly turned away and continued to study the burned sheet of paper.

"There's some coffee, Guv," Bushy Eyebrows said, "but only one."

"Oh," Baker said, "I couldn't . . ."

"Go ahead," Diana said. "I don't care for any."

"Neither do I," Tom said.

"Are you sure?"

"Perfectly sure," Diana said. Tom just nodded.

"Well all right then," Baker said, his expression warming as he raised the cardboard cup to his lips. "Still hot," he said. "Lovely."

Roberts arrived ten minutes later. Tall, with stark white hair and red cheeks, he was wearing wool trousers, a loose wool sweater, and a heavy brown jacket. His scarf was wrapped tightly around his neck, with the two ends hanging in parallel along his back.

"So . . ." he said to Baker, "out and about again, are we?"

"Thank you for coming," Baker responded.

Roberts turned to Tom and Diana, realized he didn't know them, and took a step closer. "Roberts," he said. "Deaton," Tom answered, "and Dr. Bennett."

"American, eh?"

"Yes," Tom said.

"Say something else," Roberts said.

"What would you like me to say? I hope you appreciate the fact that we're in a hurry here."

"You're from the west coast."

"Yes."

"South, not north, I'd say."

"Yes, as a matter of fact."

"Hard to be too precise."

"Orange County," Tom answered.

"Quite. What do we have?"

"A forged manuscript, we believe," Baker answered.

"What makes you think it's forged?"

"The language appears to be medieval or older, but the paper is new."

"People do still write old words on new paper," Roberts said.

"Deaton thinks it's Old English," Leonard said, with a tinge of skepticism in his voice.

"Let's have a look," Roberts said. Tom handed him the sheet of paper in its plastic folder. Roberts sat down under the light. Tom handed him the magnifying glass, but Roberts politely waved it away and took out his reading glasses. The rims were red, complimenting his bright cheeks.

"It *is* Old English," Roberts said. "Very good. It looks Scandinavian, doesn't it?"

Bushy Eyebrows scooted forward in his seat.

"But of course, it's not," Roberts said.

He studied it for at least four full minutes. "You found this here, in Sechrist's shop?"

"Yes," Baker said.

"Fascinating."

"What do you think it is?"

"I know what it is," Roberts said. "And it's either a conscious forgery or someone practicing to be a tenth-century scribe."

"What does it say?" Baker asked.

"It's quite simple, really. The first two words are really one word. The scribe often separates them. The word is *hæthstapa*. The d with the flag on top is pronounced t-h. The word itself is a kenning."

"What's that?" Baker asked.

"Deaton?" Roberts said, as if he was calling on a favored pupil.

"It's an expression. It's in apposition with the primary noun, but a more poetic rendering."

"Very good," Roberts said. "Where did you learn about such matters as apposition?"

"In high school."

"Loyola?"

"Actually no, in a Catholic high school in San Juan Capistrano," Tom said.

"I visited at UCSD for a term, back in the early nineties. We lived in Oceanside; we could barely afford *that*."

"I grew up in Laguna."

"And did you live in one of those little cottages that now cost millions?"

"Yes."

"It's all in the timing, isn't it?"

"Yes."

Baker had begun to pace. "Roberts . . . ?"

"Yes?" he answered.

"Could we trouble you . . . ?"

"It's no trouble, Charles," he said. "*Hæthstapa* is a kenning for the word *deer*. It simply means *heathstepper*. As Deaton said—a more poetic rendering. Instead of using the same word over and over the poet varies the line—not just lexically, of course, but also metrically. It's music, Charles. Quite lovely in its simplicity, isn't it? *Heathstepper*."

Baker had stopped pacing but he was clutching his cardboard coffee cup with both hands as if he was trying to squeeze the liquid from its container.

"The word a few lines lower is *stow*. The w looks like a strange p. That's the way they wrote it. *Stow* means *place*."

"That's damned little to go on," Baker said.

"Oh, I don't think so," Roberts said. "It's just enough. The passage is quite well known."

"You know the passage?"

"Why yes. You didn't want me to come all of the way down to Ludgate Circus at midnight just to waste your time, did you?"

"No, of course not," Baker said.

Leonard was tamping the ash in his pipe as if he was trying to crush some small animal.

"The description is of a lake. Actually a mere, like German *meer*. A terrible place. Wondrous. Frightening. I can't do the whole text of course, but it would go something like this: 'The heathstepper coming there—afflicted by hounds, the great hart with strong horns seeking the wood . . . will give up his life on the shore before he will put his head in those waters.'"

"What about the word *place*?" Baker asked.

"That's in the next line. The passage is actually a good bit longer. There's talk of mountain waterfalls and windy promontories, night mists and fearful wonders—all very *sturm and drang*. Then there's the business about the deer. Lovely image that. What a terrible place: one would choose death on the shore to protection inside. The poet sums up all the nastiness and then adds a final comment. I've always remembered it. He says 'Nis þæt heoru stow.'"

"Which means . . . ?" Baker asked.

"It means 'nor is that a particularly nice place.' Well, it doesn't precisely mean that, but it's close enough. And we call that . . . Deaton?"

"Litotes."

"What a waste that you're running around at all hours with the likes of Detective Chief Inspector Baker," Roberts said. "You could have been a contender. I love that film, don't you?"

"Yes," Tom said.

"Litotes?" Baker asked.

"Understatement for rhetorical effect," Roberts answered.

"It's Grendel's mere, isn't it?" Tom asked, the realization sinking in.

Baker and Leonard looked at one another in mutual incomprehension.

"Yes it is," Roberts answered. "It's Grendel's mere."

"They've stolen the Beowulf manuscript," Tom said.

"Stolen it?" Roberts asked, impatiently.

"The Beowulf manuscript?" Baker said. "Meadhalls and shaggy pants and all that?"

"Yes," Roberts said. "Meadhalls and shaggy pants, Charles. The only surviving epic poem in Old English. We are talking about the most precious literary manuscript in Britain."

"It's in the Museum," Baker said.

"Not for some twenty years or more," Roberts answered.

Baker's face fell.

"What happened to it?" Diana asked.

"They've moved the collection to the new, larger location," Roberts said, "in St Pancras."

CHAPTER FORTY-THREE
St. John's Wood, London
Sunday, 2:10 a.m.

David Roberts' flat sat above a small garden square a few blocks east of Abbey Road. It was filled with bookshelves and odd-sized tables wedged between overstuffed chairs. The musty smell of old leather from the books and chairs filled the room. Tom could taste it in his throat, along with the whiskey that Roberts had offered them.

"Here we are," Roberts said, pulling a book from the top shelf of a bookcase near the front sitting-room window. Roberts opened the book on a nearby table and turned on a lamp with a green plastic shade. It took him a few seconds to find the right page. "Now let's have the forged sheet." Leonard handed it to him and Roberts said thank you.

"Here, you see," he said. "This is a facsimile edition of the manuscript. Watch." He took a piece of tracing paper, put it on top of the forged sheet and outlined the words. Then he placed the sheet over the page of the facsimile. The words fit precisely. "The words in between and those above and below were burned. Only these three words survived. Where did you find this?"

"In the dustbin at Sechrist's office," Leonard said.

"Yes, quite. You were very lucky. Someone intended to burn this a second time."

"A second time? I don't understand," Baker said.

"Deaton?"

"I can't help you on that," Tom said.

"It's really an interesting story," Roberts said. "How is that whiskey?"

"Lovely. I could do with a bit more," Baker said, as Roberts replenished the drinks. Leonard passed, as did Bushy Eyebrows. Roberts slumped in one of the chairs, a brown leather relic with worn arms.

"It's quite fascinating really," he said. "The Beowulf manuscript was found in the library of Sir Robert Bruce Cotton, a seventeenth-century gentleman with a taste for old books and manuscripts. The original library contained a dozen bookcases; each had a bust on top of one of the Roman emperors and the manuscripts were categorized accordingly. The Beowulf text was in Cotton Vitellius A. xv, two codices joined by an early seventeenth-century binder. The resulting volume consisted of nine Old English texts, of which Beowulf is the most famous.

"We have no idea where he obtained the codices. Some people believe that they may have been preserved by a man named Laurence Nowell, the Dean of Lichfield, who died in the late 1500's, a few years after Cotton's birth. Remember—Henry VIII was paying his bills a few decades earlier by looting the monasteries. It also gave him the opportunity for a little revenge after his handling by Rome. God knows what was lost in the process. Nowell was an early student of Anglo-Saxon. Why he found and saved *these* books (if he did and if they came from one of the monasteries) and not others (if there were others) and how (indeed, *how*), we have no idea.

"The manuscript which Cotton obtained was copied by two different scribes, probably at some time near the end of the tenth century. Now comes the interesting part . . ."

Baker was beginning to pace. He was also looking at the remains of the whiskey in the bottle on Roberts' table. Diana was leaning forward in her chair, as was Tom.

"In the eighteenth century the Cotton library was in Ashburnham House, in Little Deans Yard, Westminster. In 1731 Ashburnham House burned. The manuscript was saved, of course, but it was charred around the edges. If it had been promptly rebound the damage would have been halted but unfortunately it was not. Here, look . . ."

He held the book up so they could see it more clearly. "You see the marks around the edges? What Sechrist (or someone) was trying to do was burn the edges in such a way as to replicate the original manuscript. My guess is that this particular sheet was discarded and later burned, probably in a stack of similar sheets."

"There were other burned sheets and black flakes in the dustbin," Bushy Eyebrows said.

"There you have it," Roberts said. "Some of the sheets were too close together to burn but far enough apart to scorch. You were really very lucky. Your man's work survived the flames just like the Beowulf poet's. Sechrist, do you think?"

"Possibly," Baker answered.

"You think he was doing the forgery for hire and not amusement."

"Yes, probably under duress."

"His reputation was impeccable," Roberts said. "Michael Sechrist was highly skilled and scrupulously honest. And you think this forgery is part of a larger plot?"

"We believe that it may be," Baker said. "As I said in the car, there have been other things as well."

"You mentioned the *Chevaux Ponctués*. What cheek. And what skill. What else was there?"

"We're not certain that anything else *has* been stolen," Baker said, "but we have a report that a sword has been stolen from a museum at the University of Aberdeen."

"The sword of Angus?"

"Why yes, as a matter of fact; how would you know that?"

"Your thief is a very learned man."

"Why do you say that?"

"What do you know about the sword of Angus?"

"Nothing, really," Baker said.

"Mind you, this is all theory . . ." Roberts said.

"What theory?" Baker said.

"A theory about the sword and its owner. Would you like more whiskey?"

"Yes, thank you," Baker said, sitting down and holding out his glass.

"Geoffrey of Monmouth tells us that King Arthur's coronation was attended by a king named Anguselus. However, Chrétien de Troyes, who also wrote about these matters, wrote in Old French. When the Latinized name *Anguselus* is translated into Old French it loses in perfectly regular, normal fashion its middle syllable. Thus, its second consonantal group, *gu*, which is in weak and unaccented position within the word, drops out." Roberts picked up his pencil and the sheet of tracing paper and began to write.

"We are left with this: An + sel + o. Now, since o is the normal masculine ending in French, it is often written *ot*. We pronounce the French word resulting from this syncopation: An-sel-ó."

"And the French writer could have added the article *le* and then contracted it," Tom said.

"The Angus," Roberts said.

"L'Anselot," Tom added. "Lancelot."

"But Lancelot was bloody French, not Scottish," Baker said.

"I'm afraid he wasn't," Roberts said. "And he wasn't involved with Guinevere. It's all in here . . ." Roberts took a second book down from the shelf. "I'm afraid I'm the forger here," he said, "or better, the borrower."

The book was entitled *King Arthur*, by a woman named Norma Lorre Goodrich. "Arthur was not some dreamy-eyed Englishman running about in the west country. That's all nonsense. He was half Roman and he was in the north, guarding the border country. He was close to Hadrian's Wall and no farther north than the Antonine Wall, which connected what is now Glasgow on the west to what is now Edinburgh to the east. It also connected the Firth of Clyde to the west with the Firth of Forth on the east. This is Britain's narrowest point, a ripe target for anyone considering invasion. Angus was Arthur's principal battlefield commander, not some silly, adulterous Frenchman. Besides, Guinevere was not some swoony maiden later consigned to a nunnery. She was a Pictish queen, with her own army and wealth."

"They've stolen the sword of Lancelot," Tom said.

"So it would seem," Roberts said. "His general. The military rock on Arthur's right. Above the Firth of Forth; above Stirling. Above Fife and beneath Aberdeen. Angus."

"When was this book published?" Tom asked.

Roberts opened the front of the book. "In 1986. Your man keeps up with these things."

The phone sounded and the double ring startled them. Roberts started to get out of his chair. "I gave them your number," Baker said. Bushy Eyebrows lifted the phone from its cradle at the third ring and handed it to Baker.

"Baker," he said. "Yes . . . yes . . . thanks very much." He replaced the phone in its cradle and turned toward the expectant group. "It will take awhile for full authentication," he said, "but at this point it appears that the manuscript in the possession of the British Library is a forgery."

CHAPTER FORTY-FOUR

Stratton Street, Mayfair

Sunday, 4:18 a.m.

"And was the money transferred?"

"Yes. Just before Kepler's death. His account was debited and the sum transferred to Sechrist."

"And the amount?"

"We transferred £35,000."

"Plausible enough."

"We did it electronically. The bank's computer system was child's play."

"One would expect as much from the English."

"Yes."

"Is your work finished then?"

"Yes. The Aberdeen holdings have been checked, as have those at St. Pancras. The police are running about like frightened children. They know that the objects have been replaced with substitutes, but Kepler is their only possible suspect and he is dead. Sechrist has now been suitably implicated but he is also dead, drowned in the same sea of guilt as Bennett and Kepler. A museum guard at Aberdeen has £5,000 in his personal account which he will be unable to explain."

"And in France?"

"That's finished as well. They should have our accomplice's name soon. His account contains an additional 50,000 euros, a gift from Herr Kepler. The loop is now closed."

"They will search for the antiquities rather than for us, but they will have no idea where to look."

"Precisely."

"And Deaton?"

"He returned with Bennett's sister an hour ago."

"Filled with information and suspicions, but too many steps behind."

"Yes. They can be removed at any time."

"When do you return?"

"Tomorrow."

The red glow of the digital clock was blurred. Tom blinked and refocused: **5:54**. As he rubbed his eyes the third digit flipped and revealed a third **5**. Diana was still asleep, her arm limp at the side of the bed. Her hair covered the side of her pillow. He could hear her breathing gently.

He tried to think through the evidence of the case but his mind kept returning to the stolen objects. He thought of their uniqueness, their immeasurable value, and the weight of their loss. He had never seen the originals, only copies and facsimiles. In the case of the sword he had seen nothing but a drawing which Roberts had sketched, but as he watched Roberts' hand, lovingly tracing the outline of the object, he could somehow feel its presence and its beautiful strength.

Hearing Diana's breathing and feeling the warmth of the sheets and blankets, he closed his eyes and fell back into the darkness. He awoke at 6:30 and again at 7:10. At 7:25 his phone rang. Startled, he sat up and hit the ACCEPT button. "Yes?" he said.

"Tom, it's Chris Dietrich."

"What have you got, Chief?" Tom asked, feeling the distance between them in the echo in the phone line.

"A number of things. First, we found a Laguna Beach bank account of David Bennett's. There was only one recent deposit: $175,000 dollars."

"When was the deposit made?"

"A week before his death."

"Is there a paper record?"

"No. It was an electronic transfer. The money came from a British account."

"Probably a frame. What else do you have?"

"There's more from Chile."

"Yes?"

"It *was* Karl Bachmann who was taken into custody by the Chilean police. He was detained on suspicion of arson."

"But he was released."

"Yes."

"Who sprung him?"

"We don't know. The record said there was insufficient evidence. There's more."

"What?"

"The collection that nearly burned was apparently authentic. We found a long article in a Chilean art magazine. Two of the pieces had minor smoke damage, but after they were cleaned the restorer was interviewed by the local press. The collector later claimed that the restorer had been sworn to secrecy but he must have been excited by the job because he couldn't keep his mouth shut. The two pieces he talked about had never been seen before: a Rouault self-portrait and an early Modigliani. An art historian was called in from the University and he authenticated the two paintings. That caused a real dustup. The owner charged the restorer with breach of contract and invasion of privacy and sent in his lawyers. After two weeks the story died a quiet death."

"Two lost masterpieces, both legitimate and by then very, very pricey."

"Exactly."

"That's very helpful, Chief. Please give my best to your friend at Langley."

"There's more, Tom."

"More?"

"That's right."

"I'm listening."

"How would you like a name?"

"You've got the name of the collector?"

"It just came in. The proud owner of the lost Modigliani and Rouault is one Wilfred Alec."

"You say *is*. He's still alive then."

"Yes, he's very much alive."

"In Chile?"

"Oh no. He left Chile right after the fire. He first went to Lausanne, Switzerland, where he stayed for three years. From Lausanne he went to Florence—Fiesole actually—where he stayed two and a half years. From Fiesole he went to Quito, Ecuador, then to Madrid and Nice; he even logged some time on the Greek island of Mykonos."

"He gets around, doesn't he? Where is he now?"

"I know what you're thinking; he must be in England."

"No, as a matter of fact, that's not what I'm thinking. I'm thinking that our Wilfred Alec might be in southern California."

"You'll have to be more specific."

"Newport Beach."

"Sorry, Tom."

"Where is he then?"

"San Clemente, actually just a San Clemente post office box at this point, but we're working on the rest. You were close."

"San Clemente . . ."

"Yes, and he's been there for five years. How about at your end, Tom? What have you turned?"

"Nothing much new, except for the fact that whoever stole the horses of Pech-Merle also stole the most important literary manuscript in Britain and the sword of Lancelot. Aside from that things are pretty quiet."

"The sword of Lancelot?" Dietrich said, his voice filled with wonder and skepticism.

"The question is—what does Mr. Alec have to do with all this?"

"Who is it?" Diana whispered, her voice barely but clearly audible to Chief Dietrich.

"I'll have to talk to you later, Chief," Tom said and put down the phone.

CHAPTER FORTY-FIVE
Brompton Road, Knightsbridge
Sunday, 11:00 a.m.

"Where exactly are we going?" Diana asked. The taxi was driving west, slaloming around parked delivery trucks and early *Harrods* shoppers, crossing the road to take late breakfasts or early lunches at *Richoux* and other Knightsbridge tea rooms. At the last jerk she had slid across the seat, her right leg now leaning against Tom's left.

"Chiswick," he said. "Back to the safe house where they're keeping Margaret Harrell. Baker's already there. They're questioning her about possible connections between Kepler and Sechrist and asking her if she knows anything about the Aberdeen sword. So far they haven't learned anything."

"It shouldn't take us long to get there."

"No, driving against the traffic we should be there in about ten minutes."

"Do you think she could be involved?"

"No, not really, but I think she may be holding things back. She was devoted to Kepler and she wouldn't want anything made public that could hurt his reputation. At this point that's all that he has left."

"Such as the fact that he could be under suspicion of possible collusion with thieves."

"And murderers."

The safe house was in Chiswick Mall, a row of upscale eighteenth and nineteenth-century townhouses with bow windows and balconies, overlooking the Thames. On Tom's instructions the taxi stopped a block away. He checked to make sure that they hadn't been followed before they walked the remaining distance. The river was steel gray and at low tide, the air chilly and damp. Cyclamen and pansies were in bloom in boxes along the balconies, their pink, yellow, crimson and purple flowers contrasting with the dark sky as they brought life and texture to the brick and stone facades of the townhouses. Diana held her raincoat together at the neck as they walked along the wet, black sidewalk.

Tom checked the number, which he had written on a piece of hotel stationery. He took her arm in his hand, turned slightly, and they walked toward the door of a building with a small plaque carrying the designation **Mercer House**. The doorbell was a large black knob encircled by a freshly-polished brass plate. Tom pulled it. There was no audible sound but after a few seconds the door opened. They walked into a dark hallway. The door closed and Baker's assistant, Leonard, stepped out of the shadows. He didn't speak, but simply nodded. He appeared to be perturbed at the assignment of door duty, perhaps a wrist slap for some earlier bit of dereliction. Tom asked where they should go and Leonard pointed to the stairs.

"There you are," Baker said, as they stood in the doorway of what was once the house's library, its shelves now bare of books but filled with folders, pens, notebooks, and pads. In the far corner of the room was a loveseat and three armchairs. The chintz about the windows was lush but faded and the Persian carpet was unravelling at the edges. On the table was a tea and coffee pot, a third pot for hot water, a pitcher of warm milk (slightly curdled around the edges), and an open jar of demarara sugar. "Leonard," Baker called.

Leonard appeared at the door. "Could you be so kind as to ask cook for some fresh coffee?" Baker asked. "Oh yes, and biscuits all around."

Leonard turned and disappeared. "Sit down, sit down," Baker

said. "We've just been talking about bloody Beowulf and bloody Lancelot."

Margaret Harrell was dressed in brown corduroy slacks and a light beige sweater, which hung loosely around her neck. Her hair had been cut since they last saw her but she was wearing little makeup and no jewelry. Her complexion was pale and there were lines in the corners of her eyes.

"Miss Harrell has done her best, but unfortunately she remembers very little. There was a call purporting to be from Michael Sechrist's shop, but it was some time ago and the caller was a woman. It could have come from anywhere, just someone sowing trouble. There were no contacts between Mr. Kepler and the curator at Aberdeen, at least none that Miss Harrell can remember. For that matter, there were no contacts between Mr. Kepler and anyone in Scotland, except for a dealer in Edinburgh who died three years ago and a collector in Ayrshire who moved to London last spring. So there you have it."

"Miss Harrell . . ." Tom said, nodding in greeting.

"How are you?" Diana asked.

"I'm all right," she answered. "I wish I could be of more help."

"Did you ever hear Mr. Kepler mention a man named Wilfred Alec?" Tom asked.

"Wilfred Alec?" Baker repeated.

"The collector in Chile whose collection was nearly burned," Tom said.

"So you have his name now. Jolly good."

"We also know that Bachmann was actually investigated for arson."

"Interesting," Baker said. Then, turning to Margaret Harrell, he said, "You remember the business in Chile. We spoke of it earlier."

"Yes," she said. "You say his name was Alec?"

"Wilfred Alec," Tom answered.

"That sounds English," Baker interjected. Before Margaret Harrell could answer, he called out "Leonard." When he appeared at the door

Baker asked him about their coffee and biscuits. Leonard assured him that they would be there presently. "Now, Miss Harrell . . ." he said.

She put her left hand against her cheek. "A collector of paintings, you said."

"Yes," Tom interjected. "They found a Rouault and a Modigliani in his collection. Both of them had been hitherto unknown. The Rouault was a self-portrait."

"Bloody expensive, that," Baker said.

"It *would* be expensive," Margaret added. "Were the paintings authenticated?"

"Yes," Tom said.

"And you just found that out as well?" Baker asked.

"Yes, just a short time before I called you," Tom said.

"I don't know of anyone named Wilfred Alec, but I could check Mr. Kepler's files. What would you imagine his connection with Mr. Kepler to be?"

"I have no idea," Tom said. "Alec's connection is with Bachmann. Bachmann is connected with Kepler. Kepler is dead and Bachmann has disappeared. That's all that I can tell you, I'm afraid."

"Yes," Margaret said. "Of course. Could we go into Dover Street and check the files?"

"Certainly," Baker said.

Just then Leonard appeared at the door, holding it open as a woman with a gray apron came in, carrying a steaming pot of coffee and a tray of cookies. "Hello again, Mrs. Porter," Baker said. "I'm terribly sorry, but it seems we must be off. Why don't you have a cup of that coffee and rest yourself a moment or two. The milk is still hot." She forced a thin smile as Baker slipped a handful of the cookies into his jacket pocket.

There was a smell of disinfectant in Kepler's office that Tom had not noticed the last time they were there. When he enquired about it he was told that the cleaning staff had been through the building and he was probably smelling something from the other side of the walls and floor. "We wouldn't let them in here, if that's what concerns you," Baker said. Tom just nodded.

"Well, go ahead and have a go," Baker said to Margaret. "Can we be of any help?"

"No, I can check," she said. Tom and Diana sat down at the library table. The room was cool; Diana kept on her raincoat and again held it closed at her neck. Tom took out his notepad and checked what he had jotted down during his last conversation with Dietrich, while Baker sat in a tattered armchair, slipping cookies from his pocket and nibbling on them as Margaret worked her way through the files and desk drawers.

"I'm afraid there's nothing here," she said, forty-five minutes later. "Perhaps back in Cobham . . ."

"Cobham? Right you are," Baker said. "We can't afford not to check, eh?" he said to Tom.

"No, we can't," Tom said, fearing that any evidence at Dover Street might have already disappeared.

The traffic was heavy in both directions. It had started to drizzle at midday and the streets were slick. It was 1:50 by the time they reached Kepler's house in Surrey. By then the drizzle had become light rain and they hurried to the door from the two police vehicles. Margaret let herself in with her own key, slipped her jacket over the back of a wooden chair in the kitchen, and started to work her way through Walter Kepler's cabinets, drawers, and files. The rest waited in the drawing room. Tom continued to check his notes and compare them with earlier pages in his book. Diana sat beside him, occasionally brushing her hand against the side of his leg, reassuring herself of his presence. Baker cleaned his fingernails with a miniature penknife. He seemed intent on the task. From time to time he checked his watch.

Twenty-five minutes later Margaret Harrell came down the stairs, stopping halfway. "You *did* say that his name was *Wilfred* Alec, didn't you?"

"Yes," Tom said. "Have you found something?"

"No, but I may have remembered something."

CHAPTER FORTY-SIX
Cobham, Surrey
Sunday, 2:40 p.m.

"Well, out with it," Baker said. "You're keeping us all in suspense."

"It's probably not anything," Margaret said. "I'll have to check some things. It's just that . . ."

"Yes?" Tom said.

"Mr. Kepler's assistant was named Wilhelm. At least I think it was Wilhelm."

Baker turned his head away in frustration, wrinkling his lips as he put his penknife back in his pocket.

"Back in Berlin," Tom said.

"Yes, of course. I've been his principal assistant here."

Tom flipped through his notebook. "You said earlier that his assistant was seized and taken in for questioning by the Gestapo." Tom flipped another page. "He was held for questioning for four days."

"Yes, that's right," Margaret said. "They did that sort of thing as a threat. They did it with Freud's daughter, Anna, for example."

"I understand," Tom said, "but you think the assistant's name was Wilhelm."

"Let me check," she said. "There are some old letters . . ."

The letters were kept in an unlocked steel box in Kepler's chifforobe. "He kept all of his personal papers in here," Margaret said. She took out the deed to his house and a copy of his will, setting them aside. Then she took out a packet of letters secured by a faded pink ribbon. The stamps were still intact as was some sealing wax. The smell of dried glue and foxed paper was palpable. "Let's see . . ." Margaret said, taking the letters to a nearby nightstand. She seemed uncomfortable as she sat down on Kepler's bed. It took her nearly ten minutes to find what she was looking for. "Mr. Kepler asked me to go through these several years ago. He was looking for an old Berlin address."

"Well?" Baker said.

"Yes, his name *was* Wilhelm. Wilhelm Eichen."

"Is there a middle name?" Tom asked.

She looked over the letter. "There's not much here really, just an expression of affection. Mr. Kepler's assistant is wishing him luck in his new life in London. Wait . . ." She checked the envelope again, turning it over. "Yes, here . . ." she said, "the return address—W. A. Eichen. Do you think that Mr. Kepler's assistant could be Wilfred Alec?"

"I don't know," Tom said.

"It's very doubtful, wouldn't you say?" Baker asked. "This man was an assistant. He wouldn't have the means to be a collector." Then, catching Margaret's glance, he said, "Sorry, no offense intended."

"None taken," she said. "Perhaps he was able to prosper where others had failed. Those were difficult times. Fortunes were lost but fortunes were also made. Isn't it always like that during wartime and just after?"

"Fortunes are sometimes stolen," Tom said.

"What are you saying," Baker asked, "that this assistant of Kepler's was stealing art?"

"That would account for his secretiveness. It might also account for the fact that he possessed works that no one else had ever seen. He worked for a broker. Perhaps he had access to things that had not yet surfaced. He knew the names of Kepler's clients. He knew the location of their collections. If works were hidden or shipped out of the country, Kepler would have known, and so would his assistant. So far we've been operating under the assumption that the assistant was detained by the Nazis. Perhaps that was all a ruse. He may have been negotiating with the Nazis, betraying his employer and the other members of Tenedos as well as their clients. Hitler loved art and he loved propaganda. He also used art as a prime example of the degeneracy he was personally called by God to cure. He called it *entartete kunst*. Just a second . . ."

Tom checked his notebook. "Yes, Bachmann and Erhard were involved with it; there was a story mentioning their names. They may have sold it or helped exhibit it."

"Hitler would have liked to have seen it disappear, but he would also have wanted to draw some advantage—political or financial—from its disappearance," Diana said.

"Yes," Tom added, "and Eichen could have helped him. Confiscated works could have been sold and the proceeds transferred to the coffers of the *wehrmacht*. Eichen himself might have been permitted to keep some things. Their value after the war would have continued to grow. He could have become immensely rich and still kept a core of what he considered key pieces. He may still have them, since they escaped the fire in Chile."

"And he anglicized his name to evade the authorities after the war," Diana added.

"Just a second," Baker said. "I don't mean to discourage you, Deaton, but all of this is speculative in the extreme."

"Agreed," Tom said, "but it has the virtue of covering a number of the facts. We have been discussing Tenedos as a circle of five individuals: Kepler, Bachmann, Driessen, Erhard, and Berthold. All five have either disappeared or are now dead. However, there were six individuals, counting Kepler's Berlin assistant, and that man may not only be very much alive, he may also be the same man whose home and collection Karl Bachmann may have attempted to burn. At the very least there is a connection between Bachmann and this man Wilfred Alec. Bachmann has now disappeared and Alec is known to be alive."

"That's a large number of may's," Baker said.

"True, but what else do we have?" Tom answered. "There's something else you should know."

"And what is that?" Baker said.

"Alec is living in southern California, a reasonable distance from Dr. Bennett's brother's Orange County gallery. Also no more than thirty or forty minutes from the studio where his body was found."

"And so are another—what would you say—twenty to twenty-five million other people?" Baker asked.

"I'm going to have to leave," Tom said.

"You're going back to Laguna?"

"As soon as I can."

"There's something you might do first," Baker said.

"Yes?"

"Roberts called. He wants to speak with you. I told him I couldn't give him the name of your hotel, but I agreed to give you his number and ask you to call him."

"What does he want?" Tom asked.

"He wouldn't say," Baker answered, seemingly perturbed by Roberts' desire to keep his own counsel.

Tom confirmed their flight and called Roberts. There was expectation in his voice when he answered. Tom identified himself and they agreed to meet for drinks in a pub called *The Aristocrat* in George Street. There were oil paintings on wooden panels outlining the front door, lords and dandies in bright reds and greens. Inside it was heavily Victorian with green and red velour couches, thick, bunched drapes, and etched-glass gaslights, since converted for incandescent bulbs. Tom waited for six minutes before Roberts came through the door.

His ruddy face was lined from sleeplessness and his shock of white hair had lost its body and outline. The moment he sat down he ordered a double whiskey. Tom said, "the same for me but with a little soda."

"Are you all right?" Tom asked.

"I could be polite and say yes," Roberts answered, "but the vicar told us never to lie."

"You look like hell," Tom said.

"Indeed. Baker would probably be pleased. He thinks I'm immune."

"What can I do for you?" Tom asked.

"This is not the easiest thing for me, Detective Deaton. I have a request to make of you, the nature of which you can surely anticipate. I'll be brief, and say that you simply *must* recover the manuscript. Its value is . . . beyond my ability to express." He paused and then spoke again. "Tell me, please. What have you learned? Who *is* this man who's stolen it?"

"We're not certain," Tom said, "and I'm not really at liberty to discuss the details."

"He's German, isn't he, just like Kepler and his Berlin colleagues?"

"Why would you say that?"

"Surely it's obvious to you."

"No, tell me why."

"Because they failed to take our country so they're now attempting to take our culture instead. It's the Baedeker raids of 1942 all over again."

"British culture would survive the loss of a manuscript and a sword," Tom said. "You survived the bombing of Bath and Exeter."

"Would it? It's not just the paper and the steel. It's the acknowledgment of the ease with which it could be accomplished. Tell me, did you ever see the manuscript when it was on display in the Museum?"

"Many years ago," Tom said. "On a graduation trip. It was the first thing you saw when you entered the manuscript collection."

"Precisely. It *is* the first thing. It cannot be lost. It must be found . . . at any cost. Where do you think it's been taken? Never mind, it doesn't matter. Just . . ."

"What?" Tom asked.

"Just retrieve it. Please. I'm only one man, but you must know how important this is to all of us."

"Yes, I think I know that."

The waitress brought their drinks. Roberts handed her a £10 note. "I'll get these," he said, lifting his glass and drinking more than half of it in one gulp.

"How well do you know Baker?" Tom asked.

"Well enough. He's a good detective. Likes to play it up a bit for the men, but he solves his fair share of the cases. Why do you ask?"

"No good reason. It just seemed that you were tilting with one another."

"Yes . . ."

"I just wanted some assurance that he was the best man for the job."

"Charles Baker is not a learned man, but he is diligent. That's really a good bit of it, isn't it? Continuing to look; refusing to give it up?"

"Yes, so long as you know where to look."

"It's a tricky case," Roberts said. "So much of what a man like Baker sees is the fruit of passion . . . envy, greed, lust . . . usually fed by alcohol and a sense of personal betrayal. Organized crime is conducted like business. It has its rules and its sense of order. There's blood about the edges, but there is in business as well, what? This case is different. There's greed enough but there's also organization and planning. From what Baker would say it seems to be the work of a single individual. That complicates it. There are no predictable suspects. If Baker seems a bit out of his element, that's to be understood. Don't you agree?"

"Yes, I suppose so."

Roberts signaled the waitress, holding up two fingers.

"I'll get these," Tom said. Roberts nodded in approval.

"I still don't understand why you wanted to meet with me."

"It's not easy . . ." Roberts said.

"What's not easy, Professor Roberts?" Tom asked.

"We don't do these things very well," Roberts said, "but . . ."

Tom took a sip of his drink and let Roberts finish.

"I'm not a sentimental man, at least not to any extreme, but there are certain things about which I feel rather deeply. One is language and another is Britain. You see our present condition. You see us as the shadow of what we once had been. I'm not speaking of the empire. Bugger that. I'm speaking of the general state of things—not the Britain of Mayfair and Regent's Park, but the Britain of Liverpool and Glasgow, of Manchester and Birmingham. There is a sense of impoverishment, of good times now passed. Very few really know how close we came to losing the war and fewer still are aware of the final costs of our survival.

"It was worth every last shilling of course and even though Germany is mighty again and we have faded, Hitler is dead, London is rebuilt, and this island is intact. The Russians still feel it, you know. For them it is . . . just yesterday. My father died in North Africa. I was living with my aunt then; my mother had died when I was a child. I still have his medals. They meant very little to me then; I was too young to understand the full import of what had happened and how my life had been changed irrevocably.

"Now there are winter evenings when I take them out and hold them in my hand . . . I've never done anything of that order myself, of course. I haven't sacrificed life or limb, but I like to think that in some small way I've given something, preserved something. I think of you going off to find this thief. I know that I can't be a part of it, but I wanted you to know that if there's anything I can do to help, you should feel free to call me. Call me at any time. I also wanted you to know how very much I appreciate what you're doing."

"I was in the Imperial War Museum nearly ten years ago," Tom said. "I was in the World War II display, standing in a mockup of a bunker with a sound and light demonstration. A man came up behind me, an elderly man. I could see from the corner of my eye that he was not well-dressed. He was old, doing his best to balance himself on arthritic feet and knees. He stepped closer to me and whispered something in my ear. He said, 'You bombed them during the day and we bombed them at night.' I turned to say something to him, but he was gone. Children were running around, people were handing out leaflets, soliciting contributions. It was a very strange experience. He somehow appeared, spoke, and then, instantly, he was gone. I've never forgotten it."

"Are you a religious man, Detective Deaton?"

"I believe in the force of evil," Tom said. "It's very hard not to. I hope that there's something or someone on the other side as well, someone in addition to ourselves."

Roberts took a deep drink, finishing off his whiskey, as the waitress brought the second round. "I believe that there is some force for goodness which enables us to discover and create beautiful things. The preservation of those things then becomes our responsibility. Sometimes we give a good account of ourselves and sometimes we do not. Our ability to see that beauty and preserve it is what constitutes civilization. All of the rest of it is so much trumpery: crowns and palaces, silks, gold, and diamonds. The beauty comes from the spirit, not the substance itself, and it is the spirit which evil seeks to corrode and defeat."

"To civilization," Tom said, "as much of it as we can salvage."

Roberts took another deep drink. "I was in Boston once for an academic term. The people there called it the 'hub of the universe'. I was not anxious to contradict them, for they were my hosts and while I can be an irascible man, I do my best not to be an impolite one. In all honesty, however, I cannot say that they were right.

"A few blocks north of us on Baker Street is 221-B, the fanciful creation of an Edinburgh physician. Letters are still received at that address, desperate letters, asking for help from a character in fiction. He has given pleasure to people all over the world and still defines, for many, the ratiocinative process. And *he* is a fiction.

"From where we are sitting I could take you—in a matter of minutes—to the houses of Dickens, Keats, and Carlyle, to the building where Johnson made his dictionary, the square where Reynolds painted his portraits, and the street where Hogarth set up his painting academy. We could stand beside the graves of Milton, of Bunyan, of Defoe, and of

Blake. This is the city of Marx and of Freud, of Newton and of Darwin. Chaucer was controller of customs in this port; Pepys was the founder of this nation's civil service. Handel's music was played on our great river and Mozart gave recitals in our pleasure gardens. This is the country of Alfred and of Arthur, of Harold, of Lawrence, Harris, Montgomery, and Churchill. This is the place to which one comes to hear the language of Shakespeare . . ."

He paused and took another drink. "Forgive me, I didn't intend to run on like that."

"That's all right," Tom said. "I was taught that soldiers should have a liberal education. They started as engineers, you know, at least in America. The principal problems were always engineering problems, at least of some sort. That's changed to some degree. When I was studying military history as a college junior our instructor told us that a liberal education was essential for their task. He was an older man, a veteran as I recall, with something of a southern accent and a flair for language. He told us that soldiers needed an education to appreciate what they someday might have to destroy. 'But that is not their primary mission,' he said. 'Their principal task is to protect and preserve—not just words, not just platitudes about some system of government—but to protect and preserve books and paintings, libraries and cathedrals, vineyards, gardens and parks: the most beautiful works of man.' I've always found that to be idealistic and, in its way, quaint. I've also always believed it to be true. Do you think that I'm being sentimental or silly?"

"I think there is a kind of madness in sentiment, just as there is a madness in love. The Elizabethans were right about these things. They froze and burned in their love of unattainable mistresses and they understood the world through the sounds of the planets and the meaning of flowers and herbs."

"Good fighters though," Tom said.

"Yes. With precious little tolerance for pirates and mutineers. They put their bodies on the bank of the Thames at Wapping Dock. It's one of

Charles Baker's favorite sites . . ."

"He pointed it out to me," Tom said.

"I thought he might have. The bodies stayed there until three tides had washed over them. A lesson. Wherever you are, whatever you do, wherever you should go, we shall find you, return you to this place, and this shall be your end. Not very pretty, of course. Some would call it barbaric. The practice did have the twin virtues of clarity and finality."

"Nice counters to sentiment, wouldn't you say?"

"I should say *essential* counters," Roberts answered.

V

THE FIFTH CHAMBER

CHAPTER FORTY-SEVEN
John Wayne Airport
Monday, 7:12 p.m.

Their connecting flight from Chicago arrived at John Wayne Airport on time. Its turnaround time was short and when Tom and Diana deplaned the waiting area was already crowded. Chris Dietrich was standing with his back against a pillar with detectives flanking him on either side. They spaced out as Tom and Diana approached Chris, bracketing them as they moved through the airport.

"Diana, Tom . . ." Dietrich said. "Welcome back to sunny southern California. We're parked in the ramp."

When they reached the baggage area their luggage was already on the conveyor. Tom picked up the bags, showed their baggage checks to an elderly attendant named Marta and followed the Chief to the ramp. As dusk settled in the sky was orange and gray with the remains of the day's smog still hovering to the east and filtering through the pockets of buildings marking the skyline. The air was calm and the airport roadway thick with sounds and catalytic converter smells. The palms scattered between the traffic lanes and ramps offered a perfunctory welcome. The detectives who were standing by Dietrich at the gate moved in closer as they approached their cars. A third detective was on the ramp level where Dietrich had parked his car. He was drinking coffee from a Starbucks cup with a high plastic lid and Tommee Tippee spout. After Dietrich, Diana, and Tom got into the Chief's blue sedan the other three got into a similar model in dark green and followed them through the parking attendant gates.

"I'll take the coastal road," Dietrich said, driving toward Newport Beach. Considering the time, there was a large volume of airport-related traffic that did not begin to thin out until they were nearly a mile and a half beyond the exit.

"Where are we, Chief?" Tom asked.

"About a block and a half from the new *Courtyard by Marriott.*"

"Sorry, I meant in the case."

"Well, for one thing we've found his house."

"Which is?"

"Just above the coast on something called Seaview Lane."

"Overlooking the water?"

"Oh yes. An entry ticket to his neighborhood starts at about 10 mil. Alec sits at the end of a short, asphalt road. Going in and out will be tight. The road's very narrow, barely wide enough for two cars, if that. There are nice circular drives for each house, once you leave the roadway, but the street itself is narrow. Alec's house looks small from the front but the back sections of it sort of cascade down the side of the cliff."

"How many levels?"

"Four, but the top one's just an entryway, a few steps above the first real level."

"How long has he lived there?"

"He's owned the property for five years, but he's only occupied it for two."

"How so?"

"It was under construction for three years before he could move in."

"That's a long time. I wonder what he's got in there besides wood, glass, and a lot of square footage."

"Since you asked . . ." Dietrich said, pulling a tube from beneath the seat.

"You got the construction blueprints, Chief?"

"As a matter of fact we did. Several of the floors are half-underground."

"Galleries probably. Security would be much less of a problem if there was only one side to worry about sealing. What's the electronic system like?"

"Slightly more advanced than Ft. Knox's. He's got a lot more in that house than blacklight Elvis portraits and poker-playing bulldogs."

"We figured that," Tom said.

"Yes," Dietrich said. "By the way, there's more."

"Yes?"

"What would you think of a building plan that would call for a ventilation system powerful enough to pull the smog out of the San Fernando Valley and a hydraulic system large enough to protect the Rose Bowl from the results of a double-digit earthquake?"

"He's built a cave underneath the house."

"Yes, and a rather large and secure one, I'd say."

"He must have a lot in there to protect," Tom said.

"That's a fair assumption," Dietrich answered, "since the actual assessed value of the shell that contains it is $28,000,000 plus change."

"I'd like a closer look."

"Hector tried to get in yesterday," Dietrich said. "He dressed up like a deliveryman. We put him in a van, gave him a handful of parcels, and sent him to the door. The address on the boxes was Seaview Trail. If anybody came to the door he was supposed to act confused and in need of directions."

"What happened?"

"Nothing really. He was greeted a few seconds after he pushed the bell. A woman answered, told him she wasn't expecting anything, told him she didn't know where Seaview Trail was, and told him to have a nice day."

"Did she seem suspicious?"

"Hard to say. She was the modern type: high heels, a chalk-stripe power suit—all business. Not a hausfrau."

"German?"

"As German as the Brandenburg Gate and just as cold. Stark blonde hair, ice-blue eyes, no makeup."

"How old?" Tom asked.

"Thirty or so. Very fit."

"Maybe a granddaughter. Did Hector say anything else?"

"He said she smelled good."

"Did she smell of gardenias?" Diana asked, the first words she had spoken since getting into the car.

"How did you know that?" Dietrich asked.

"She broke into my house. Her scent was still in the air."

"When?"

"It was Sunday afternoon, right after I found David's body. The scent was heavy; it filled the whole house. When I got in my car to leave I realized I had carried some of it with me. I had to open the window in order to get rid of it. I remember at the time feeling nausea and anger. Someone had entered my house without permission and gone through my things. She was looking for David's pictures, I suppose. What else did Officer Campo say?"

"I asked him if she identified herself and he said no," Dietrich answered. "He couldn't really see anything in the house. They were standing in some kind of anteroom or hallway. He said it was stucco with some exposed beams. There was no furniture except for a hanging light fixture and a single table of dark walnut. He did comment on the security system. He could see signal-trips along the window sills and some openings along the floorboards for light beams. He also said that the circular driveway in front of the property was gravel."

"A natural alarm system," Tom said.

"Yes. There were also some thick, rose arbors covering the ground floor windows. Very rustic and quaint, but also good natural barriers."

The sign for the PCH was welcome, after slogging through the boulevards of Irvine. Dietrich signaled, moved to the exit lane, turned, merged, and began to drive south along the coast. The office buildings on the left contrasted with the glow of the lights shimmering along the water. The traffic was heavy, but moving steadily.

Dietrich picked up his cell phone, hit the speed dial, waited, and said something in numerical code to the detectives in the car following them. Diana turned toward Tom, seeking answers.

"They're going to take some back streets and alleys, close off any possibilities of our being followed, and then head into Laguna. The Chief will take us to a safe house; the tail car will split off and go in another direction."

"How do you know that?" she asked.

"Standard operating procedure," Tom said.

When they got to the safe house in the Hills they could see a shadowy figure in the rear of the garage. Dietrich drove directly in and parked the police sedan. The door was closing behind them before he had turned off the ignition.

"Hector probably parked several blocks away and then walked in. He left the garage space for the Chief. When they're certain that we weren't followed, the Chief will take off."

"He always does this?" Diana asked, as she closed her car door.

"Just about always," Hector said, stepping out of the shadows, opening the side door of the garage and leading them to the back porch.

"Nap or talk?" he asked.

"Talk," Diana said.

"Talk," Tom added.

"Hungry?" Hector asked.

"Yes," Tom said, "thanks."

Hector went into the kitchen and returned a few minutes later with a six-pack of Pacifico, a plate of rye bread, and a bowl filled with small pieces of roast beef. The scent was spicey. Tom made Diana a sandwich and handed it to her. "This is delicious," she said.

"Hector cooks and shreds the beef, heats it in a pan with Italian dressing and chops in some pepperoncini," Tom said. "He always does that. Beer?"

Diana nodded. He handed her a Pacifico and she put it next to her plate without taking a drink. Tom put the blueprints of the house on the edge of the table. "How do we get in?" she asked.

"Good question," Dietrich answered. "Depends on the purpose."

"The purpose is to find the stolen art in his possession and arrest him for murder and theft," Diana said.

"What if it's not there? Then we look ridiculous and we've put him on his guard," Dietrich said.

"Then we go in surreptitiously, see what's there, and make the formal arrest later."

"And what if we're caught? We get hauled before an Internal Affairs hearing board and face possible arrest for breaking and entering," Hector said.

"We'll have to show probable cause and get a warrant," Dietrich added. "When we serve it we'll be announcing to him that we know who he is and what he's been doing."

"What's wrong with you two?" Diana asked. "You suddenly sound as risk-averse as a pair of White House aides."

Dietrich took a drink of his Pacifico and let that pass. Hector looked at Tom.

"You see," Tom said, "we have to think this through."

"Think what through?" Diana said. "That man killed my brother."

"The man . . . or the woman?" Tom asked.

Diana sat silent.

"You said that the woman was in your house. Perhaps she was looking for your brother's pictures because she was the one who actually killed him. At this point we don't know. If we go in we go in prepared to do whatever's necessary. In other words we go in prepared to kill. They'll defend themselves and we'll do the same. It would be nice to know that we're not killing any innocent people in the process. It would also be nice to know that the evidence is there to convict your brother's killer and explain the circumstances of his death. When we do go in we won't hold anything back. That's why we try to be as certain as we can before we move."

"How can we do that?" Diana asked, impatiently.

"Why don't you enjoy your sandwich," Hector said. "Let your food digest a little. Enjoy your drink. Then we can take a few minutes and plan something."

CHAPTER FORTY-EIGHT
Agoura Way, Laguna Hills
Monday, 11:38 p.m.

"So we're decided then, Chief?" Hector said.

"We are," Dietrich answered. "I'll get the warrant from Judge Kyle and pick up Bill Brighton. Tom and Diana will go in as advisors to consult on the investigation and to help identify whatever the four of us can find. You'll stay out on the road and watch the clock. We should bring Alec and the woman out in just a few minutes, but give us a full half hour. If we haven't surfaced by then, tell the backups to stand by. We'll have a half dozen squad cars within a quarter mile of the house and choppers just over the ridge. At forty-five minutes the dismounteds will come in and the choppers will be in the air—earlier if there's any suspicious movement."

"Will you arrest him?" Diana asked.

"That depends on what we find," Dietrich answered. "At the very least he'll be taken in for extensive questioning while we take a long, slow look at his house. We'll have our own interrogation team ready and the French and English police available by phone. We'll be able to hold him for hours while we do a thorough search of the house and grounds."

"Or hold *her*," Tom added. "Or both of them."

"Right," Dietrich said.

"Hector can't go in with us since she's already seen him," Tom said, "but I like having him outside as backup."

"How soon? Tomorrow?" Diana asked.

"More likely the day after," Dietrich said. I have to reach the judge, the DA, the feds and the British and French. In the meantime, you and Tom should have a long look at the blueprints of the house before going in. Hector, Bill and I have already studied them."

"When will you know?"

"Give me a couple of hours at least. It may take a little while to reach the British and French police. You two should get some rest in the meantime." Tom nodded in agreement and started to get up.

"Where are you going?" Diana asked.

"There's not enough room for all of us here," he answered. "Besides, you could probably use some privacy for a change."

"Where will you stay?" she asked Tom.

"If there's no one suspicious in the area I'll stay on my boat."

"I'm going with you," she said.

Hector and Dietrich watched for Tom's response.

"I think you'll be safer here," he said.

"I'd rather go with you."

"OK. Let's go then," he said.

Hector took his car keys out of his pocket and handed them to Tom. "It's just down the street," he said, "on the south side, about a block and a half."

Tom smiled, thanked him, and patted Dietrich on the side of his arm with his open hand. He was already on the phone. "I'll call you in the morning," Tom said to Hector. Dietrich raised his hand in a gesture of good-bye as they opened the door to leave.

As they drove down to the marina Diana was staring straight ahead into the headlights of the oncoming traffic, but her left hand was on Tom's leg. "Are you all right?" she asked. "Are you ready for this?"

"What do you mean?" he answered.

"You were rubbing your head and neck when we were walking toward Hector's car."

"I'm just a little stiff. I'll be OK. Sometimes when I sit too long in one position I have to work it out a little."

"You're sure?"

"Yes, I am, but thanks for asking."

The streets were clear around the marina. Tom checked in with the harbor master before going to his boat.

"What was that all about?" Diana asked, as they walked to Tom's slip.

"What do you mean?"

"The whispering."

"Oh, I asked him if he had seen anyone suspicious around. He said no one other than the usual boaters. He also said that he won't say anything about you being here. I think he must be worried about your reputation."

"That's very gentlemanly of him," Diana said.

The lock on the partition between the cabin and the aft section of the boat had not been disturbed. Tom and Diana entered the cabin and Tom slid the sunlight-blocking drapes in place before turning on the light. "You can have the first shower," he said.

"Do you think I need it?"

"No, but I thought you'd like one."

"You're right. Before that, let me see the back of your head," Diana said.

Tom sat down on one of the chairs outside the galley, turning his head toward the wall lamp.

"It looks irritated," Diana said. "Are you sure it doesn't hurt?"

"It doesn't. Really."

"How's your vision?"

"Fine."

"Stay there," she said, getting a moist washcloth and a dry towel.

She daubed at the incision for several minutes and then dried it with the towel, rinsing out the wash cloth and repeating the process in areas adjacent to it. "Where's that salve they gave you?"

He poked around in his bag, found the tube, and handed it to her.

Her look and tone were skeptical. "This is over-the-counter stuff; it's not going to do very much." She smoothed it on with her fingertip, gently and thoroughly. "Just let it dry," she said. "I'll check it again in a little while."

"Thanks," he said.

"You're welcome," she answered, as she returned the towel and wash cloth to the head. She seemed fresh and rested. He found himself following her every move as she hung the wash cloth to dry and slipped the towel beside it. When she turned she realized he'd been watching her.

Without saying anything she slipped off her skirt and blouse, walked toward him, sat down beside him on the edge of the bed and kissed him on the cheek. "Move over, Detective," she said. "I'm not going to spend this night alone, particularly when it could be our last."

An hour and a half later as she fell asleep beside him he stared at the glow at the edge of the drapes and the faint shadows cast by the nightlight. He thought of the other women he'd known, all special in their own ways. None were quite like Diana. She was attractive and intelligent but most of all she was driven—not just by events, but also in her dreams and desires. She showed him everything and yet in certain ways she showed him nothing. He had talked to her, held her and been held by her, shared her search and now something more. He wondered what would be left when that search was over. He was useful to her now, but they were walking into the dark and there was no way to know what they would find there or whether they would emerge together afterwards.

CHAPTER FORTY-NINE
The Harbor at Dana Point
Tuesday 6:53 a.m.

"Where do we stand, Hector?" Tom was sitting on the side of the bed, cradling the phone against his shoulder as he slipped on his shoes and socks. Diana was standing in the head, drying her face. When Tom looked up at her she returned his smile.

"The Chief's going to pick up the warrant from the judge and return to us here at the safe house. Brighton's on his way. With the Chief running point all the barriers fell. We're clear with the DA's office and with the Orange County Sheriff's Department. The interrogation team is in place and they're ready to start. The French and English police are standing by. The choppers will be ready and the backup's been assigned. Brighton has been checking on the equipment and I've been going over the architectural drawings of the house one last time."

"So we're going in *today?*"

"Yes. We're shooting for 9:30. We don't want him to think he's being rousted in the middle of the night. He might get jumpy, do something dangerous. Both the Chief and the Lieutenant thought it would be best to lowkey it and I agree. The cavalry will be just around the corner if we need them. How soon can you get here?"

"Just a second." He checked with Diana and then got back on the phone. "We'll be there by twenty after seven."

"Good. We'll take you through the drawings and you can work with Brighton on weapons and equipment."

"Has he got flashlights, Hector?"

"Yes. I talked to him about ten minutes ago. He mentioned that he had just changed the batteries."

"How about rope?"

"Yes, but there's only so much you can put in the bottom of a briefcase."

"Matches?"

"Relax, Tom, the Lieutenant will have everything, even down to the flares and knives."

"Have you got your usual collection of unauthorized weapons?"

"I've always got those."

"We'll see you in a few minutes then."

Diana was at the foot of the bed, dressing. She was wearing a sports bra and a tanktop for extra warmth, then a sweater with long sleeves over dark slacks. She put on a poplin jacket but when she looked in the mirror she thought it was too informal. She put it back in her bag and took out a wool blazer.

She watched Tom as he slid a turtleneck sweater over a long-sleeved tee shirt, trying to detect any hints of pain as the fabric passed over his head. He put on leather shoes with rubber soles, and a loose-fitting, wool sports jacket.

"Going for the yuppie rather than the burglar look?" she asked.

"Yes. The trick is to keep him thinking we know less than we do. If we can keep him from reacting at the house we can get him out of there quickly and have him taken downtown. That gives us free rein to go through his place without him calling in reinforcements or setting off any protective devices."

"You mean explosives."

"Possibly, but I doubt that he'd want to destroy his own place, particularly if the art is there. There might be something else—gas, for example." He paused, then spoke again.

"When we're there . . ."

"Yes?" Diana responded.

"I really don't want you in the middle of it."

"Why shouldn't I be in the middle of it? It's my brother they killed."

"Call me selfish."

"Don't you want to see me happy?"

"Yes, but I don't want to see you hurt or worse."

"I'll be all right. Will Lieutenant Brighton allow me to use my personal weapon?"

"Reluctantly, yes. What you or he doesn't have, Hector will."

The oncoming traffic was steady as they drove up into the Hills—principally people leaving for work, a few cars full of kids getting an early start for beaches and parks, an SUV or two with golfers in bright-colored shirts with visors and ballcaps, boyfriends heading home after an extended weekend, kids beginning a day of unplanned drifting and cruising.

Tom noticed the unmarked vans on opposite sides and opposite ends of the street as he turned into the driveway of the safe house. He parked the car in the space on the side of the garage. Diana was out before he could open the door for her and together they climbed the porch steps at the rear of the house. Tom raised his hand to knock but the door opened before his knuckles hit the frame. Hector handed him a cup of coffee when he entered the kitchen. "Dr. Bennett?" he said.

"Coffee, thanks," she answered. "Where's the Chief?"

"In the dining room with the Lieutenant."

"I'll get my coffee and join them."

When she returned with the steaming-hot coffee, Tom and the Chief were going over the architectural drawings of the house. Brighton was sitting opposite them; he had a street map. "Hector will be *here* . . ." (pointing) "and we'll enter . . . *here*. We'll have the other units on these side streets . . . *here* . . . and *there*. The choppers will be in the fields below the eastern slope of the elevation. We don't want him to hear them coming in. If we need them we can call them in in a matter of seconds."

Tom looked closely, fixing the street names in his memory and estimating distances. "It's pretty steep around there, no place to land the choppers."

"No, we'd use them to follow him if he tried to make a break," Brighton said.

"If he had the firepower to get past our people."

"Yes. Sometimes they help to intimidate. They make inexperienced people jumpy. They could give us an edge."

Tom checked his watch. It was 8:17. "Let's have one last cup of coffee and then saddle up," the Chief said.

"Bill and I will go in," Dietrich said. "I'll do the talking. They'll know this is hardly routine but I want it to appear to be as routine as possible. If they see a lot of people they might bolt and start firing. As soon as we get Alec and his people out of there I'll hand them over to the backup to bring downtown. Then you two can come in and we'll start going through the house."

Diana looked at Tom. "It was our understanding that we could go in at the outset."

"Too dangerous," Dietrich said. "Perps don't like crowds."

"Perps like numbers in their favor though," Tom said. "If there are only two of you and a half dozen of them you'll be squeezed."

"And if you go in with a squad of police they might open up immediately," Diana said.

"Dr. Bennett . . ." Dietrich said, lowering his voice, "I appreciate your courage but you must also appreciate the fact of your inexperience."

"So will they," Diana responded. "They may be less guarded."

"Bill?" Dietrich said, soliciting an opinion.

"They're both still alive," he answered.

Dietrich took a deep drink of his black coffee, then put down the cup. "OK," he said, "but no heroics. Understood?"

He took their nods as Hector stepped outside the room for a second. Tom noticed him checking on something in his pocket, outside of Dietrich's line of sight. He was dressed in dark brown twill pants, a brown turtleneck, and a loose tan jacket. When he was satisfied that he had everything, he stepped back in and said, "Everybody about ready?"

"Let's do it," Dietrich said. "Let's be smart and cautious and do this by the book, but let's also take this guy down."

"And remember what I said," he added, "no heroics." Hector looked at him and smiled. "I didn't mean you," Dietrich said.

CHAPTER FIFTY
San Clemente
Tuesday, 9:28 a.m.

Seaview Lane wound its way along the inland side of a steep hillside; it was no more than a lane and a half wide, with security walls and entry gates wedged against its curbs and angled tributaries spoking from the main road, all marked **Private Drive** in bold letters. Above them the sharp blue of the coastal sky was punctuated by a handful of clouds, all moving east rapidly, as if they suspected something violent was about to occur and they wanted no part of it. By the time they approached the end of the lane and Alec's property they could see silver glimmers on the Pacific and the edge of the distant horizon.

"That's it," Dietrich said. From a distance the top level of the house looked like a midwest funeral home with a modest square exterior and a simple porte-cochère. As they got closer they saw that what appeared to be rough marble or stucco was actually formed cement with etched, parallel ridges—retro-brutalist, like college libraries and student centers from the early seventies. Softened somewhat by the blooms on the rose arbors around the windows, the basic structure and materials suggested a mausoleum or medium-security prison. They heard the gravel crunching under the wheels of their sedan as they drove up to the front of the house.

Dietrich led the way, his posture all boredom and nonchalance. Brighton stood at his side, with Tom and Diana in the rear. He pulled the steel handle for the bell and waited, his eyes on the red and yellow roses around the windows, his hand near the grip of his automatic.

After fifteen or twenty seconds the door opened. A young woman greeted them. She was wearing a white lab coat. Her eyes were silver blue, her hair a stark straw blonde that could have been mistaken for dyed were it not for her faint, nearly white eyebrows. "May I help you?" she asked.

"Yes," the Chief said, showing her his badge. "My name is Dietrich. I'm from the Laguna Beach Police Department. This is one of my lieutenants, Bill Brighton, and these are consultants on a case, Mr. Deaton and Dr. Bennett. We'd like to speak with Mr. Alec."

"Come in, please," she said. She took them through the entryway which Hector had described and down a short flight of stairs to a semicircular sitting room. The front of the room was underground, the rear looking out over a garden with desert plants. A narrow stairway at the side of the window descended to the level below. In the center of the room was a curved leather couch. Except for a table on the rear wall and parallel sconces on either side of the window there were no other furnishings in the room.

"Please make yourselves comfortable," she said. "It will take me a moment or two to bring in Mr. Alec." She opened a door that was flush with the front wall and closed it behind her. Dietrich looked at them and signaled with his eyes to spread out. Tom and Diana sat on the couch, while Dietrich and Brighton stood by the windows. "The view is really exceptional," Dietrich said, folding his hands behind him and continuing to project a sense of detachment from the case.

It was at least a minute and a half before the door opened again. The blonde came through first. Tom was thinking of her as Lorelei now. It seemed like a good name—half Rhine maiden, half moll. Behind her was an elderly man in a wheelchair with an attendant behind him. The attendant had a stethoscope around his neck and a thermometer next to the pens in the pocket of his lab coat. He looked sufficiently Nordic to qualify for the Hitler-Jugend, but the hornrims and pony tail were more west L.A. and the hint of a tic might have posed a problem for the Third Reich. He wheeled the man who called himself Wilfred Alec toward the front of the couch as Dietrich and Brighton walked forward and took up positions behind it. The man was old and frail, dressed in a purple silk robe with matching silk pyjamas that fell away from his shrivelled neck. His skin was practically translucent, his few gray hairs dotting his head and the top of his chest like so much chance growth. His eyes were closed, his liver-spotted hands folded peacefully in his lap. He seemed to be either napping or readying himself for the embalmer.

"Grandfather," Lorelei said, putting her hand on his shoulder, "this is Chief Dietrich of the Laguna Beach Police Department."

Alec's chest and shoulders lurched slightly to the left as he shifted position, unfolded his hands and raised his head. As his eyelids moved they realized he was staring blankly through glazed sockets that looked like shattered, blue-veined eggshells. The scars around his eyes were now fully visible, the remaining adhesions distorting his face into a twisted mask. He waited for the image to take its full effect—raising questions, casting doubts. "How do you do. And please don't be concerned; I expected your silence. I lost my sight in a fire . . . saving beautiful things. You needn't be shocked or feel any embarrassment. I assure you that *I* am reconciled to my condition. It was many years ago, but as you can see it managed to change my life forever. A terrible but somehow necessary moment. Who of us knows what he would do in a similar situation? Impossible choices. I had the courage to make the choice, but now, as you see, I live with the result. But you did not come here to talk about my blindness. What did you come here to do, if I may ask? Please, you will have to identify yourselves."

His voice was high-pitched and annoying. It was the voice of an opinionated lecturer, raised to an uncomfortable level by either hearing impairment or the desire to luxuriate in the sounds of his own speech.

"I'm Dietrich," one voice said, the others following in turn from the darkness. He tilted his head at each sound, recording the location, the timbre, the associated name.

"And what division of the Laguna Beach Police Department are you with today, Chief Dietrich?" Alec asked, his voice surprisingly strong considering his physical appearance.

"The investigations division, Mr. Alec. The case is robbery/homicide."

"And which are you investigating, Chief Dietrich, a theft or a murder?"

"We're investigating both."

"And how may *I* be of service?"

"We have a number of questions to ask you, but we would prefer to do that downtown. Your attendants can come with you, of course."

"My *attendants*? Yes . . . well . . . I am afraid that is quite impossible, Chief Dietrich. I am an elderly man and a sick man. I never leave my home. You will have to ask your questions here. How many questions do you have, if I might ask?"

"We'll bring in an ambulance," Dietrich said.

"I already told you no," Alec said, insistently. "If you persist in not listening to me we will have a difficult time of it, Chief Dietrich. Karl . . ."

The attendant's hands came out from behind the wheelchair, accompanied by two Glock pistols. Lorelei simultaneously pulled a .32 automatic from beneath her lab coat.

"We've actually been expecting you, Chief. Perhaps I should have said something earlier, but you were playing your part so well that I thought I might play a part as well. At this age and under these circumstances one has so few amusements. By the way, we know about the other men accompanying you. I suspect my neighbors are already calling your superiors to complain about the illegally-parked cars on their streets. They're quite protective, you know. These homes are not inexpensive and every bit of land is precious."

"You'll need more than a few handguns to keep them all out,"

Dietrich said.

"Will I? I don't think so," Alec said. "They wouldn't be coming in for a few minutes in any event and a few minutes is all we'll really need. If they attempt anything earlier I've made contingency plans. I can jam their radio and cell phone signals and I've posted marksmen at both ends of the lane if they attempt to escape. They're quite cut off, you see. It is always striking when one thinks what a little planning can do, don't you think? You shouldn't have sent that delivery man in the other day by the way; did you really believe we would fail to see through such obvious theatrics?

"So, as I said, you can put away any thoughts about the men you believe to be in reserve. We have you here and they'll be of no help to you. By the way, there are more surprises coming, surprises you would be too naive to anticipate."

"There are too many of them for you," Dietrich said.

"Yes, of course, but that will be no problem, for all will go as planned. When all of this is over I'll have someone contact the mayor and explain to him what has happened. The mayor is a reasonable man. He'll find the story quite plausible. I'm well-acquainted with him, of course. Are you? My charitable work, you see. This will be an extension of that work, as it were."

Tom was watching his lips and hands, seeing how he twisted his fingers together, relishing the silence of his audience as he spoke each word. Karl and Lorelei were listening too, their attention fixed on each successive syllable. Tom looked at their hands. They each had a firm grip on their weapons but from moment to moment they broke eye contact with their captives, charmed somehow by the sound of the old man's voice. Tom felt like a bored student in the class of a martinet, while they, the teacher's toadies, listened worshipfully.

"Worried about stolen art, are you?" Alec asked, initiating more conversation.

"And about the men who died because of it," Dietrich said.

"You shouldn't concern yourselves with them," Alec said. "Life is short, art is long. They were tools that, unfortunately, became impediments."

Tom waited and listened, hoping for a pause, an opening, some sudden opportunity. Alec droned on, his tongue curling around each syllable. Tom continued to wait, holding his expression. Alec spoke of civilization and the current, unpleasant lack of it, implying that his house had been invaded by philistines who must now pay for their impertinence. He was delighting in every word. Tom's eyes were on those of Karl and Lorelei. As they exhibited the hint of a smile at Alec's choice of words and nodded at one another in self-satisfied agreement, Tom found his moment. He threw himself forward from the couch, driving the wheelchair into Karl and throwing him against the wall. Lorelei jerked toward him, raising her weapon, as he whip-kicked her right arm. Her automatic discharged as she fell off-balance, but the rounds hit the ceiling and wall. Diana was up in an instant, driving her fist into her cheek and eye and sidestepping her before she had a chance to recover. By now Dietrich and Brighton had taken out their weapons as Karl opened fire on them. Tom and Diana dove toward the narrow, curving staircase beside the picture window as Lorelei spun around to shoot them. Overhead they heard the rounds penetrating the stairwell. A split-second later they heard multiple additional gunshots. Tom's gun was out as he tripped down the final set of stairs, Diana right behind him. When he rolled behind the stairs and out of any possible line of fire Diana could see that his pantsleg was spotted with blood.

The shooting stopped momentarily. "I'm going up," Tom whispered. "You stay here."

"No, I'm coming with you."

"Somebody has to escape and counter their story," he said. "That's you. I'm going up to see if I can help Bill and the Chief."

"I'll give you thirty seconds and then I'm following you," she said, her Walther in her hand now. Tom looked at her as if to ask whether or not she knew how to use it. She bent her wrist and showed him that the safety was off.

Taking his time initially, his .45 aimed at the top of the stairs, Tom took the last steps three at a time, bolting into the room with his weapon extended at arm's length. There was no one there, but the wall behind the couch where Brighton and Dietrich had been standing was splattered with blood. Tom went to the door through which Lorelei and Karl had brought Alec. Standing to the side he threw it open with his left hand, his leg now throbbing with pain, his sock wet with blood.

There was no response. Beyond the door was a short semicircular hallway leading to a large steel door with a call-button beside it and a small light above the button. An elevator. They had brought Alec up from another level. Tom hit the button but there was no response. The door or gate on the car were ajar or the elevator's electrical connection had been broken. Tom came back through the sitting room, heard movement on the steps and as he turned he again felt the pain shooting down his leg through his ankle to his foot. Lightheaded at the loss of blood he hobbled toward the stairs. Diana was nowhere in sight as he braced himself with his left arm, making his way down as quickly as he could before his vision began to cloud and he felt his leg give out beneath him.

CHAPTER FIFTY-ONE
San Clemente
Tuesday, 9:52 a.m.

Tom awoke a few moments later to find himself beneath a long walnut table. He couldn't remember dragging himself across the room in search of cover, but he was there. The French silk carpet that filled three-quarters of the room was stained with uneven streaks of his blood. He turned abruptly, looking for Diana, but she was nowhere in sight. He crawled to a sideboard, found a drawer filled with linen napkins, pulled up his pantsleg, and tied one of the napkins around his leg. He kept his hand pressed firmly against the wound in an attempt to stop the bleeding. He started to stand but his leg would not yet support his weight. With his back to the bottom of the sideboard he looked around.

The second level was the kitchen and dining area. To his left was a door leading to the elevator. To his far right was a door leading, he imagined, to a bathroom. The dining room proper overlooked the garden. To the left front was a kitchen with what appeared to be oversized work surfaces and large appliances. Copper pots and pans were shelved in the open, side-compartments of a large island that included a sink with a goose-neck faucet. He could see the outline of a black, Aga oven and the break in the cherry cabinetry that marked the doors to a Sub-Zero refrigerator. The slight whirr of its motor was the only audible sound on that level of the house.

Where was Diana? She would not have left him voluntarily and she would not have allowed herself to be taken easily, but there was no blood visible except for his own and there were no signs of a struggle. The sounds he had heard on the steps were faint—the slightest shuffling. Perhaps she was coming to help him when she was seized from behind. It would have taken two people to do that so quietly. That meant that either Karl and Lorelei were free to take Diana (and Brighton and Dietrich were down) or there were others in the house working for Alec. She wouldn't have abandoned him. She couldn't.

Perhaps she had heard or seen something on the dining-room level. Coming up the steps to help him she turned abruptly and hurried back down the steps to . . . where? To escape? To pursue someone or something? Perhaps she had barricaded herself in the room he assumed was a bathroom. He dragged himself across the carpet, sat at the side of the door to that room and whispered her name.

There was no response. He whispered her name a second time but still there was no answer. Wedging his back against the wall and putting his weight on his good leg he got to his feet, raised his pistol, and threw open the door. He had been right. It was a half-bath with sickroom support bars on either side of the toilet and a call-button on the wall above. The room was papered in a floral pattern with tones of peach and yellow. The hand towels on the sink bar accented the colors of the walls and a wooden shelf above the sink contained a pair of stacked wash cloths and a tray of scented soap with hints of lilac and cinnamon. Diana, however, was not there. Either she was waiting on the floor below, she had been taken prisoner, or she was indulging in the kind of heroics against which Dietrich had warned.

As he started to make his way back to the dining room he heard a sound. At first he thought it could have been the motor of the elevator, but it seemed intermittent, less steady. Either way it was too distant to be identified. Balancing himself on the backs of the chairs around the walnut table he moved as quickly as he could to the opposite side of the room and opened the hallway door leading to the elevator. The light above the call-button was dark. He touched it. It was still slightly warm. He hit the call-button but there was no response.

Returning to the dining room he leaned against the wall, listening. He could hear nothing. Again balancing himself on the backs of the chairs he hobbled toward the stairs to the next level below. Perhaps they were waiting for him there. There was no sound above him. If they had returned to the top level they were able to do so in absolute silence. He sat down at the top of the stairs, raised his pistol to his cheek, and slipped down a step at a time, denying them an easy shot if they were waiting for him.

It suddenly struck him that something was radically wrong with the house of Wilhelm Eichen, aka Wilfred Alec. There were no artworks anywhere. Even though the view of the garden commanded attention in each of the rooms there was ample wall space to carry the works of art which Alec presumably possessed. Had they all been sold after he lost his sight? At the bottom of the stairs to the lower level there was a large foyer, another door to the elevator hallway, and doors leading to what he expected to be bedrooms. In the foyer was an ornately-carved walnut table with fauns and satyrs serving as supports for the flat surface, also a set of brass wall sconces, and another silk, French rug. The items were all rare and expensive, but nowhere near the price bracket of old master paintings. They were the kinds of things you would find in every San Clemente home, not the kinds of things you would find only in museums and the homes of billionaires.

Moving behind the stairs and against the wall, Tom continued to listen. There was nothing audible except the tick of a small brass clock on the carved table. Tom explored each bedroom in turn. There were three. None of them had windows, since they were at the front of the house and hence, underground. Recessed lighting and floorboard electric heaters had been installed in each room and each had a separate bath.

The first was done in simple fruitwoods with dark wool carpeting and leather-upholstered chairs. Karl's no doubt. The second was much larger, with bright lights and pastels. Lorelei's. She had installed a corner greenhouse with artificial light and tropical plants. The enclosure was warm and slightly humid, with condensation clinging to the glass walls. Tom could hear the buzz of the lights. There was a dehumidifier on the floor beneath the greenhouse but it had been turned off.

Lorelei's bathroom was in yellow, with complementary wallpaper, tile, fixtures, towels, and soap. Above the tub was a window box with indirect, artificial lighting and some small plants. It glowed like an oversized nightlight.

Eichen/Alec's bedroom was the largest and when Tom entered he found himself in darkness. The room was lit by a large ceiling fixture with a rheostat switch, but when Tom pushed the button the light barely glowed. He turned it up and was struck by what he found.

The furnishings were simple enough: a cherry bed with extra pillows and a large eiderdown comforter; a plain walnut work table with a telephone and a keyboard with braille buttons and keys. The bathroom was simplicity itself: tub, toilet, and sink, with support bars everywhere, and simple white cotton towels and wash cloths.

It was the open wall across from the bed that seized Tom's interest. There were two oil paintings hung in parallel, each by Van Gogh, each never seen before. The first was a spray of fuji mums, the second a sunset over a field of wheat. The oils were so thick you could trace the paintings' lines and swirls with your fingertips, doubtless their possessor's desire.

A few feet from the paintings was a large leather chair surrounded by bronze statuary, some by Degas, some by Giacometti, some by Brancusi. The pieces were positioned on a half-moon shaped table which partially encircled the front of the chair, so that Alec could sit among them and touch them endlessly. Each was a human figure, the great majority female.

The tick of the clock in the foyer seemed louder when Tom returned. He checked the elevator hallway. The light was cool, the elevator inoperable. The steel door—like those above—was locked tight and could not be opened unless the car was at that floor. Tom probed it with the point of his pocket knife and quickly realized that the door could not be jimmied without causing sounds that would immediately disclose his position.

He returned to the foyer. There were no more steps. They were all in the cave below and there was no way he could reach them. The Chief and Bill Brighton were probably down if not dead. They had taken Diana or were about to and they would come for him next. His leg was throbbing with pain and while the napkin had helped, he was leaving smears of blood from his pantsleg and shoe. If they were able to remove Dietrich, Brighton, and Diana as well as Alec, they were in good enough shape to take care of him.

The window opposite the foyer was tightly sealed, probably bullet-proof, and at least fifteen feet above the cliff below. He couldn't leave. He couldn't stay in place and wait. He couldn't attack. For the moment all he could do was listen to the tick of the clock, which seemed to grow louder and louder.

CHAPTER FIFTY-TWO
San Clemente
Tuesday, 10:12 a.m.

Tom looked at the clock and compared the time with that on his watch. In a few minutes the backups would come in. If Karl and Lorelei were still here with their captives and there was any problem subduing the backups they would kill all three of them immediately.

He rested his leg for ten seconds, counting off the last three, and then hobbled back to the elevator, trying to keep as much weight off of it as he could. The elevator light was cool. He got down on the floor and felt along the bottom edge of the elevator door. There was a steady, cool breeze all along the frame. The air from the cave. High School Earth Science. What was the constant temperature—54 degrees?

There had to be another way down. What happened when the elevator was inoperable? A simple power outage or tripped circuit breaker would trap the occupants of the car. A repairman would have to be able to get at the elevator motor and cabling system. That would have to be at the bottom, deep in the cave, since the elevator's works were inaudible throughout the house. They couldn't be sealed in some soundproofed wall; how could they then be repaired? But where was the alternate way down? And if he found it, wouldn't that be the logical spot for them to be waiting for him?

He returned to Alec's bedroom. An ego like his would seek control of everything. Tom checked the walls, looking for moving panels; then he slid along the floor, probing the toe moulding with his pocket knife, feeling for cool air. The room was warm; it would have been easy to detect any break in the air temperature, but he found nothing. He checked the linen closet in Alec's bathroom, feeling along the tiles. Nothing.

But Alec was in a wheelchair. Unless the alternate route was another elevator or a very long inclined plane it wouldn't do him any good. Forget the hidden panels and all that Nancy Drew stuff. Kick out the cobwebs and the confusion and think rationally. What area of the house had he not checked?

He pulled himself up the stairs by the oak bannister, again braced himself on the dining room chairs, and made his way back to the kitchen. He was back on the level from which Diana had presumably disappeared. He didn't have to look far. To the right of the island, behind the arch that had outlined the entrance to the kitchen, was a door. It looked like a simple broom closet. A plausible place to hide? Perhaps Diana was just beyond. He put the palm of his hand against the frame. The cool air outlined the door, unimpeded by its thin and rippled weather stripping.

He whispered Diana's name but there was no answer. She wouldn't have waited; she would have pursued. Now she needed him. She was doubtless expecting him, but so were they. Lorelei with her .32, Karl with his twin Glocks. He stood to the side, raised his automatic, and turned the knob.

The door was unlocked and ajar. It opened easily. The light from the kitchen illuminated the first few yards of the passageway but the rest remained in darkness. Its floor was stone for the first few steps, with bristle mats to clean the shoes of those using it. The floor beyond was earth. Tom ran his palm over the wall just beyond the door. It was uneven, the material manmade, some compound used to simulate the walls of an underground cavern. There was also a crude wooden railing on either side. The angle of incline was steep. The support would be necessary for most.

Tom reached inside his jacket pocket and took out a penlight.

He pressed down the button and partially illuminated the rest of the passageway. It was at least thirty yards long, with a large wooden door at the end. He shined the light against the ceiling and along the edges of the floor, behind the railing and around the kitchen doorframe. No wires. No apparent sensors. There was a single bulb in a fixture halfway down the passageway and a switch just to the right of the kitchen door. Before reaching for it he asked himself, what else does it turn on besides that light?

Checking to make sure that the kitchen door remained unlocked, Tom depressed the button on his penlight and entered the passage to Alec's cave. The earth was firm beneath his feet and the air was damp. As he got closer to the door at the end of the passage he turned off the penlight, blinking it periodically to assure himself of his position and his distance from the door. The whole place was nothing but doors, with uncertainty always waiting on the other side.

This one somehow seemed easier. It was heavier, but it was old and out of square, with the remnants of a once-functioning keyhole and narrow separations at the corners of three of the panels. A grand wormy relic, it was probably also stolen from a cave in France. There was even, faint light on the other side, more a glow than a beam, and silence. He could stroll right through, play Captain America, and wait for the interviewers from Channel 7 to listen to his war stories.

Too easy. Too damned easy. He checked the edges of the door for wires. Then he stood in the darkness, waiting for his eyes to adjust. Looking through the ancient keyhole then, trying to see something aimed at the door: an abrupt greeting. Hello. Goodbye.

CHAPTER FIFTY-THREE

San Clemente
Tuesday, 10:34 a.m.

The lower left corner of the door was attached to a steel channel in the floor by a single iron bar. As Tom leaned against it the bar moved freely and noiselessly in the channel, the only sound being the slight rush of air as the door opened into the cave.

He pressed the door just far enough for him to slip through. Moving to the side he let the door slip back into place on its track. He could now see the source of the glow—lighting along a path leading to the left whose reflection had struck the opposite cavern wall. His eyes slowly adjusted as he realized what Alec had recreated: the Pech-Merle cave, in every detail.

The tones were all yellow and brown and peach, with great pillars of streaked stone connecting the ceiling to the floor below, the apparent products of patient millenia. The sparse lights created shadow effects that were all the more haunting because of the number and sheer size of the stalagmites and stalactites. In the back of his mind Tom could nearly hear the sounds of a preternatural organ announcing the onset of some great rite or ceremony. Despite the obvious fact of its artificiality the immediate effect was powerful and overwhelmingly real, probably because the original was itself so haunting and otherworldly.

The path to the left led to the *Frise Noire*, the Chapel of the Mammoths. From there the horses would be visible below. Tom turned to the right. At Pech-Merle there had been a chamber where the bones of bears had been found, a chamber with an ancient tree whose roots ran all the way to the cave from the sunlit world above. Backing against the wall Tom hit the penlight briefly. The size of the chamber was similar but there was no tree root and there were no bear bones. Alec had no interest in nature; he was interested only in art.

Moving to the left, past the door to the cave, Tom felt an uneven iron bannister. It was designed both for support for those walking along the moist earthen floor and as a barrier, to keep the tourists on the intended track. Alec had reproduced it exactly, choosing to endure a difficult wheelchair path in the interest of authenticity.

Approaching the *Frise Noire* Tom realized that there were no lights to illuminate the position where the drawings of the mammoths would have been found. Why? Because Alec would not have been able to experience them, painted above him, out of reach. Even if he had attempted to touch them he would feel relatively little. The cool, damp air of the cave, the moist earthen floor, the bumps and ruts, the texture of a large oak door—they were his reality.

And so were the horses. While he couldn't feel the drawings themselves he could feel the outline of their magnificent stone canvas and he could trace the prominent nose, forehead, forelock, poll, and mane of the great horse on the right, its lines deftly following the curve of the stone slab.

He moved a few feet farther and turned to the right. There were the horses, the centerpiece of the limestone cathedral. The lighting was soft and direct, the horses glowing, seizing and commanding attention. As he looked closer he could see the outline of a large plexiglas chamber, protecting the stone from interlopers. Even in his own home Alec had to possess the artefact more completely. To the side of the horses were the reflections of two shadowy figures. He tried to make them out, but the light was too faint and their outlines too vague.

Then, suddenly, a sound. A voice. Alec's. Coming from the left, out of the darkness. At Pech-Merle the path would have curved off to the right, circling behind the horses and then bringing viewers back to the horses themselves, the climax of their journey, but Alec had created an addition.

What? A private apartment to bring him closer to his precious horses, away from human contact? Tom moved closer and could see a trace of distant light emerging from what looked like a tunnel. Inside there was reflecting light and the corner of some frame that looked like plexiglas. What was this, a series of chambers or galleries? For what? The Beowulf manuscript of course, and the sword of Angus. The entire collection must be in the cave. That was why the house was empty except for the Van Goghs and the statuary over which Alec could run his fingertips, taking his delight. This was the treasure room, the final chamber.

Alec's voice became more pronounced, but as Tom shifted position, trying to fix its origin, he realized that he had been hearing echoes. The plexiglas chamber enclosing the horses had deflected Alec's voice, making it appear to be coming from the left. Tom moved closer. He could see now that Alec was inside, next to the horses. He was propped against the side of his chair, speaking to Diana, who was standing before him in the semidarkness, her hands behind her, the two of them protected by the front panel of the plexiglas chamber enclosing the horses. His hands were on her face, tracing its shape and outline.

Tom started to move more quickly. Where were Karl and Lorelei? Diana was the bait to lure him closer; that much was clear. They knew he would be there sooner or later. Why waste time tracking him through the house and risk being shot? Far easier to put the old man in plain view, have him run his hands over the helpless woman as she waits for the knight errant to show himself, proclaiming his love and dedication as he plunges into the center of the crosshairs.

Where were they in the darkness? Behind the wall curving to the left? Beyond the parallel stalactites a few yards to the right of the horses? Somehow he would have to take them out first. Only then could he free her and see the sweet tableau of Diana released from her bonds as her brother's murderer cried out pathetically for help, the realization becoming increasingly clear that he was finally alone and unprotected. And, of course, they would be counting on all of this, counting on his trying to find them before freeing Diana. They would be counting on his desire for justice and revenge. They would have anticipated each of these steps, each of these emotions, planned for them, prepared for them. They knew every inch of the cave, its paths and dark corners. They had the weaponry. And, perhaps most crucial of all, they controlled the lighting within the cave. Perhaps they were now sitting next to a bank of switches, ready to throw floodlights on him or to plunge them all into total darkness.

Standing with his back to the wall, the cool, moist curve of the stone against his neck, he looked beyond the plexiglas chamber where Alec held Diana. In the shadows he thought he saw a glint of light, a reflection. He concentrated, focusing his eyes. Then he saw a second and a third. Reflections from eyeglasses? There were at least three or four figures standing in the darkness. Or were there? Neither Karl nor Lorelei had worn glasses. There could be many more of them than he had thought. Their glasses were more obvious now as they seemed to be leaning forward, watching the old man, his hands moving over Diana's neck and shoulders, finding her throat and breasts.

CHAPTER FIFTY-FOUR
San Clemente
Tuesday, 10:41 a.m.

The plexiglas screen protecting the horses was approximately twelve feet wide and eight deep, with ample room for Alec to maneuver his wheelchair. It was at least ten feet in height, too high to scale. Tom couldn't come in from the right, putting Alec in the likely line of fire. He would have to come in from the left, where the door to the plexiglas chamber permitted him access, and that was directly in the line of fire, if not from Karl and Lorelei, then from the voyeurs with the eyeglasses hiding in the shadows.

Keeping his back to the wall and wiping the cool moisture from his forehead he inched around to the left, trying to keep the weight off of his bad leg whenever possible. The ground was drier now as the path rose above the floor of the cave. He watched each step, trying desperately to insure his silence. In the distance he could see Alec. He was seated, leaning forward in his wheelchair now, as if he wished to rise up. Even though Tom was at least thirty yards from Diana and the light was faint he could see the expression of disgust on her face as she bent her body sidewards in an attempt to elude Alec's touch.

After ten or twelve seconds of lateral movement Tom could see the light reflecting on the far left wall of the cave. There was no sign of Karl or Lorelei. Ready to risk that the area behind him was clear, he only needed to concern himself with the voyeurs to his front-left. They were at 10:00, Alec at 2:00. They had an unimpeded line of fire on the door to the plexiglas chamber. If Tom could just crawl forward along the path that right-angled out from the wall and get close enough to the plexiglas and the horses he might get into the chamber, free Diana, and use Alec for cover. At any rate, Alec would have ordered his people not to fire indiscriminately, lest their rounds strike himself or his possession.

Alternatively, he might get close enough to the chamber to protect himself inside after laying down some unexpected fire in the general direction of the glistening eyeglasses. From there he could either shoot his way out behind Alec or negotiate, using Alec's life as his bargaining chip.

Either way he had time to decide and to react to circumstances. The upside now was that while Diana was in an unpleasant position it was not a position of immediate physical danger. She had to endure the old man's hands but that was far less serious than the weapons' fire of his subordinates.

As Tom lowered himself to the ground and began a slow, low crawl, the cool, moist earth felt good against his face. He had enough strength in his arms to pull himself forward without putting undue stress on his leg while the stalagmites provided him both cover and concealment.

Within minutes he was in earshot of Alec's voice. Its shrill ugliness urged him forward. Tom could see that he had slid Diana's sweater and tank top above her bra.

"Are you cold, Miss Bennett? It makes the nipples rise, of course. An added benefit. The Hollywood starlets used to apply ice to their nipples to make them erect under their satin gowns. Did you know that? Nipples fascinate me—the manner in which they can both feed children and attract men. So functional and yet so lovely. So common, really. They're not like faces. They differ from woman to woman, but not greatly. Yet they still interest us and stir our imaginations."

Diana didn't respond.

"I myself have grown used to the temperature of the cave. It is my home now. I find the constancy of the temperature very reassuring." He paused, returning his fingers to her breasts. "You're quite lovely, you know. I suppose Detective Deaton would have told you that by now. I was surprised by your nose and ears—long, but not pronounced. Different from your brother's. Of course, I could feel his only in death.

"The fingertips are quite amazing, don't you think? I read four languages in braille. By touching your face for no more than a few seconds I can recall it forever. I could draw it and it would be accurate to the last detail, except for the colors. You could wear your hair longer, you know. You're young enough and it would complement the rest of your figure.

"I don't understand that confining brassiere. Your breasts are full and well-formed. Why hide them under all that cloth and elastic. If you were with me I should touch them constantly. The buttocks are very nice as well . . . and the waist and back. Backs are too often forgotten, don't you think? I love the line of a woman's back. I had a Modigliani once that could bring me to orgasm. It was a painting of a woman reclining on the grass. Its subject was the curve of her back. The side of her face was in view. Also, her right arm and left elbow. The portrait ended just below her hips and buttocks. It was absolutely lovely. Five years ago, or perhaps ten, you could have served as the model."

His hands and fingertips continued to touch her as he described the painting. Diana's expression was one of revulsion. Tom could see now that there was a post in the ground to which she had been secured. Her arms were behind her back and she was unable to move her legs more than an inch or two. It exposed her at the same time that it constricted her.

Alec's hands were now around her bare waist. "He will come, you know. He won't allow me to touch you like this. Perhaps he's here already, contemplating his next step. Still, if he's not . . . that's all right. I can be quite patient. I won't tire of touching you. It's been so long since I had an opportunity such as this. There is always Helena, but I've grown so accustomed to her. I know her body like my own. It is like staring at oneself in a mirror. It has its purposes but they are no longer aesthetic."

"Helena. Your granddaughter?" Diana said.

"Yes."

"You touch and fondle your granddaughter?"

"Of course. How else am I to appreciate her beauty?"

"You don't find it odd that you should do that to your own granddaughter?"

Tom pulled himself closer. He could see Diana's eyes. She was only half engaged in the conversation. She was also playing for time. She knew that the backup would be coming in or at least attempting to and she knew that Tom would eventually find her. Alec's willingness to talk was an opportunity.

"She is not actually my granddaughter. My wife, you see, died shortly after the war, before we had the opportunity to have a family. I knew that I would need someone upon whom I could rely absolutely, someone who could aid me in difficult times."

"And you adopted her?"

"Oh no, I would never adopt. Too uncertain. There was a German girl in Athens, an art student. She was very bright and very fit, also very poor. I persuaded her to do me this service."

"Have your child."

"Yes."

"Which you then took from her."

"*Took* from her? She was *my* child."

"And the art student's."

"She was paid. It was a business arrangement, one of the best I've ever made, by the way. Helena has pleased me in so many ways. She has helped me acquire so many beautiful things. She has also helped me destroy my enemies."

"And she has no life of her own?"

"Why should she? What other life would she want?"

"What will she do after you die?"

"I don't think of that. Why should I?"

"Perhaps she has."

"Perhaps."

"And who is this Karl?"

"An employee."

"Nothing more?"

"What are you inferring?"

"He shares your home."

"Only as a matter of convenience. His presence in this country is not something he is anxious to reveal to the authorities."

"Why? Is he a criminal?"

"I would say he has been . . . misunderstood."

"And Helena . . . the irony of the name would not be lost upon the Tenedos partners."

"Irony? There is more of it than you could possibly imagine, Miss Bennett."

"In what way?"

"Never mind," he said, teasing her.

"I would appreciate it if you would pull my sweater down," she said.

"Certainly," Alec said, beginning with the bra and tanktop and then proceeding to slowly pull the sweater across her breasts, down to her waist.

"The vulva, you see, is of less interest to the artist. There is line but little form, unless one proceeds to the clinical. To the painter there must be both. The curves and swells, the extremities, the eyes, nose, ears, mouth and hair are everything. That is why I have not proceeded to touch you everywhere. You see, I am being quite honest with you. My appreciation of your beauty is that of the true connoisseur."

"Tell me something," Diana said.

"What is it?"

"Why did my brother agree to paint the horses for you?"

"Why do you think?"

"You threatened him."

"Yes, he was quite stubborn, you know. I offered a cash arrangement but that was of no interest to him. I was forced to give him an ultimatum, something I personally abhor, but I had to have my horses and he was the only artist capable of helping me secure them. When our negotiations broke down I informed him (actually Helena informed him) that your death would follow upon his recalcitrance and that the death would be a lingering and unpleasant one. Another irony. He died to save you and now you see what little good it did him. He should have taken my offer of money."

Diana was literally shaking with rage as the small chain that was wrapped around her wrists rattled against the post to which it had been secured. Alec was silent, enjoying her anger and helplessness. With the interruption of their conversation Tom knew that he would have to make his move. Otherwise, Alec might proceed to the next step in his plan and the opportunity would be lost.

Getting up on his knees he high-crawled toward the plexiglas enclosure. His leg was throbbing and his pantsleg was sodden with blood and the damp earth from the cavern floor. Moving into the open doorway Diana saw him. Her eyes opened in surprise but she tried not to move her head and signal his presence. Suddenly her eyes darted from left to right. He cocked his head to the side, as if to ask "What?" Her lips formed the word "No."

A second later he was inside the chamber. He spun Alec's wheelchair to the left and put his left arm around Alec's throat, putting the old man between himself and the line of fire. "Speak and I'll crush your windpipe," he said, using his right hand to work at the connection between the chains on Diana's hands and the ring on the post to which they had been attached.

"No, Tom!" Diana said.

He looked up at her just as the crop came down on his wrist. It was thin leather with a steel core, a combination whip and sap. The sound of steel against bone was audible. Tom tried to reach inside his jacket for his automatic as the crop came down a second time, now across the bridge of his nose. As he fell backward he felt the boot on his throat and the muzzle of the gun against his temple.

CHAPTER FIFTY-FIVE
San Clemente
Tuesday, 10:52 a.m.

"Why not give him another stroke, Karl. I think the added remind-er might prove useful." Alec's voice. Tom could just make it out. The crop came down a third time, this time across his cheek and mouth, tearing into his lip and cracking his teeth. The blood was now running freely from Tom's nose and mouth. Karl—who had been waiting for him behind the slab—removed Tom's automatic and ordered him to his feet. As he rose slowly Karl kicked him in his bloodied leg with the toe of his boot and Tom barely suppressed the gasp of pain. He turned, trying to see Diana, but his vision was blurred and Karl was pushing him forward.

Alec remained with Diana and was joined by Helena a few seconds later. Helena unlatched Diana's chains from the post and pushed her away, in the direction of Tom and Karl. Alec followed behind, his wheelchair moving smoothly along the edges of the path. When he got outside the chamber he turned in his chair and locked the plexiglas door. Diana turned and looked at the horses directly for the first time. Her mouth fell open as her eyes darted across the paintings, counting the red and black dots in the bodies and along the edges of the horses.

Helena slapped her hard across the face and shoved her forward. Diana's ear was ringing, her jaw numb. The edge of Helena's nail had cut her cheek just below her right eye. She refocused again, staring as best she could at the tableau of the horses.

Helena slapped her a second time. "Would you like me to borrow Karl's rod?" she asked. "It would turn that little neck and chest of yours to bloodied pulp."

Diana looked ahead, walking quicker now, trying to keep an eye on Tom as Karl pushed and kicked him into the darkness ahead. "Alec," she said, in a voice loud enough for Tom to hear.

"What is it?" he asked.

"Your paintings are forgeries."

"Of course they are," he answered. "I forced your brother to make two sets."

"You built all of this and then risked your life and the life of your daughter for forgeries?"

"Silence her, Helena," he responded. "I don't want to hear any more of this."

Helena kicked her at the base of her spine, hurtling her forward. As Diana started to fall, Helena grabbed the end of the chain hanging from her hands and jerked her upright. "I can do that until you're unable to walk and then we'll drag you," Helena said.

Diana stumbled forward in silence, the pain in her legs and back nearly unendurable. She tried to balance her pace, breathing deeply and exhaling quietly through her mouth.

They were heading away from the center of the cave, past the break in the ceiling where Tom had thought he had seen the reflections in human eyeglasses. As he passed he might have seen that they were actually shiny lumps of imitation calcite. Diana tried to stay close enough to be able to see him. He was walking uncertainly, swabbing at his face with the sleeve of his jacket, trying to clear the blood so that he could see and breathe more clearly. She heard an occasional retching cough and saw Karl poke him in the back with the tip of the crop. Trying to keep her own balance and shake off the pain burning at the base of her spine, she tried to walk a little straighter. At the same time she wanted to look as weakened as possible, so she rubbed her ear and cheek with her right shoulder and breathed heavier as the path rose before her.

It appeared to her now that there might be another path, circling the rear of the cave. She could see a clearing off to her right, but she did her best not to turn her head. Tom had come in at the entrance below the kitchen and turned left, with Diana in the chamber to his right. Continuing to circle to the left he eventually found the path that led to the center of the cave and the tableau of the horses. Now they were walking to the left of the plexiglas chamber, back in the direction of the path that Tom had followed when he entered. Perhaps that path circled the cave, with the path to the horses and the path on which they were now walking each bisecting it.

What was in the darkened corner beyond the artificial light? Where were the two of them being taken? Moving through the shadows she could now barely see the back of Karl's jacket. Then, suddenly, he appeared closer to her. He had slowed or stopped. She dipped her head down and increased her breathing as her eyes rose, scanning the area.

"Keep moving," Helena said, striking her in the back with the butt of her pistol. The pain shot up and down her spine as if she had been struck with electrified barbwire. She distracted herself with thoughts of high school physics—the students all holding hands, conducting electricity around the room in an elongated circle. It rippled across their hands and wrists like a tremor under the southern California desert.

Karl was clearly visible now, no more than thirty feet ahead of them. Tom was visible as well; he seemed to be leaning against the side of the cave. As she got closer she saw Karl pull him back and small shafts of light appear in the cave wall.

The wall was covered with artificial calcite which masked the seams and edges of a sliding door. The chamber beyond was not yet visible, though she could see a bright glow and shadowy reflections. Karl and Tom went inside, Tom bracing himself against the edge of the open door. When Diana paused, Helena hit her again with the barrel of her pistol. She winced and walked more quickly, wondering what awaited them there.

As she got closer to the open passageway to the inner chamber things began to come into focus. Tom was on the floor now, his body in a vaguely fetal position, Karl standing above him with his crop in his left hand, his pistol in his right. Tom's automatic was stuffed into Karl's pants, the handle hanging over the top of his belt.

The reflections were brighter now. The room appeared to contain more plexiglas chambers. Diana heard some scuffling behind her. Alec had bumped into Helena with the side of his wheelchair. Helena apologized for being in his path and then struck Diana in the back, telling her to move forward, out of the way. "Get in there, you stupid bitch," she said. Diana remained silent.

Diana moved forward, into the passageway. The tunnel was short, no more than a few yards in length. Diana approached its end, turned slowly, and beheld a vision of hell.

CHAPTER FIFTY-SIX
San Clemente
Tuesday, 11:05 a.m.

Alec had lifted himself out of his wheelchair and into a leather chair at the center of the room. "The true *Chevaux Ponctués*," he said, pointing to a chamber to his left. "The plastic capsule protects them against moisture and cold, but I can touch them whenever I choose. I'll return them to their rightful place in the center of the cave after this unpleasantness is over. I touch all of my possessions. Touch is all that remains, but I love the textures—stone, paper, steel, bronze, wood. Flesh.

"The dotted horses are my special prize. In the chamber to their left, the single surviving copy of the manuscript of the *Beowulf*. We kept the capsule the same size for purposes of symmetry. To its left the sword of Angus or, as the vulgar would say, the sword of Lancelot. You were not aware of the contents of the fourth chamber. You could not have been. Regrettably its condition has deteriorated seriously, but it is quite authentic."

Diana was staring at the walls and ceiling and the shapes projecting from them, her mouth frozen open in horror, but Helena struck her ear and cheek with the butt of her pistol, ordering her to listen to Alec's words. Stunned and shaking with pain she turned, tried to focus on the fourth plexiglass chamber, and began to make out the outlines of the head of a horse, ending in the front at the forearm and projecting at the top as far as the withers. It was constructed of planks of wood that were now warped and worm-eaten.

"Of course it was never of the size depicted in films. The walls of Troy were not that high. It is a great source of pain to me that so little remains, but what can one do when authenticity is demanded. Would you like to know how I secured it?"

Diana remained silent as Alec continued.

"It was in the possession of the Vatican. It had been there since the fourteenth century, as a matter of fact. Therein lies a story, of course. It is a pity we have so little time. Suffice to say that the Vatican was anxious to keep the horse's existence a secret. The story of the siege of Troy had long been known, of course, but somehow the actual existence of the horse added a reality that the Vatican preferred not to provide.

"All pre-Christian, of course, so where was the harm? I believe it all had to do with the power of pagan myth and story. That was the word that the cardinal used: *pagan*. I have no idea what it is they feared. The best guess is that Homer's Trojan war really had nothing to do with Helen or Paris. Oh, there may have been a stolen slave or concubine, some event which set things off, but the war was really over trade. Access to the Black Sea. They fought for control of the Dardanelles, not for some lost girl.

"One would think that the Vatican might have played that up. The true reality of paganism, you see. Material wealth, lust, theft, piracy, whatever. *Godlessness*. Well, who can understand *them*? I was the beneficiary in the end. I have the horse and they have a second-rate El Greco and a third-rate Titian, if anything of Titian's can be said to be third-rate. They also have a chest full of my gold, but less of it than they had originally wished."

Karl and Helena were fixed by the sound of his voice, drawn to it like birds to an overflowing winter feeder. Diana tried to look at Tom from the corner of her eye, but she could see nothing but a motionless shape.

"And in between your plastic chambers are the remains of the Tenedos partners," Diana said, suppressing her emotions as she stared at the heads and limbs projecting from the cavern walls and ceiling, fragments of human gargoyles, gaunt, distorted with silent pain.

"Yes, these too are now my possessions. That is Bachmann there, the first on your right. The pigheaded one with the pointed ears. To his right, next to the *Beowulf*, is Driessen, then Berthold, and finally Erhard. I tried to preserve some of their most memorable features: Berthold's heavy peasant feet, Driessen's hands, the hands of a woman, lovely in their way, but anxious to take all that you have, Erhard's thick arms and broad, stupid forehead.

"Erhard called me *Willy*. Time and again I asked him not to, but he persisted. He treated me like an errand boy; they all did, but he especially. 'Willy, do this . . . Willy, do that; whatever else you're doing can wait.' His needs always came first; mine were inconsequential. He introduced me to clients as Willy, never as Wilhelm. They came to believe that I had no last name, like some foolish lab assistant in a bad film. *Willy*. As if I were some servant. He especially enjoyed humiliating me before women. *Willy. Willy.* He stopped saying it when Helena removed his tongue. She used the small clippers, taking a piece at a time, ever so slowly. When it was finished and the screaming had stopped he tried to curse me, but all he could do was choke on his own blood and make the ah and oh sounds of an idiot boy. It was a moment I shall always cherish.

"They tried to ruin me, to destroy my collection, to destroy *me*. I lost my sight protecting my beautiful things. Bachmann! We took out his eyes in reprisal, one first, then, days later, the second. For me there are now only shapes and textures. It is the textures which I prize most. So pure. So basic. We cut off Bachmann's fingers, to deny him that pleasure. After the fire I withdrew, waiting, healing, planning. Then we hunted them down one by one. Karl was not with us yet. What you see is the result of Helena's work and my plans. It would have been impossible without her. Her sense of revenge is exquisite and she takes pleasure in the work."

Her eyes were fixed on his lips, her ears on the sounds of his voice; she was worshipful, entranced.

"For a moment I thought about adding you and Deaton to my human gallery. It might have been quite interesting—Deaton frozen forever in time, staring at you in frustrated desire, no more than an inch away, while your eyes and lips and breasts and nipples were mine, mine to touch at any time. A pity we need your bodies elsewhere. I shall miss the scent and feel of yours."

"I wouldn't count on escaping. I wouldn't count on *anything* if I were you," Diana said.

Alec laughed. "Look at the remains of Tenedos. They attempted to hide from us and after we seized and killed them the police attempted to discover the identities of their abductors. Needless to say, all of their attempts failed. The Tenedos partners are mine. Look at them. *Look* at them! The triumph is mine. Their bodies are mine, fixed in time, displayed on my walls like impaled bugs beneath collector's glass. Kepler would have joined them, but I needed him for other purposes. Kepler and his orders, his endless little personal requests, the obnoxious sound of his voice, his cheap suits and scuffed shoes . . .

"I touch them often . . . to remember them . . . and to savor my victories over them. Thoughts of former times, sweeter now by far. The touch and the memories of you might have been sweeter still, but there will be memories nonetheless. And memories you should now realize, are all that you will be able to provide."

"You collaborated with the Russians, betraying the Tenedos partners' clients," Diana said. "You told the Russians where the best collections were hidden and in return they gave you the opportunity to escape. They also gave you enough of the artworks themselves to enable you to become a rich man."

"Is that the way you see it?" Alec asked. "How shortsighted. How small-minded. To me the art is everything. Its temporary ownership is immaterial. There is nothing else of value. Art is life. Without it there is nothing. The art had to be protected from the shelling, from the fires, and from the looters. It went to Russia and now you see the result. The art is preserved and the world may see it again. I am happy to have played some role in accomplishing that. That I should be rewarded in some small way seems only just."

"The Tenedos partners saw it differently," Diana said.

"Yes, they were embarrassed. They felt that confidences had been betrayed. They were fools. They put their personal reputations above the preservation of the art."

"And now you will lose everything anyway," Diana said.

"I beg your pardon . . ."

"Our police backup will be here any second. Unless you have an army protecting you the police will keep adding men until they succeed."

"Of course they will," Alec said. Diana could see the beginnings of a smirk on his lips.

Helena walked toward a corner of the room. Diana could hear the click of a switch and saw the glow of a television monitor. "They are talking over bullhorns now," she said.

"Excellent," Alec said. "We have at least another thirty minutes. Take these two with the others and position them."

"Killing us will only add to your list of charges," Diana said. "All of you will die for this."

"I don't think so," Alec said. "Planning is everything. I would not be sitting here among the treasures of the world and the dead bodies of my enemies if I were not able to anticipate my enemies' moves and adjust to them. You see, Miss Bennett, our guards are simple criminals, hired for this occasion. They are not aware of it yet, but the trunks of their vehicles contain artworks. Nothing that I couldn't spare, of course. A minor Goya, some Picasso prints, a Rouault *Miserere* . . .

"If any of them survive they will protest that they were working for me, but the evidence will suggest otherwise. They were burglars, you see, caught in the act, contriving a preposterous story to save themselves. My own preference would be for total success on the side of the brave police. Far tidier that way. You see, Miss Bennett, Helena and I have actually been absent all the while; we've been thousands of miles from this place. Charges are being made on my credit card at the Royal Opera even as we speak. Today my beautiful Helena shopped at *Harrods, Selfridge's,* and the *Burberry* shop in the Haymarket. Phone calls have been made, faxes have been sent, orders have been placed. You see, Miss Bennett, we are not here.

"But *you*, Miss Bennett, you and Detective Deaton and Lieutenant Brighton and Chief Dietrich *are* here. You surprised the burglars and they did precisely what they would be expected to do. They killed you. That is what the positioning of your bodies will show. You see, you will be little more than detritus—rubbish in their wake. They killed you and then left the building to return the fire of the police. We've been waiting for the escalation of the violence, you see. We've planned for it, counted on it. It's all quite simple really."

Diana heard a door slide open behind her. The terminus of the elevator. The standard elevator door opened on the other side of the cavern wall, in the common area, but this provided Alec and his assistants access to the elevator car from inside the private chamber. The sliding door would later be returned to its original position and the chamber sealed. When the police found the cave they would find a forged painting of the horses rather than the original, a legal forgery, prepared for the quaint amusement of a harmless, rich old man. With the right lighting and the right compound to seal the artificial calcite they would never discover the cave within a cave with its four gallery chambers. From inside the car of the elevator they would see a blank wall and have no idea that there was a space beyond it.

"They won't all fit," Helena said.

Diana turned and saw the bodies of Chris Dietrich and Bill Brighton slumped against the side of the elevator car. Each was bloodied. She couldn't see if either of them was still breathing. She looked at Tom. He still hadn't moved.

"Take those two up and come down for the other two," Alec said. "Karl will stay here with me."

Helena opened the gate at the back of the car and got on, a pistol in each hand, aimed at the heads of the unconscious men below her. The door closed and Diana could hear the motor turn the cable that pulled the elevator car to the floors above.

CHAPTER FIFTY-SEVEN
San Clemente
Tuesday, 11:18 a.m.

Karl was standing above Tom, his weapon at his side. Alec was running on about the Tenedos partners, how they had abused him earlier and underestimated him later. Diana stood patiently, her wrists behind her, still secured by the steel chain. Back in the cave she had tried to bend the links by pressing them against the steel post to which she was attached, but without success. With every sentence of Alec's she had twisted the links in her fingers, applying all of the pressure she could manage with her thumbs and index fingers, but they refused to bend. If she could sit down now she thought she could pull her wrists under her feet and bring her hands in front of her, but to what purpose when Karl was standing ten feet away, armed with a lethal weapon?

Karl continued to listen to Alec's words as he talked about the Russians, how misunderstood they were, how helpful they had been, how their love of art had done so much to enrich the world. She feigned interest in what he was saying as she tried to catch a glimpse of Tom. Her eyes darted to the right as if she were blinking and refocusing. She couldn't turn and stare directly. As Alec droned on about the czar and his Fabergé eggs, then about the Hermitage and its treasures, she thought she might have seen something. She stared at Alec for a moment and then blinked again, trying to get a look at the side of Tom's face.

His right eye was open. He appeared conscious. For an instant she thought he nodded to her, confirming her hopes. A few seconds later she looked again. His eye was opened wider, his nod more insistent, as if he were saying, "Do it!"

But what could she do? She couldn't attack, not with her hands behind her and Karl armed. She could kick out at Alec, but what would that accomplish? She couldn't kick Karl; he was too far away and he had the advantage of ample reaction time. Her only hope was to somehow divert Karl's attention and give Tom a few inches and seconds in which to make some move.

Alec was talking about the impressionist works at the Hermitage, comparing them with the 'paltry' holdings of the Norton Simon. "And that Burghers of Calais tripe at the entrance," he said. "Think about it, really . . ."

"Think about *what*?" Diana blurted out. "About your arrogance and pretense? About your insecurity and your ignorance? How dare you even mention Rodin's name?"

Karl tensed up, his spine stiffening. Alec laughed.

"Laugh, you foolish little man," she said. "You're nothing more than a common thief."

"That will be enough," Alec said.

"Enough of what?" Diana responded. "Enough of the truth? I think you could use more of that. You'll never hear it from this pair you've hired to fawn over you. No. I'll tell you what you are. You're a disgusting little troll, groping at dead bodies and sitting pathetically in a room full of stolen goods."

"Silence!" Alec said.

"*You* be silent," she said. "I'm sick of your maundering on about things you don't begin to understand and I'm sick of your petty orders. I won't obey you like this hired help and that daughter out of a bad Nazi propaganda film."

He was rocking back and forth in anger. "Karl!" he said. Karl stepped forward, anxious to be released, anxious to be permitted to strike her, to hurt her in some terrible way.

As he took his third step Tom bolted to a sitting position. At the same time he grabbed Karl by the ankles, jerking them back and up. Then, as Karl fell forward in a helpless rage, he tried to break his fall, extending his hands desperately, bracing himself, even if it meant crushing the fingers of his right hand beneath his pistol. Tom leaned forward in a second burst of energy. Somehow he found the strength to hurl himself across Karl's back, his hands at the back of Karl's head and neck, driving his face into the hard floor with even greater force.

The thud of the pistol grip and the piercing cry which came from Karl's trembling lips further masked the already-muffled snap of his nose and cheekbones as they split and shattered like twigs in a soft paste of flesh and blood. Using the back of Karl's head for leverage as he rose, Tom lifted his head by his hair and drove his face against the floor a second time and then a third.

Alec knew what had happened. He seemed to be collapsing into his chair, seeking sanctuary in its folds and creases, terrified of what might happen next. Tom stood behind him in silence, catching his breath and absorbing the pain pulsing from the side of his leg to the top of his head. Diana could see the toll that his actions had taken. After a moment he stepped to the front of Alec's chair and thrust his hand into Alec's throat. "Don't speak and don't move," he said. "If you do either one I'll hold you in the air by your throat until you bleed from every orifice in your body. That is a promise you know I'll keep. Do you understand what I'm saying?"

Alec nodded, his chin jerking spasmodically, and Tom released his grip. He then moved toward the chamber containing the sword. He removed it from its velvet-covered stand and returned to Diana, who was watching Alec. "Here," he said, "put your wrists there." She spread her hands over the top of a steel table adjoining Alec's chair. It was sculpted of brass, tin and steel—a set of geometrical shapes that looked like a frozen mobile.

Tom stood back, took the handle of the sword in both hands, lifted it into the air and brought it down in a single violent stroke, shattering the links of the chain and bending the table in the process. Then he handed Diana the sword and positioned her to the side of Alec. "If he moves or speaks, drive the point of the blade into the center of his throat."

Then he retrieved his automatic and Karl's pistol, first peeling back Karl's bloodied fingers from its grip, and hobbled toward the passageway leading to the main cave. "I'm going after her," he said. "I may be able to be of some good to Bill and the Chief. If she gets past me . . ."

"Don't worry," Diana said. "I'm not going down alone."

CHAPTER FIFTY-EIGHT

San Clemente
Tuesday, 11:26 a.m.

At the rear of the cave—behind the room where Diana was holding Alec—was the door to the elevator. The call light to the left of the handle was not lit. Tom walked further into the darkness, using his penlight to find the works for the elevator. To the left of the motor and cable assembly was a box with circuit boards which drove the elevator's electronics. Below that was the circuit-breaker box. Attached to the right of the box was a handle which was connected to the motor by a taut chain. When there was a problem with any part of the system the device was programmed so that the chain would jerk automatically, pulling down the handle, breaking the circuit and stopping the car. Tom thought about the fact that the assembly seemed so complex and yet so crude. Pulling down the handle he immobilized the elevator.

Opening the circuit-breaker box he compulsively flipped the switches. Then he proceeded toward the door. Helena would not be able to slip by him on the elevator and get to Diana. She would have to get past him on the stairs.

The kitchen and dining level was empty. Tom had worked his way through that area as quickly and quietly as his leg would permit, and there were no bodies, no bloodstains, no smell of cordite. There was also no sign of Helena.

He went to the stairs leading down to the bedroom level. If Helena was below him she would have to come back to the middle level in order to return to the cave. The most plausible place to put the bodies was on the upper level, but Tom didn't want to go there immediately and be forced to risk her slipping behind him. Instead he decided to return to the kitchen. He quickly checked the drawers, found some large metal spoons and measuring cups, and a ball of twine.

Cutting a piece of the twine and attaching the ends to the metal utensils, he returned to the door to the cave. Gently hanging the objects on the doorknob on the cave side of the door, he closed the door quietly and then pulled the knob slowly but firmly, forcing the warped door against the jamb. If Helena Alec did slip past him he would hear her the moment she attempted to open the door.

Pausing for a moment at the base of the steps, he tested his leg, braced himself on the railing with his left hand, raised his automatic, and began his climb to the top level. Looking behind him from time to time he noticed the trail of blood droplets he was leaving in his wake.

The stairway wound more steeply to the right as he got closer to the top. He was moving a step at a time, waiting and listening. Staying as close to the floor as possible, he leaned forward to see as much of the entry level as he could. To the right he could see a pair of legs. The body was slumped against the wall, the shoes large. Bill Brighton. On the left was the top of a man's head. The hair short and gray. Chris Dietrich.

There was no sign of Helena. Beyond the hall leading to the entry foyer he could hear the sound of gunshots and bullhorns. Was she just beyond, listening and watching? Was she hiding on the elevator? If the car was on this level the door would have opened even if the car was immobilized. She had several choices. If she had chosen to hide inside the elevator car or, perhaps, above it, the steel door would afford her some protection, forcing Tom to commit and giving her some slight advantage.

Toward the center of the room was the leather couch. She could be laying behind it, her body hidden from view. If he went in too quickly she would hear or see him and he could be shot. If he waited too long he might lose the chance to keep Bill and the Chief from bleeding to death, assuming they were still alive.

He put that thought out of his mind, leaned forward, still saw no sign of her, and pulled himself to his feet. He stumbled toward the short set of steps up to the foyer, climbed them as silently as possible, saw that she was not there, and returned to the first level. Dietrich was on his left and he walked toward him first, keeping his weapon aimed in the general direction of the elevator door.

As he approached him he paused for a second to check the stairs. He leaned to the right and as he did the sound of the shots and the realization that one round was ripping through his shoulder came simultaneously.

CHAPTER FIFTY-NINE
San Clemente
Tuesday, 11:41 a.m.

"What are you doing here?" she asked, her words edged with surprise and contempt.

Tom lay still, his eyes partly closed. "It doesn't matter," she said. "You can stay here with your friends. One more body will add to the effect."

His vision was blurred but when she turned he could see that she had changed her clothes. The white lab coat was gone. She was wearing a dark suit and had a purse hanging from her left shoulder. It swung back and forth in a short arc, like the hypnotic device of a Saturday-serial villain. He realized what had happened. She had positioned the bodies, then returned to her room on the lower level to change. When she had called the elevator there was no response. Figuring that the gate or door were not closed tight she returned to the top level, hearing Tom and then shooting him.

"If I don't return, he dies," Tom said, the words coming slowly and deliberately.

By now she was standing above him, her gun aimed at his head. She walked backwards to the elevator, opened the door, slid back the gate, and flipped the toggle switch for the light. The car remained dark.

"You've disabled the elevator," she said. "Just as well. You can walk the whole way then. Get up."

When he hesitated she kicked him in the side and he suppressed the groan. He was trying to assess the damage. His whole right side was soaked with blood. There was also a dull, throbbing pain farther down, as if one had struck his waist or hip.

He tried to get to his feet but he could barely stand. Off in the distance beyond the house he heard the blades of helicopters and the sound of bullhorns. There was also intermittent gunfire.

"Hurry up," she said.

He braced himself on the bannister and moved down a step at a time. His arm and shoulder were raw with pain but he thought of Diana and of Brighton and Dietrich. If he couldn't hold on they would all be lost.

When they got to the kitchen and the door leading to the cave he grasped the knob with his left hand as firmly as he could and jerked it hard. The pain shot through his body, but the noise resounded through the passageway. If Diana was anywhere in earshot she would know that they were coming.

"How very cute," Helena said. "Is that the way you thought you were going to defeat us, with childish signals?"

Tom didn't respond. He kept moving, taking a step at a time, but more slowly now. At least he was leaving a trail of blood that someone might later follow. The cold air rushing from the cave enveloped him, tightening his muscles and amplifying his pain. By now he felt as if he was dragging himself, but he knew that if he could just reach the door to the cave and open it, any further gunshots would be heard by Diana and she could better guard herself against any eventuality.

The door opened easily and there was a second wave of cold air, this time more damp. Something else had changed. The light in the passageway reflected on the walls of the cave, but when Helena switched it off they were suddenly plunged into darkness. She turned it back on so that they were standing among the shadows and reflections.

"What . . . ?" she blurted out and then paused, the realization sinking in. Tom turned and thought he caught a glimpse of an ugly smile. "Now you are in my father's world," she said. "No one but he and Karl would know how to turn off the lights in the cave. They have retaken their prisoner and now they are ready for you. Give me that flashlight you were using earlier. Hurry or I will put a bullet in your spine."

He hesitated.

"Don't be a fool," she said. "I was observing you all the while with our security camera. I know you have it."

The penlight was in his right pants pocket. He reached across with his left hand and took it out. Offering it to her he dropped it on the floor of the cave. She stepped back immediately, the pistol still aimed at his eyes.

"You become more pathetic by the moment," she said. "Take two steps backward." When he did she picked up the penlight and pressed down on the button on its top. The light came on. She had thought he had hoped to surprise her when all he had hoped to do, all he was *able* to do, was attempt to break the bulb.

"Now keep moving," she said.

As she walked and he stumbled he could see that she was holding the penlight at her side, keeping the light on the ground, just a few paces ahead of him. She didn't want to give anyone an easy shot at her and she didn't want him to be seen in profile. Whatever was waiting for her ahead was still a source of some apprehension. Perhaps Alec did turn off all of the lights, but then he was struck immediately for his pains. She had to be concerned. If Karl was still functional Deaton would never have made it to the top level of the house and for all his intelligence her blind father would be no match for a young woman whose hands and feet were free.

Her vaunting about their now being in her father's world was a whistle in the dark. The only things she could really count on were the fact that Tom was wounded badly and she was armed.

Three minutes later they were on the path between the forged tableau and the inner cave. Tom tried to walk at an even pace though his mind was cloudy and his vision was betraying him. The light just before his feet seemed to be moving in kaleidoscopic patterns. He felt like some ghost or lost spirit, wending his way through brownish yellow plastic, like a forgotten actor on an abandoned movie set. Since he was unable to see clearly, he tried to listen, but the only sounds were the squish and shuffle of his feet as he moved through gravel and damp clay.

At the mouth of the passageway Helena told him to stop and move to the left, staying close to the wall. "Slowly," she said, poking his bloodied side with the end of her pistol.

A few seconds later they stood at the entrance to the inner cave. She shined the penlight methodically, beginning on the right and moving up and down the cave wall. The heads and arms and legs of the Tenedos partners were unreal in the faint glow of the penlight, like funhouse figures designed to frighten infants. The light illuminated the four plexiglas chambers. Tom couldn't see whether the sword had been replaced or not. Finally Helena shined the light on the chair and the floor beyond.

She noticed that the table next to the chair had been damaged, pausing to examine it as the beam traversed the room. Tom was trying to maintain his balance, trying to see whatever she saw without passing out at the time that he might be needed most.

The beam moved to the left of the table and illuminated an empty chair. Then it moved from side to side covering the earthen floor. Tom focused. The light had seemed independent, disembodied, as if it had left Helena's hand and was doing its work deliberately and efficiently. But Helena was there. Tom could smell the thick, nearly sickly scent of gardenias. The scent revived him. It focused his thoughts and senses. He followed the beam of light, looking at the floor. He blinked his eyes and refocused. As the beam passed beyond the left of the chair he was sure of it: Karl was no longer there and there was no sign of Diana.

CHAPTER SIXTY
San Clemente
Tuesday, 11:54 a.m.

"Good, they've gone," she said. "Turn around. We're leaving."

He braced himself on the wall of the passageway, his body outlined by the glow of the penlight. He felt as if he was emerging from some giant, lifeless sewer.

"Keep moving," she said. As she reached the entrance to the passageway he heard a clicking sound and the movement of the panel as it slid back into place, walling off the inner cave. "Don't stop," she said. "Just keep moving forward."

The beam of the penlight was higher now, his body fully illuminated, casting shadows against the giant stalactites to his left. He saw the gleam again, the light that he thought was a reflection from a row of eyeglasses.

For a second he thought he heard Helena stop, as if she were listening for some word or signal. "Stop," she said; then, after a few seconds, she said, "Go on."

A few feet from the forged tableau she told him to stop again. "That's far enough," she said. "This is where I must leave you." She raised the pistol higher, aiming for the head. He thought of diving for cover behind the plexiglas, but he could barely move, much less outrun a set of bullets.

"I always enjoy the death of a fool," she said. "A pity I can't prolong it."

He was ready to offer her some parting thought, some curse or threat, some final, decisive promise, when his blurred vision caught a gleam in the darkness and he heard the weapon discharge, scattering rounds to the side of his bloodied right leg.

Then came the scream: piercing, soul-searing.

The penlight was on the cave floor, turning them to spectral figures of light and shadow. He blinked and then squeezed his eyes shut, opening them again, trying desperately to see what had happened. He thought he saw the muzzle of the automatic pistol on the ground, next to Helena's feet. She was staggering back and forth, screaming again in pain. He saw the rush of blood running down her leg and then, looking up, he saw its source: the remains of her right hand, twitching desperately as it hung by a single shred of flesh and shattered bone.

Diana emerged into the light, the sword at her side. Helena was staring at her in mute horror. "My hand," she cried, "my hand!"

"Justice for thieves," Diana said. Picking up the penlight, she shined it against the tableau. "My brother's final work," she said. "His final work before you murdered him. There will be justice for that as well."

Helena was clutching at what was left of her hand, gathering her strength, her lips opening in a bitter sneer. "You need courage to take revenge," she said. "Your brother died in fear. You will also."

Without a second's hesitation Diana lunged forward, driving the sword deeply into Helena's sternum, the sheer weight of it fixing her in place, like a waxwork statue, ready for the exhibitor's case. Her voice was now a series of gasps, her eyes moving wildly in the semidarkness. She reached out toward the edge of the sword as if she might somehow remove it with her left hand, but once extended the hand merely came to rest against it.

Diana braced her foot against Helena's belly, pulled slowly on the sword until it was fully released, then watched as Helena stumbled in the dark, finally falling against a row of stalactites before collapsing to the floor. Standing above her she stared into her dying eyes, paused, spat, and walked away.

"Can you move?" she said to Tom, who was trying to slip Helena's weapon behind his belt as the pain shot through his arm and shoulder.

"Yes, but not very quickly." He put his left arm around her for support, squeezing her left shoulder with the little strength he had remaining.

"I'm so glad you survived . . . and came back," he said, his voice shrinking to a whisper. "Where . . . did they . . . go?"

"I don't know. Alec flipped some switch or pushed some button and suddenly everything was in darkness. I hurried out of the room, thinking he might have some weapon and start shooting wildly. After a few minutes I heard him rouse Karl. Then I heard Karl's footsteps, but they grew fainter and fainter. I couldn't follow them in the dark without bumping into something and giving away my position. The next thing I knew you had returned with her, so I waited to see what I could do to help."

"You did it . . . all," he whispered, trying somehow to kiss her in the blurred haze.

"They couldn't have followed you or you would have found them on the steps," she said. "What about the elevator?"

"Dis . . . abled," Tom said. The words were coming harder now. "There has to be . . . another . . . way. Of course . . ."

CHAPTER SIXTY-ONE
San Clemente
Tuesday, 12:05 p.m.

"Check her pockets," Tom whispered, each word coming with a separate breath.

"For what?"

"A . . . key."

Diana returned in a few seconds. "It was in her purse. It's electronic." She raised the penlight so that Tom could see the object. It looked like a miniature TV remote, with four small buttons.

"One . . . for the inner . . . cave," he said, "another for the . . . the real entrance."

"What do you mean, the real entrance?"

"Like . . . Pech-Merle," he said, his voice slowing. The . . . real entrance . . . behind . . . the horses. How the . . . c- cave was . . . discovered. This . . . is . . . an . . . au-then-tic . . . copy. The second exit for . . . escape."

"The floors of the house are over there," she said, "on the side of the cave with the elevator. If the other entrance is back here, back behind the horses, it would come out somewhere lower, down the side of the slope. On another street. That must have been their escape route. They probably had a car waiting. Damn! Why didn't we anticipate that?"

"Don't . . . w- worry about . . . that," Tom said. "Go . . . back there." He nodded his head in the direction of the stalactites with the bright calcite, the eyeglass stalactites.

He slumped forward, half leading her, half falling. Together they worked their way back between the formations, taking a short cut to the path rather than backtracking to the area of the inner cave.

"There," Diana said, aiming the penlight, its light beginning to flicker and fade. Behind some grillwork of stalactites and stalagmites she could see a smooth wall behind a low ceiling. "Careful," she said.

It was no more than six feet and a few inches in height. When Tom stepped forward he could feel the top of his hair brushing against the top of the passageway. "How far?" she said.

"Fifty . . . feet . . . off to . . . the . . . left."

The light was faint now. "Hu-r-r-y," he said, unconscious of the fact that she was holding him up, pulling him along. "See . . . anything?"

"No," she said, as the light finally faded. She tapped the penlight against the side of her leg, shaking the batteries, hoping for some kind of miracle. She depressed the button at the top, there was a final flicker, and then nothing.

"Damn," she said.

"My . . . left . . . pocket," he said.

She reached inside and found a pack of matches. Lighting one and holding it in front of them she started to move forward, but the damp cave air extinguished the flame. Lighting a second one she held her left hand around it, protecting it. They moved forward, more slowly this time. The light was faint and there were only five matches remaining in the pack.

"Look . . . there." He pointed to the end of the path. There were only another ten or twelve feet of passageway, then an abrupt, inclined wall of damp earth.

"Door is . . . close," Tom said, measuring out the words.

"Too much . . . slope for . . . wheelchair."

Diana took out the electronic device and started pushing buttons. Nothing happened.

"Damn," she said again. "They're gone. I just know they're gone." She showed him the device, turning it so that he could see it.

"Look," he said, "see . . . this?"

It was a small, tubular extension at the top of the device with a single prong at the center.

"The transmitter," she said. "So? It's not transmitting."

"Close to . . . the . . . re-cei-ving unit," he said.

"Or attached to it," she said. There were two matches left. She lit one and started going over the wall.

"Lo-wer," he said. "He'd be reaching . . . from . . . the . . . chair."

Diana knelt down. The floor was cool against her knees. The match was almost burned out but she thought she saw something near the base of the wall. She let the light go out, then felt around the rim with her fingertip. There was a piece of imitation calcite covering it, but beneath the calcite she could feel metal. Inserting the transmitter into the opening she could feel the sleeve around the prong sliding surely. When it would go no further she pressed a button. Nothing. Then a second. Still nothing. As she pushed the third button she heard a click. When she pushed the fourth she felt a rush of warm air.

CHAPTER SIXTY-TWO
San Clemente
Tuesday, 12:18 p.m.

The open door revealed a passageway that angled sharply to the right. At first the light was faint, but as they got closer to the end of the passageway they could see a glow.

"The wall's translucent," she said. "Maybe the stuff inside is too, but with the earth covering it you couldn't tell. There must be only a few feet of earth around us here. It's much warmer than in the cave."

She turned to look at Tom, wondering why he hadn't responded. He was leaning against the wall of the passageway, his eyes closed.

"Tom! Tom!" she said.

He opened one eye and tried to walk toward the end of the passageway, but collapsed against the side of the wall. "Be . . . careful," he said.

She took off her blazer and covered Tom's arm and shoulder with it, pressing it against his wounds as he winced. With his left hand he tried to remove Helena's pistol from beneath his belt. "That's OK," Diana said, covering his hand with hers, then slipping it aside and removing the weapon.

She hurried down the passageway, the pistol raised, her heart pounding. The artificial slab was loose on its hinges. The electronic device which had opened the inner door had also opened the outer. She pressed against it slowly and could see the earth and dry grass along the edge of the door.

The door itself was low, just high enough for Alec to go through in his wheelchair. Figuring that they would not have waited to watch the door but rather have made a quick escape, she pushed the door open. For a moment her view was obstructed. Then she realized that there were several boulders just beyond the door to mask its outline from prying eyes.

Stepping around the side of the largest boulder she saw a narrow indentation in the scrub that could serve as a trail. Beyond that was a street ending in a cul-de-sac. The houses on the street were surrounded by redwood fences and in between the last houses on the west side of the cul-de-sac was a black Lincoln Town Car. Its back was toward her, ready to start up, ready to accelerate, ready to leave.

At first she thought of aiming for the tires and shooting, but decided to try to get closer first. If it *was* Alec's escape car—and she was sure that it was—there would be time for a shot or two. If they escaped she wanted to get the license number if she possibly could. She took a deep breath and started running down the path.

Tom braced himself on the wall of the passageway; Diana's blazer hung over his shoulder like a bloodied serape. As he approached the final door he saw the boulders beyond and the hard-packed yellow gravel of the path. As he got closer he could see Diana in the distance, running toward the black Town Car. He tried to call out to her but there was no breath behind the words.

Emerging into the full sunlight of midday he fell back against the side of the largest boulder. His face, which was splattered with blood, was suddenly warm in the bright sun. He tried to wipe his forehead and eyes, but he couldn't raise his right arm. Leaning back toward his left he suddenly saw something beyond the shrubs.

Leaning his back against the boulder and pushing off in short steps, he made it to the far side of the rock. There he saw the body. It was Karl. Resting comfortably behind some scrub, out of sight of anyone on the road above and anyone on the nearby street across the open area, the body had been sprinkled with dirt and dry grass for light camouflage. The arms were at the sides, the legs extended, the clothes all in place. All was in order except for the fact that the head was nearly severed from the body. A clean cut extended from ear to ear, the blood now stilled after its first, even wave. There was no sign of a struggle, not even a bent branch or a footprint.

As Diana approached the Town Car she realized that the motor was running. She ran faster, her body now damp with perspiration, her hand gripping the pistol even more firmly, her heart racing. She saw the license plate and stopped for a moment, scratching the number into the dirt in case she did not survive to report it. Then she ran to the side of the car, the pistol extended, pointing directly beyond the smoked glass at the shape in the driver's seat.

CHAPTER SIXTY-THREE
San Clemente
Tuesday, 12:27 p.m.

The electric window had begun to move the moment she raised the pistol.

"Dr. Bennett," a voice said.

"Hector?" she answered.

"Of course," he said, turning toward her. "I saw you running, but I knew you were safe and I didn't want to leave my friend here."

Alec was in the front passenger seat, his hands cuffed to the handle above the door. There were pieces of wire around his thighs and calves. In the back seat was a uniformed driver. There was an angry bruise on his forehead, a sponge rubber ball wedged in his mouth, secured by a double ring of duct tape. His hands were behind him, his feet raised in the air, tied to the courtesy handle on the opposite door. There was wire around his knees and ankles.

"I believe you've already met Mr. Alec," Hector said. "We've been having a very interesting conversation."

The ring tone came from Hector's cell phone. Excusing himself, he picked it up, listened, and spoke. "Yes . . . yes . . . good," he said. "How soon? . . . good . . . and Tom? . . . good . . . yes . . . no, we're fine . . . thanks for the message . . . OK . . . right." Diana was impatiently shifting from foot to foot. "Turn around," he said to her.

She turned and saw a dozen armed men. Tom was being lifted onto a stretcher by two officers in plain clothes.

"They just took the Chief and the Lieutenant to the hospital," Hector said. "They're both pretty chewed up but they should be OK. They're both type B's; I called for blood and some ambulances as soon as we thought there might be trouble. I'm surprised you didn't see anybody inside. They must have come in just as you were going out."

"Do you have blood for Tom too?"

"Yes. He's an O. They'll put him in the second ambulance. They say he's conscious. He's shot up, but it doesn't look as if anything important's been hit. The EMT said that he's in better condition than the Chief and Lieutenant. The Lieutenant's left lung collapsed and the Chief came within a pint or so of buying it. My friend here has a good bit to answer for."

"You'll never convict me, you stupid man," Alec said, his head turned vaguely in Hector's direction.

"He keeps talking like that," Hector said. "I call that true optimism. What do you think?"

"He killed my brother," Diana said. "He killed them all, directly or indirectly."

"No, he says that's all part of a plot to steal his artworks. He says that he bought everything fair and square and that someone is buying forgeries to put in the place of his treasures."

"How would he know they were forgeries? He can't see them," Diana said.

"Exactly," Hector said. "That's what I keep telling him. If anybody wanted to steal his stuff they could just load it on the truck and shove him over the side of the hill."

"Don't be ridiculous. They're devoted to me," Alec said.

"Now there you go again," Hector said. "If they were devoted to you, why would they steal from you?"

"I wouldn't expect you to understand," he said.

"Because of the art?" Hector said. "Because they were obsessed with the art? They had it anyway and they knew you weren't going to be around too much longer. All they needed was a little patience. In the meantime they could see it every day. After you're planted they would have it outright. I don't see any motive. Like I said, all they needed was to be patient. It took a long time to put the collection together. I'm sure they could wait a little longer. That's something *you're* going to need, by the way. I hope you've given some thought to that."

"What do you mean?" he said, curtly.

"Since I joined the force I've acquired some experience in this area and the detectives and I have had many discussions about what educated persons such as yourself would call the contemporary system of justice. For a number of years you're going to be one hell of a bother, but eventually there will come a day when the system will run its course and you'll hit the *high wall*, the one you can't get over, the one you can't get around. I figure with the trial and all the appeals and all the lawyer whining, you may have five or more years to wait before they move you to the cell at the end of the block, maybe even ten or more, but believe me, they *will* move you. You've been running around the world, killing people, hiding out in your big house with your cave and all your little secret rooms and chambers—let me tell you something, my little friend, the chamber that's waiting for you is bare except for a center table with some straps and a side table for the needles and the poison. There're no windows, no rugs, no flowers, no artworks, not even any color except for the white along your knuckles and the yellow and green mess that may come up from the pit of your stomach. First they'll strap you down. Then they'll have to find the vein. With you shaking and screaming it can be a little tricky, but they'll hold you down until they find it and then they'll slip in the pointy steel. If you listen real hard you might even hear the puncture. It's louder than a simple pinprick. Think about a 6 or 8-penny finishing nail being shoved into the thick peel of an orange. But when that time comes, don't worry if you can't hear it, because you won't have any trouble feeling it. You'll know it's there. A little conduit, your last link to the outside before they turn loose the poison. It will hit your veins and arteries like an angry river. Then, in little more than a matter of seconds, your lungs will feel like they want to come through the front of your blue shirt. The veins on the side of your head will be popping and your mouth will be gulping for something that's no longer there. You'll feel heat down your throat and your heart will suddenly be banging like a thick wooden stick against a tin drum. You'll want to scream out but there won't be any breath. You'll just gasp and struggle and whimper and finally collapse into yourself, into the silence."

Alec was straining against the wire around his legs. His hands were jerking against the cuffs. The Lincoln was rocking slightly as he thrashed back and forth.

"I would like to ask you for a favor," Hector said. "Would you do a favor for me?"

Alec sat silent.

"When that time comes, I would like you to remember the details of this little talk we're having. You'll be yelling and cursing and wrenching in pain and fear and you won't want to say what you should say, namely, that that Latino man whose friends you tried to kill was speaking the truth when he told you that the state would collect on every outstanding debt. And they *will* collect. You can be sure of that. You think about the pain you've caused. You think about the greed and the arrogance and the betrayals and then you think about that table. And that needle. And that poison flowing into your body. And the hollow screams that no one will ever hear."

"You fool," Alec said, his lips shaking. "Do you think someone like you could ever be capable of frightening someone like me with cheap threats and half truths?"

Diana walked around to Alec's side of the Town Car as Hector lowered the window. She reached in and ran the tip of her fingernail over the inside of his elbow, across his veins.

He bolted and twitched, sweat now covering his face as his body started to convulse. There was drivel at the corners of his lips.

"I believe the answer to your question is yes," Hector answered, "and remember—those weren't empty threats or lies. Those were promises and each of them will be kept."

CHAPTER SIXTY-FOUR
Saddleback Memorial Medical Center
Three Weeks Later, Tuesday, 9:45 a.m.

"You're here," Tom said.

"Of course I'm here," Diana answered. "How do you feel?"

He reached out for her hand and gripped it hard when she offered her own. "Terrific, but they won't let me out of this thing," he said. The orderly pushing his wheelchair was impassive. "It has to do with liability. Once they put me in your car I'm your problem."

Diana smiled. "You look like somebody who's had a skiing accident. Lots of bandages but you're still smiling, trying to find some happiness in the fact that you're still on vacation. How's your leg?"

"Much better since they took all the tape and gauze off. You know what the doctors say about problems with skin: 'If it's wet, dry it; if it's dry, wet it. If all else fails, prescribe steroids.' Personally, I think the fresh air is the best medicine."

"The last time I saw you you had more tubes in you than I could count. I was there for three hours and you slept through it all, even when I whispered in your ear."

"It's great to see you."

She was still holding his hand as the orderly rolled the chair toward the entrance of the hospital. "I understand Chief Dietrich responded immediately to the transfusions," she said. "I saw him last night and he was smiling."

"Yes. I told him he was like my old high school Plymouth. Everything else was as good as it was ever going to get, but a change of oil could work wonders."

"They had to move Brighton to another room."

"Yes, they work well together but neither of them was designed to share the same space around the clock. They both wanted to reorganize the stuff on the chest between them and they kept fighting over the TV remote. Also, they couldn't hear themselves think because the other was always on the telephone obsessing about something back at the station."

"You know something," she said, "you've said more in the last few minutes than you usually say in a day."

"Nobody's shooting at us now. Did I mention how good it is to see you?"

"Yes, and for me too. Hector told me that you had some special meals brought in for the three of you."

"Yes," Tom said, "I actually got reprimanded by the hospital administrator, the head nurse, two surgeons, and the lawyer for the people with the cafeteria concession. Not bad for one day's work."

"I don't think people who have had major surgery are supposed to be eating pastrami and swiss cheese sandwiches and drinking Bull's Breath beer. I understand the dill pickles were the size of zucchinis."

"I thought they needed something to motivate them to get well. What really made the whitecoats mad was the fact that they couldn't wrestle the food away from them. See, that's the problem. The patients start giving them some indication that they really *are* getting well and it makes them mad. Better they should lay there with their behinds sticking out of their gowns, trying to suck on ice chips as they get in the mood for the rust-colored jello and the fruit cocktail with the pieces of stem left in the grapes. I gave them hope and what did I get in return—snotty phone calls from doctors and not-very-subtle threats from lawyers."

"What did Brighton and Dietrich say?"

"They wanted to know what happened to the cheesecake."

"I also saw Professor Roberts the other day. Here, in the hospital."

"I recommended they use him to authenticate the *Beowulf* manuscript," Tom said. "They couldn't prosecute Alec for art theft without verifying that the works were legitimate. There's no crime in owning forgeries. I figured Roberts would like to return to California for awhile. We had a nice chat. In the meantime the people at the British Library have sent an armed guard for the manuscript, but, officially, they've put it in Roberts' personal care. He looks like somebody who just hit the PowerBall lottery."

The doors opened automatically and the orderly pushed Tom to the side of Diana's car.

"This is where I get off," Tom said.

The orderly handed him a clipboard with a form to sign.

Two and a half hours later they were on the 101, heading toward Carpinteria.

"What's our first stop?" Tom asked.

"Santa Barbara, I thought. Maybe a day or two of rest there. I'll prop you up on the beach, replenish your fluids. Then maybe Carmel. Somewhere up in the mountains."

"And then?"

"Do you always have to plan things this carefully? They're not shooting anymore, remember?"

"I remember it all," he said. "Your brother would have been as proud of you as I was."

As they drove into Montecito Tom could feel the warmth of the sun against his face. "What are you going to do with the horses?" he asked.

"They've been taken as evidence for the time being, but when they're returned I'll keep them. Despite the memories they're David's last work. He painted them to save me. They're like a final wish or a last message.

Somehow I can't get them out of my mind. I thought that if I continued to look at them I'd dream about the cave and the violence, but I really haven't. They're so very beautiful."

"How could they not be?" Tom said, as he reached for her hand. "How could they not be?"

❧❧❧